About the author

It still remains unclear as to wh
C M Vassie is a work of fiction
doomed attempt to document a troubling moment in the
hidden history of Whitby.

The introduction published in this long-awaited new edition
may finally tell us something about its author. Or not ...

What *is* certain is that Whitby's Goth Festival takes place
spring and autumn, pandemics notwithstanding, and that the
event has witnessed incidents of an unsettling nature.

It is also clear, as revered Victorian journalist Bram Stoker
observed in 1897 in his meticulously researched scientific
paper regarding a harbour shipwreck during a violent storm,
that the old whaling town on the North Yorkshire coast has
played host to a dark plethora of curious events.

For those keen to understand how it was that a group
of skeletally-thin cadavers appeared in the town during
the Autumn 2016 festival, this somewhat dry but well
researched and informative work may prove of interest.
Many souls died or disappeared during the festival that
year, and in subsequent years, so this account, complete
with autopsy reports, continues to serve some purpose. The
whereabouts and backgrounds of singer Thor Lupei and Mr
Murray, are explored in SCRAVIR II - Lacklight, we are
assured, and a third book is published anon.

Finally, if you insist on reading this work and afterwards feel
drawn to make a lacklit visit to Arguments Yard or the area
at the foot of 199 Steps to the Abbey, we implore you not to
walk alone.

C.M.VASSIE

SCRAVIR

While Whitby Sleeps

injini press

First published in Great Britain in 2021 by injini press
Reprinted 2021, 2022 (twice)

Cover illustrations: D.K.Vassie
Map of Whitby: C.M.Vassie

A catalogue record for this book is available from the British
Library

This Edition 2025

ISBN: 978 - 1 - 7391132-7-8

WHITBY

Lighthouse

West Pier

East Pier

Whitby Pavilion

Whalebone Arch

Royal Crescent

Khyber Pass

Pier Road

Henrietta Street

Church o
St Mary

199 Steps

Cliff Street

Dracula
Experience

Sandgate

Church Street

Swing
Bridge

Church Street

The Ropery

North Sea

Daniel's tent

Campsite
Field

The
Yard

Dog
house

The Barn

Farview
Farm

Endeavor
Wharf

Railway
Station

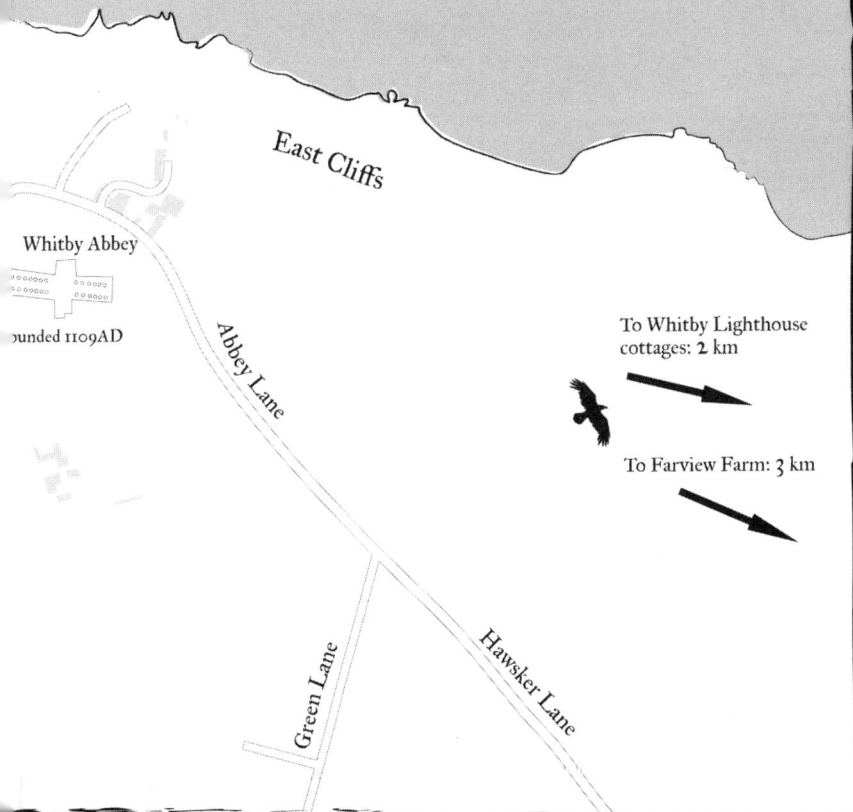

N

W   E

S

NORTH SEA

East Cliffs

Whitby Abbey

founded 1109AD

Abbey Lane

To Whitby Lighthouse
cottages: 2 km

To Farview Farm: 3 km

Green Lane

Hawsker Lane

INTRODUCTION

When Injini Press asked me to interview C M Vassie, following the publication of Scravir II - Lacklight the second book in the trilogy, I was confused. Who wants to learn about such obscure and degenerate fiction? Who reads contemporary Gothic horror and, in heaven's name, why?

The publishers were nothing if not persistent, praising my other work and even lauding articles that I myself considered mediocre at best and little more than plagiarism at worst. With mixed feelings, I accepted the assignment (I confess that the fee helped assuage my concerns regarding the merits of the exercise).

Regrettably, there is no overnight train to Yorkshire so, leaving my comfortable apartments in West London, I was obliged to rub shoulders with the hoi polloi on a locomotive that trudged the dreary landscape northwards to York where, late morning, I found the author in the backroom bar of a hostelry a mile from the station. They live in a village close to that city.

It would be satisfying to be able to report upon the singular appearance of the author; the magnetic intelligent gaze emerging from beneath turbulent eyebrows perhaps, the arcane aura accompanying their presence, the erudition betrayed in their each and every utterance. Sadly, none of this was the case. The backroom bar contained an ordinary-looking individual who was evidently as distracted at the thought of being subjected to an interview as I was disappointed to be conducting one.

Various pleasantries behind us (I did my best to agree with their analysis that there was more to life than London), we got down to business.

It has not been my experience that authors are particularly

interesting when talking about their own work. Manicured anecdotes about the influence of early childhood usually ring hollow or are packed with self-aggrandising details. So it was that I learned of Vassie's childhood visits to Whitby, the anonymous little harbour town where the stories are set, their joy at paddling in the icy waters of the North Sea, a naughty attempt (probably made up) to break into a lighthouse 'to see the harbour from a different viewpoint', and a dull tale about the 'amazing' way the wind erodes and pockmarks tombstones in the churchyard above the east cliff.

I listened politely. Eventually we turned to the books themselves. Without suggesting any literary merit in the works (that I confess I had not read), I asked what had inspired them. My interest must have appeared genuine because there followed a long exposition on the 'fascinating' history of Whitby's old town, the hard lives endured by its inhabitants, and the associations the place has with gaudy horror stories.

The first Scravir story is set in the present-day festival of excess that is the Whitby Goth Weekend. A cursory 'online' exploration of this event reveals photographs of thousands of happy souls of all ages who parade the old streets in gloomy costumes - blacks, purples, and crimsons - complete with bustles, top hats, crinolines, cloaks and veils in a celebration of all things Gothic. Far too much puffy flesh is on display for my taste. People push prams in which sit infant skeletons. Dogs are adorned with bat wings. Exhibitionists lurk in every alley. It won't surprise the reader to learn that prodigious amounts of alcohol are drunk, or that over a three-day period every last fish and chip in the sea is hauled out of the water, tossed in boiling fat and fried to a crisp to sate the gourmet Goths. At nightfall these gluttons of gloom congregate in the Whitby Pavilion, an architectural mishmash of buildings that hang precariously on the lip of the west cliff, where they twist and jive into the night like ghouls in a dance macabre.

Vassie explains that this was the genesis of Scravir; an idle thought as to what might happen at such a festival if real corpses were slumped against a wall in one of the alleys, ginnels or yards that criss-cross the old town. Would passers-by shriek or call the police? Would paramedics be called to attend to the dead or dying, or would a feckless public assume the bodies to be props provided for their entertainment?

The author decided the latter response more likely and thus was born a story. Evil is running amok among a group of revellers. So intent are the Goths on indulging their fantasy of evil that they fail to recognise real horror in their midst. Not having read Scravir I could only nod indulgently and mumble my bravos at the product of so prodigious an imagination.

That said, I had at least read the first and last pages of the book and could therefore ask if it was deliberate that the story starts with the words 'Let me finish' and ends with the words 'Start again. From the top.' I was assured that it was and, as a reward, the author suggested that I look carefully at the names of the characters as, apparently, many relate to the names of characters in Dracula. They cited, as an example, the name of the pathologist Dr Nigella Shaveling. N Shaveling being an anagram of ...

Very drole, if you like that kind of thing, I suppose.

One thing puzzled me. Why on earth create original monsters; what was wrong with vampires? Or Dracula? Most horror stories are happy to go with the pointy fangs, the old man who gets up late and does little else than sink his teeth into innocent necks. I am told that in the Scravir books the nemesis is original; an intelligent, gifted individual making moral judgements about who shall live and who shall die, and the scravir themselves are more than killing machines, and the hero a difficult mix of competing motivations. Why abandon the clichés of the genre? What is the point? To 'create a contemporary gothic tale' was the self-serving reply.

Aside from foolish word games and morally ambivalent characters, a key element to Vassie's Whitby tales is the old town itself. Research was allegedly undertaken prior to the writing, the better part of it in the Whitby Museum, a quirky establishment situated in the town's Pannett Park. There ancient dinosaurs lie side by side with model whaling ships, fossils, dolls, stuffed animals, a mummified *Hand of Glory*, and the *Tempest Prognosticator*, a silly Victorian device that used leeches to forecast weather conditions on the North Sea.

It was in this same museum's archives that Vassie researched the harsh lives of fisherwomen in 1820s Whitby, as preparation for their time-travelling adventure The Whitby Trap.

Any introduction such as this should not provide what are nowadays known as spoilers. In any event, any exposition would be predicated on my having read the stories. While I did promise the author that I would read Scravir on my journey home, I did not promise to describe penny dreadful potboiler scribblings as literature and am thus spared from pretending that these tales are other than coarse sensationalist adventures designed to generate a frisson of fear and page-turning excitement for those who like to indulge such emotions. To conclude, the discerning reader is, as ever, probably better served reading an academic treatise on John Bunyan's Pilgrim's Progress or any of the Slough Chronicles by Sir Ernest Drinkwater; upright intelligent works that serve some moral purpose.

My meeting concluded and my expenses taken care of by the publisher, I procured the services of a taxi to take me to Whitby, in the hope of obtaining some local colour to add to this introduction, not realising the town was some fifty miles to the east. Another dreary journey, this time in the company of a morose local driver who spoke only to complain about the weather. Eventually I was disgourged by the harbour and for a couple of hours I trudged here and there among the chip chompers, shove-a-ha'penny amusement arcaders, and those who find comfort and meaning in a distant horizon where featureless grey sea meets dull grey sky.

Duty done I went to the station to begin my journey home.

I write the last of these lines on the train from Whitby to Middlesborough, having now read the first few chapters of Scravir.

Night has fallen. The empty train keeps stopping at godforsaken little stations in the middle of nowhere: Ruswarp, Grosmont, Egton, Castleton Moor, Commondale. The doors hiss open and a frigid wind howls through the carriage. Minutes pass as rain spits insolently at the windows like a drunken lout itching for a fight.

All most disagreeable.

An ugly chill in the carriage is irritating the hairs at the back of my neck. This, combined with the nasty undercurrents of the story in my hands, is leaving me, I confess, somewhat unsettled. Why on earth do fictional characters insist on venturing into places that they should patently be avoiding? Scravir is awakening frankly uncomfortable emotions. How could this young hero, Daniel, not understand the dangers he is courting? For peace of mind I think it prudent to stop reading for now and to revisit the book once I am safely returned to the bosom of civilisation ...

Brian Suet
Glen Vanish,
Goring
Wessex
November 2024

CHAPTER 1

Miss D's Bar of Mysteries, West London

"Let me finish,' Daniel says. 'All that horror stuff - castles, howling wolves, vampires, buckets of blood, "*give me a sign, master*", steampunk, clockwork goggles, top hats, eeevil. I don't believe in any of it so why would I go to a Goth festival?'

'Good music,' Alex suggests, good-naturedly. 'A weekend with your mates? Crimson corsets and amazing babes?'

Daniel's eyes fail to light up.

'OK. Whatever.' Alex stands up and wobbles his empty pint jar. 'Shall I get another round in?'

'I'll get my own,' Daniel answers.

'Suit yourself.'

Alex threads his way between the tables, dumps his glass on the bar and waves a tenner back and forth in front of his hipster beard in the hope of attracting attention.

Daniel runs a finger round the inside of his crisp packet on the off-chance he'll find a few crumbs. It's not that he doesn't enjoy Alex's company, they have been friends as long as he can remember, but Daniel is skint. That is the issue. That and all the gothic stuff. He would rather spend what little splash he has on real things. The supernatural is for little kids.

He cannot know it yet but in a few sleeps manchild Daniel will either revise his view of what is and what is not real, or lose his life.

The bar is heaving. Tuesdays are the new Saturdays in *Miss D's Bar of Mysteries*. Only a few weeks into term and students' pockets, like Alex's, are still stuffed with loan money. Money that is desperate to escape and see the world.

'Hey, Daniel, check this out.'

Daniel turns round, straight into the face of a gargoyle nightmare in fluorescent green shorts and a purple hoodie.

'This is Katie.' Alex steps out from behind the nightmare.

'Hi Danny,' says Katie whose face is weirdly half-visible beneath a transparent plastic mask; zombie meets evil woman in a Miyazaki animation. 'Looking forward to Whitby?'

'Tell her I'm working.' Daniel addresses Alex, ignoring Katie.

'You're right, he is a miserable git,' Katie says. 'This is *the* Daniel, right, the guy whose mum ran away with the milkman?'

'Nothing to do with me.' Alex throws up his hands, a picture of innocence. 'I swear, Dan.'

'Right.' Daniel turns to the gargoyle. 'I'm not a miserable git, Katie-Watey. Some of us work for a living.'

'Ow, you're killing me,' Katie gasps, clutching her heart. She turns to Alex. 'I know!' Her voice now gleams with enthusiasm. 'He could go as Scrooge, stand on the pier, and shout at tourists.' The energy ebbs as quickly as it flowed. 'Second thoughts, with that face he'd scare the pelicans.'

'Pelicans?' Daniel scoffs. 'In Yorkshire?'

Alex is laughing like a set of clockwork false teeth. Like Katie is the queen of stand-up. Daniel shakes his head sadly. With her mask, Katie makes Quasimodo look like Superman. Not that Daniel fancies Superman any more than he fancies Quasimodo. Or bloody Alex. Or rollercoaster emotions Katie 'pelican' crater-face.

'But you are coming, right?' Alex refuses to let it go. 'Like when did you last have a holiday? We could ...'

'No.'

Alex's smile slips.

Katie tugs Alex's arm. 'Forget him. Come and meet the

other guys. They've got this great ...'

'In a minute.' Alex is still looking at Daniel.

Katie saunters away to join a bunch of girls giggling at an iPhone screen at the long table in the bay window.

'If it's just the dosh,' Alex says, 'I can lend you ...'

'We'll catch up next week. You can tell me how it went.'

Alex finally accepts reality. 'OK. Catch you later, mate.'

Torn between relief and regret, Daniel watches Alex join Katie and the others. She is all over him, peeling up the lower half of her mask to give him a kiss. Black lipstick meets brown whiskers. Alex can't have known her more than two weeks. It must be his blue and yellow jacket, flashy as a kingfisher. Some girls are such suckers for bright colours.

It is fifteen degrees colder outside the pub. Daniel doesn't do waiting for buses. He walks and, twenty minutes later, has almost reached his bedsit when his phone rings.

'Hi Dad,' he says.

'Where were you?'

'Sorry?'

'Sod sorry. I've been waiting an hour.'

'What for?'

'Clearing out your room so the lodger can move in. Remember?'

Daniel has completely forgotten the arrangement. Funny how you forget stuff you don't want to do. Stuff like moving all your childhood posessions out of the family home.

'I'll be there in half an hour. I was working late.'

'Don't bother.'

'What about my things?'

'They'll be in a cardboard box in the alley.'

'They'll get nicked.'

'What would anyone want with your old crap?'

Daniel changes the subject. 'Alex invited me to spend the weekend with him up north. In Whitby.'

'So you weren't at work. You were in a pub with your mates.'

'Where was it Mum grew up?'

'I don't talk about that.'

'Middleham, wasn't it?'

'Middlesbrough. She isn't there son.'

'Take Street she called it. "All they did was take take take."
She used to sing that while she was cooking breakfast.'

'Don't poke old scabs.'

'Did you ever go there? To meet her family ...'

'Don't be stupid.'

'... or to see what the place was like?'

'Listen, if it was Shangri-bloody-La up there why did she
bugger off down here the day she turned sixteen?'

'I'm just saying ...'

'I don't have time. Your old stuff'll be in the ...'

'Wait.'

'It's always all about you, Daniel. What about me? How
d'you think I felt when she run off and dumped you on me?'

The well-trodden path to self-pity city; it happens every
time Daniel tries to talk about mum. Which isn't often.

'I only wondered where she ...'

'Look, if you want to go then be my guest. They're tribal
up there. One big happy family. You'll find her no time. OK?'

'I didn't say I wanted to go.'

'We weren't interesting enough son. End of. One day she
wakes up and thinks sod this for a lark and she's gone. Just like
that. You were eight so you can't remember but ...'

Suddenly Daniel does remember. For the first time in over
a decade he remembers. He sees himself in the front room,
a snotty-nosed kid staring at her photo on the wall, tiny fists
clenched, trying to understand what he has done to bore and
disappoint his Mum and make her leave forever.

'... and that was that,' his Dad is saying. 'So when you're

ready to grow up and accept reality ...'

Daniel has heard enough. He cuts the call and presses Alex's number into his mobile.

'Hey. Dan, sorry about earlier, bruv. I shouldn't have ...'

'I'm coming.'

If she closed her eyes tightly to block out the harsh glare of the streetlights, the woosh of lorries speeding away from Rotterdam docks sounded like the sea.

The fever was getting worse, her shaking limbs causing the acrid smell to spill from the lining of the filthy sleeping bag she had retrieved from by the canal. She had not eaten for two days. Over the weeks she had lost a great deal of weight. Her hair was matted and dirty, but she had not forgotten her name. She was called Grace and she was determined to find a way of getting aboard a ship to England.

Like her grandmother back in Africa, Grace would never have believed that ice could exist outside the freezers of the expensive shops in Monrovia, the Liberian capital, but there it was hanging like carrots from the bridge above her head. She wished she could tell her parents, brothers and sister what she had found but Ebola had stolen them. She was alone in the world

The concrete wall at her back sucked what little heat remained in her skinny frame, in spite of the triple-layered cardboard chrysalis she had wrapped around herself. How many pupae emerged as butterflies and how many shrivelled and died alone and unmissed?

The ground beneath her was peppered with pigeon shit but here in the shadows she was at least dry and relatively safe. Vagrants, drunks, and other asylum seekers might turn up, driven by the same need for shelter, but while she remained hidden Grace was unlikely to attract the casual violence of local youths and angry old men.

Hearing footsteps, she opened her eyes and pushed the woollen hat up off her face. A tall stranger had left the path and was pushing through the bushes towards her. He looked well dressed. Not a vagrant or asylum seeker then. Grace shrank back, hoping he would see only a pile of rotten cardboard and turn away.

But he kept coming. Her flimsy shelter trembled as he knelt centimetres from her face. She held her breath and prayed. Suddenly the cardboard lifted, his face centimetres from her own and she was petrified. In her home country she had been taught to be fearful of his kind, they were often killed and their bones used to make powerful magic.

But this one placed a paper bag beside her.

'Eat it quickly while it is hot,' he urged her in English and in French.

She could smell the food. Nothing made sense. She was so hungry. Grace propped herself up, opened the bag, reached inside and grabbed the takeaway cup, smelling the soup and feeling its heat spreading into her hands. One eye on the stranger, one eye on the food, she wolfed down the sandwich, the fries, the soup, the croissant.

When he put his hand on her shoulder; she cursed herself for having been stupid enough to believe that he might be different to the others. At fourteen, she knew what he wanted. What they all wanted. Everything was a contract; I give you something, you give me something. Her body in exchange for a shelter or a biscuit.

Then she felt the surge, like the heat that had found her fingers through the sides of the soup cup, growing so quickly she thought she would burst into flames. She looked up at him, her brown eyes ablaze with fear and astonishment. His eyes were closed.

The heat rippled and grew. Gasping, Grace fell back, her limbs jerking out involuntarily, as stiff as if in a fit, throbbing with the rampaging heat. Staring blindly up at the underside of the bridge, her mind swam with fragmentary images of her journey, tumbling like coloured shards in a kaleidoscope. Then, as suddenly as it had started, it stopped.

For a moment he was standing above her then the branches of the bushes were creaking as he pushed through them and, without a word, he was gone.

And she felt better than she had in weeks.

CHAPTER 2

The Journey – Daniel Murray

Friday 4th November Ealing, London

I ran to Ealing Broadway station, rucksack on my back, hopped onto the Central Line and checked my messages. There was one from Alex:

"Brilliant! C U in the Middle Earth Tavern. 9.30"

Hobbits. Brilliant. Not. Beneath that was the previous evening's message from Kerplunk Katey:

"Number 13, Three Kippers Cottage, Henrietta Street. Alex says you can sleep on the sofa. But no being boring, we're there to paaarty! And you have to be in costume. A creature of the night. We're really strict about that."

I had sent a four word reply: "Really strict. Got it."

No point telling her I had the self-respect to make other arrangements. I had searched *Whitby Goth Weekend, places to stay* certain that there would be something cheap and moderately cheerful in a small town on the edges of the Arctic Circle in November.

Wrong.

Every room in Whitby was booked, except the grand hotels at the top of the hill. £250 a night.

Then I spotted it. Right at the bottom of the list. From the map it meant a bit of a walk along a dark road but so what? A tenner a night. In the back of the net perfect.

It was touch and go but I made it to Kings Cross and hopped aboard the two o'clock train just as the doors were closing. I had half-expected everyone heading north to be in period costume but, except for a hysteria of Harry Potter fans dribbling in front of a wall in the middle of the station, everyone seemed normal: tired and keen to get home for the weekend.

The journey was boring but dull. Gas towers, Arsenal Football ground, a few miles of terraced streets then, leaving London behind us, the sun came out briefly, lighting empty fields and a couple of church steeples, stone tributes to a rural space programme that had never quite taken off.

One so-what sandwich and one hundred and sixteen minutes later we arrived in York. With sixteen minutes to burn, I stuck my head out of the station hoping to pack a glimpse of the famous Minster, the largest Gothic building in Europe. Turned out that you couldn't glimpse the famous Minster because the famous city walls were in the way. (You should have the photos by now. Pretty rubbish I know, sorry.) I could have gone for a walk but I didn't want to risk missing my connection.

Train number two. As the train pulled out of York I allowed myself to think about what lay ahead. Goth Weekend was only part of it, I was conducting research.

While all my mates, including Alex, had gone straight from school to university and were debt-surfing to destitution, I was living the dream, earning the minimum wage in a nine to five and somehow stashing pennies away to join the housing ladder. Not in London, where my savings would never buy more than an outside toilet in Mile End, but a proper house, in a city where young people could still buy a house. I had checked everything out online. Street after street of terraced houses, a new university campus with thousands of students. The perfect opportunity for Daniel Murray, aka me, to scramble up, like Jack on the beanstalk, to a new land of property and success. In eighteen months I would have a deposit, buy a house and rent it out to students and use the income to buy the next one.

Ten years and I would be primping my plump property portfolio while Alex and Katie and the others were clutching useless media-studies degrees, adrift in a sea of loan repayments.

The train rolled northwards in the darkness and by the time we passed through a wasteland packed with graffiti covered cargo trains and overgrown bushes I had scribbled down the addresses of a dozen terraced properties, ten times cheaper than in London. A discarded shopping trolley loomed out of the darkness like a prehistoric shark scavenging on the sea floor, followed by huge billboards carrying smiling two-meter high faces where none of the components quite lined up. Finally the cop shop swung into view, brightly lit and gaudy as a box of Quality Street, and the train slowed and stopped.

Middlesbrough. As lovely and glamorous as Luton. I got off the train, ran to the exit and legged it out of the station. Forty-five minutes later I was back on the platform, out of breath and confused. I'll tell you about it sometime.

I hate journeys, especially travelling alone. Which is how I travel. Only so much staring at my phone I can stand. Either I eat non-stop, stuffing myself with crap like a pedal bin on acid, or I'm trying to sleep with my face vibrating against the window while the person next to me is stuffing her face with pickled eggs.

London to York: two hundred miles in one hour fifty-six minutes. Middlesbrough to Whitby: thirty miles in one hour forty-nine minutes.

Sixteen bloody stations; I counted them. Never more than five houses, a cattle shed, and a few desiccated weeds trembling beside bored-looking stones.

Assuming there was meant to be heating … it had died. I played at making breath clouds in the cold air until someone caught my eye and gave me that pitying look that people give saddos who are wearing novelty antlers on a bus.

My fellow passengers were a jumble: flat-capped locals

with dour buttoned-down faces and shapeless homemade clothes (camouflaged in greens and browns to avoid attracting the attention of predators when they stepped off the train), and a few outsiders going Goth. I was the only one with a rucksack; everyone else had cases. And hatboxes. I had brought a hat myself but it was a crushable special, stashed in my rucksack.

A group of students at the far end of the carriage were playing Open Drains; you drink as many bottles of Newcastle Brown Ale as you can in five minutes while singing "We are the Barnsley, the mighty mighty Barnsley" at the top of your voice. The other passengers all pretend nothing is happening, as people do in England until someone finally snaps, purple in the face, and starts screaming *will you please shut up* before apologising profusely and throwing themselves off the train or hiding in the toilets to avoid any further unpleasantness.

I almost said something, but who listens to me?

And so we trundled: Kildale, Commondale, Castleton Moor, Danby, Lealholm, Glaisdale, Egton, Grosmont, Sleights, Ruswarp, Timewarp ... until eventually the countryside ran out of cowsheds and we slipped down the hill into Whitby.

It was half past seven as I grabbed a visitor's map at the information desk and stepped out of the station into a gale gritty with horizontal rain. Parka zipped, I hurried along the harbour towards narrow streets and hot food.

The town was adequately catered for in terms of fish and chips. The sweet smell of frying fat billowed from every second door. I had expected streets heaving with Goths but the weather had driven most of them indoors. A hardy group of steampunks in platform shoes, top hats and velvet jackets spattered with brass buttons like green olives on a pizza were posing in front of the Dracula Experience. As I passed, one of the party produced a fob watch from his waistcoat pocket and declared 'My word, is that the time, Sir?' to raucous laughter from his friends. Already pissed. Easily amused.

The famous spiritualist and clairvoyant's shack was just where they showed it on Google. How could someone with even ten percent of the talents advertised in capitals above the door be operating from a tatty shed beside a crabstick stall?

It was warm in the fish and chip shop.

'How do I get to Hawkser?' I asked the girl shovelling my chips into a cardboard box.

'You mean Hawsker?' she asked, her Yorkshire accent thick as treacle. 'You in a car, love?'

I turned to show her the massive rucksack on my back. 'I'm walking.'

'What's quickest way to Hawsker, Bob?' the girl shouted over the fish fryer.

'Lose your job and miss a rent payment,' came the helpful reply from an individual of whom only the hat was visible. 'There's no way back so don't try it.'

The girl's purse-lipped smile and arched eyebrow suggested that stupid remarks were all you ever got from whomever was on the other side of the frying fish.

'I'd take a taxi,' she said.

'Can't I walk there?'

She made big blue eyes at me as she placed the battered fish on top of my chips. Wearing normal clothes instead of an ugly green nylon uniform she would be really pretty.

'Are you training to reach North Pole?'

'Less than five kilometres, according to Google,' I told her.

'How far's five kilometres, Bob?' she shouted to the hat on the other side of the fryer.

'More than four but less than six.'

'About three miles,' I told her.

'I know that. I were wondering if *you* have any idea. Where are you going?'

'A campsite. Farview Farm.'

Her expression changed again. 'Farview? Don't you know

about …' her voice trailed off. She sighed and changed tack. 'It's November, in case you hadn't noticed.'

'Everything else was booked.'

'You'll freeze to death. Or worse.' She hesitated. 'Look, I wouldn't normally, but in our flat we've a futon. You could …'

'I'll be fine.'

She shrugged. 'Suit yourself. Nowt as daft as folk. Especially southerners. Cross the swing bridge and follow signs to abbey steps. At the top, the abbey's on your right. Keep going and you're onto Hawsker Lane.' She leaned forwards and whispered, 'I'm giving you a few extra chips,' then straightened up. 'You'll need them. That's six pounds ninety.'

'What will he need?' asked the voice behind the fryer.

'Wellies and a canoe. He's heading up abbey steps,' the girl answered, winking at me.

I was halfway down the street and stuffing my face when she shouted 'Here, take this.' Shoes clattering, she ran up. 'Bob'd kill me if he saw me give it you.' She handed me a small pink plastic fish. 'I bet you don't have one.'

'Yeah, right. Why would I?' I was confused.

'It's a torch. Look, you push its eyeball. Like this.'

'Is this a fish and chip thing or a Whitby thing?'

'Just one of Bob's stupid gadgets. We use it to go to the store at the back. It's pitch black up on the headland.'

'OK. Thanks. Does it need feeding? Are you going to the festival by the way? To watch the bands?'

'We're open while ten o'clock when it's busy ... Maybe.'

'Might see you there then. Tomorrow night?'

Her smile was radiant but fleeting. She looked anxious again. 'Here's my phone number, in case you get into trouble.' She scribbled on a slip of paper. 'What's your name?'

'Daniel. Dan.'

'I'm Tiffany. Take care, Daft Dan.'

The bridge over the river Esk, though it was not really a

river at that point, was a cast iron swing job designed to let tall ships pass through to the back of the harbour. I wondered what it looked like open, with a stretch of road complete with double yellow lines hanging over the water, leading nowhere.

Narrow footstreets led through the old town. Sandgate, with its Goth shops, fishmongers and Victorian photographer's parlour, led to Market Square. Past the squat sandstone clock tower onto Church Street crowded with shops selling old-fashioned sweets, hiking gear, rocks and fossils, rude postcards, buckets, paintings; all that junk that people have to buy when they see the sea. Spilling out from a couple of pubs were twenty or thirty people, all beer glasses and laughter. Top hats everywhere, long purple dresses, red bodices, face tattoos, earplugs the size of dinner plates, telescopes, and dogs in ruffs.

The Internet guide said that it was important to visit Argument Yard, an alley off Church Street. I disagreed.

I had finished my fish and chips and was still hungry and disappointed that "Justin's famous fudge shop" was closed. A hundred different types of chocolate, fudge and toffee, according to the Guide. Given the walk ahead and the fact that my entire provisions consisted of a small bottle of lemonade, I was relying on the campsite shop being well stocked.

The steps up to Whitby Abbey were sick. The sign at the bottom said that there were one hundred and ninety-nine steps. I must have climbed at least five hundred by the time I reached the top and stopped to catch my breath.

The view was spectacular. Across the dark waters of the harbour, houses, shops and games arcades lit up the hill opposite like fairy lights on a Christmas tree and, in spite of the rain and the journey ahead, I felt a real buzz of adventure. It was going to be an exciting weekend.

Turning back into the rain, I faced a choice. To the left a path led through the graveyard towards a church squatting on its haunches, its eager flagpole shaking like a dog's tail. To the right, the second path, thick with running water, led on towards the abbey. Desperate for a couple of minutes out of the elements, I headed briskly between the blank-faced wind-blasted tombstones towards the shelter of the church entrance.

I fished my phone out of my pocket to ring Alex; it was already obvious that I wouldn't reach the campsite, pitch my tent and walk back into town to meet him at the Middle Earth Tavern by half past nine.

Voicemail.

My fingers were poised to type a text when my head was whipped back as my hood was yanked from behind. The phone flew out of my hand.

'How dare you. How DARE you! On hallowed ground. You devil.' shouted a woman's voice trembling with rage.

I tried to wriggle free but the grip on my jacket intensified. Something sharp as a blade pressed against my Adam's apple.

'Urinating on the souls of the departed, smoking your drugs, desecrating the churchyard.' the voice shrieked behind me, in a thick accent. 'I abjure you and fight fire with fire!'

She was strong and moved quickly, cracking my elbow against a tombstone as she dragged me backward away from the steps and the church, away from the light. My shoes slipped in the sodden grass.

'Cleanse him, oh Lord, that the evil be purged and sanctity restored to thy holy place.'

'Stop,' I tried to shout but the excruciating pressure against my throat reduced my voice to a pathetic gurgle.

The land sloped down. Was that the sound of the sea? I lurched to my right, twisting and dropping a shoulder. Instead of escaping the woman's clutches, I lost my footing and crashed to the ground. I saw her briefly, silhouetted against rough rushing clouds, as she spun me round on my back. A mountain of a woman with calves as thick as telegraph posts.

'Not far now.' Her voice now calm, almost sing song.

She marched across the headland, down the slope, still hauling me by the neck. Suddenly I understood that the sharp metal cutting into my skin was not a knife but the zip slider on my parka. The church was disappearing from view as I flailed about, reaching out for something, anything, to stop our progress. Handfuls of wet grass. Struggling to breathe. I reached for the edges of my hood, desperate to prise it away from my windpipe but my fingers could not force their way between the fabric and my neck.

My tormentor meanwhile was humming cheerfully.

The breeze was chill on my face as rain clattered like nails being hammered into a coffin lid. My head was spinning and I began to seriously consider that this mad bitch might actually throw me over the edge of a cliff.

'Alice. Alice! That's enough,' shouted a male voice.

A moment's hesitation, then the dragging recommenced. Running footsteps now.

'Enough! Let him go!' said the male voice.

The dragging stopped.

'Let him go!'

'The Lord's work,' she mumbled.

The vice-like grip on my hood ceased and I lay in the slick wet grass gulping air like a drowning fish.

'Back away, Alice. Sit down,' ordered the male voice. 'Hi, is that Charlie?'

Charlie? I rolled over onto my side and saw a tall thin man dressed as a vicar talking into his phone.

'Yes, I've got her. In the churchyard … Three minutes. OK. That's fine.'

The man leant towards me and stretched out a hand. 'I'm so sorry. Reverend Allstairs. Let me help you.'

The man dressed as a vicar was a vicar and hauled me to my feet. His hand was warm and dry. Sitting three metres away was Alice in a black plastic mac, glowering at the ground, her demons evaporating into the night. Mid-fifties, grey hair hanging in girlish plaits, her mouth puckered in a pout.

'I am afraid Alice gets agitated by the Goth festival and has a tendency to wander from the unit. She's mostly harmless.'

'Mostly?' I spluttered.

'On this occasion she has, I confess, somewhat exceeded her ...'

'How many people has she killed?' I asked.

Alice lay back in the grass, sighing like a deflating balloon.

'No sleeping on hallowed ground, Alice,' Allstairs said, then turned to me. 'Unless you are enjoying the eternal sleep that comes to us all.' His stern features softened into the faintest of smiles. 'The social workers should be here any minute. Can I help you? You are staying in a hotel perhaps?'

I shook my head. 'Is there somewhere I can dry off a bit?'

'The church is closed, I'm afraid. But if you are looking for accommodation I recommend a local hostelry.'

'It's OK,' I answered. 'I'm sorted. I'm heading for Farview Farm, in Hawsker.'

The clergyman gave me a curious look. He studied my rucksack. 'It is a long trek lad, and the roads are dark.'

'I've got a torch. Of sorts.'

'I am sorry I cannot be of more assistance,' he said, looking genuinely distraught.

Alice had sat back up and was rocking back and forth, hugging her knees.

'Will she be all right?' I asked.

'She'll be fine,' the vicar reassured me. 'Well done you for asking.'

I shrugged.

A couple of men in raincoats were striding purposefully towards us. They stopped in front of Alice and pulled her to her feet. She offered no resistance and stood meekly between them, head bowed.

'Bloody Fridays,' said one of the men. 'Someone rung earlier to say "I bet Mad Alice'll be off" but nowt we could do. There's no staff.'

'We keep telling them,' the other man agreed. 'No-one bloody listens. How's the lad?'

'I'm OK,' I said, assuming they meant me. 'No worries. I'm on my way.'

No point wasting half an hour in an awkward conversation. I left them to it and strode off up the hill to the church. My phone was in the grass by the path close to where Mad Alice must have leapt out from behind a grave.

Bloody Gothic weekend. Still, I'd have something to talk about later.

My laryngeal prominence was hurting like hell. I knew it was called that because I had checked up about Adam's apples; people at work kept banging on about the size of mine, telling me I looked like I had swallowed a coffee cup.

Turns out knowing the posh name for a body part makes sod all difference to the pain.

It was eight o'clock and I could smell the sea. The path ended at the abbey entrance, as Tiffany had said, alongside a large car park surrounded on three sides by high stone walls. A single road led away towards the south-east.

I admit I hesitated.

Should I go back into town instead of wandering off into the wilderness drenched to the skin? Who else was out there hiding in the dark? Then I remembered Katey-Watey. Begging her to let me kip on their sofa would be worse than being throttled. I'd never hear the end of it.

Anyway, there was no such thing as evil, just the occasional nasty bastard and a few lost souls like Mad Alice. Odds on bumping into more bad shit must be a million to one.

The footpath hugged the abbey's perimeter wall, affording my person a welcome respite from the malevolent attentions of the elements. The place was so gothic I was talking to myself like the sad steampunks outside the Dracula Experience; those old late night horror movies had made more of an impression on me than I had realised. It felt fun so I rolled with it.

The carcass of the desecrated edifice festered beyond the wall, a tenebrous jagged presence against the pit of darkness and the solitude that had enveloped my flagging soul. I avowed to an extreme discomfiture that propelled me to hasten away from that haunt of malediction. Twice I fancied I heard the ugly animal rasp, a black cry in the grim gloom of those sepulchrous stones. Crow, wolf, or denizen of the night?

Or, put another way, the on-line guide said that, in the horror story, Dracula had climbed the 199 steps and disappeared into the abbey.

The further I walked the bleaker and more exposed the landscape became; an infinite expanse of wind-swept grass cowering beneath a bruised, brooding sky.

The wall came to an end, as all walls do, and I was again faced with a choice.

I had saved a screenshot of this junction on my phone before leaving London. Just as well because there was no signal on this edge of emptiness. Green Lane, to my right, and Hawsker Lane, going straight ahead. I knew which road to take but the loss of a signal bothered me. I could not remember ever being disconnected from the rest of the world. Cut off from the Collective. It didn't happen in London. No-one would know where to find me if I went missing. No GPS signal. Nothing. I might as well be at the North Pole though, on second thoughts, since that was called a pole it was probably bristling with mobile phone antennas.

The path had shrunk to a dotted line of irregular flagstones, thin as a trail of breadcrumbs in a forest. I followed it past a line of squat buildings with corrugated roofs, then the buildings were gone, leaving only the night sky, the wet road, and a tatty broken hedgerow through which the gale howled and moaned.

I abandoned the path for the road, better to walk in safety than risk tripping in the undergrowth. I had not seen a single vehicle since starting my climb to the church and I felt sure that even with my ears covered I would hear any approaching car, or at least see the beam cast by its headlights. I chose not to use the dead fish torch Tiffany had given me; in that vast darkness I'd be as exposed as a luminous prawn floating in the Marianna Trench.

After a few minutes I passed a turning on my left. The scribbled sign read *caravans for sale*. The jagged crest faintly silhouetted on the horizon might be a farm. For a moment I fancied that I might have reached my destination but the name on the gate said otherwise.

The monotony of the terrain was getting to me. I don't scare easily but I did find myself spinning around more than once, having had the strangest sensation that I was being followed.

The road was empty.

I had to take the seventh turning on the left. In the lack-light, there being no moon, I stuck to the middle of the lane, keeeping both verges equidistant. I had gone some consider-able distance beyond the second turning when I was startled by a blaring barrage of noise. Throwing myself into the hedge, I turned to find a double decker bus at my heels. One of those old Routemaster buses they used to have in London, with that half-cab at the front. There was no light to see the colour of the bus but I knew instinctively that it was black. The headlights were off and the sidelights scarcely brighter than a flickering match. The bus inched forward until the cab drew level then stopped. Protected from the rain by the overhang provided by the upper deck, the driver's cab window slid open.

'The night is chill,' said a booming and resonant voice from within. 'Allow us to carry you to your destination.'

'Thanks for the offer but I'm almost there,' I answered. 'No worries.'

'No-one should walk in this weather. Hop on the back and I can at least take you the next kilometre down the lane. There are blankets on board. Coffee and whisky. We are heading left presently but we cannot leave you drowning in the dark.'

I could not see into either the cab or the bus, there being curtains in the windows. The voice sounded friendly enough but the incident with Mad Alice had put me off strangers for the evening.

'Honestly, I'm fine. I'm walking to the campsite, it can't be more than a mile now.'

'What a coincidence. Farview Farm?'

'Yes, that's right.'

'That is where we are heading. The offer still stands, my friend.'

The diesel engine was ticking over. I looked up and down the lane, trying to imagine how often a bus appeared here in the middle of nowhere. If I refused I might be walking for another thirty minutes, or more.

'I'm soaking wet.'

'That is why I stopped, my friend.'

'OK. Thanks. Where do I get on?'

'At the back. It's a bus,' the driver laughed.

I walked towards the back of the bus. It was not an open platform bus; there were doors at the back that folded open on my approach. As I stepped forward to climb aboard I saw the destination board above the doors.

HOUNDS OF HELLBANE
WORLD TOUR

On the doors were a succession of stickers marking music festivals in Germany, Denmark, Netherlands, Slovakia, Bulgaria and so on. A tour bus belonging, presumably, to one of the bands playing at the Goth Weekend. I might, amazingly, be closer to the action than Alex, Katie and the others!

I stepped on board.

The bus had been adapted. A chain was hung across the stairs, along with a sign that read:

STRICTLY NO ADMITTANCE

ON PAIN OF DEATH

A bit gothic. At the top of the stairwell was a mirror, designed to allow the bus conductor to see onto the upper deck from down below. It was so dark that I could not say with any certainty what I saw but, if pushed, I would venture the opinion that there were chairs and long tables and that on the tables, or boxes perhaps, were long sinuous forms writhing like a kelp forest in the sea pushed back and forth by shifting currents.

Downstairs seemed nice.

Part of the seating had been replaced with storage space. The space that remained had been converted into an open-plan kitchen and lounge area. Warm as toast.

Everything was black: curtains, cupboards, table, chairs, small sink and taps … everything. The only lighting came from three pencil thin slithers of light that shone from the ceiling down onto a jet black worktop on which stood a black cafetiere, from which drifted the delicious aroma of fresh coffee. Black coffee.

'Please take a seat and we can be on our way,' said the driver.

I could see the top of the driver's back above his chair through a partially open window but nothing more. Removing my rucksack, I took a seat by the cafetiere and the bus set off. There were mugs in a cupboard under the worktop and in no time I was warming my hands round a steaming cup of coffee and feeling almost ready to smile at my good fortune.

'Where are the band? Are they…' I started.

'Resting," the driver cut me off. 'We've had a long journey.

There's a bottle of slivovitz in the cupboard to your right, should you desire a pick-me-up.'

According to the label, slivovitz was the finest plum brandy in the world and made of damsons grown in the mountains of Moravia. I poured a small slug into my coffee and replaced the bottle in the cupboard.

Barely had I put the mug to my lips when the bus slowed right down and turned onto a potholed track that shook the suspension and rattled the mugs in the cupboard. Seeing the cafetiere sliding across the worktop, I wrapped it in a tea towel (also black), and placed it in the sink.

Parting the curtains I saw that the track had entered a farm. Thinking we had arrived, I stood up and pulled the bell cord, for the hell of it. I hadn't been on an old Routemaster bus since I was ten years old and, back then, I had to stand on a seat to reach the cord. The bell went ting but the bus kept going, straight through the farm and out the other side. I sat down again.

Along the sides of the bus, just below the ceiling, where the advert posters would be on a London bus, there was a long line of cryptic signs and symbols, dark grey against the black of the overall décor. Some of these looked vaguely familiar, variations of astrological symbols, others resembled nothing I had ever seen. One in particular drew my eye. It showed what looked like the head of a bird of prey, the beak tugging on a loose bag on which were written a jumble of letters in a jagged script that resembled a collection of tiny bones. I was musing on this and drinking the last of my coffee when the bus slowed again then came to a stop.

The diesel engine ticked over for a few seconds then died. In the ensuing silence I fancied I heard the hollow tock of a grandfather clock. I waited for the driver to announce our arrival then, when nothing was said, I turned towards the cab. The driver had gone; I had been so absorbed in the image of the hawk that I had failed to hear him open his door and climb out.

Drawing back a curtain, I peered outside. It was deep sea trench black. I was tempted to stay on the bus and await the return of the driver, who must no doubt be discussing where to park with the owner. On the other hand, I did not wish to appear rude. Shouldering my rucksack I went to the back of the bus and pressed the luminous exit button. The doors folded back on themselves with a pneumatic hiss and I stepped out.

The rain had stopped, which was excellent news, and the rolling clouds had parted to reveal a whisker of moon, but that was as far as the good news went. I had been camping before, in Devon and in France, two star sites and no star sites. I was ready for rudimentary facilities but Farview was in a class of its own. The place was deserted; no reception block, no lighting, no signposts, nothing. Fortunately, I didn't need much: a toilet block and a patch of ground that could take a dozen tent pegs. My tent was cosy and easy to erect. My sleeping bag had, according to the makers, saved lives on Everest and on Svalbard, so give me some grass free of cowpats and sheep shit and I was sorted.

The thin light of the moon outlined a large delapidated house with a jagged and possible broken roofline and chimneys all at different heights.

Behind me stood a huge barn with rusted corrugated iron sheeting for walls. Two doors, tall enough to allow a bus to pass beneath them, were slid back to reveal a gaping maw as black as the empty void of space. Flapping back and forth in the wind on the right hand door was a small, frayed and mud-spattered poster bearing three words in Comic Sans ...

Welcome to Farview!

CHAPTER 3

Text message from Miss Katie South
to Miss Chloe Carter

Sent: Fri. 4th November 2016: 8.53 p.m.

Hi C! Made it. Sorry forgot to mssg earlier.
Everything is brill! Hope you liked selfies,
Megan says I look big cute on pier. Walked
on beach and to lighthouse at end of harbour
wall while still light. Quite creepy … huge
gaps between planks. U can see down
between them to the sea!
Gorging on fab chocolate and chips every 2
hours. Only live once!
Goths everywhere. Cottage stinks of fish cos
we're only few doors down from old smoke
house where they make kippers all night
while we are kipping. Geddit? Seeing band
and pubs later. Creepy thing … saw really
skinny old guy dressed as steampunk in
alley called Arguments Yard (I know, totally
goth!). Shivering and coughing in a corner.
Tried to grab us while we were taking pix.
Muttering like totally mad. Made us all jump.
Alex shouted at him 2 back off. My knight in
shining armour ha ha. Is it love? Blushing.
Can see yr face thinking about it! Ha ha.
Hope u have gd weekend. K <3

CHAPTER 4

Farview – Daniel Murray

Friday, 4th November 2016, 9.00pm

I do not scare easily, as you know. More than anything I was angry. I was paying good money, twenty quid is twenty quid, for a plot on a campsite during the famous Whitby Goth Weekend. It had been advertised on the internet. Paid by credit card, and I had the right to expect a proper service to be delivered, complete with washroom facilities including hot showers, a campsite shop – open between 7am and 11 am every day, including Sundays – and free WiFi. The place was completely deserted. There wasn't even a bloody mobile signal, never mind free bloody WiFi.

I crossed over to the far side of the yard, passing a large pile of ancient manure (I think) that hummed and honked like dirty nappies. An open gateway gave onto a large field in which there was a grand total of three tents and one camper van. No lights on in any of them.

Back to the main farm building, which was beyond grim and foreboding. Not acceptable. They might not yet have electricity and they might go to bed at seven o'clock but they were damn well going to come downstairs and make me feel welcome.

The front door had neither bell nor knocker so I banged my fist on its surface several times and waited.

Sullen silence. I knocked again, more loudly this time. The windows to either side of the door were dull and dirty, I could not even see my silhouette reflected in them. In the mud by the door was a metal boot scraper, I wondered casually what noise it would make flying through the window.

Where was the bus driver? Aside from whisper thin slithers of light escaping the edges of the curtains on the lower and upper decks there was no sign of life on the bus either.

I had a choice. I could make the best of a bad job, pitch my tent and in the morning walk back into town to ring the bank to cancel the payment, and post a really bad online review to save any other sucker from making the mistake I had made, or I could keep banging on the door until someone answered.

To my great surprise, as I brought my fist down once again the door clicked open. I pushed it cautiously with my shoe, half-expecting a grotesque and protracted creaking echo in a cavernous void, accompanied by hysterical cackling. It being Goth weekend. Instead the door swung silently to reveal a small vestibule, empty save for a large pair of wellington boots and a couple of pegs on which hung an assortment of jackets and hats.

'Hello. Hello?'

I crossed the threshold. The inner door opened as silently as the first. Beyond was a narrow hall, at the far end of which was a staircase. A window or skylight, I could not see which, washed the stairs in a pale light, enabling me to see the frowning walls upon which hung a couple of stag heads. The doors, of which there were two to my left and three to my right, were all of dark wood. On a small table stood a gas lamp and what looked like a display stand of tourist leaflets. From my parka pocket I fished out the torch Tiffany had given me and looked for a light switch; if I was going to intrude upon the farmer's family I should at least ensure that they could see I was harmless rather than risk being on the receiving end of shotgun barrels. The light switch was the size of half an orange and made of scalloped brass and brought a dusty chandelier to flickering life above my head. Of the six bulbs only one was alive but it was better than nothing.

'Hello. Hello?'

My voice echoed in the empty stairwell. After three minutes of repeated attempts to contact the occupants, the house remained as silent as a crypt. I decided to try opening the doors. They were all locked. Should I venture upstairs? Perhaps someone had died or needed medical assistance. My foot barely on the first step, I was startled by a spine-chilling noise.

Even now I cannot find adequate words to describe it; a skin-crawling mixture of the mechanical and the visceral, as if a living machine were foraging for food, sniffing and scratching and snarling under its breath, accompanied by the sighing of pistons releasing steam and the rhythmic whining of a laser printer. Every hair on my body bristled and I feared I might lose control of my bowels. Reluctantly I turned towards the front door, dreading what apparition might be standing in the doorway but the moon had once again been swallowed up behind the clouds and I could see nothing at all.

Fumbling my way back to the front door I stepped outside, the torch switched off and clenched in my fist, ready to be used as a weapon if circumstances demanded. I could barely make out my own feet but knew immediately that one thing had unquestionably changed.

The bus had gone.

Rain again, icy and hard as spikes spat at my cheeks as I took a deep breath and considered my options. There were others camping in the field, it couldn't be that bad. What had I expected for a tenner a night? Time to man up and pitch my tent.

I crossed the squelching yard, through the crooked gate-posts and over the cattle grid, stepping carefully from bar to bar, torch in hand, then waded wet grass to a spot between the far wall of an outhouse and a hedge and there I pitched my tent.

My pop-up tent worked perfectly. Released from its bag, it sprang into shape and four tent pegs later it was securely fixed to the ground. I shoved my rucksack inside, crawled in after it, zipped the door, rolled out my camper mat and sleeping bag, and climbed out of my wet clothes.

It wasn't even ten o'clock but I was shagged out and there was no way I was walking back into town. My throat was sore but nothing was broken so all in all I was OK. I wriggled into my sleeping bag and, in a matter of minutes, I was ready to sleep.

From inside the tent, the falling rain was soothing. The wind rattling the fabric did not worry me; with a hedge on one side, a building on the other and my weight on the inside, the tent wasn't going anywhere. I confess that I did wonder about the sound that had frightened me, and what had become of the bus, but the moment passed and I slipped into a dreamless sleep, blissfully unaware of the violence taking place just a few miles from where I lay.

CHAPTER 5

Farview – Daniel Murray

Saturday, 5th November 2016

It was still dark and I was immediately alert. My phone read 2.37 a.m. I knew I was in a tent and how I had come to be there. The wind and rain had stopped and all was quiet, so what had woken me? I was still speculating when, just inches from my face, on the other side of the flimsy fabric of the tent, something began to sniff and scratch. As with the noise at the farmhouse door there was a mechanical edge to the sound only this time, instead of the muffled snarl I had heard, there was an even more alarming sound, a tuneless humming. No animal could make such a noise; a sentient being was scratching and sniffing outside my tent! I pinched myself. Maybe I was at home in London trapped in a horrible nightmare. Maybe I would wake up and find myself in bed with thirty minutes to shave, down a cup of coffee and trudge off to work. But the more I pinched the more my thigh hurt, I was already awake.

The clouds must have parted because the walls and roof of the tent became brighter as if the slender moon were shining down. I gripped my sleeping bag with both hands, if whatever was out there lifted its head, its silhouette would appear on the tent wall. Terrified of what I might see, I closed my eyes and kept them shut. How long I lay there listening to the feral scratching I do not know. I even fancied that I smelled its fetid breath as it foraged outside my tent, inches from my face, tormenting me with its evil presence until I wanted to scream.

Either the creature eventually left or I passed out because next thing I knew morning had arrived. I opened my eyes and saw only the orange glow of the tent's plastic fabric above my face. A small bird was chirping. I consulted my phone: 6.55am. Sunrise was round the corner. Desperate to relieve myself, I climbed out of my sleeping bag, pulled on my clothes, put on my wet shoes, unzipped the tent and crawled out. Feeling a fool for the fear that had gripped me during the night, I stood and stretched beneath a metal grey sky, heavy with cloud. Some three metres away was the end of the outbuilding; I could either go round the corner to empty my bladder discretely or crawl through to the other side of the hedge. I crawled through the hedge and froze.

I was less than a metre from the jagged edge of a cliff; the sea spread like a five hundred lane grey motorway complete with commuting seagulls gliding past way below. I had pitched my tent beside a fifty metre drop!

On the plus side, standing right by the hedge I had a flappy crappy mobile signal.

I typed Whitby Goth Weekend News into the search engine. Hangovers notwithstanding the day kicked off with the Bizarre Bazaar at around 11am. Festival goes were reminded that while anything from jeans to 'Full Victorian' were acceptable, a level of taste and decency were expected. Which meant that Alex and Katie had probably been sent home. The Whitby Goth Weekend Virgins meeting had taken place on Friday morning so whatever treasures they bestowed upon the participants I would have to do without.

Rather than attempting to download the festival programme I decided to wait until I had a reliable signal but there was a news item, posted only minutes earlier, that caught my eye. It was from the Whitby Gazette. Under the headline "BREAK-ING NEWS - While Whitby Sleeps - poverty scandal", the report highlighted the increasing number of destitute people dying in the town centre, a development that shamed Whitby, the article said. Three bodies, thought to be victims of hypothermia, had been discovered between 1am and 3am in two ginnels in the old town. I had no idea what a ginnel was but the dead were all elderly, two men and a woman. A source at Whitby Community Hospital on Spring Hill said there had been a slow but steady increase in homelessness over the past decade and that the Goth festival attracted beggars from as far away as Middlesbrough and Bridlington. I was expecting the next sentence to claim that they were all foreigners from Romania or some similar rubbish but what came next was surprising. All three bodies had been dressed in full Goth costume. A police source was quoted as saying nothing was being ruled in or out at this stage.

Whitby Goth weekend was plainly not just the student thing I had assumed.

By this time the urge to piss could no longer be refused. I crawled back through the hedge and used the outhouse wall. I was starving. Hoping that the farmer might finally be awake, I headed for the farmyard. Someone must be up, milking cows, polishing turnips or whatever else they did that was so important that the whole country had to have its clocks turned backwards and forwards every six months. The three tents and camper van I had seen the night before were still there at the other end of the field though, apparently, I was the only one awake as there was still no sign of life.

As I passed through the field gate I was surprised to see the black Routemaster bus parked up alongside the large barn. Hadn't the vehicle left while I was in the farmhouse attempting to make contact with the farmer?

My path was blocked momentarily by a speeding chicken that rushed out from beneath the broken door of an outbuilding, almost causing me to measure my length in the mud as I lurched backwards. Regaining my composure, and hoping that my pathetic yelp had not been witnessed, I knocked on the farmhouse door. Still no sign of activity: no lights, no smell of frying bacon, no radio playing the shipping forecast. I decided to try my luck round the back, following the path that led between the buildings. There had to be a shop, it said so on the website. As I walked I thought idly about what Tiffany, the girl in the chip shop, did on Saturday mornings. Did she wake up wondering when her life would begin? Like I did. Did she live alone? Was she at college? Did she dream of achieving something big, of making her mark on the world? Was she the kind who would walk away from a boyfriend who wasn't making anything of himself?

There was a door at the side of the house but it was locked. The back of the house was like the face of a dementia patient, a wide sandstone surface as blank as a sheet of paper. Vacant windows, no curtains, no potted plants on windowsills; opaque apertures to an edifice without a soul. The door did not even have a handle. Following a path between the dried heads of dead gladioli, their flowers faded to the colour of old paper, I climbed the steps, approached the door and found that the featureless wooden slab did at least have a keyhole. But that was it. I knocked and shouted, more out of habit than expectation.

Beyond the short garden there was nothing but open fields as far as the eye could see. While my attempts to communicate fell on deaf ears within the house, and I was beginning to doubt that anyone lived there, I did provoke a response from the outbuilding that ran along the alley.

A dog made a noise. To call it barking would have been to aggrandise what was a low and piteous whimpering; the sound of an animal abandoned rather than a fierce watchman defending life and limb. I retraced my steps and followed my ears. How had the magnificent howling of wolves been reduced, in this pathetic descendent, to a monotonous and miserable whining more associated with a snivelling six-year-old trying to force a tired parent into buying them a bag of crisps? The trail led to two whitewashed doors beside a derelict greenhouse whose pained and warped condition was offset by the paneless nature of its superstructure. One of the planks of the nearer whitewashed door had perished and fallen away. Peering inside I beheld the wretched hound, its bedraggled dull coat betraying signs of serious neglect, its eyes rheumy, its muscles twitching uncontrollably. The room contained a large stack of wooden pallets and stank of dog shit. On seeing me, the dog made an attempt to bare its teeth and snarl but it was so enfeebled that I imagined a person might suffer greater injury being gummed by a snail.

There were two bolts on the door and I toyed briefly with the idea of releasing the hapless creature from incarceration but decided, on reflection, that it would be safer to find the owners and raise the matter with them.

Behind the second whitewashed door was a storeroom. Spotting a sack of dog biscuits and several tins of dog food I started the day with a good deed. I grabbed two plant pot bases from the derelict greenhouse and manoeuvred them through the gap in the whitewashed door. The dog snarled.

'Not letting you out, mate, but here's some nosh.'

I filled one improvised bowl with handfuls of dog biscuits and emptied a tin of dog food onto the other.

'There you go. And I'll ring the RSPCA, all right?'

The famished dog paused long enough to lick my hand. I dropped the sack of dog biscuits in the greenhouse and§ walked away to the sound of busy munching.

Back in the farmyard, The Hounds of Hellbane bus was locked up, curtains drawn, no signs of life. I peered into the large barn that had unsettled me the previous night. Without the partitioning, it was large enough to house a sixty seater plane. Even in daylight the barn still filled me with an inexplicable foreboding. What was hiding there in the gloom, patient as a spider with legs poised on its web, awaiting the vibration that signalled the arrival of its prey?

Suddenly, I snapped.

This was absolutely the worst campsite I had ever visited. I still hadn't found a toilet or a supply of fresh water or the farm shop. My clothes were damp and I was hungry. Yes, I had come to the frozen north for a gothic experience, but not to die of consumption on a sodding wind-swept moor. I had allowed my brain to slow to a trudge and was consumed by fear of monsters and ghouls.

In broad daylight, for the love of God.

I straightened my shoulders, showed the farmhouse two fingers and strode purposefully back to my tent. I was here to enjoy myself and that started with getting out of this miserable shithole and heading into town to join the action.

As I changed into my festival clothes I discovered a cereal bar in one of the side pockets of my rucksack, eight months out of date but fairly edible. I pulled my crushable hat into shape, grabbed my wallet and phone, and clambered outside, leaving my parka on my sleeping bag. It was only as I zipped up the tent that I realised I had unconsciously made the decision to stay on the campsite. Maybe it was the realisation that all the alternatives were going to be more expensive and the truth was that I had not been eaten alive in the night and, as long as I made sure I brought food and drink with me and had a dump in town before I left, I didn't need facilities.

My phone said 7.47am.

Passing the barn, no longer in a pathetic state of apprehension, I stuck my head inside. A huge pile of large turnips on one side and a clapped out old tractor on the other. And no doubt it would be just as scary all the way to the end. Thank God no-one had seen me shaking like a four-year-old. I was still congratulating myself when my gaze fell on the bicycle partially hidden under hessian sacks.

I was never a thief. Except for a couple of chocolate bars when I was twelve, which you know all about because you were there. The bike could not have been worth more than a tenner. It was rusty, the paintwork was chipped, the tyres as slick as soap bubbles. There was even a spring poking up out of the saddle, held down with masking tape. And it wasn't like I would be stealing it. I'd just cycle into town, leave it somewhere and then cycle back on it later. No-one would even know.

I had the wind in my sails as I pedalled along the single-track road on my two-wheeled squeak wagon. The air was fresh, the grey sky huge. Catching a glimpse of the sea, rippling on my right, I sensed I was starting an adventure. Food, music, a new town to explore.

And Tiffany.

I would keep it casual. 'Just popping in to return the torch, thanks.' Or, 'I woke up wanting to eat fifty three of something so I thought why not have more chips?'

Maybe not.

Besides, chip shops aren't open in the morning.

Fifteen minutes later, the bike was behind a hedge and I was at the top of the 199 steps and five minutes away from a cooked breakfast. St Mary Church was still squatting on its haunches on the headland. In daylight the tombstones were just tombstones and didn't remind me of anything at all. I took the steps two at a time, except the wide ones they used to rest coffins on. Below, in the harbour, fishing boats chugged towards the jaws of the harbour and the open sea. A dozen seagulls shouted at each other over the rooftops.

At the bottom of the steps was a street sign for Henrietta Street. After I had eaten I would knock on the door of number 13. Wake them up. Being students they probably wouldn't get out of bed till midday. Then I noticed the yellow tape stretched between the railings on either side of the street.

CRIME SCENE – DO NOT CROSS

A group of people in white protective suits and gloves were bent over, making their way along the cobbled street. A tent had been erected where the land fell away to the left of the cobbles.

'Can I help you, Partner?' a police officer called out from the other side of the tape.

'My friends are staying on Henrietta Street,' I said, feeling obliged to say something. 'For the weekend.'

'Y'all can reach the far end of the street by moseying along the beach and up the other side. You take care, you hear?'

She and a colleague were laughing as I hurried away before anyone decided it was worth taking me in for questioning.

Minutes later I was in a café round the corner eating a massive breakfast of sausages, beans, Yorkshire pudding, bacon, and eggs. No mushrooms or tomatoes or any other pointless vegetable they liked to shove on your plate because they were cheap. In less than twenty minutes I would feel human again and ready for the day. And it wasn't yet nine o'clock. I was rummaging in my backpack for my wallet when the front door opened, the bell rang, and a police officer stepped inside.

'Five, please, Angie,' he said, 'and a couple of black coffees. It'll be chaos here later on.'

'It was chaos yesterday,' Angie answered, pushing a lock of bleached blond hair back up under her hat. 'So, Simon, tea-cakes or butties?'

'Four of each, Love. I'll eat the spare on my way back.'

'Get bored with the beard?'

'It were the Mrs fed up with me bristles scratching her foundation, if you follow me.'

'Cheeky.'

They shared a laugh.

'You've gone from desert island castaway to cuddly Bradley Wiggins lookalike,' Angie observed. 'Minus the lycra, thank God. I couldn't cope with seeing you in lycra. So what's going on out there?'

Simon scratched the back of his head. 'I wish I knew, Pet. Never seen owt like it. We know most of our dossers. Brian, Mad John, Curful Clive, Alice, and the rest of them. But this one, no-one has any idea who he is. And there's two more.'

'I know, they were saying on the news.'

'Strangest thing is their togs. This one here is in Victorian keks, a stripy waistcoat and top hat. And so skinny. His bum's like two boiled eggs in a hanky.'

'Maybe he's a Goth.'

'There's a couple of them saying that, including the Inspector, but it doesn't make sense. Not to me, anyroad. I mean, if you've got brass to buy a fancy suit you're not going to be sleeping rough under a bush, are you?'

'Fair point. Shall I wrap these? Are you there all morning?'

'Not up to me but I doubt it. Leave them open; everyone's so hungry they'd end up eating t'paper bags. We've been there while four o'clock this morning. Anyroad, not long now, we're all jiggered.' Simon turned to look at me, as if noticing me for the first time. 'D'you think he knows it's *Goth* weekend? He's done all right though. You've given him enough Yorkshire pudding to flag Market Square.'

'He looked hungry. They need their strength when they're his age,' Angie said, winking at me. 'You can bring back tray when you're finished,' she told Simon as she placed the last of the five cups of tea on the tray. 'I'll hold door.'

She closed the door behind the policeman and turned to me. 'Bad business,' she said, as if passing the final verdict on the affair, before disappearing under the arch into the kitchen.

CHAPTER 6

Message from Miss Katie South to Miss Chloe Carter

Sent: Sat. 5th November 2016: 9.26 a.m.

Hi C! You're not going to believe this. Just been woken up by police. It's like something out of Crimewatch outside. That's them behind me in the selfie. Sorry about my hair, haven't brushed it yet. Ha ha. Someone found dead thirty metres down the street. They wouldn't tell us anything but the street was closed off and we had to use a backway down some steps and along beach if we want to get into town. Had we heard any noises in the night or noticed anything strange?
On dirty weekend? As if.
Just switched on the local news. 3 people died during the night!!! In Whitby. How Gothic is that? Cud be wind up.
Anyway, we're all OK, so tell my Mum not to worry ;-) Daren't ring her myself, she'll just do a number. Back Monday. Great gig last night. Mad. Really, really mad! See ya, K

CHAPTER 7

Whitby – Daniel Murray

Saturday, 5th November

Having breakfasted handsomely I spent the morning wandering the streets of Whitby old town taking in the sights, sounds and smells. The sun was breaking through the clouds from time to time and there were even a few patches of blue sky. I told myself that I was looking for presents but in truth I was nosey-parkering. Who had I got to buy presents for?

There were a few Goths around but not many, hangovers would keep them out of action until lunchtime.

Three shops stood out that morning. The first was Justin's fudge and toffee shop where I purchased two large cannonballs, potent rum truffles of extraordinary qualities, allegedly. I promised myself that I would eat them a slither at a time since it was clear that a single cannonball contained at least a week's recommended calories for a normal adult. Not that it's really an issue for a skinny git like me.

The second shop, Oddson's Seven Wonders, was packed with ephemera from around the world, Maori masks, spirit-catchers, Goth bodices and coats, steam-punk goggles and telescopes, leather ties, herbal remedies, orgasmic gobstoppers, driftwood placemats, macramé nipple clamps, kidney jewellery (visible only on intimate x-rays), temporary genital tattoo kits, (who has temporary genitals?), chuckle charms, armpit hair-crimping tongs, edible nightdresses, authentic Aztec butt plugs, fresh fruit pacifiers, books on how to use your urine for astral projection, and enough incense to perfume a sumo wrestler convention. Spent so long in there that I was surprised they didn't charge me admission. I promised myself that I would find Tiffany and bring her in to choose a small gift in gratitude for the loan of the torch.

Worried that the cannonballs might be melting I left Oddson's Seven Wonders and made my way down to the east beach. Chalked on a board, it said that low tide was at 1pm so I strolled happily along the sand collecting stones and fragments of dead crab and watching the small wading birds scampering back and forth at the water's edge. I know it's a big word but I caught myself realising that I was happy.

The chocolate cannonball pledge was a failure; I finished the first before I left the east beach, and the second by the time I reached the end of the east harbour wall where the wind hurled huge waves about with such force that I felt obliged to remove my hat and stuff it in my backpack. Given the size of the chocolates and the amount of rum soaked into the raisins I was probably drunk.

Having followed a narrow path up from the beach, the third shop I visited was Fortune's Kippers on Henrietta Street. 'Shop' was a grand word for a place the size of a single garage. Like the chocolate shop, the windows and doors were painted a rich burgundy red. *Cured kippers sold only here* read the sign. Tucked in between the shop and the hill, a pair of large doors were open, revealing the smoke house. The smell of smoked fish was overpowering but not unpleasant. The walls were black as a chain smoker's lungs and glistening with tar. Fish hung from the roof in rows, like caramel-coated bats. I didn't know what I would do with a pair of kippers but I knew I must buy them immediately. I could work out who deserved them when I got back to London. Bending my head to enter the shop, I saw that choosing what to buy would not be difficult. The choice was simple: large or small. I handed over my money and watched a large pair of Whitby's finest being wrapped in old newspaper. As I left the shop I went back to have another look into the smoke house. While it was overcast outside, the room was not very deep and I could see right to the back. I was turning away when something caught my eye; a movement close to the rear wall. Uncertain as to what I had seen, I leaned forwards. This may seem strange but I swear the wall shimmered, as if a man were there, moving beneath the kippers, his shadow projected upon the wall. But the smoke house contained only racks of fish; there was no-one there to cast a shadow and, in any event, the room was dark and every surface painted black so how could a shadow make itself visible? How could there be a black darker than black? I was staring at the wall trying to make sense of this illusion when I felt a hand on my shoulder.

'Can I help you, son?'

I shook my head and left. Back on Henrietta Street I saw that I was now on the other side of the police incident tape and that I would have to go back onto the beach if I wanted to get into town. On the plus side however was the fact that I was now almost outside number thirteen. I crossed the cobbles and rang the doorbell. It was way past eleven o'clock so when nobody came to the door, I pushed the letterbox open and shouted 'Little Pigs, Little Pigs, open up or I'll huff and I'll puff and I'll blow your house in.'

The front door opened with a gothic creak.

'Bloody hell! What are you wearing?' Alex said, his hair dishevelled.

'He looks like an extra at a Trump rally,' giggled Katie, appearing behind Alex. At least I assumed it was Katie; the only other time we'd met she had worn a Quasimodo plastic mask.

'Given that neither of you is wearing more than a towel, I am not taking lectures. I'll come back when you've finished.'

'Is he a prude?' Katie asked Alex.

'No, I am not a sodding prude.'

'In which case, put the kettle on while we get dressed,' Alex said cheerfully.

'He can't come in dressed like that. I said *creature of the night*, Daniel. Remember?'

'What's your problem?'

'You're wearing a stetson, jeans, and a bandana.'

'Midnight Cowboy,' I explained, pushing past her.

'Yeah, owned,' Alex laughed. 'Classic film. Nice one, mate.'

Katie pouted angrily.

We spent the rest of the morning drinking coffee and playing cards by the window that overlooked the harbour. There were two other girls in the cottage, Hannah and Megan, both friends of Katie's that I hadn't met before. Everyone thought my kippers looked disgusting and ordered me to put them in the fridge, except for Hannah who said they should go straight in the bin. Instead of the fish we ate cookies and cakes, except for Hannah who said she was on a grape diet because refined carbs were practically a poison.

Hannah kept popping out to the kitchen. No-one else commented on the cake crumbs that had mysteriously appeared on her top whenever she returned from the kitchen, so I kept my mouth shut too. Megan was quite hot, in a Twilight vampire tramp kind of way but, to be honest, I was still fancying my chances with Tiffany.

'Have you lot been out in daylight yet?' I asked shortly after one o'clock, 'or does this Goth thing mean you can only leave the house after sunset?'

Katie bared her fangs and went *Aaargh*.

'Yeah. I am super-scared,' I dead-panned.

'You ought to be,' said Katie returning her gaze to her smart phone 'Wait till it gets dark, big boy.'

'Oooooh,' chorused the others.

'Only I was thinking it might be good to walk to the end of the pier or have a paddle in the sea,' I suggested.

'Count me out,' Katie said. 'You know the new Disney film comes out soon? The trailer's amazing.'

'It's the same bloody story as the last film,' I said. 'And the one before that. Princess separated from her parents is led on a scary but amazing adventure by a scheming traitor who has somehow …'

'How would you know, dreary Daniel?' Katie cut me off.

'They're like takeaway baked potatoes. Different fillings but same old stodge.'

'We did the beach thing yesterday,' Hannah wrinkled her nose. 'It was disgusting. Like walking on the edge of a huge dustbin with scraps of someone's seafood dinner all over the place ...'

'Don't be coy, Hannah,' Katie said. 'I bet you're dying to walk through town on a cowboy's arm.'

Megan didn't look best pleased at the suggestion, but she good-naturedly joined the *take the piss out of Dan* fest. 'Look at his little face. You've scared the pants off him.'

'I just thought we could all do with some fresh air,' I said.

'You sound like my mum! Doesn't he sound like my mum?' Megan teased.

'Give him a break,' Alex said, finally coming to my defence. 'I'll go with you, mate. We can grab a pint while we're there.'

He grabbed his coat and we left the girls to it. The police tape and the sunshine had gone. Collars turned up against the cold, we hurried beneath thick dark clouds through narrow streets towards the bridge. The gusting wind shook the newsagent's A-board carrying a headline about the mysterious deaths overnight. I went in and bought a paper to read later on.

'So what made you change your mind?' Alex asked when I re-emerged. 'I mean it's great to see you and ...'

'The old man was pulling his miserable old fart number and I suddenly realised that could be me in twenty years' time. Have you read this?' I showed him the lead article.

'So you decided it was time to become a goth.'

'I decided to do what he never did and visit Middlesbrough. Where my mum's from.' I pushed the paper in his face a second time. 'It says here that the bodies were ...'

'I never said anything to Kate, you know. I've been ...'

'Doesn't matter.' I folded the newspaper and shoved it in my jacket pocket; it would keep.

There were Goths everywhere: top hats, brass goggles, thick-soled boots, straining bodices, silver topped walking sticks. Every second bloke was a banker or a railway fat controller on his way to a funeral, while all the women had stepped off a burlesque stage.

Almost all.

Suddenly a mad blond was walking straight at me, looking like she had been buried in her wedding dress. Bedraggled hair, face white as a snow-bleached skull, a faded rose clutched in her left hand, a hand caked with blood from where the thorns had pierced her fragile skin. I dodged out of her path. People applauded as she passed.

On the swing bridge the wind was snatching people's hats off their heads and causing costumes to flap and billow like flags.

'Did you find her?' Alex asked above the noise.

I turned towards him with no idea what he was talking about.

'Your mum. I'm assuming you stopped in Middlesbrough, right?'

His face betrayed his thoughts; a jumble of curiosity and concern.

I gathered my thoughts. 'You know, when she was pissed off she'd tell me: "There you go again. Take, take, take. Just like back home on Take Street." But there isn't a Take Street, It's Teak Street. It was her accent.'

'You spoke with her?' Alex asked. 'After all this time?'

I shook my head. 'I'm talking about when I was a little kid. Yesterday, I told myself I was just looking to buy a house. Took the edge off it. There's twenty terraced houses on the street. No trees, no front gardens, nothing. Even worse than down our way. I know it's the right street, I asked some old geezer if there had ever been a takeaway that sold parmos.'

'What the hell's a parmo?'

'Dunno, but mum used to say she'd be sent down the street to buy parmos.'

'And?'

'And the old boy showed me where it had been. Student flats now.'

Alex grabbed my arm and pulled me out of the way as a huge guy in tails and a pink jelly brain under a glass cloche strapped to the top of his head, staggered past, pissed as a fart.

'You all right?' Alex asked me.

'She'd run away from a boring terraced street in the north and ended up in a boring terraced street in West London. With a pesky kid and my old man for company. No wonder she walked out. '

'You'll find her,' Alex reassured me.

I turned away, it had all got a little too personal.

Over Alex's shoulder, as still as a post box in the chaos of the street, a man stood gazing down at the cold waters of the harbour. Red hair and mutton chop sideburns tumbled out from beneath his top hat. The right sleeve of his morning suit was missing, revealing a mechanical arm made of brass, mahogany, transparent plastic and, within this sleeve, what looked like real bone or possibly ivory along with an intricate system of pulleys and sinews that opened and closed a hand concealed within a black silk glove. Whether he genuinely had only one arm or was hiding the other in his jacket I couldn't tell but I was mesmerised.

I suddenly realised that the bloke was looking straight at me. Assuming that someone behind me had caught his attention, I turned, but there was no one there; he was staring at me with an intensity that made me uncomfortable.

'Hey, Dan.' Alex had moved on across the bridge.

'Do you see that guy staring?' I said as I caught up with him.

'Just a nutter,' Alex said. 'It's worse when the pubs close. Last night some old codger's screaming at us that his life's blood is being sucked away by devils. Pissed as a fart.'

I had expected the Goths to be a bunch of students in face paint but there were people of all ages. People old enough to be my nan and granddad were wandering about with blow-up Dracula bat wings sticking up out of the back of their black jackets. Even the dogs had black ruffs. Somebody, presumably a local inhabitant, was wheeling their shopping home in a child's coffin. It looked a bit odd; cucumbers, a cauliflower, carrots, potatoes, and a turquoise bathroom carpet and toilet seat cover set drifting past in an open casket.

'Wait!' a female voice shouted behind us. 'Wait. Alex.'

Katie, Megan and Hannah, wearing masks but not in full costume, pushed their way through the crowds towards us.

'Creatures of the night,' Katie sang, wrapping her arms round Alex.

'I thought you lot didn't want to ...'

'Changed our minds, didn't we?' Hannah cut me off while ogling the coffin éclairs in a bakery window.

The café next door advertised black coffee weekend with the slogan:

Don't even think of asking for it white!

It seemed like the whole town had morphed into an enormous selfie machine. Katie, Megan and Hannah were glued to their phones, the town little more than a background for their gurning faces.

'Anyone fancy chips?' I asked innocently as we passed the Dracula Experience and reached Pier Road.

Just me and Alex; the rest said they had only just finished breakfast.

'It's all right, mate. I'll get these,' I told Alex on the threshold.

He looked at me as if it was the first time I had ever offered to pay for anything, which in fairness it was, then he shrugged and left me to it.

It wasn't Tiffany at the counter, just some greasy-faced kid covered in pregnant zits about to pop. I ordered two large chips and read the poster about sustainable fish stocks.

'Two large chips,' said the greasy-faced kid.

I looked up. 'Thanks ,' I said, taking the boxes from him and helping myself to salt and vinegar. 'Is Tiffany around?' I asked casually.

'Tiffany?'

'About so tall, blue eyes, brown hair and a freckle just here.' I pointed at my left cheek. 'Oh, and a really big smile.'

'Oh her. She never starts while five. We're on shifts.'

'What was that?' asked a voice on the other side of the fryer.

'A customer asking what sachets we do,' the youth shouted, and winked at me.

'Chums and chair legs, you tell him,' said the manager. 'Or you could squeeze your zits and …'

'Ketchup, tartar sauce and mustard,' the youth said, embarrassed and disgusted.

'I'll have two ketchups,' I said aloud then mouthed the word, 'Thanks.'

I should have guessed that half our chips would be eaten by Hannah, Katie and Megan. In that order. Opportunists. Worse than the seagulls. By the time we had passed the amusement arcades I was tempted to pop into another chippie but it would just be throwing money in someone else's mouth and, besides, I wanted to be hungry again just after five o'clock.

Seagulls are made for Gothic settings: those evil yellow eyes that follow every move, waiting for someone to trip and fall so that they can swoop down, peck the victim's eyes out and feast on the body until there's only an empty ribcage. And if they weren't staring insolently at humans they were fighting amongst themselves, screaming and shouting, strutting and shoving like drunks at a football match.

As we stepped onto the pier two couples were taking photos of each other. Elegant black dresses for the women, long tailcoats, knee-length black leather boots and top hats for the men. One of the women called over and asked if we would take a photo of them all together. They gave Alex a camera and a smart phone and posed in a line with the lighthouse behind them.

I saw it coming but was too slow to respond. Maybe five metres back, sitting on the handrail, two seagulls whispered something in each other's ears. They rose into the air, catching the breeze, soared and turned and came in like dive bombers, dropping their payloads in a synchronised display, managing to splatter white streaks over both couples' hats and shoulders before any of us could even think of warning them. And we couldn't even point out the culprits because, their bombing raid completed, the two birds had dropped behind the harbour wall and left the crime scene. All in less than a second. Alex handed over the cameras and we moved on. In our wake we could hear from the comments that his photos had caught the moment in all its visceral ugliness.

We walked towards the lighthouse, passing strange structures that looked like wooden Daleks but were, according to Megan, capstans, revolving cylinders for winding the ropes that moored ships in the harbour. The temperature had risen all afternoon and although the sun remained invisible it felt almost muggy. On the beach to our left an optimistic ice-cream van loitered for customers.

The surface of the sandstone lighthouse was gouged and hollowed like the walls of the Grand Canyon, rasped away by the rough tongue of the wind. Having posed for photos – various combinations of three Goths and a cowboy – we were about to step onto the wooden walkway that led to the green beacon at the end of the pier when we heard sirens. A police van and two police cars screeched to a halt at the end of the pier and eight or nine officers in DayGlo jackets leapt out. Everyone on the pier froze as the police thundered past, two of them pausing on the wooden walkway to stretch a roll of yellow scene of crime tape between the handrails.

There were maybe a dozen people ahead of us. The police rounded them up and sent them towards us. As they walked, people were staring down at their feet, looking down through the gaps between the planks.

'All make your way off the pier,' said the female officer on the walkway. 'We need access for emergency vehicles. Thank you for your cooperation.'

We turned away as the first members of the public ducked beneath the crime scene tape.

'What happened?' Megan asked a young guy who was looking physically sick as his girlfriend led him away, her arm around him.

'He saw it, on the lower deck resting against a pillar,' the girlfriend explained. 'We thought it was a fisherman having a nap or something.'

The boyfriend broke away and threw up over the railing into the sea. The girlfriend smiled weakly at us.

Other people who had been out on the pier were passing us, some confused, others ashen-faced. A middle-aged Goth couple wandered past, her face haunted, his face angry.

'Some joker's only gone and stuck a zombie skeleton down there all dressed up,' the man said in a thick Cockney accent. 'Eyes pecked out and everything. Bloody disgrace. Scared the hell out of her. And we was going to bring the kids. Can you imagine? Whoever done that, they should lock 'em up and toss the bloody key. Come on, Love, it's all right.'

The couple walked away, his arm around her shoulder.

'Anyone fancy a walk on the beach then?' Katie asked brightly, trying to keep everything from getting too dark.

'We might see a pelican,' I told her.

Katie stuck her tongue out.

We ran down the ramp. Sea foam skimmed and flew across the sand like tumbleweed in a two-horse western town. The waves snuck in behind us like pickpockets out to steal the heat from our feet. We shouted ourselves hoarse, scratched our names with our heels, jumped up and down till the sand around our shoes turned to jelly, and we ran some more.

By the time we returned to the cottage to dry out and veg in front of the TV, the afternoon light was fading. The news was a horror show. British politicians tearing each other apart over Brexit, and an even bigger punch up on the other side of the Atlantic with Americans screaming at each other over who should become president, conspiracy theories flying around like flies over sewage. Pretending darkness and mayhem was limited to zombies staggering around graveyards seemed a little pathetic given what was happening in the real world, but I kept my mouth shut; after all I was the cowboy wearing a Stetson to a Goth festival!

Even the local news was bleak. It turned out that the corpse on the pier was indeed a prank but Chief Inspector David Rawes of the Whitby police was incandescent and we could all sort of see his point. There were three real corpses in the morgue, he explained, and thousands of visitors who had come to the town to have a fun weekend. What Whitby did not need was a bunch of tosspots deliberately trying to spread fear. When the perpetrators were found the whole force would work to ensure they were brought to book.

He explained about the bodies found earlier in the day. The deaths were being treated as tragedies and not crimes. The victims had been very elderly, in one case possibly in his nineties, and all three appeared to have died of hypothermia, there being no obvious signs of violence or homicide.

'It is a stark warning to us all to remember to dress warmly and to drink responsibly,' the inspector concluded. 'Autopsies are being carried out and we hope to know more in the next twenty four hours.'

The story then shifted to an interview with George Sadwright, a city councillor who was calling for the entire festival to be cancelled.

'This cannot be allowed to continue,' said the jowly old git whose veined nose suggested he was not beyond enjoying the odd drink himself. 'We have people traipsing around in graveyards for selfies, bands making a god-awful noise through the night, grown men and women staggering around in ugly masks and people treating litterbins as urinals. I don't care how much money it brings the local economy, it's got to stop.'

'There speaks someone who no longer has to earn a living and hasn't enjoyed himself since he served in the trenches,' said festival organiser Sarah Plinth, a cheerful round-faced woman in a crimson Victorian bodice and black lipstick. 'We would echo the police's advice that people drink responsibly and dress warmly. It is November and we want everyone to enjoy themselves safely.'

Hannah plugged in her iPad and insisted playing the Rocky Horror Show on the television, to which the girls all sang along, while Alex and I stood in the kitchen eating cheese and talking about the old days at school. Apparently two other classmates were up in Whitby, Darren and Jordan. They had left Alex a message. We rang Jordan.

'Yo, how's it hanging, man?'

'Cool. We're cool,' Alex answered. 'How about you? Where are you?'

'Oh, you know. Lighting up the world, as usual.'

'Where?'

'Whitby Lighthouse. There's a cottage on top of the cliff. Darren blagged his dad. The views, man, I can't tell you. Is that Daniel?'

Alex turned his phone slightly so that Jordan could see me better.

'Wow, the Milky Bar Kid! Wazzup, Dan?'

I gave him a thumbs up.

'Where are you all?' Jordan asked. 'And more importantly, how many chicks are there with you?'

'We got a cottage bang in the middle of Whitby. I say we, me and the girls, Katie, Hannah and Megan are in the cottage but … Oh, and Dan is … I don't know where exactly …'

'He probably needed somewhere to stable his horse,' Jordan laughed.

'You're right, I'm on a farm.'

'Chill.'

'Yeah, chill,' I agreed.

'Anyway, where shall we meet?' Alex stepped in. 'How about the Dracula Experience?'

'Where's that?'

'On the harbour. Just ask. Eight o'clock?'

'Hang on a second. I'll ask Darren …'

We waited a couple of seconds.

'Yeah. He's good for that. See you there.' Jordan said, cutting the call.

Alex turned to me. 'Jordan is a twat, isn't he?'

'No, Jordan is an opportunist. Darren is a twat.'

While the others got busy with their makeup, I went out for a walk. A group of Goths were gathered round the lamp-post at the end of the street, laughing and chatting. I wanted to buy some chips from a certain shop across the harbour but it was only just five o'clock and it would look bad to appear too eager, so I headed in the opposite direction up the hill towards the sea.

The night air was chill. Smoke from Fortune's kipperhouse skulked the walls. In seconds I had the wind in my hair and was overlooking the harbour lighthouse, yellow against an ink blue sea. The view wouldn't have changed for hundreds of years. I imagined Captain James Cook heading out of the harbour on the Endeavour; men climbing the rigging to unfurl the sails, wives standing on the harbour wall waving their hats and shouting their goodbyes while children tugged at their skirts.

The tide was in. Waves crashed against the sea wall as large black birds flew languidly across the calmer water of the harbour. Cormorants perhaps? I wasn't sure. To reach the harbour wall you had to descend a steep path where dinosaur footprints had been set into the concrete. I could not conjure up an image of a T-Rex sauntering towards the beach, though I wasn't going to swear it hadn't happened.

The weather was brewing, dark clouds blooming rapidly over the sea to cover the town in a black pall as I watched. Having been in town all day, and in the cottage much of the afternoon, I had conveniently forgotten that later on I would have to make my way back to the farmhouse in the middle of nowhere. At least I had the bicycle, hidden behind the hedge at the junction of Green Lane and Hawsker Lane.

On the horizon a flash of fork lightning spanned sky and sea, quickly followed by another and another. Too far to hear the thunder. I thought again of Captain Cook and his crew out on the ocean, hundreds of miles from land, heading into the unknown, afloat in an outsized wooden coffin as an epic tropical storm engulfed the ship and tossed them about like gravel in a cement mixer.

Another story came to mind; hadn't Count Dracula's ship run aground on the narrow stretch of beach beneath me in another epic storm?

The storm grew with terrifying speed. In minutes huge waves were crashing against the harbour wall, sending water five metres into the air. Having walked some little way down I became transfixed by the relentless power of the sea, a force so brutal that I could imagine the giant lumps of stone the size of cars that flanked the ramp being hurled into the air. I retreated up the slope, away from this primal savagery until, at a safe distance, I could again enjoy the power of it without fearing for my existence. Finally, tiring of the noise and the overwhelming sense of personal irrelevance this monstrous seascape engendered in me, I made my way back to the street where the cottages were at least built on a human scale and where the span of a human life did not seem as trivial as a mayfly's.

The street was empty save for three puddles of light clinging to their lampposts, but there were lights on in many of the cottages, which cheered me up more than I would care to admit. I was passing Fortune's Kippers when I thought I heard something move in the shadows. I turned and stared cautiously into the space between cottage and smokehouse, my muscles tight as springs. I sneered at my readiness to swallow purple myths and creepy stories like some snivelling eight year old, but the sense of foreboding clung to me like a wet shirt.

Fifteen minutes later I was heading across town with four Goths; two with grotesque latex masks for faces, two with sunken grey cheeks and steam-punk eye wear, all four in top hats, purple silk, crimson lace and black velvet.

Darren and Jordan were waiting for us, as promised, outside the Dracula Experience. Darren, being Darren, his suit wasn't a fake, he was wearing genuine Victorian clothes. God only knew how much they had cost his dad. The trouble was that Darren was on the *fill-her-up* side of twenty stone and his costume was quietly weeping under the strain and praying he didn't sit down. Oblivious to the textile tension about his person, Darren made a point of showing us all his new tongue barbell; 18 carat gold with a large diamond at one end. He said it was a diamond anyway, and no-one felt inclined to dive into his mouth to check.

Jordan had gone for steam punk meets Rasta meets Goth. It was the first time I had seen a black Goth and I had to admit he did look chill.

As we passed my favourite chip shop I sidelonged inside, discretely so no one would notice, but couldn't see her. Maybe she had just been letting me down gently.

Maybe I would try again later on. Hope springs eternal.

We passed the lifeboat museum and made our way up the steps, passing under the whalebone arch, to the West Cliff. To our right was the sea and on our left were all the big hotels I had wisely turned down in favour of camping on the edge of a cliff on an abandoned farm in the middle of sodding nowhere.

Soft pillows, heating and minibars make a man weak as Wednesdays.

Turned out Darren had parked his dad's Land Rover on North Terrace opposite the posh hotels, so we all had to endure a tour of what I can only describe as a boring box with leather seats.

'What are *you* driving?' Darren asked me, sensing I was not overly impressed with his wheels.

'A stolen rust bucket bike without mudguards. It's not as fast the cruiser 2.12 turbo but the running costs are way cheaper and I look less of a prick when I'm using it.'

Darren was the only one who didn't find that funny.

I was the only one who knew it was actually true.

Pleasantries and introductions completed, we headed down Cleveland Way to the Pavilion. The place was heaving, you couldn't move for top hats, vampire tattoos, and earplugs.

Advice: if you want to stand out in a crowd, wear a Stetson. I was not usually obsessed with drawing attention to myself but at that moment it felt good to be a little different. Not wearing-a-tutu-pink-wig-and-shrieking-Land-of-Hope-and-Glory-in-Japanese-on-a-unicycle different, but not-quite-the-same-as-everyone-else different. Which is, I think, better on the whole.

The queue was long and much interest was being directed towards a black Routemaster bus parked near the entrance. I don't know why I didn't immediately recognise the bus but the truth is that I didn't; I was worrying about how much the tickets would be and whether I had brought enough splash or if I was going to embarrass myself in front of everyone.

We were level with the bus when Katie, who was taking selfies like the craze was about to end, started banging on about Hounds of Hellbane being her favourite underground band.

'Seriously, there's one YouTube film where the lead singer is like swinging from a chain and he's got this lizard in his hand and …' Katie was saying when the doors at the back of the Hounds of Hellbane bus opened.

Standing in the doorway, backlit by a single spotlight, stood a man who must be two metres tall. He was dressed in what looked like a black crocodile skin suit but couldn't be because that stuff had all been banned years ago. His black shirt was shiny as silk. His fingers were encrusted with huge silver rings of skulls and leering masks. Everything was black or silver, except his long hair, eyebrows and trimmed beard which were pure white and his irises which were pink. He wore a huge watermelon smile like the Joker in a Batman movie.

All around us people were murmuring and pointing.

'OMG, that's him! It's Thor Lupei!' Katie said, desperately trying to create a selfie with the man in the background, her face locked in a rictus grimace of fan-gasm.

People up and down the queue were taking photos on their phones.

The man on the bus looked straight at me and said in a booming voice, 'Daniel, so pleased you made it. Step on board, I've got your backstage pass.'

CHAPTER 8

Message from Miss Katie South
to Miss Chloe Carter

Sent: Sat. 5th November 2016: 8.07 p.m.

Get ready for total madness! You know
Daniel, the nerd who hangs around with Alex
in the pub sometimes? Well he is here in
Whitby. Not in our cottage obviously. Anyway,
we're standing outside the venue about 2
see the bands and everyone is going mad
cos there's this black bus, totally Goth, and
on the side it says Hounds of Hellbane. I
know! They aren't even on the programme
but it looks like they are playing.
Like WHAT!
And this is CRAZY. We're standing outside
the bus and the doors open and he's there.
Thor Lupei! SERIOUSLY. Check my selfie,
it's awesome.
I look like 'wow'. ¯\(°_o)/¯
But this is really freaky. He looks straight
at us and says 'Hi, Daniel, I've got your
backstage pass'!!!!! I mean WTF?
And now Daniel is on the bus and we're like
WHAT IS GOING ON? Stay tuned!!!!

CHAPTER 9

Whitby – Daniel Murray

Saturday, 5th November

Daniel, please. Take a seat.' Thor Lupei ushered me onto the lower deck as the bus doors hissed shut behind me. 'Welcome, welcome. You must forgive my manners but I have much to do before we leave for the venue. You will, I hope, find food and coffee to your liking on the worktop.' He went to the foot of the stairs, turned, and after a moment's pause said, 'If you will allow me, I must request you to remain on the lower deck, for your own safety. But please make yourself at home.' He indicated the lower deck with a grand sweep of his hand. 'Everything is at your disposal. I shall be as quick as I can.'

I sat in the chair I had occupied the previous night. I poured myself a coffee and waited. The ceiling creaked above my head as Thor Lupei moved about the upper deck. As soon as he had spoken to me in front of the crowd, I recognised the voice and knew that he had been driving the bus the day before. How and why he had picked Farview Farm? Had he gone online like I had? Had he actually met the farmer?

Hearing the crowd outside, I pulled a curtain open far enough to peer out. The queue was starting to move toward the entrance but Hannah and Jordan spotted me immediately and waved excitedly. I waved back casually and let go of the curtain.

'So Daniel, how has your day been? Did the campsite match your expectations?'

I hadn't heard him come down the stairs. Lupei was now wearing a long black leather coat, over the crocodile skin suit, with the collar turned up.

'Honestly? No. It's quiet. That's about all I can say for it.'

Lupei smiled his watermelon smile. 'Quiet. Yes, indeed.'

'But Whitby is nice.'

'You are right. A charming town. One almost wants to eat it … to swallow it whole and chew it.' His eyes gleamed.

'How did you find the campsite?' I asked.

Lupei appeared not to hear me. I watched as he poured himself a coffee. He was not as young as I had at first thought. I had thought maybe forty but he might even be in his sixties I realised; while his jawline was firm, the pale skin of his cheeks and close to his ears was a mass of thin wrinkles that contrasted with the dynamic vitality he exuded from his every pore. His hair being white, his eyebrows were not hugely in evidence but, up close, I saw that they were thick and bushy. His nose was straight, with nostrils that seem permanently flared. Like the skin of his face, the backs of his hands also showed the signs of age. He downed his coffee in a single gulp, cleared his throat and snarled like a lion.

'Vocal exercises,' he explained, seeing my nervous expression. 'Nothing to alarm you, Daniel. Shall we make our entrance?'

I finished my cup of coffee and nodded. 'Are the band coming with us?'

He looked confused momentarily. 'Ah, the band. Yes, of course. No, no, they will be joining us in … in a little while. Come.'

As we made our way to the doors he said. 'All these Goths, do you find them tiresome?'

'No, no. Well, yes, a little. I mean they are all very nice. It's just … I find it weird when everyone tries so hard to look the same because they want to be different.'

Lupei laughed out loud, his resonant voice filling the bus. 'Quite so. Which is why you have dressed for the Wild West.'

'I don't mean you, of course,' backtracking furiously, in case I had upset him.

'Oh, please. I am not offended,' he brushed aside my concerns. 'Like you I am playing a part upon the stage. Satisfying expectations. Offering a feast of gloom, gruesome malevolence, and unnatural sensations to orchestrate a frenzy of passion and terror.' As he spoke his voice grew in volume and pitch and tempo. 'And all to the raucous cacophony of the world's wildest thrash metal extravaganza!'

It was pure Rocky Horror Show kitsch and I knew then that he would have the crowd eating out of his hand.

We stepped off the bus. Lupei took my arm in a dramatic gesture and together we strode to the stage door. Alex, Katie and the others must already be in the building, but there were plenty of other Goths to stare and take photos on their phones as we swept past. If there were others in Whitby, aside from me, who had not heard of Hounds of Hellbane, they certainly weren't anywhere near the Whitby Pavilion.

Lupei banged on the stage door the way a baron might to gain access to a castle, three huge thumps as heavy as a battering ram. Almost immediately the door was opened from inside and I realised that maybe I had simply failed to knock correctly on the door of Farview Farm. What my nan would called a cheekie chappie opened the door, a tiny bloke not much more than five foot high, round as an egg and wearing an orange uniform, white gloves, a dickie bow and huge black-frame spectacles as thick as the ends of pint glasses. He looked to be around sixty but had dyed his hair jet black in the hope that it made him look as though he had just left school; which sort of worked if you thought of school as a life sentence without parole.

'Ay up, there's one on stilts and the other straight in from

Little House on the Prairie,' he chortled, his voice as Yorkshire as a pudding. 'Come in, lads. Lovely to see you. I'm Eric. I knew a cowboy once, he were that bandy-legged he couldn't stop a pig in a passage.' Eric consulted the list on his clipboard. 'Hounds of Hellbane and maybe …' He turned the pages back and forth, 'Devil's Truckers?'

Lupei smiled indulgently. 'He's not a band, Eric. He's my guest. Daniel.'

'Ah. There you go. Got him.'

We followed tiny Eric along a corridor, while I wondered how I was on the guest list.

'Room Five. Everything should be gradely, gentlemen. If you have any worries just shout.'

The room was very ordinary if irregular in shape. Large mirrors encrusted with a perimeter of light bulbs for makeup artists to do their magic, half a dozen chairs, a sink, fridge, microwave, and a table on which stood a large cardboard box marked "Hounds of Hellbane – 5/11/16 Rider". Lupei rubbed his hands together happily as I wondered what he might have ordered for the band. Sixty bottles of designer beer, a fine single malt from the Outer Hebrides, or several litres of cola, a pile of junk food, burgers, crisps, taco wraps, and a dozen curries from a restaurant in India? I had never been backstage before but the excesses of rock bands were legendary. To be honest, I was miffed that there was no sign of groupies.

Lupei leaned forwards and opened the box. He smiled and reached inside and lifted out what I can only describe as a fuzzy wooden melon. Holding it in both hands he lifted it above his head, as if offering a newborn baby to the gods, and chuckled contentedly in that resonant baritone voice, seemingly oblivious to my presence. I had a quick look in the box; it was empty.

'You are in for a rare treat, Daniel. You can leave your backpack here, by the way. It will be quite safe. A rare treat.'

'I am?' I said, dropping my backpack on the floor by the fridge.

'Cupuaçu, from ten thousand kilometres away in the very heart of the Brazilian rainforest. Secret of the Amazon Indians.'

He produced a long and frankly scary knife from within the folds of his coat, placed the cupu-whatever-it-was on the table and, in a single violent downward sweep of the blade, split the object in two unequal halves, to reveal a creamy off-white pulp as wrinkled as a brain concealed within.

'Amino acids, antioxidants, vitamins, polyphenols, phosphorus, selenium, theacrines,' Lupei said, bringing one half of the fruit to his nose and sniffing languidly. 'And other mysterious trace elements. While the other bands lounge around and sink into an inebriated haze, we indulge the elixir of health. The shamans use this to lower blood pressure, improve brain function, strengthen the heart, increase libido, stimulate skin rejuvenation and immunosuppression, and boost the gastro-intestinal system. It is the world's most compact pharmacy. And to top it all, the taste is exquisite: melon, chocolate, banana and bubble gum all rolled into one.'

He spun round, spotted a drawer beneath the microwave and from it produced two spoons, one of which he tossed to me. Grabbing the larger half, he sunk his spoon into the creamy pulp and wolfed it down greedily.

'That is for you,' he pointed at the smaller piece still on the table.

I picked up the fruit and smelled it. Like chocolate and pineapple at the same time. The inside was divided into five segments of equal size, each appearing to contain a pip or stone. I spooned out a piece and put it in my mouth. Lupei laughed as I grimaced at the sourness. As well as the flavours he had mentioned there was a faint hint of aniseed and the gingery taste found in some mangoes. Not wishing to offend him, and realising the fruit was quite possibly more expensive than the finest single malt, I ate the whole thing.

'Well?'

'The weirdest thing I've ever tasted,' I confessed. 'Is it a drug? Am I going to suddenly think I can fly?'

Lupei shook his head and smiled indulgently. 'Shall we go and see the warm-up acts?'

We stepped out of the dressing room and Lupei shouted "Eric!" at the top of his voice. In seconds Eric appeared, led us up the stairs and left us in front of a door that bore the sign "Strictly Artists Only".

'I'll knock on your door, ten minutes before you are due on-stage,' Eric told Lupei. He consulted his watch. 'In around seventy minutes. Don't mean to pressurise you but … the rest of the band?'

'All taken care of,' Lupei waved him away. 'You'll see them soon enough.'

Eric smiled back but it was clear he was a little anxious. 'Four songs?'

'Not one more nor one less. You have my word.'

Eric took his leave and we pulled open the door and stepped into the hall. We stood in the shadows behind the screen to the side of the band and watched. It was all guitars and drums, a post punk barrage of sound in front of which a guy with what I would call a pretty weedy voice was exhorting the crowd to travel with him to a world of darkness. It seemed to me that the closest the singer could have been to the world of darkness was losing himself in a fridge at college, but being more of a hillbilly blues and country man myself, I was not the best judge.

Thor Lupei beside me appeared to have sunk into a trance. His body was completely still as he stared at the band and, beyond them, the audience. In the coloured lighting on the stage, his face resembled a mask. He could have been any-thing from thirty-five to sixty-five. His pink irises appeared to have disappeared altogether, leaving only his pupils staring out of the centre of his eyeballs, which was more than a little creepy. I understood, obviously, that he was albino. I wondered if he saw the lights differently to everyone else. A vein was pulsing in the side of his neck so slowly he might almost be hibernating.

Where we were, to the side of the stage, we were voyeurs; neither with the band nor with the crowd but, rather, in a bizarre middle ground, detached and analytical, observing humanity performing a ritual. I was no longer even hearing the music as anything more meaningful than the noise of the air conditioning on an aeroplane when you peer through the triple-glazed windows at the lights of a city ten thousand meters below. Was that how Thor Lupei was feeling?

One song finished and another began. The lights strobed red then blue then green. The drummer noticed us and frowned. I waved then, suddenly, the drummer recognised Lupei. He started to hit the drums with more intensity, causing one of the guitarists to turn. Guitarist and drummer exchanged glances, the guitarist turned and spotted Lupei and grinned like he had just won the lottery.

Lupei, for his part, remained as calm and focused as a meditating monk. A couple of songs later the band finished their set and trooped off the stage, high on adrenalin, to rapturous applause. Coming up to us the lead singer offered Lupei his hand. For a moment it looked that Lupei was ignoring him then he seemed to snap out of his trance. He gave the singer his widest watermelon smile.

'They're up for it,' he said, glaring into the singer's eyes. 'Particularly that little group to the left. You could have jumped down and taken any one of them there and then on the floor.' Lupei raised his hand and made a gesture of someone picking a fruit from a tree. 'Male and female alike; you owned them all my friend.'

Evidently flattered, the singer smiled and nodded vigorously and seemed about to speak when Lupei's interest in him appeared to vanish, as quickly as it had arrived. Lupei turned away to fix his gaze once more on the audience, as if memorising each and every face. The singer continued to look up excitedly at Lupei for a few seconds then his expression changed to one of humiliation and he pushed past me without a word.

Within a couple of minutes the drum kits had been swapped over and the next band gathered beside us behind the curtain. The compere came on and introduced the next act, mopping his brow theatrically with a huge handkerchief to convey just how hot the band were, then made his way past us to exit the stage. In the opposite direction came the band, Ant Acid: guitarist, bass player and drummer who, between them, were sporting enough tattoos to fill an art gallery. Behind them was the lead singer, in her late twenties, Goth glam, head to toe in skin-tight black leather, lip jewellery and flame red hair.

'Have fun,' Lupei said, his face radiant, his smile wide as Wednesdays.

As she drew level with Lupei he put his arm behind her as if to help steer her past and suddenly she was in his arms. It was quite a move and, for a second, it was unclear as to whether Lupei would receive a kiss or a slap in the face. Pulling her towards him, her breasts pressed against his chest, he whispered something in her ear. The look in her eyes suggested surprise, irritation, lust and excitement in equal measure. She pulled herself away, gave Lupei an Elvis sneer and ran onto the stage. We stood and watched the first couple of songs. The band were tighter than the previous one, maybe I just preferred watching female singers from behind, and the audience excitement was ramping up steadily. As before, Lupei was staring past the band at the large crowd of jumping, dancing fans as the lasers swept back and forth.

'Watch the sheep, always watch the sheep. A good shepherd must know his flock,' Lupei whispered in my ear before the third song began. 'Please forgive me, I must go now to prepare myself. I notice you were standing with a group of people earlier. Your friends, perhaps?'

'Yeah.'

'Wonderful. If you should like to invite them to join us backstage after my little spot, I would be delighted to meet them all. How many are there?'

I counted them off in my head. 'Six.'

'Perfect. I will have a word with Eric. Just scribble the names down for him.'

And with that, and a dramatic sweep of his long leather coat, he was gone.

I watched the "sheep", wondering what on earth he meant by it. By the stage the fans were all pressed up together, dancing, singing along, lost in the moment. The further back you went the more passive the audience appeared, not that they weren't also dancing and buzzing, but less so. There was a tight group of maybe a dozen people on the left, maybe ten metres back, who were dancing in formation and calling out to each other. From my vantage point I could see only a fraction of the hall but I knew from the queue outside the venue that there must be a thousand people at the concert. Wanting to see my friends I moved closer to the stage, to the edge of the screens that hid the artists waiting to go on from the crowd. A middle-aged couple, in full Goth, were bobbing along to the beat. The woman, who was on the large side and in some danger of bursting out of her costume, pointed at the singer and mouthed the words "that's our kid" her face oozing pride and pleasure. I gave her a thumbs up and turned my attention to the crowd. Finally I spotted Alex and Katie and the others, on the right and quite close to the stage. As the song came to an end I waved discretely in the hope of catching their attention. It was

Jordan who spotted me, pulling Darren's sleeve and pointing me out. Darren looked sick as a parrot and who could blame him; he or rather his dad had splashed out thousands to get to the gig and it was the loser who hadn't even gone to college and was riding on a stolen bike who had got in free and now had the best seat in the house.

Not that I wallowed in that kind of thing, not my style. Really.

Alex seemed happy for me, which was nice. I felt guilty because it would have meant more to him to be where I was than it did to me. Put me on a stage with Arthur 'guitar boogie' Smith or Darius Rucker and it would be a whole different ball game; not least because Arthur 'guitar boogie' Smith was long dead.

The set came to an end. The band took their bows and came down the stage steps towards us. The compere came back on.

'Well, well, well. She's something, isn't she? Wow! I'll bet seagulls fly backwards when they see her. Eh? So, Whitby, are we all having a good one?'

The crowd roared their pleasure.

'Grand. Well, boy do we have a treat for you now! It's not on your programmes. To be honest the amount you cheapskates are paying it would never be on the programme but I'll tell you this: there won't be a dry seat in the house when I tell you …' the compere's voice was rising to an hysterical crescendo. 'It's only the biggest Goth band in the world! … With the amazing Thor … Lupei!'

The crowd were stamping their feet and chanting.

'It's … wait for it … wait for it …'

'Now, now, now, now,' screamed the crowd with one voice. 'HOUNDS OF HELLBANE!'

The compere had barely finished speaking when the stage erupted in light and sound. I hadn't even noticed the band go on stage, and I was next to the bloody steps! There were four band members: drums, bass, guitar and keytar. Two men, two women, all tall and lanky, dressed head to toe in black leather with long black hair, steam punk paraphernalia and face masks. They were instantly playing faster than the wind, the notes flying out from the stage like a storm of locusts engulfing the crowd who stood transfixed, jaws dropped. I have zero idea how they transformed the lighting in just three minutes while I was standing behind a bloody curtain not three metres from the drum kit but, out of nowhere, Whitby Pavilion had become as bright as the main stage at Glastonbury.

And Lupei wasn't even on stage yet!

The music hit an end note then as everyone started to applaud, changed key and went off in another direction. Suddenly the melody seemed to be in two keys at once, as if two formula one cars were chasing each other through hairpin bends. The drums pounded away in a rhythm that all made sense but didn't sound like anything I had ever heard.

Then it stopped.

The lights cut out and the whole hall was left in absolute silence. You could hear the sharp intake of breath. People could not have been more disorientated if the venue had suddenly slid off the cliff and down onto the beach below.

And just when we all made the decision to breathe again a massive chord from the band brought the stage back to life and in the middle of the stage, all two metres of him, holding his jet black Gibson guitar aloft in his left hand, that watermelon grin spreading from ear to ear, stood Thor Lupei.

With the index finger of his right hand he singled out individual members of the crowd, as if choosing his biggest fans. A woman fainted. The music stopped.

'Hello, Goths,' Lupei said in his deepest baritone.

The music erupted afresh with a fury that sent an electric pulse up and down my spine. I didn't really know what Goth music was and I suspect that after a few minutes much of the audience realised that they didn't know either as the band seg-ued seamlessly from one song to another. "Watch the sheep" Lupei had told me. Faces lit up as the crowd recognised a tune and started to sing along, their faces uplifted in ecstasy. After a couple of choruses the song would shapeshift into another song and again recognition would spread across the sea of faces and they would allow themselves to be bathed in the cascade of notes pouring from the stage.

Lupei had a vocal range three singers would have been happy to share; from Johnny Cash through Robert Smith and on to Prince. Watching him from the side of the stage I could see that even while he sang and danced, his voice soaring above the band, his face wracked with passion, there was still an extraordinary stillness about his eyes, a sense that he was animating a puppet, fashioning a performance and sitting far far away in a quiet place.

The idea that Lupei was both present and absent unsettled me hugely. I felt that I was inside the tent at a seaside Punch and Judy show seeing the performer's hands animating the characters as they ran back and forth chasing sausages and hitting each other. And that realisation caused me to look at the rest of the band. They were all amazing performers, it was impossible to imagine any of them making a mistake, their movements effortless and perfect. And yet, somehow, also too perfect. They barely looked at each other, keeping their eyes fixed on Lupei, slaves to his every whim.

I was feeling more than a little overwhelmed. And dehy-drated. I wonder if the cupuaçu, was more potent than Lupei had let on. I slipped behind the screen and made my way to the door that led to the artists' dressing rooms.

The singer from the last band was standing in the corner staring at Hounds of Hellbane. I could tell from her face that she was both mesmerised and thinking about how far she had to go before she could perform like Thor Lupei.

'Off to get a glass of water,' I explained, pulling open the door.

The bored look in her eyes betrayed that she did not give a toss what I did. I stood next to her for a few seconds, looking at the guitarist punching power chords in a relentless frenzy of attack and it dawned on me; I had not seen a single member of the band blink in all the time I had been watching them. Weird.

The stairs were empty. Eric was waiting in the corridor.

'Mr Lupei said you had six friends to bring back stage after his set is finished.'

'Yeah, yeah, of course. Do you have a pen?'

I scribbled the names down for him. 'I was just about to go and find them.'

'Make sure they all have ID.'

'Yeah, no worries. Which way is it to the hall?'

Eric showed me out, explaining that we had to go right round to the stage door outside to get back in.

A smack of fresh air and I was in the foyer. It felt like I had landed back on Earth after a weird time in another galaxy. The sound of the gig was audible but low enough to hear conversations, people talking about where they had parked their car or where to get something to eat. All very reassuringly boring and normal, except for the goggles, top hats and mahogany waistcoats. I went to the bar and asked for a glass of water.

The clock above the bar read five to ten.

'Two pounds?' the barman said, as if wanting to give me the option of reconsidering.

'You're right. I'll be back.'

I found the gents and drank a pint from the tap then went back to the bar and ordered half a pint of Jet Black. In little more than a couple of minutes I had sorted out the rehydration and quaffed a finely balanced porter packed with liquorice, coffee and sweet toffee (according to the label) and all for less than two quid. Bargain.

No such luck when I tried to get past hall security to find Alex, Katie and the others.

I explained to a man the size of a shed and the easy going manner of an overgrown alligator with toothache, that I had been backstage with Thor Lupei and Hounds of Hellbane and that I simply wanted enter the hall to collect my friends.

He explained to me that if unless I could produce a valid ticket I could sod off.

We were enjoying what could only be described as a stand-off when, to my great relief, Megan appeared on the other side of the door. The music had stopped. Seconds later the doors opened and Alex and the others poured out of the hall. Behind them the crowd were facing the stage, stamping their feet and chanting "Hellbane! Hellbane! Hellbane!"

'Dan! What the ...' Alex was grinning and shaking his head in disbelief. 'What a gig. Glad you came?'

I nodded, I owed him one. Maybe I'd spend some of my savings on going to see Arsenal with him.

Behind Alex, Darren looked miserable.

'I've got a surprise,' I told them all, as Jordan and I exchanged high-fives.

'No offence, Dan, but how the bloody hell do you, of all people know Thor Lupei?' Jordan asked.

'Maybe the *Midnight Cowboy* is also a dark horse,' Alex suggested cryptically.

'See what you did there,' Megan said.

'You're all invited backstage. To meet Thor,' I said.

The looks on their faces were priceless. Mostly ecstatic, except for Darren who looked physically sick; he wasn't used to being trumped.

'Cheer up Darren,' Alex said, 'you can spend daddy's money on something else.'

'For real? He's invited us backstage?' Katie demanded, her face flushed from dancing.

'You know what? When Lupei shouts out "Daniel, so pleased you made it. Step on board" Katie nearly wet herself!' Hannah laughed.

'Did not.'

'We have to go round to the stage door,' I explained, leading them outside and past Hellbane's black Routemaster bus. I knocked three times with a heavy fist, as Lupei had done.

'What's it like on the bus? I bet it is totally Goth,' Hannah said.

'Yeah, like black velvet everywhere,' Megan said.

'And freaky dwarves handing out drinks in cups made from monkey skulls,' Jordan suggested.

'No, Jordan. Yuck,' Hannah and Megan said in unison.

Jordan looked at me and shrugged.

The door opened.

'Daniel,' said Eric. 'Mr Lupei has just arrived off stage. Names please and I hope everyone has ID.'

Eric checked all the student cards and allowed us in.

'Room Five,' I said.

'You know your way?'

'Yes, I think I remember.'

'I still don't get this,' Darren was muttering unhappily. 'I mean he's dressed as the sodding Lone Ranger. This suit cost five grand. And I still think Alexi Liaho is a better ...'

'Chill, man,' Jordon cut him off. 'Just chill.'

We reached Room Five. I knocked.

'Come.'

I pushed open the door. Lupei was lying full length on the carpet, eyes closed, white hair like a swirling mass of snakes around his head. Straddling him was the singer with the red hair, still in her leathers. Which was kind of awkward.

'Welcome to you all. You will forgive me. The exigencies of performance require a little moment's relaxation. And Catherine is an excellent masseuse. I have tasked the glorious

Eric with acquiring beverages and snacks for one and all. I trust you all enjoyed the gig.'

He said the word "gig" playfully as if savouring the sound of it across his tongue. I was not a masseur but I felt fairly certain that the services Catherine was offering Lupei were not the standard package. She whispered something in his ear and the two exchanged conspiratorial smiles. She stood up, adjusted her clothing, tousled her hair and flounced from the room.

'It was amazing,' gushed Katie before anyone could feel uncomfortable. 'The best gig I have ever seen. In my entire life.'

Eyes still closed, Lupei smiled broadly. 'Marvellous.'

'Are the band .?.' Jordan started.

'Back in their boxes,' Lupei said. 'So to speak.'

I was going to say something when I remembered the time. 'I need to make a call.'

Lupei's eyes opened and he turned his head to look at me.

'I promised someone I would call. Do you mind?'

'Not at all. I will endeavour to entertain our guests while you are otherwise occupied,' he said without a trace of irony.

'I'll be back in a few minutes,' I said.

The door opened as I turned towards it and Eric came in bearing a huge tray.

'Eric, you are a tiny spherical angel,' Lupei said sitting up.

The others were so gobsmacked at being in Thor Lupei's dressing room and seeing the collection of beers, wines, spirits, fruit juices, crisps, nuts, cakes and so on the Eric was depositing on the table, that I might as well have been invisible again. I had served my purpose. I grabbed my backpack from beside the fridge and left, running down the corridor, rummaging in my pocket as I went. I keyed the number into my phone and hoped I wasn't too late.

'Who's this?' she answered.

'It's Daniel. You said to ring you after ten when you came off shift.'

'Hey Daniel! Are you OK, love?'

'I'm fine,' I said, imagining what it might be like if Tiffany, or anyone else for that matter, called me "love" and meant it. 'I was wondering if you wanted to go to the Goth gig at the Pavilion? … Sorry, can't hear you. What?' I had reached the stage door so I pushed it open and stepped outside, hoping to get a better signal. I did get a better signal but the door slammed behind me, the wind had picked up and it was beginning to rain. Dead leaves were flying everywhere.

'I said, I don't know. I stink of chips and haddock and it's quite expensive and most of the acts have already played.'

'That's OK. I can get us in at the stage door.' I shouted into the phone.

'Really? How?'

'It's a long story. Let's just say that show business has taken a shine to me. Where can we meet?'

'Do you know the whale bone arch?'

'At the top of the cliff. Yes.'

'I'll be five minutes,' she said.

I ran.

CHAPTER 10

Whitby – Email from Dr Nigela Shaveling
to Chief Inspector David Rawes

Sent: Sat. 5th November. 8.52 p.m.

Chief Inspector, please find prelim. report attached.

To save time and, I hope you will forgive me, to ensure that
the technical language in my report does not obfuscate my
findings, I present here a summary of the salient points in
plain English. I should say at the outset that this is quite the
most remarkable case I have seen in nearly forty years' work.

I say 'case', there are three victims in the morgue. While I
have as yet completed only the first autopsy, my first and
superficial overview would indicate a high correlation in
the condition of all three victims. The similarities have led
me to conclude that all three cases may be related and that
immediate action is required to protect the public. It is not
my place to do your work, Chief Inspector, but, if asked, I
would venture the opinion that all three persons were victims
of murder, committed by the same perpetrator/s.

Henrietta Street – unidentified male
Visual inspection confirmed that the man was, at first
sight, in his mid to late eighties and severely
malnourished. Time of death occurred around 2am. The
man appeared to have been in good health until very

shortly before death. (I shall return to this.)
Distinguishing marks included three tattoos:

• an anchor on the left upper arm, beneath which was written the word FOREVER

• a text tattoo containing the letters MUFC (presumably Manchester United Football Club) on the left lower arm

• an abstract 'tribal' tattoo on the right shoulder

All three tattoos were monochrome and in blue ink. The tribal tattoo appeared to be less than two weeks old. (I shall return to this later)

Feet

It is customary with older people to have problems with the feet: corns, bunions, hammertoes, thickened and discoloured toenails. Much of this is related to older/thinning skin becoming more fragile. It is therefore surprising to me that while the skin of the feet looked as old as the rest of the body, there were no signs at all of the wear and tear that is normally associated with old age. It is as if the man has grown old without wearing shoes or walking anywhere, which self-evidently does not tally with assumption that he was either homeless or living on the streets. To put it differently, it is as if he had the old feet of a young man or vice versa.

Weight - 44 kg

The man was 1 metre 75 in height (5 feet 9 inches) but weighed just 44kg. Context: Irish hunger striker Bobby Sands (5 feet 9 ½ inches) weighed 43kg at the time of death. Ergo it is doubtful that he walked to the place of his death; he would not have had the strength to lift one leg in front of the other.

Clothing

Dressed in Goth clothing, all of it new and showing no signs of wear and tear. The clothes were too large and the belt was set for a man with an 86 centimetre waist and a weight of around 68 kg. In other words, if the man in Henrietta Street had stood up his trousers would have puddled around his ankles.

Dental work

The teeth show no signs of decay, nor any fillings. While this is not unusual in many twenty-year-olds, thanks to the fluorides in toothpastes and better diets, etc., it is all but unheard of in an 80-year-old male who has lived his life in the United Kingdom.

Toxicology

We are still awaiting toxicology reports from the labs, but I think you need to know now that the body was missing both its kidneys. There were no outward signs of violence, scarring or incision, save some signs of petechial rash in the eyes, often an indicator of choking or strangulation.

Conclusion

The following is not for release to the public as I know this will sound extraordinary, and possibly lead to panic, but it is my finding that the body found in Henrietta Street, while initially appearing to be that of an 80 to 90 year old man, is, in fact, that of a young man, possibly only 25 years old. (The tribal tattoo is of a type only found v. recently and inked on healthy bodies, typically gym users). Its grossly collapsed condition on the sagging skin suggests that as recently as two weeks ago the victim had a normal body weight of 68-72kg.

At the risk of having my license to practice removed on the grounds of insanity by those with more timid minds, it is my belief that all three people who died last night were not elderly vagrants but younger people.

I have just established that the female victim is lacking both uterus and pancreas. In some inexplicable way all three victims appear to have aged forty to sixty years or more and lost a third of their body weight, in a matter of hours or minutes. You will, I hope, understand why I am contacting you while my work is still incomplete.

Of particular concern is the fact that with the festival coming so close to Halloween, one of the bodies was lying in the street for several hours, ignored and unrecognised by passers-by who mistook it for a ghoulish theatrical prop. Without wishing to sound alarmist, I urge you to consider that there is someone or something murdering people on Whitby's streets and that the public, including the thousands attending the Goth festival, are in grave danger.

Preliminary reports on the other two victims will be forwarded to you as I complete them.

Dr N.Shaveling, FRCPath

CHAPTER 11

Whitby Pier – Daniel Murray

Saturday, 5th November. 10.04 p.m.

The squalls that had battered the harbour wall during the course of the afternoon had returned with a vengeance, each smack of the waves sending a surge of white foam skywards, casting the handful of thrill-seekers on the pier into brief silhouette.

On the cliff top, where I stood, the leafless cages of the low bushes were being shaken so violently that it could only be a matter of time before they were ripped out of the ground and swept away. I stepped back from Captain James Cook's statue; his head was made of granite and I didn't want to lose my head if he lost his. I had positioned myself on the cliff, with the town to my right and the harbour jaws to my left, in order to catch the earliest glimpse of Tiffany when she appeared around the corner of Pier Road down below, but my eyes kept being drawn back to the intensifying storm over the sea.

Suddenly the sky around the harbour lighthouse was thick with seagulls as they arose en masse and flew inland at speed, seeking sanctuary among the chimneys and rooftops of the old town. Their cries carried faintly in the wind as they passed beneath me.

A bellowing horn turned my attention back again towards the sea. To my horror, a boat was trying to pass between the harbour jaws. From my vantage point, the vessel looked no larger than a pleasure craft designed for two or three fair weather fishermen, but we had been down by the lighthouse earlier and I knew that the boat must be eight metres or more in length. Thrown this way and that, it was unable to hold a course between the green and red lanthorns at the end of the piers. The lanthorns disappeared repeatedly beneath huge columns of spume as the roaring wind ripped a satellite dish from the boat's cabin before hurling the vessel itself against the left hand pier.

Hearing shouts I turned my attention back to the street below where a crowd was gathering. There was much gesticulation, with people pointing towards the pier, and men running. Suddenly I spotted a girl I thought must be Tiffany. Without a second thought I left my crows nest view, leapt over the low wall and ran down the steps towards the harbour, holding my hat and ignoring the protestations of people coming in the other direction, who had to press themselves against the cliff to let me pass.

In less than a minute I had reached Pier Road. The girl I had identified from above was not Tiffany but my disappointment was short-lived. Someone was shouting my name. Tiffany was running towards me, lit by the bright lights of the amusement arcades. Behind her, an ambulance was coming along the road, lights flashing to shift the dozens of on-lookers.

The background vanished and I stood there, a helpless adoring puppy, noticing the way the light caressed her cheek, the light in her eyes. Hoping I wasn't too obvious. Not giving a sod if I was obvious. She was beautiful and I ...

The siren made us jump. We stepped off the road and onto the pavement. The spell was broken. Tiffany looked confused.

'A boat hit the pier. I saw it all from up on the hill.'

Her face blanched. 'What did it look like?'

'I couldn't see much, it's too far away. Dark bottom bit and ... lighter on top. The cabin ... isn't it? Anyway, how was work?'

Tiffany ran straight past me towards the pier.

'What is it?' I rushed after her.

'Uncle Ted,' she shouted. 'He were out this evening.'

As we ran it began to rain like it had the previous evening, torrential rain, cold and hard as shards of glass. My hat flew off. I saw it briefly as it swept over the railing into the harbour, swooping out of sight like a gull. I could not have cared less. In less than a minute all my plans for the evening had fallen apart and I'd made a total twat of myself. There were maybe fifty of us running. A few Goths mingled with local people. A couple of men had stopped to grab lifebuoys from their holders and were charging towards the harbour lighthouse.

'Tiffany,' shouted one of them. 'What are you doing?'

'Me uncle Ted, he's out there!'

'Nowt you can do down there, lass. Go back.'

Tiffany ignored him and kept running, and I stayed with her. Behind the lighthouse, safe from the full force of the storm, the waters of the harbour rose and fell more than a metre. Beyond the lighthouse were the harbour jaws, the piers embracing an oval space not much larger than a swimming pool. It appeared that enough water to fill several Olympic pools was entering and leaving this space every couple of seconds as the swell lifted three or four metres then withdrew, sucking the water out again until you felt you should see the pebbles and silt on the bottom, before spewing back to engulf the lower platform of the pier in an orgy of violence.

Beyond the jaws, on the seaward side, the waves smacking the piers dwarfed the drama within. We crossed the wooden bridge onto the pier. I was by now fearing for my life and for Tiffany's. I grabbed her hand.

'Stop. The sea's coming up between the planks.'

'He's my uncle. This is my life. Go back or shut up.'

The men ahead of us were sailors, strong men used to fighting an angry sea, skilled in dodging or riding the blows, bracing themselves against the elements like St George facing the dragon. I was a soft Londoner, dressed as a sodding cow-boy and Tiffany was a girl who sold fish and chips. But she belonged.

'Let's take this,' I said, trying to release the lifebuoy nearest us from its stand.

Tiffany shoved me aside and showed me how to do it. She tied herself to one end of the rope with some fancy knot and passed me the life buoy. 'You'd better put that on, landlubber,' she said with a twinkle in her eye. 'We don't want to lose you.'

I felt ridiculous but somewhat safer. We were by now both completely drenched. Ahead of us a dozen men with biceps thick as telegraph poles were clinging to the railings by the green lanthorn. We could barely hear their voices above the wind as, clinging to the rail, we advanced hand over hand towards them. Below us, wrestling the clammy talons of the sea, the boat was trying to enter the harbour, it's engines strain-ing against the brute force of the elements. It was clear from Tiffany's face that the boat was indeed the one her uncle had left on earlier in the evening. A hollow boom sounded each time the ship's hull crashed the pier. The waves covered our shoes every few seconds. Tiffany lashed the centre of the rope that linked us together to the rail; she was not just a girl who sold fish and chips.

'Tiffany, I told you to fuck off,' shouted one of the men by the lanthorn.

'Don't waste your tongue shouting at women, you bastard. Save the fucking boat,' she screamed back.

How long we stood there staring into the abyss, watching brave men walk the tightrope of life and death, I cannot say. I lost all sense of time. Three times our hearts sank as it seemed that all was lost. The boat was crumpling before our eyes as it was thrown against the pier time and again. Piece by piece every external fitting on the boat was ripped off and sucked into the furious swell. Inside the boat's cabin we saw three men working as one, struggling desperately to hold the ship's wheel and steer a course to safety. The sea was a monster, roaring and devouring everything in its path, determined never to release the men from its grim clasp. In the wind I heard snatches of women and men screaming from near the harbour lighthouse, and saw the flashing blue lights of ambulances and fire engines gathered at the end of the pier. There was a light in the sky above the harbour, speeding towards us. As it drew nearer, the sound of a helicopter became audible above the howling wind.

That evening, watching the helicopter hovering above the damaged boat, seeing a man lowered on a winch towards the convulsing sea and the fragile boat, its gunwale underwater, its cabin swaying left and right like a set of windscreen wipers, I learned the meaning of courage and fortitude. I feared for the helicopter. I feared for the men. The man on the winch hung in the darkness above the deck with the sea throwing itself at him like a polar bear slashing a seal with its claws. Suddenly he was lit up, yellow against the blue night. On the deck of the boat the cabin door opened and a man lurched toward the lifeguard who caught him and secured him to the winch. Immediately the helicopter backed away, pulling the two men up and out of harm's way. In less than a minute the lifeguard was back in place above the submerged deck. The cabin door opened again and another man threw himself at the lifeguard.

'Why isn't it backing away?' I shouted at Tiffany.

Her face was white with fear. At that moment a third man ran out onto the swirling deck. He launched himself towards the lifeguard but lost his balance, slipped and shot across the deck on his back. Tiffany screamed, her voice so bestial that I recoiled and, in so doing, lost my footing as a wave surged upwards between the planks. In one movement I hit the deck and, carried by the malevolent liquid tendrils of the sea, disappeared beneath the bottom rail toward the black waters in the harbour jaws. I fell so quickly that I did not even think to make a sound, either in fear or in protest.

My downward path came to an abrupt end as the lifebuoy, which had been around my waist, snapped tight under my armpits, winding me and pitching me back and smacking my head against a concrete column. For an instant I feared that my arms had both been wrenched from their sockets, so intense was the pain. I was swinging at the end of the rope maybe two metres beneath the upper deck of the pier, spinning slowly and swallowing vast quantities of seawater. I was groggy, my senses so dangerously overloaded by a vortex of noise, light, smell, taste, and movement that I was struggling to form any semblance of coherent thought. Confused and disorientated, I imagined myself back behind the stage curtain at the Pavilion, watching Thor Lupei's pyrotechnics. The crashing waves became a thrash metal frenzy of drums, guitar and keyboards serenading a vast crowd. The flashing, dancing lights were a spectacular light show.

In the darkness beneath the upper deck I thought I saw Lupei's band standing beneath me, looking up, inquisitive, calm, observing me from behind their masks with unblinking eyes.

'Dan! Dan! Daniel!'

I awakened as from a dream, sucked back into the real world in a rush. I was coughing up water and aware of intense cold. My body was being pounded on all sides, the seawater stinging my eyes and sloshing into my ears.

'Dan!'

I looked up towards the noise and saw a girl waving. Beside her, one on either side, were two large men. I blinked as another truckload of water swallowed me and I felt myself slowly rising up and away from the mayhem. As I travelled upwards in a series of jarring movements I saw a boat falling apart, the cabin shearing in half to reveal for the briefest instant two chairs and a table on which lay coffee mugs, a box and a playing card. The two of clubs. Then a wave passed through, swirling everything away and the ship disappeared beneath the swell leaving only the briefest trail of bubbles. Continuing to spin slowly I saw under the pier deck one last time. The vertical pillars and floor seemed to shimmer for a moment as if a shadow of someone walking were passing over them, the shadow of a terrible supernatural force looking at me, cold and calm in the midst of chaos.

The two men lifted me over the handrail and carried me back along the pier. Too exhausted to protest, I closed my eyes and said nothing. When next I opened them the harbour lighthouse was behind us and I was being lowered onto a stretcher. I tried to sit up. Tiffany was there pushing me back.

'Don't move,' she said, smiling sweetly. 'It's all OK. They got Uncle Ted off the boat just before it broke up.' She turned to someone I couldn't see. 'Does he really need to go to hospital? He's just got wet keks, that's all.'

'He needs checking for broken bones and concussion.'

'I feel fine,' I said. 'And so does my brain. She's Tiffany and she deserves a medal for saving my life. I'm a stupid southerner who went too close to the edge. Are keks something you have with a nice cup of Rosie Lee? Can I go now?'

I sat up before anyone could stop me and swung my legs off the stretcher. The paramedic looked almost disappointed.

'I'll look after him,' Tiffany reassured her.

'I meant it about you saving my life.' I told Tiffany as we walked away. 'Do you do this kind of thing every week?'

'Couldn't let a London townie die on Goth weekend. Besides, you told me you had a backstage pass.'

'Like they'll let me in the building in this state,' I said, lifting my arm to show her the water dripping from my clothes. I flinched from the pain in my shoulder.

Tiffany did a twirl to show me she was as wet as I was.

'No, but I were thinking, they might let me in if you ask them nicely. Come on, love, I'll buy you some chips.'

We walked away from the pier and the howling sea. There was a queue outside the chip shop she said was better than the one she worked at. I couldn't have cared less. Although I'm sure the narrow streets were very picturesque, all I was seeing was Tiffany, the way her nostrils flared when she smiled, the way her wet clothes clung to her, the way she said "were" instead of "was".

'So what's it like being a student in London?' she asked.

'I wouldn't know.'

'You said your friends were all students.'

'They are. You'll meet them tonight. But I'm not, I've got a job. Of sorts.'

'Doing what?'

'Let's pretend I'm a lion tamer or something.'

She pulled my sleeve playfully. 'Come on, tell me.'

I shook my head. 'You'll say I'm boring and walk away.'

'Daniel, I work in a fish and chip shop. Am I boring?'

'I didn't mean that. I was just ...'

She pulled me to a stop. 'It can't be that bad. Spill the beans.'

I took a deep breath. 'I'm a trainee lettings negotiator at an real estate brokers.'

'Oh, thank God for that.' Tiffany set off up the street. 'I thought you were going to say you were an estate agent.'

'I just bloody did!'

'No you didn't. You said trainee. Plenty of time to switch to lion taming.'

'Now you're taking the piss.'

She took my hand. 'I don't care what you are Dan. I care about who you are. Work is just work. We've arrived by the way.'

We were outside a terraced house on Cliff Street. Tiffany

pressed the intercom button beside the front door.

'Hiya, is that pizza delivery?' asked a woman's voice after a few seconds.

'Are you decent, Tina?' Tiffany said. 'I need to pop in and grab a set of clothes for a drowned cowboy.'

The door clicked open. Turned out Tiffany lived in a flat with two girlfriends, one of whom had a boyfriend around my size. While I stepped into dry jeans, a dark-blue hoodie and a t-shirt that declared *I love Baby Strange*, Tiffany changed out of her green and cream uniform into black jeans and a Goth bodice. I had to pinch myself; she was so beautiful a bird of paradise would have been sick as a parrot to see her.

Tiffany had rang her parents to check on uncle Ted; he'd been airlifted to Scarborough Hospital. They were on their way there in the car. Her mum was still worried but the doctors had told her he was in good hands and already receiving the best possible care.

We left our clothes drying on radiators. I left my backpack, happy to have an excuse to return later on, not that there was much in it, and we set off to the Whitby Pavilion. It was just after eleven and the rain had stopped, though the wind was still rattling the lampposts.

'This way.' Tiffany pulled me back. 'There's a ginnel.'

'A what?'

'A ginnel, a short cut. You southerners don't know owt.'

'As long as Mad Alice isn't hiding somewhere.'

'You know about Mad Alice?' Tiffany looked genuinely surprised.

'Let's just say we bumped into each other last night. In the churchyard up on the hill. I'll tell you about it sometime.'

We had reached the Pavilion. I headed straight down the side path.

'Wait, it's this way,' Tiffany said.

'We're going to the stage door,' I explained.

I knocked three times. The door opened and Eric stood before us, looking a little taken aback.

'Daniel. What a pleasure. A new costume I see. Have you forgotten something?'

'I came back to join the others. This is Tiffany, by the way.'

'Evening Tiffany. Have I seen you somewhere?' He turned back to me. 'Your friends and Mr Lupei all left together, some twenty-five minutes ago. I assumed …'

I spun round and realised that we hadn't passed the bus in the car park.

'… and you were meeting them elsewhere,' Eric was saying.

'You're right, I did leave my coat in the room. Do you mind if we pop in to collect it? Mr Lupei said he would leave a message for me if I wasn't back.'

Eric did not seem entirely convinced by my performance but I formed the impression that maybe he remembered being my age and took pity on me.

'Aye, all right,' he said.

'Brilliant.' I indicated to Tiffany that she could go first.

As I followed her inside, Eric caught my eye and winked. 'Don't be too long now,' he called after us. 'It's open. By the way, I'm sure he's coming back, he's left several boxes of equipment.'

'I've never been round back before,' Tiffany said, clearly impressed. Which was a start.

We arrived outside Room Five.

'You didn't really leave your coat, did you?'

I shook my head, turned the handle and we stepped inside. The room was empty, though there were still unopened drinks on the table.

'Do you want a beer?' I asked, banging the top off a bottle on the edge of the table.

Tiffany held her hand out. I passed her the bottle and

grabbed another.

'Shame they've gone. I wanted you to meet Alex and Jordan. They called us the "Gristle Gang" at primary school. You'd like them.'

'So you really know Thor Lupei?'

'Yeah. We watched the other bands from the side of the stage. Then he went on. He was unbelievable. He just …'

'You can get to the side of the stage from here?'

'I'll show you, if you want.'

'Go on then.'

'I'll bring a couple more beers.'

'What's that?' she asked, pointing at the husk on the worktop.

'He called it a cupuasoo or something.

'Cupasoup? You sure?'

'Cupuasoo. It's a fruit from the Amazon jungle. Tastes really weird, like banana, mango, bubble gum and chocolate all at the same time.'

"Looks like he left you a note.' She passed me a folded slip of paper on which was scribbled 'my good friend Daniel'.

I opened it and we read it together.

"My Dear Daniel,

I once again have to crave your forgiveness. What must you think of me, leaving before your return? Your friends are charming company. I trust we will meet later on at Farview?

Eternally yours, Thor Lupei."

'Sounds a bit camp,' Tiffany observed.

'I don't think so,' I said, a little too defensively.

'Only teasing. Anyway, what's that stuff about Farview? He doesn't mean the farm, does he?'

'I'll tell you later. Do you want to see the bands?'

Moments later we were stood at the side of the stage,

drinking our beers and watching the headline act. Tiffany was in seventh heaven and took a bunch of photos on her phone, sending them to friends along with a spray of emojis. In fairness, the band were great, but my idea of what constituted a headline act had been forever altered by witnessing Hounds of Hellbane in full flow. The bar had been raised so high I doubted that I could ever enjoy a goth gig as much again.

Standing there side by side I became aware of another sensation. While my head was full of Tiffany, my body was still in shock from my accident. I felt a growing sense that I was drowning, back in the barrage of noise, spinning uncontrollably beneath the pier, the cold claws of the sea leaping up to drag me to my grave. And there was something else; a growing feeling that Lupei had been there watching me.

'Are you all right, love?' Tiffany shouted as a song came to an end. 'You look like you seen a ghost.'

'It's the noise. Like a flashback.'

I was shaking from ear to ankle. Tiffany reached a hand up to my cheek, concern written all over her face. 'Oh Daniel, you should have said.'

'You're really beautiful, you know that?' I said.

'Get away, you wazzock,' she said happily. 'Let's get you out of here.'

She took my hand and steered me towards the door that led down to the dressing rooms.

CHAPTER 12

Message from Miss Chloe Carter
to Miss Katie South

Sent: Sat. 5th November 2016: 11.13 p.m.

K. OMG! Thor Lupei! Only just got your mssg.
Unreal, girl. Loved selfies. When I saw yr hair
I was like what!!!! Have you taken loads of pix
of gig? Can't wait 2 see them.
I checked – he wasn't even on the prog. U
must have been like oh wow!
Where r u now? I called Hannah and she
said they went back through town to cottage
cos Darren and Jordan were being a pain.
Like Darren is so binary he doesn't respect
anyone's boundaries. Hannah got Megan to
send me her pix.
Nice one of that friend of Alex's getting on
the Goth bus. WHAT is he doing dressed as
Woody in that cartoon? !!! We were totally …
WTF.
Let us know you're back safe. See ya xxxxx
C <3

CHAPTER 13

Whitby - Email from Chief Inspector David Rawes to Dr Nigela Shaveling

Sent: Saturday, 5th November. 10.28 p.m.

Dr Shaveling, with respect, I suggest you need a holiday. I accept that your lab is grossly understaffed and that privatisation is impacting negatively on both your service and mine, and I appreciate that Whitby is home to the Dracula Experience, but we are now living in the 21st century. I cannot accept your conclusions as anything other than hysteria or a temporary loss of reason.

As you must surely know, Goths come in all ages and sizes.

Don't bother sending me the other reports. I will pretend I have received nothing from you as yet and we'll sit down and take a clear look at everything when the toxicology reports are back from the lab. Get a good night's sleep and cut back on the gin and tonics.

Best
CI D.Rawes

CHAPTER 14

Whitby - Email from Dr Nigela Shaveling to Chief Inspector David Rawes

Sent: Saturday 5th November. 10.52 p.m.

Chief Inspector, I have long since understood that thinking outside the box is outwith your list of talents. Nonetheless, I would urge you to ask your staff to consult the list of missing persons. If my deductions are correct, you will find that amongst those persons reported missing over the past 24 hours are individuals who broadly match the descriptions of the victims in my report. Check for clothing, tattoos and other distinguishing features, height, etc.

You will have noted from my report, the male had a distinctive gold and silver earplug containing a vintage watch movement. The female, autopsy now completed (report attached), had gold nipple rings, from one of which hung a small black chameleon. Not typical for 80 year old woman.

I do not require these reports to be filed away discretely, copies have already been sent to the Royal College of Pathology. If this situation escalates over the coming hours I will be able to demonstrate that any reluctance on the part of the police to take action was not the result of any failure on my part.

Dr N.Shaveling, FRCPath

CHAPTER 15

Whitby Pavilion - Daniel Murray

Saturday, 5th November 11.55 p.m.

If Eric was still around we didn't see him as we walked the empty corridors to the stage door.

Stepping outside, away from the noise and into the fresh air, I felt the pressure lift from my shoulders. Clouds, lit orange from below, hurried inland spitting softly as they went. Ahead of us pools of streetlight connected the Pavilion to the rest of Whitby like a set of stepping stones across a black stream.

'How is he?' Tiffany said beside me, holding her mobile in front of her face.

A tinny female voice, presumably her mum's answered.

'They've put him in an induced coma, love. Said it were best. I hit roof but Dad says doctors are doing right thing.'

'What does he know?'

'Don't be rude, Tiff. It's just a precaution. The consultant said everything looks normal. Are you at home?'

'I've been at Pavilion with Daniel.'

'Who? The lad who fell off pier?'

'Say hello to me mam,' Tiffany told me.

'Hello, me mam,' I obliged.

'We've been watching the bands but Daniel were feeling poorly.'

'Why am I not surprised? Where's he sleeping tonight?'

Tiffany made eyes at me. Protective mothers going a bit heavy with the obvious subtext.

'They're all in a cottage. On Henrietta Street. A bunch of them from London.'

'Well you see he gets home safely. And you do the same. Is Tina there this weekend?'

'I'm not a baby, Mum.'

'You are. You're my baby.'

'Give Uncle Ted a kiss from me. Bye Mum.' Tiffany cut the call and turned towards me. 'Sorry about that.'

'Don't be sorry. You're lucky, I wish I had a mum who cared about me. What do you want to do? How about coming back to *my* cottage on Henrietta Street?'

'Couldn't tell her you were camping at Farview Farm.'

'I understand. No worries. I'll walk you back afterwards. If you want. I just don't want tonight to end. '

It was quieter than before but there were still people out on the streets, a few open pubs, a couple of chip shops attracting passing Goths, like streetlights attract moths. Along Pier Road a couple of bikes padlocked to railings had been blown over by the gusting wind, or kicked over for a laugh. Sooner or later I would have to climb the hill and cycle back to Farview, unless I could blag my way to staying the night in town. But then my tent was up there on the cliff top, and Lupei had said "I trust we will meet later on at Farview."

'After midnight the chippies sell crap,' Tiffany confided. 'They've switched fryers off and the chips are limp as farts or hard as bullets.'

'Everyone's pissed,' I told her. 'No-one cares what they shove in their face when they leave a pub.'

The lights were on at the cottage. I rang the bell. Megan opened. The door creaked. Megan looked a little surprised to see us, if I'm honest, but she let us in.

'This is Tiffany. Tiffany, Megan.'

Hannah poked her head round the kitchen door. 'Did you see Jordan? He said he was on his way.'

'He's not bringing Darren, is he?' I asked.

Hannah shook her head.

'Thank God. Have Alex and Katie gone to bed?'

'Didn't you read the message Thor Lupei left you?' Hannah asked.

'I assumed they're all back.' I said.

'They went off for a spin on the Hellbane bus. Darren's with them,' Megan explained. 'Hannah didn't fancy it. Neither did Jordan. He said he would hang out at the Pavilion until they got back. Hannah and I came back here. We said we might go back later on.'

Lupei's message hadn't mentioned any of that.

'Anyone want coffee?' Hannah called from the kitchen.

'Where are you staying?' Megan asked Tiffany.

'She lives here,' I explained.

'I was asking Tiffany.'

'Do you want a coffee?' I asked Tiffany.

'White, no sugar.'

I went into the kitchen to help fix the coffee. Hannah was shoving a couple of biscuits in her mouth while she thought no-one was looking.

'What did you think of him?' I asked.

'Who?' she spluttered as she span round guiltily. 'Darren? He's a …'

'Not him. Lupei.'

She studied me for a few seconds before answering. 'Honestly? He frightened me. I mean the music was great and he was the perfect host. Polite but really creepy. In his eyes. I know what you're going to say but you're wrong. It's not because he's albino. I'm not prejudiced. It's the way he looks at you. I don't know how to put it but …'

'Watch the sheep, always watch the sheep,' I suggested.

'Yeah, that's it. He's like looking down on you from far away, like we're woodlice crawling on the pavement and he can crush us with his boot.'

'Text from Alex,' Megan called out from the next room. 'Just reached the Pavilion and they're walking back across town. They dropped Darren off at the lighthouse. He was too drunk to drive and feeling sick.'

Hannah looked relieved.

'The bus ride was great, he says. And Katie says "best Goth night ever".'

I was rummaging in the fridge for milk when the doorbell went. It was Jordan. The kitchen clock said twelve sixteen.

'This town is insane,' he announced, collapsing on the sofa. 'Like a film set. I swear, if we had a Whitby theme park in Acton we'd mint it, I'm telling you. Fifty quid a ticket. Have you seen the sea, Dan the man? Waves five metres high? Crazy. There's this boat in pieces. Someone said it was smacked against the pier till there's only matchsticks left.' Jordan laughed as he spoke. 'Unbelievable!'

'Tiffany's uncle was on that boat,' I told him.

Jordan's face crumpled like a house of cards. 'Oh God, I'm really sorry. I didn't mean …'

'It's OK, they all got off alive,' Tiffany reassured him. 'The chopper winched them up, just in time.'

'I didn't know. Sorry. I'm Jordan,' he said, grabbing a coffee from the tray I was carrying, meaning I would have to make a fresh one. 'Is Alex ..?'

'They just texted,' Megan told Jordan. 'You'll have to get a taxi. Darren's feeling sick so they dropped him off.'

'Blood claat, I'll bell him in a minute. So Dan, how does a nerd from Ealing create a bromance with a Goth superstar? And what happened to the cowboy vibe by the way?'

'It got wet. And to answer your first question: on the camp-site …'

'What campsite?'

'Farview. Where I'm staying on the …'

'You're on a campsite?' Jordan said incredulously. 'Like in a tent?'

'It's a farm south east of the town, past the abbey.'

They were all looking at me as if I was deranged, except Tiffany who just looked worried.

'Everything in town was booked, or two hundred quid a night and …'

'It's No … vem … ber,' Jordan mouthed each syllable.

'And you're in a luxury apartment in a sodding lighthouse because you're happy sponging off that twat Darren. Some of us have principles … but not much splash. All right? Do you want to know about me and the Hounds of Hellbane or what?'

'OK, OK, chill out, dude.'

'Let's play cards,' Megan suggested. 'While we're waiting for the others'

We played knockout whist and I explained about the night before. I was a blind dog with piles and distemper by the time we reached round three; I nominated Tiffany to play my single card. It was the two of clubs. I was out of the game.

'So you didn't see the upper deck of the bus?' Hannah asked.

'That was the card of your uncle's boat. The two of clubs,' I muttered as the flashback hit me.

'The upper deck of the bus?' Hannah repeated.

'What? Oh, I don't know. He said it was out of bounds.'

'And there's no-one at the farm?' Megan said.

'There were three other tents in the field and a campervan, but I didn't see anyone. Just me and the Hellbane tour bus.'

'The whole band are on the bus?'

I shrugged; I had no idea. Tiffany had listened without saying a word. She had won the round and was picking trumps.

'Hearts,' she said.

Everyone grumbled half-heartedly about Megan and dodgy shuffling, except me since I was out.

'Farview farm were closed back in August,' Tiffany said quietly, as she played her cards. 'Two campers died. They had pitched their tent too close to the edge. The cliff collapsed in a storm and they were buried under tonnes of rock and mud. When police got there they found the farmer had also died weeks earlier. His wife, Helen, were alone in the big house with his corpse in one of the bedrooms. People would push money through the letterbox or pay online or not pay at all, then park wherever they liked. Some people would see the place and simply drive away again. Others wouldn't care. And then there were the bad people. Stories about girls being taken there and abused. They arrested four men at the end of September. It were in the papers and on the news. Maybe not in London,' she said, looking at the rest of us. 'A month ago the paper said Helen had disappeared.'

'How long does it take to walk?' Megan asked, looking at her watch.

'From Farview?' I asked.

'From the Pavilion, idiot.'

'It took us fifteen minutes,' Hannah told her.

'They should have been here by now.'

'Maybe they've stopped off,' I suggested.

'Text her,' Hannah said.

Megan looked worried. Maybe it was all the talk about Farview Farm. She grabbed her phone and sent a message, then tried ringing. No answer.

'Try Darren.'

'What's he going to do? He's in bed or he's wrapped round the big white tuba, counting the lumps in his vomit.' Jordan said. 'They dropped him off.'

'Just try him.'

Jordan tried Darren. No answer. 'The bus must have broken down; it must be fifty years old. They're out on the moors and the wind is howling and the jelly-eyed ghost of …'

'Not funny, Jordan,' Megan cut him off.

We continued playing cards or, rather, the others continued playing and I walked over to the windows that overlooked the harbour. The reflections on the windows were too bright so I wrapped the curtain behind me. The gale was still whipping the waters of the harbour. Huge mountains of water were crashing against the harbour wall, as they had been for hours.

'I don't think you should go back to the farm,' Tiffany said gently, taking my hand at the window. 'You can stay with me, but no funny business,' she whispered.

'Do you think we should ring the police?' Megan said behind us. 'It's been thirty four minutes since she sent that text and …'

At that moment her phone pinged.

'Oh, thank God,' she said. She was silent as she read the text. 'Bloody hell.'

'What is it?'

'I don't know.' Megan passed the phone to Hannah who read the screen and passed the phone to Jordan.

'It doesn't make sense,' Hannah said. 'That was sent over an hour ago and he's sent a message since then. Why has this only just arrived?'

'I don't know,' Megan shouted. 'How would I bloody know?'

'So maybe it's a joke and …'

'Shut up Jordan.'

'What's a joke?' I asked, holding my hand out to take the phone from Jordan.

The message was short and if it wasn't a joke …

CHAPTER 16

Whitby Pavilion - Daniel Murray

Sunday, 6th November 00.52 a.m.

We ran all the way. There were still plenty of people about, most of them totally wasted. We must have spoken with thirty people hanging around outside the Pavilion. Nobody had seen anything. We went inside.

'Have you seen the Hounds of Hellbane bus?' Hannah asked a middle-aged Goth couple with skulls painted on their faces and so drunk they could barely stand. 'The black double decker?'

'You were on it, love,' said the woman who was wearing a big badge that read Laura – 46 years young today! 'And he was on it,' she said pointing at Jordan. 'You were all on it.'

'I meant have you seen the bus since midnight?'

'They were all on it, weren't they?' Laura asked her partner.

'Everyone's on something,' he answered and they fell about laughing.

We're all geniuses and comedians when we're wasted.

We had no more joy with the Goths inside. Hannah and Megan were increasingly anxious; if the bus had not come back to the Pavilion where had it gone? Why would Alex have sent a message saying they were back in Whitby if they weren't?

'I can help you,' said a man with his back to us, at the bar.

I recognised him immediately; the red hair and mutton chop sideburns, the morning suit missing a sleeve, and the mechanical arm that ended in a black silk glove. The man from the bridge. He was carrying a long leather coat over his shoulder.

'But he is not to be trusted,' he said pointing at me. His accent was foreign.

'Another wino,' Jordan muttered. 'Thanks but no thanks, man.'

We turned to walk away.

'Three of them left with the wolf on the bus and three got off before it left.'

We stopped.

'You, you and you.' The man pointed at Hannah, Jordan and Megan. 'I saw everything. If we hurry we may still find your friends alive. But this one is not on your side.' He added, staring straight at me.

'What's that supposed to mean?' I said angrily.

'The wolf uses people like you, my friend. You are already tainted; the tethered goat that draws the tiger, the bait that sets the trap. Do you have transport?'

'We've got a car,' Jordan volunteered.

'You don't have a car,' I said.

'Darren does,' Jordan replied, producing a set of keys and swinging them in front of my face. 'He gave me the spare set, in case he ended up drinking too much.'

'You've drunk as much as him.'

'No alcohol has touched my lips.'

'Since when?' I asked, remembering his fondness for Red Stripe lager.

'Since I grew these,' Jordan shook his dreadlocks. 'Strictly Ital, vegetarianism and a clear mind and spirit. And a lickle spliff. But not tonight.'

'Do you know where they went?' asked the man with the mechanical arm.

'Who are you?' Megan demanded.

'I am Emile Noir. I hunt scravir. I'll ask again, do you know where they went?'

'Lupei was talking about taking us for a short drive up the coast,' Megan explained, 'We didn't fancy it. Half an hour ago I got a text saying that Darren was feeling ill and they were dropping him off at home.'

'Which is?'

'Darren and Jordan are staying at the lighthouse, but there's something you need to know about the text. There was another …'

'We leave now,' Noir said to Jordan. 'I can help but we have to hurry.'

'We're all coming,' Megan reassured Jordan.

'Not a good idea,' Noir said.

'Daniel,' Megan grabbed my arm.

I was still wondering what Noir meant. What the hell were scravir, and what was his thing with me? And the more I looked the weirder his arm appeared. Was that real bone in the middle of his mechanical arm?

'I agree with Megan, let's stick together,' I said.

'Drop me off,' Hannah said. 'I'll stay in the cottage. In case they come back there.'

'On your own?' Megan asked.

'I've got my phone. I'm tired and I'm cold.' Hannah pouted. 'All right?'

Tiffany grabbed my arm. 'I'm coming with you,' she told Jordan, her face resolute.

Jordan appeared visibly relieved. Noir looked irritated but was keen to get going. We ran from the Pavilion to North Terrace and piled into the Land Rover, Noir sitting at the front with Jordan who got busy with the satnav. Megan insisted we drop Hannah off outside the front door of the cottage and then wait until she was safely inside. Nobody protested. We then followed the road along the east side of the river where dozens of small sailing boats rocked back and forth in their moorings, their masts shaking in the wind. Left onto a road that led up a hill, eventually hitting a junction where we turned sharp right. All at once I knew where we were. My stolen bike was hidden just behind the hedge; we were on Hawsker Lane.

'Are you sure this is right?' I asked, alarmed as to where Jordan was taking us. 'This is the road to Farview Farm.'

Emile Noir turned to study my face, his gaze probing and intimidating, then turned to Megan 'Tell me about the other text.'

'It was from Katie. She was hearing screams coming from inside the cottage.'

'Who was inside?' Noir asked.

'Didn't say. It was just "Screaming inside the cottage. Come quickly. Help."

Jordan swung the car left onto a rough track heading east towards the cliffs. No-one spoke as he threw the car through the gears, weaving left and right along the narrow lane, slamming the brakes at every corner. A brief moment of light as the lane passed through the middle of a farm then we were plunged again into a hedge-flanked blur of darkness.

My logical brain was convinced that everything was a misunderstanding or a prank and that we'd arrive and find Alex, Katie, Darren and Thor Lupei sitting in front of a warm fire in the lighthouse cottage, laughing and drinking. Or maybe they were all back at Henrietta Street. But my emotional brain was far less confident; I was freediving into a morass of disturbing doubts and fears that I did not want to face.

A mile further on Jordan took a sharp left and we left the fields behind us and entered wilder terrain, driving between banks of gorse and dead fern. The charcoal sea appeared beyond a low dry stone wall; distant white horses glowing below us as far as the eye could see. The road bore right and after a hundred metres the way ahead was blocked by a gate.

Noir climbed out and opened the gate and we passed through. Hemmed in between a freshly painted white wall to our left and a hill to our right we drove towards a group of white buildings at the centre of which stood the lighthouse, flashing from white to red every few seconds and sending out a beam of light so bright it lit the clouds. Jordan turned into the parking area and cut the engine.

There was no sign of the black double decker bus. We could hear the whistling wind, even with the doors closed. The grasses on the hill were pressed flat.

A washing line was vibrating like a guitar string.

I had expected the lighthouse to be a tall structure towering forty or fifty metres into the air. It wasn't much higher than a three-storey building. It didn't have to be, it was perched on top of a sixty-metre cliff overlooking the North Sea. It could be seen from thirty-three kilometres away, someone told me later. Nestled beside the lighthouse on either side were the two keepers' cottages that had been converted into holiday lets once the lighthouse had been automated and the keepers made redundant.

We climbed out of the car as Emile Noir caught up. He was now wearing his long leather coat. The clouds were rushing over us, heading inland. The smell of smoke hung in the air.

'It's that one,' Jordan said, pointing at the cottage beyond the lighthouse.

'OK you and you, come with me,' Noir said, pointing at Jordan and me. 'I'm keeping an eye on you. You two, stay in the car and lock the doors.'

Noir and I followed Jordan. We heard the car doors open and close behind us. Why were we allowing Noir to dictate our actions? Who was he? What did he know? Our path was illuminated by light spilling from the lighthouse. Nothing looked untoward until we opened the front door and stepped inside the cottage.

There were signs of a struggle everywhere: smashed flower pots in the vestibule, a chair on its back in the hall, cutlery strewn across the floor in the kitchen where a drawer had been ripped out of a kitchen unit. Jordan ran ahead, calling out Darren's name.

'Alex,' I shouted. 'Katie.'

Noir tugged my sleeve and put his finger to his lips. Standing silently, he listened attentively. I followed him into the lounge as Jordan caught up with us.

Jordan shook his head. 'Place is empty.'

'Shh,' Noir put his finger to his lips a second time.

A coffee table lay smashed against the wall, the sofa had been overturned and the curtains were billowing in and out. Jordan walked over to the window and pulled back the curtains.

The window was in pieces, glass and wood leaning out into the night, as if someone had been thrown through it. Jordan looked anxiously back at me, climbed up onto the window ledge and jumped out. I crossed to the window and looked out. Behind the cottage an expanse of lawn dropped away towards the cliff edge. Jordan was running towards a low dry stone wall in the shadow of which lay an irregular-shaped lump. Behind me Noir ran out of the room. I caught up with him as he threw open the front door and raced out.

The grass was slippery. Jordan had stopped by the wall and was staring at the ground.

'Makes no sense,' he said.

The irregular lump was in fact a body, face down in the grass. From the side, the head looked wizened and lined. Noir rolled the man onto his back. A skinny old man. Dead, his face frozen in a grimace of pain, his eyes staring vacantly up at the sky, his skin so thin it was translucent and might have been made of parchment.

Jordan turned away and threw up.

It wasn't just the face, the old man's body was beyond

skinny. The hands, hooked and thin as vulture's claws, reached out from the ends of crumpled sleeves, as if to push something or someone away. Who had attacked him and why? And where were Darren, Alex, Katie and Lupei?

Then something else struck me.

'The question is, where's Darren?' Jordan said.

'No, that's not the question,' I said, trying to make sense of what I was seeing. 'The question is how come this old man is wearing Darren's clothes?'

Jordan did a double take then scratched his chin. 'Maybe Darren's having a shower when this guy breaks in, they have a fight, the man jumps through the window and Darren chases after him.'

'You are both wrong,' Noir said. He had pulled up one of the corpse's trouser legs to reveal the almost non-existent calf muscles of a body that resembled a mummy from the British Museum. 'Nobody has stolen Darren's clothes and Darren has not escaped anywhere.' He paused to make sure he had our full attention. 'This is Darren. You're looking at him.'

'No way,' Jordan scoffed. 'End of.'

'You're insane,' I told Noir. 'Darren's only twenty.'

'Does he have any distinguishing features?' Noir asked calmly. 'Birthmarks, scars, earrings, that kind of thing.'

Jordan and I looked at each other. I shrugged.

'Nor me.' Jordan said. Then his face changed. 'There is one thing.' He looked down at the body. 'Nah.'

'What?' Noir probed.

Jordan looked at me then down at the old man's face then back at me.

'Do it,' Noir barked.

Jordan took a deep breath, grabbed the old man's chin and pulled open the jaw.

There, nestling against the shrivelled tongue, was a gold barbell with a large diamond at the end of it. Jordon lurched backwards, like he had received an electric shock, his face torn between disbelief and disgust. He collapsed to his knees and threw up in the grass, over and over until his stomach was empty and he was gagging only bile.

My fists were clenched so tightly that my fingernails were breaking the skin.

At that moment we heard raised voices.

Megan and Tiffany were alone in the car.

I jumped up, hauled Jordan to his feet and ran back up the slope, Jordan just behind me. Skirting the large oil tank at the end of the house, we raced towards the car then stopped; their voices weren't coming from the car but from a different direction. Up on the hill, I spotted the light of a torch. We scrambled up the bank, oblivious to the gorse bush thorns ripping into our hands and legs.

The girls were on the narrow coastal path overlooking the lighthouse, some little distance south of the cottages. The gravel path, no wider than a laptop, snaked away towards the horizon with nothing more than a line of barbed wire to keep hikers from tumbling over the cliff edge.

Megan was clutching something. 'She must have dropped it.' She handed me a blue purse.

'You sure it's Katie's?' Tiffany asked.

I unclipped the purse and pulled out a bankcard that read Ms Katherine South. As Noir made his way up the slope towards us, we were all thinking the same thing.

'Do you think Alex is with her?' Megan asked, shining her torch in the grass as she followed the path. She bent down to pick something from under the bracken. A smart phone.

'Whitby's that way, isn't it?' Jordan said, pointing northwards. 'There's nothing for miles in that direction, is there?'

'Yes, there is,' Noir said.

Tiffany spoke the words as they were forming in my mind. 'Farview farm.'

CHAPTER 17

Message from Miss Katie South to Miss Megan Holmwood

Sent: Sat. 5th November 11.09 p.m.

Megan, you were right not to come. Thor and Darren have had a fight. Darren such a prick when he's pissed. We're at a lighthouse (the one on the cliff BTW.) Thor drove him home because Darren said he was feeling sick and then Darren is rude about the bus, like it's an old wreck and why can't he go upstairs and so on. So Thor asks him to leave. Darren goes off shouting stuff back at Thor. Then Thor gets off the bus and follows him. And Alex chases after Thor, apologising for Darren, and they all disappear into the cottage.

Stayed on the bus but phone signal's crap ... might as well be in the jungle. Plus weird noises on the upper deck that freaked me out so now I'm sitting on the hill. The lighthouse is amazing, prob lights Holland from here. Everything is quiet so I guess they've all calmed down. I'll text when we are heading

OMG a window's just got smashed. They're all screaming. Text again in a minute. K

Unsent – no signal
Send again?

CHAPTER 18

Whitby Lighthouse - Daniel Murray

Sunday, 6th November – 01.30 a.m. 'Oh my god, he is evil. We have to stop him,' Megan said as soon as Noir had finished telling her and Tiffany about the body. 'He has to be stopped or killed or something.'

'Hang on a minute,' I said. 'We don't know that Lupei is responsible for any of this. We don't really know what is going on. All you have is his explanation. I know everyone is gothing out and on a Dracula trip but there is a rational explanation for everything.'

'You read her message,' Megan insisted, holding up Katie's smart phone.

'How do you know her pin?' Jordan asked.

Megan shook her head pityingly at Jordan.

'The message does not say anything about Lupei being the evil one,' I countered. 'It just says they had an argument. I have arguments with Darren; he's a twat. It doesn't make me the devil's spawn.'

Jordan looked like he was going to say something then stopped himself.

'She's got no money or ID or cards.' Megan switched back to Katie's circumstances. 'She's dropped her phone and is heading in completely the wrong direction. She could have fallen off the cliff. Oh my God!'

'We should split up,' I suggested. 'I'll take the path because I have already been to the farm and know the layout. It can't be more than a kilometre. You lot take the car, we can meet there.'

'You're not going alone,' Noir said.

At first I thought he wanted to protect me, but something in his eyes made it clear that Noir wasn't protecting me, he wanted to protect Katie from me.

'OK,' Jordan said. 'You and Emile go along the path, and I drive with Megan and Tiffany. Do you know how to get there?' he asked Tiffany.

She nodded.

'There's still a dead body down there,' Megan said, pointing at the cottage. 'What about the police?'

'Let's find your friends,' Tiffany suggested, 'then worry about the rest of it. If we drive back to Green Lane there'll be a signal and we can trying ringing Alex.'

Megan gave me her torch and we split up. We heard the car start up behind us as Emile Noir and I ran in single file along the narrow cliff top path away from the lighthouse and into the darkness.

Though Noir was beyond weird, I was glad not to be heading towards Farview alone. Except for the barbed wire that curled treacherously beside our racing feet there was no sign of human presence; we could have been on a wild inihabited world. Plunged into that howling wind-swept dark, shadows of a hill on one side and raging sea far below on the other, I longed for the tame streets of West London, a lamppost every fifteen metres, each one numbered and accounted for, every hazard quantified and minimised.

The heavens opened and rain beat down, making the path slipperous underfoot. I had experienced the dark drench on Hawsker Lane the previous night but this was immeasurably worse. We were two or three metres from the edge of a cliff, with a sixty-metre drop to the rocks in a gusting wind, racing towards a deserted farmhouse with no idea of where we might find Katie or what state she would be in when we found her. My lungs were burning as we staggered up a steep embankment. Almost at the top, I slipped and fell headlong in the mud, cracking my hip painfully against a rock. Noir hauled me to my feet and I thanked him and, for the first time, he looked at me as if I were a normal human being.

'Is Katie short-sighted?' he asked, reaching into the long grass and picking up a pair of black-rimmed glasses.

'No idea,' I answered.

A dry stone wall ran the length of the ridge, at right angles to the cliff. I followed Noir over the stile that straddled the wall, pausing at the top to take in my surroundings and to catch my breath. Breaking the crest of the hill ahead of us was the blunt black silhouette of a building that I recognised. Farview Farm.

We cut across the fields towards the farm. The ground dropped quickly and we found ourselves trudging through boggy ground, ankle deep in freezing water, vegetation snagging our legs.

'Those are the tents I saw last night,' I told Noir, pointing up the slope ahead of us.

When we reached them I saw how badly I had misjudged the scene the previous night. Up close it was easy to see that there were no happy campers sharing the field with me; the grass in front of the entrances was over a foot high. No-one had entered these tents in weeks, maybe months.

'We check each one,' Noir insisted.

The first tent, a two-man pop-up not unlike my own, was empty, with no sign of ever having been occupied. The second tent, no larger than the first, smelled bad as we approached and I confess I was nervous as Noir leaned forward and unzipped it.

The smell exuding from inside was overpowering, sickly sweet and fetid. Noir turned away to breathe fresher air. From a coat pocket he produced a leather half-face mask to cover his mouth and nose. Pressing a button on his gloved mechanical hand, the tip of one of his fingers lit up like a torch. He poked his head back through the tent entrance.

The pitch of night had enveloped us in a heavy fist. Though Noir's torch beam was only pencil thin and entirely contained within the fabric of the tent, I worried the light advertised our presence and would draw evil towards us. The fears that had gripped me the previous night returned, reinforced by what Tiffany had told us about the farm's recent past, and when Noir dropped to his knees and crawled into the tent, I would have shouted at him to stop had my voice not dried in my throat. The back of Noir's head made a lump in the canvas as he moved about within. The rain fell ever more heavily, drumming the taut skins of the tents. The farmhouse squatted brutishly against a backdrop of black marauding clouds moving inland like a pack of wolves. I wanted to be a thousand miles away.

Noir was reversing out and the noisome stench was increasing exponentially. I braced myself as he leaned back and stood up.

'If this is as bad as it gets, we will be the happiest men in the universe,' he declared. In his hand he held the carcass of a plucked chicken on its plastic tray, green and yellow with slime, disgusting putrid liquid overflowing the tray and spilling to the ground. 'Looks like they left in a hurry.'

He hurled the chicken away from us, back down the field, then wiped his hand clean in the wet grass.

The third tent was larger than the other two. I decided to show willing and open it myself. I ripped the zip upward and, torch in hand, stepped inside without having to crawl or bend over.

It was a time capsule to summer. A partially deflated beach ball, bamboo canes with small fishing nets for rummaging in rock pools, four pairs of flip flops - two adult pairs and two smaller pairs – and a pack of cards. Swimming costumes hanging on a string that spanned the roof. A small plastic table carried plastic cups and plates.

On either side of the central area there were two sleeping compartments. They were dry; everything laid out as if the family could arrive at any moment: sleeping bags, pillows, a teddy bear, a quiz book, some colouring crayons.

Noir had entered the tent behind me.

'What happened to these people?' I asked, my voice thick with emotion.

It was a question neither of us could answer. We zipped the tent up and covered the short distance to the camper van. The curtains were drawn at every window including the windscreen. The grass was long around its wheels.

'This was here when you arrived?' Noir whispered, rattling the locks on each door.

I nodded.

'OK,' Noir shrugged and carried on towards the farmhouse.

'That's mine over there,' I whispered, pointing my tent out, barely visible as a blob of grey wedged between a shed and a hedge. 'And there's a cattle grid at the gate,' I warned him.

We trod carefully over the cattle grid and into the farmyard and there, at last, we saw evidence of Katie's presence; a set of footprints in the mud leading away from the gate, made by trainers clearly smaller than a man's feet. Why wasn't Alex with her? I opened my mouth to shout but before I could utter a sound, Noir clamped a hand over my mouth. He shook his face and put a finger of his mechanical hand to his lips.

'If she is hiding she needs to remain safe,' he whispered, leaning in close. 'She is young and her spirit is strong. We must move carefully. I feel the scravir. There is danger here.'

I had no idea what he was banging on about but, as Noir spoke, I noticed his mechanical arm was glowing more brightly. I was again drawn to the structure of this prosthesis because although I knew my imaginings to be absurd I could not dispel the feeling that the bones were fakery designed for aesthetic effect for what remained of Noir's real arm. But how could that be? It made no sense.

Noir moved silently away from the farmhouse, passing behind the rear of the large barn. As I followed, the small hairs on the back of my neck bristled. We neared the farm entrance, keeping to the shadows of a tall and unkempt hedge until, finally, we stepped onto a road and I understood Noir's intentions. In the distance across the open landscape we saw the twin beams of an approaching vehicle. We hurried along the road, away from the farm. It was at first unclear as to where the vehicle was travelling or how large it was but, over the space of half a minute, it drew closer until we recognised the Land Rover. Noir waved Jordan to a stop and signalled to him that he should cut the engine. We were maybe a hundred metres from the farm.

Megan's window opened. On the back seat, Tiffany looked relieved to see me. Rain was drumming on the car roof.

'Where is she?' Megan demanded.

'Did you get through to Alex?' I asked.

Tiffany shook her head.

'Quiet and listen.' Noir took command. 'The good news is that we have not found a body on the path,' he whispered. 'It appears that your friend made it safely as far as the farm. Now I must beg you to remain calm and quiet. She is in grave danger. I have detected the presence of scravir and ...'

Megan cut him off. 'Forget the steam punk crap, it isn't funny anymore. I just want to find my friends.'

'What I am about to tell you will seem very strange but I must ask you to trust me and allow my words to reach you both here and here.' Noir leaned across and touched my head and heart. 'The arcane knowledge I possess is not new.' He opened his coat and took from within it a short sword, maybe fifty centimetres in length. 'The danger your friends face is real. I carry the ghastly paraphernalia of my trade and am alert to perils that you will not see until it is too late.' Replacing the sword within the folds of his coat, he produced a row of tiny transparent vials on a rack, arranged like bullets in a magazine. 'Even faced with the terrors ahead of us, it is our good fortune that Nature, in its mercy, has provided us with the skills to fashion agents of destruction to kill the most formidable foes and to heal those touched by their evil.'

'Yeah, yeah. Have you seen the bus?' Jordan asked, interrupting Noir's gothic weirdness.

Noir looked at each of us in turn. I was soaked to the skin for the second time in the evening and my teeth were chattering.

'Tell me, did you just see your friend reduced to the corpse of a skinny old man?' he challenged Jordan. 'Or was that just gothic weirdness?'

Jordan said nothing.

'We saw a body wearing his clothes,' I said. 'We don't know more than ...'

'I understand that this is all completely outside your experience but you must trust that I am here to help,' Noir said earnestly. 'May I continue?'

No-one spoke.

'Park the car out of sight from the road,' Noir told Jordan. 'Keep watch and warn us of any approach.'

'There's no phone signal out here,' I said.

Noir reached into a pocket and produced two small boxes made of brass and mahogany. Each device had what resembled a miniature Victorian telephone handset, with brass receiver and mouthpiece, a short antenna and various buttons and dials. Steampunk walkie-talkies! I didn't know whether to laugh or cry. Noir gave one to me and one to Megan and took us all through the controls, including the vibrate setting, to ensure the holder's location wasn't given away by someone calling.

'I'm coming with you,' Megan announced, stepping out

of the car. 'Katie's my friend.' She passed the walkie-talkie to Tiffany.

'Call every ten minutes,' I told Tiffany. 'If I can't talk I'll signal back to let you know we are OK.'

Noir, Megan and I headed back towards the farm. Behind us we heard the car manoeuvring then, after a few brief seconds, the engine was switched off again. We walked three abreast in the deeper gloom beneath the hedge. Megan had thankfully left her top hat in the car. Dressed in black from head to toe, she was dressed for skulking in the dark. Passing through a gap in the hedge we hugged the wall of the barn to make our way to the farmyard. No lights on anywhere, the house was as empty as when I had arrived the night before.

'That passage leads to the back of the farmhouse,' I whispered, 'but there's a sick dog in an outhouse who might start barking. The front door is open, so is the barn and when ...'

Noir held up a finger to silence me. He pointed in the direction of the barn doors then cupped his ear, suggesting we listen carefully. All I could hear was the rain clattering around us. I flinched as freezing water dripping from the barn roof found the back of my neck. Noir walked silently to the barn entrance. From a pocket in his coat he produced a strange pair of telescopic goggles, which he put on. He beckoned us to follow him. It was only when we crossed the threshold and stepped out of the rain that I heard what he must have heard; a faint scratching and sniffing sound, distorted and mechanical.

Lost immediately in the thick blind void of the barn, we were bold as braille. I stepped forwards focused on what was real. I drew on my memory of what I had seen the previous morning, the huge pile of turnips to the right, the old tractor to the left. Or was it the other way round? Katie was an airhead but would she really have come in here, even to escape the rain?

We had not lit our torches but, as my eyes adjusted, the

glow from Noir's arm provided just enough light for us to see each other's faces. But if we could see each other who else could see us? Noir swept his arm back and forth slowly as if using a sensor.

'Stay behind me,' he ordered.

We followed the dim light of his arm as Noir crept further and further into the gloom, Megan behind him and me behind her. In the absence of sensory input my brain was behaving like a car radio searching for a signal. Something. Anything. To the point that I could no longer trust my eyes, my nose, my ears. Could I really smell sweet cherries and burning fat? Was the luminous glow of Noir's arm slowly changing colour, or was my mind confabulating wildly? Was I really hearing a gentle articulated mechanical movement rushing along the rafters above my head?

'What's that sound?' I asked Megan.

'What sound?'

The vibration in my pocket was real. I felt the contours of the walkie-talkie and found the answer button. I pressed it twice to let Tiffany know we were OK. Moments later the walkie-talkie vibrated twice to let me know that they were also OK.

Twenty-five steps inside the barn Noir stopped and sniffed the air. Suddenly I understood; he wasn't looking for Katie at all, he was hunting. What had he said about using bait? Were we the bait, Megan and I? Was Noir using us to draw something towards him? Too far in to flee, I put my hand gently on Megan's shoulder. She flinched, then relaxed. I leaned forwards and found her ear.

'We stick together,' I whispered.

She said nothing, but I felt her hand press upon my own.

Noir opened his coat and, in the lacklight, I saw a device that might have been a syringe or a pistol into which he fed the magazine of tiny glass vials he had shown us earlier. The magazine slipped into place with the gentlest of clicks. From another pocket, he produced a second set of brass telescopic goggles. He separated them into two and handed us each a single eyepiece.

Without a word Noir stepped beyond the next partition leaving us in total darkness. Holding the eyepiece against my right eye I saw Megan glowing brightly, and my own hand was white with heat. An infra-red detector. Megan, who had done as I had, was staring back at me, a grim smile forming beneath the brass optic. We exchanged a thumbs-up and followed after Noir. Rounding the corner of the plyboard wall we were confronted with a sight that stopped us in our tracks.

The only thing I had ever seen that remotely resembled the scene before us was night-time film footage on the internet of thousands of crabs crawling over each other on a beach. Writhing on the floor of the barn was a jumbled mass of naked and painfully emaciated figures, their limbs moving back and forth, one over the other. I guessed they were human though they did not resemble any humans I had previously seen. Interlocked as they were it was hard to say how many individuals there were: six, seven, eight? Eyes white with heat, as seen through my infra-red optic, the figures struggled to lift their faces on scrawny necks too weak to bear the weight of their heads. Could they see us? I didn't think so.

Where a normal human is soft of form - bones hidden beneath muscle and fat - these creatures were like stick insects, all angles and jutting bones pressing against translucent and blotchy skin.

Their laboured breathing was rasping and dry, like that of asthmatics. Was this what I had heard crawling outside my tent the previous night? As Noir took three rapid steps toward the squirming mass, Megan gripped my arm so tightly that she was cutting off the blood supply to my hand.

Were these the scravir?

How long had they been in the barn and how did they get here? We watched in gruesome fascination while Noir lifted the syringe gun and poked it into the nearest body and pulled a trigger that in turn activated an ornate piston that pushed the contents of a vial into the abdomen of the creature. Like a boxer who had just thrown a successful punch, Noir stepped back, avoiding a grasping hand.

He pressed a button on the pistol, ejecting the spent vial and loading another into the delivery chamber, and stepped forward a second time. Watching Noir in action, his long skinny limbs poised over his victims, the syringe hovering over the bodies as he picked his spot, I was reminded of a parasitic wasp squirting its eggs into a hapless caterpillar.

With the aid of the infra-red eyepiece I could see that the small quantity of liquid Noir had injected into the first creature was growing exponentially, causing the victim's skin to bubble and crawl as the foreign substance spread through the body at ferocious speed. The remaining tissue of the creature was being eaten away before our very eyes. Sensing the threat, the other creatures hissed malevolently, their hands flaying in the darkness, long-nailed fingers reaching blindly towards their assailant.

It seemed an uneven contest, the able-bodied Noir, armed and fleet of foot, dispatching one by one this writhing but impotent nest of bones and sinews. Injecting a second creature, Noir stepped back and reloaded.

As I watched through my optic I noticed that within Noir's mechanical arm the bone or ivory was lighter in colour than the outer surface that encapsulated it. It made no sense. The infra-red spectrum registered by my optic presented a visualisation of heat; why would the inanimate core of a mechanical arm be hot? What purpose could be served by such a phenomenon?

Before I could find a rational explanation, my attention was distracted by what was happening on the floor behind

Noir and beyond his peripheral vision. Of the eight creatures, four were no longer writhing helplessly. Behind Noir's back, they had linked hands, their heads turning slowly towards each other in the darkness. My blood ran cold as I saw what they were doing. Three of the four creatures were wasting away before my eyes, their remaining muscles disappearing from beneath their skin to leave their limbs as thin as sticks and their abdomens as empty and taut as drums. The fourth, on the other hand was rapidly gaining weight and strength, stretching its limbs and lifting its head off the floor. In horror, I realised that by some diabolical method I did not understand, three of the creatures were sacrificing themselves, the flesh slipping out of their bodies and transferring into that of the fourth. Through my eyepiece I could see the light fading within the three even as white heat burgeoned in the fourth.

Megan had noticed it too. Her fingernails were digging so painfully into my arm that I was obliged to wrench it away. The noise of our movement caused the reassembling creature to turn its head towards us in the darkness. Its nostrils flared as it sniffed the air. Instinctively I sniffed the air myself. I could not smell human but I could most definitely smell the same odour I had noticed on entering the barn; sweet cherries and burning fat.

'Emile! EMILE!' Megan hissed. 'Behind you!'

Noir turned having injected a third or fourth creature, as the reconstituting scravir (for I now admitted to myself that this was what Noir must have meant) let out a rasping roar and rose to its feet. Beside it, the three remaining creatures were now no more than husks of skin and bone, as dry as three-thousand-year-old mummies. The scravir was as tall as Noir and could clearly see his glowing mechanical arm. Its face broke into a lop-sided smile. In one movement, it bent forward and grabbed the leg of one of its fellow creatures, ripped it cleanly from the body at the knee then drew itself up to its full height, bone in hand, swiping it violently in an arc that smashed against Noir's shoulder, sending him reeling backwards. As Noir collapsed, the sword he had shown us earlier fell from his coat, clattering to the floor.

The scravir stepped quickly towards Noir, catching him while he was still off balance and hurling him back against the wall. Any dream I had harboured that I was witnessing a television stunt had vanished, we were fighting for our lives and as soon as Noir was killed the monster would turn its attention on us. Megan had reached the same conclusion. She leaned over, picked up a large stone and hurled it at the scravir.

'Leave him alone, you bastard,' she screamed.

While the scravir turned towards her, I rushed forwards and picked up the sword that Noir had dropped. We had the advantage of being able to see more than our enemy. The scravir was still turning when I smashed the sword blade down onto its shoulder with all my strength. With a crunch of breaking bones, his arm fell out of the shoulder socket and sagged, a gaping wound revealing the broken collarbone and torn ligaments. Beside me Noir was clambering to his feet and reloading his syringe.

It wasn't clear whether the scravir felt any pain from its injury; there was little blood. Stumbling over the bodies of its fellows, it lunged towards Megan, swinging the leg bone as it came. Megan stepped back to avoid the blow and tripped, falling heavily onto her back. In a shot the scravir had closed the gap and stood over her, its mouth breaking into an ugly grin as it raised the leg bone high above its head in preparation for delivering the mortal blow. I threw myself forwards and slashed at its thigh, slicing the muscle right through to the bone. The creature having no clothes to contain it, the muscle simply fell away, flapping and twitching in the air behind its calf as the scravir wobbled and rocked.

Finally we heard its voice, a deep roar, primal as a landslide, evil as genocide. In a fury of energy it brought the bone down to crush Megan's head, but she rolled away and the bone struck the floor of the barn, the aftershock rippling back up the monster's arm. Unable to walk the scravir could not protect itself from Noir who thrust his syringe deep into the monster's back. As soon as the vial was emptied, Noir withdrew the needle, recharged the pistol and plunged the syringe in a second time.

The scravir howled with rage as the contents of the vial raced through its muscles and vital organs. Skin rippling with lumps and bumps as muscles dissolved and organs failed and strength vanished, the creature collapsed to the floor, its vocalisations beginning to sound almost like words. Through my eyepiece I could see the heat shrinking until its limbs were as black as the enveloping gloom. It writhed for a minute more until the remaining life force flickered and was extinguished.

I helped Megan to her feet.

'You have both shown immense courage,' Emile Noire told us. 'We must get these bones outside and set fire to them.'

If there were other scravir in the barn that night I did not see them. Maybe we were reckless to assume our job in that dark place was done but, as ordered, we turned our attentions to building a fire. Thankfully the rain had let up. We laid a large sheet of plastic in the mud of the farmyard then collected straw, hessian sacks and timber from within the barn and constructed a pyre. Noir, having checked that all the scravir were dead, helped us drag the corpses outside and toss them onto the pyre. He handed Megan a box of matches.

As we watched the flames streaming high into the night, I was struggling to think coherently. I had just witnessed the destruction of what I took to be eight emaciated human beings. True they had been transformed into monsters but they were, nonetheless, human beings. Who had they been? Where had they lived? Where were their families and friends? Who had reported them missing? Would we all end up like them?

The walkie-talkie vibrated in my pocket. Jordan and Tiffany had seen the smoke rising from the farm. I gave Tiffany the bare facts and said I would explain properly later. She told me Jordan had rung the police and left an anonymous message about the body at the lighthouse cottage. Was that a good thing? I could not decide, but it was too late to change it. Jordan and Tiffany wanted to join us but Noir refused. He insisted our work was not yet done; there may be more evil lurking in the farm, and we had still not begun our search for Katie. He needed them to remain on watch.

The pyre crackled with heat, the flames burned green and red, then purple. The smell was disgusting; all three of us found ourselves gagging helplessly.

'You know what I'm thinking?' Megan said. 'Where does Thor Lupei fit into all this? You said his bus was parked here last night. Where is he from? Did he just arrive for the gig, or has he been here for days, or even weeks?'

I thought of telling her about Lupei's band, Hounds of Hellbane, how strange they had seemed to me on the stage at the Pavilion, playing like robots, never blinking. Were they scravir? But first I had a question for Noir..

'Are you going to tell us what's going on?' I asked him. 'You fit in great at a steampunk festival, with that arm made of brass and mahogany and all the little cogs and pulleys, but that isn't a toy, is it? You're just like Thor Lupei; using a festival to hide in broad daylight. Who are you? What are you? '

Noir smiled as he gazed into the flames, as if he were remembering an amusing anecdote.

'When we are young,' he said eventually, 'we are invincible, immortal, nothing is beyond our reach. We don't see the myriad of tiny imperfections that incrementally eat away at us. We cannot imagine ever needing to wear glasses or seeking a helping hand to cross the road. We look at weakness or fragility and feel sick. We flock to those who tell us everything bad in our lives is someone else's fault. We grab the hand of those who promise to attack our enemies. We struggle to imagine the Long Now and our place in the continuum of history. Lupei feeds all those desires and, yes, I once underestimated him and it cost me my arm. They say that the best things can cost an arm and a leg …' He paused. 'I got off lightly, don't you think?' Noir smiled grimly, looking up at Megan and I. 'Lupei groomed my home town, like he is grooming you, Daniel. Making you feel special. Using you to get at your friends. Telling you that you are different to the others.'

'Watch the sheep,' I muttered.

'Always watch the sheep,' Noir finished the sentence. 'But maybe you are not like me. Maybe you are stronger.'

'So what are scravir?' Megan asked.

'You already know more than almost anyone alive,' Noir told her. 'They are the husks of human beings, trapped and weakened like paralysed flies in a web. Their muscles, strength and vitality, and sometimes their organs are sucked out of them, rendering them helpless, their lives entirely dependent on sustenance provided by their master who can replenish them and deplete them at will.'

'Hang on,' Megan said incredulously. 'You're telling me that the master - I'm assuming you mean Lupei, right? – can siphon out a person's muscles or liver or whatever without cutting a person open and then just as magically put it all back in when he feels like it?'

'More than that. He can put one person's vitality, organs, muscles into another person and thereby …'

'That might have made sense in the eighteenth century,' I interrupted Noir, 'but we all know that just doesn't work. The tissues would be rejected. You can't just shove one person's kidneys into someone else.'

'Very clever, Daniel. But allow yourself a moment to reflect that the force that can remove a kidney without breaking the skin might also be able to control a body's immune responses. The fact that medicine took until the late 20th century to understand the immune system does not preclude arcane and esoteric knowledge from having mastered the same subject thousands of years ago. Does anyone claim that birds could not fly until Clément Ader's steam-powered linen bat, the Avion, took off from a French airfield in 1897? Anyway, let us find Katie. If she is here and still alive she will be in desperate need of our help. Megan, you know your friend better than I, where would she hide?'

The walkie-talkie vibrated in my pocket.

'Hi Tiffany.'

'There's a vehicle heading towards us.'

'OK. Got you.'

'It's a lorry or a bus and it's moving really fast. Over.'

'OK. Over and out.' I turned to Megan and Noir. 'We have to move.'

CHAPTER 19

Whitby Police Station, phone transcript

Sunday, 6th November 02.11am

Operator: Hello, emergency service operator, which service do you require? Fire, police, or ambulance?

Shaveling: This is Dr Nigela Shaveling, forensic pathologist, I wish to speak with DC Simon Cook. I understand he led the team on Henrietta Street yesterday morning.

Operator: What is the nature of the emergency?

Shaveling: I've told you who I am. His direct line is busy and I am fed up of waiting in limbo listening to bloody Mozart on your wretched automated service.

Operator: I'm sorry, Maam, but I have to ...

Shaveling: Just put me through to the SOCO team.

Operator: Connecting you now ...

DC S Shapps: Hello, where are you calling from?

Shaveling: I wish to speak with Simon Cook. Is he on duty?

Shapps: What is the nature of your emergency?

<u>Shaveling</u>: Oh for God's sake. The direct line is busy and I have to speak with him. Just take down this number and ask him to ring me back. It is a matter of extreme urgency.

(Phone number redacted)

Caller terminated call.

CHAPTER 20

Transcript - mobile phone call from
DC Simon Cook to Dr Nigela Shaveling

6th November 02.13am

Cook: Dr Shaveling? DC Cook. What can I do for you?

Shaveling: Thank God. Have you seen my preliminary report on the murder in Henrietta Street?

Cook: I think you're overestimating my rank.

Shaveling: Give me an email address and I'll send it to you.

Cook: It might be better to follow protocol.

Shaveling: Forget protocol. If we leave it to that puffed up halfwit Rawes ... Sorry I'll rephrase that ... If we leave it to the detective inspector, it may be too late.

Cook: OK, but I may not be able to look at it for an hour or more. We are on our way to an incident.

Shaveling: Another body?

Cook: Appears so.

Shaveling: Where?

Cook: Whitby lighthouse.

Shaveling: I'm on my way.

CHAPTER 21

Farview Farm - Katie South

Sunday, 6th November, 01.42am

If you are reading this - whoever you are - it is probably because I am missing or dead. Sorry for scribbling on kitchen towel. I dropped my phone and this is the only paper around.

I am stuck in this abandoned campervan in the middle of nowhere because I made a stupid bloody mistake. We were at the lighthouse cottage when everything went weird. Lupei and Darren were fighting and Alex was trying to break them up. Then Darren was lying on the ground and not moving and I panicked, but I went the wrong way and now I am on this farm. I am tired and wet so I'm staying put till it gets light.

TBH this place gives me the creeps. Like something off the Horror Channel. I've locked myself in and drawn the curtains. A while ago two men tried to open the doors. I was terrified they would smash the windows but they gave up and walked away. They were both quite tall but I can't say more than that; I dropped my glasses and my bloody phone and my fucking purse while I was running. This is a total nightmare and I wish we never came. On the plus side, I found some blankets in a cupboard so I am not going to freeze to death.

Katie South.

PS: Please tell my boyfriend Alex that I really loved him.

CHAPTER 22

Farview Farm - Daniel Murray

Sunday, 6th November

"Get back!" Noir yanked me away from the window, where our faces were lit by the orange glow from the fire below, and back into the shadows.

Not before time as, seconds later, the Hounds of Hellbane bus thundered into the farmyard and shriek-braked in front of the burning pyre.

With little time at our disposal, my knowledge of the farm had proved decisive. I had opened the front door of the farmhouse and led Noir and Megan inside. Knowing all the downstairs rooms were locked, I took them straight upstairs. Given what Tiffany had told us, it was strange that the building had not been broken into. The story had been all over the local media and it wouldn't have been that surprising if a bunch of kids had come to throw bricks through the windows or to generally trash the place. Were people afraid? What of?

There were six doors on the landing. The first door opened onto more stairs, far less grand than the main staircase, leading both up and down. The second door revealed a large bathroom containing a cast iron bath resting on lions' paws, but frosted windows that gave no outside view. In the next room, a large space with no carpet and no bed, an ugly smell lingered beneath the pungent odour of disinfectant, and a large stain covered a third of the floor. Presumably the master bedroom in which the wife had kept her husband's body for weeks.

The third room was more to our liking. The torch on Megan's phone picked out a spartan bedroom with faded blue and cream floral wallpaper, mahogany wardrobe, a clumsy chest of drawers on which sat several weathered copies of Farmers Weekly and what I think was a chamber pot. A metal framed single bed and a broken dining room chair. The room smelled OK, the window looked down on the farmyard, and there were curtains, which we left partially drawn.

As the bus came to a halt, a movement in the periphery of my vision drew my attention to the field. Maybe it was just the flickering light of the fire reflected on the side of the white campervan, some eighty metres away, but I thought I had seen one of the doors open and close.

Lupei leapt down from the cab of the bus and ran forward. He stood before the fire, staring at the blazing bodies engulfed in crackling flames as glowing embers danced and rose in the heat to be whipped away in the wind. There was nothing of the showman. Turned in on himself, his body posture was that of someone consumed by apprehension or sadness. Noir's assessment of Lupei seemed, at that moment, absurd, unfair, grotesque even. Was Noir simply bitter at Lupei's talents and success? Why should we believe that the monsters in the barn had anything to do with the singer?

I was lost in these doubts when, silhouetted against the conflagration and suddenly trembling with rage, Lupei tossed his head back and let out a furious primal howl, lips drawn back like a wolf, before turning heel and charging out of sight around the back of the bus.

None of us spoke. We could only wait and watch. From our vantage point we could see across to the upper deck of the bus but the black curtains prevented us from seeing within. Where had Lupei gone? Was he in the barn?

I jumped as a visceral ear-splitting shriek was followed by Lupei's reappearance round the back of the bus, dragging a cowering human figure by the ear. Lupei was shouting as he frogmarched the pathetic individual towards the fire and while we could not make out the words their tone was clear enough, a torrent of snarling menace. He pushed the person forwards until they were standing directly before the flames then Lupei stepped back and stood behind his victim who, like a fly in a web, made no attempt to move away. Hunched, passive and compliant, the victim seemed resigned to their fate. Had they been drugged or hypnotised?

Lupei's face was contorted in an evil grimace. The suave sophistication, big smile and scrupulous manners had vanished; a thug had replaced the gentleman.

Finally the victim appeared to awaken to the danger, lifting their head and turning away from the flames and towards the farmhouse. Megan gasped and grabbed my arm as I flinched back from the window.

Alex.

I was falling into the bowels of a nightmaze, disgusted by the horrors I had witnessed, my emotions swinging the pendulum between rage and despair. I turned to Noir, now desperately relying on him to outline a plan. Of the three of us, he alone understood the logic, the rules of engagement, that governed this mad reality into which we had been plunged.

But, like Megan and I, Noir seemed paralysed with fear. Below us in the farmyard, Lupei took a step forward, talking to Alex as he grabbed his arms. Was he about to shove my friend into the flames?

Suddenly Pharrell Williams was singing "That's why I'm Happy", his voice echoing in the room as Megan wrestled to pull her phone from her pocket to switch it off. Noir tried to wrap his coat around her to mute the sound but Megan pushed him away. Down in the yard Lupei had let go of Alex's arms. He was hearing the phone above the noise of the fire and moving his head this way and that, trying to pinpoint the source.

His face was lost in shadow as he turned away from the fire to look directly towards the farmhouse. Beside me Megan finally managed to kill the sound, but it was too late.

'Shit!' I spluttered.

Noir snapped out of his stasis. Rummaging within the folds of his leather coat he produced various objects, which he thrust into my hands: a drawstring pouch, what looked like a weird pistol and a leather bound book.

"Take the back stairs and get out. I will draw him to me to buy you time. Go!"

The last I saw of Noir as we fled the bedroom, he was by the wardrobe, clutching the sword in his mechanical arm, his face resolute. Megan's torch lit our path as we raced across the landing, pulled open the first door and, closing it behind us, headed downstairs as quickly and as quietly as we were able. Behind us, muffled through the door, we heard Noir shouting and goading Lupei from his vantage point on the landing.

At the bottom of the stairs we threw open each of the three doors only to find dank rooms without windows. In one room a man in an old suit, wellingtons and a flat cap was standing in the darkness with his back to us, leaning against the wall. It was all either of us could do to stifle our screams.

'Shit, it's a fucking scarecrow!' Megan hissed.

'We're in the basement.'

We turned tail and raced back upstairs, opening the first door we reached, and stepped into the kitchen.

It was the only moment I spent on Farview Farm where I got a sense that it had indeed once been a campsite. Against one wall were a stack of shelves on which were pots of jam, bags of sugar, tins of ham and tomatoes, boxes of rice and pasta, tea towels and cooking oil, all marked up and ready for sale. Alongside them was an empty chill cabinet, carrying labels for vegetables and cheese, and a table on which stood an old mechanical till. We didn't have to think about which door to use to leave the kitchen; the muffled sound of fighting and shouting through one door steered us towards the other and we stepped out into the alley along the side of the house. To our left lay the farmyard and the burning pyre, orange light flickering against the walls of the alley, the smell of burning thick in the air.

Maybe we could rescue Alex and run with him towards the tents and the coastal path beyond them, I thought to myself. But before Megan and I could decide what to do or which way to go, the decision was taken from us. A door banged open and Lupei shouted at the top of his voice, his cry echoing across the yard. We retreated along the alley towards the back of the house where we were confronted with the reality that there were no hedges or trees to hide behind, just those open fields that stretched on forever, bathed in the rheumy light of a sickle moon that had emerged from behind skating clouds.

The abandoned dog was barking and, knowing it was only a matter of time before Lupei came running down the alley, there was only one thing we could do. I dragged Megan towards the outhouses, grabbing the bag of dog biscuits from the greenhouse and pulling back the bolts on the whitewashed door.

'You're insane,' she said, shining her torch inside to reveal the snarling salivating jaws of the hound. 'Forget it.'

'Trust me,' I said, pulling the door open just long enough to step inside without releasing the dog.

It was immediately upon me, teeth bared and growling.

'All right, mate? Easy, easy. How were those biscuits I gave you yesterday? OK?'

I held out my hand. The dog attacked then stopped, its teeth just inches from my fingers. It sniffed them and looked up at me.

'Good dog,' I gave him some more biscuits from my other hand. 'Megan come in. Easy, mate, she's a friend. OK. Easy.'

The dog snarled but did not attack.

'It stinks of shit,' Megan observed.

'Reach through the gap and push the bolts back in place,' I told her.

A few seconds later we had moved the pallets forwards a little and were hidden from view. Not a moment too soon, because suddenly Lupei was at the door, peering through the crack, and the dog was snarling and growling, barking and lunging forwards.

'Shut up, you miserable runt,' Lupei growled in his deep resonant voice. He peered beyond the dog into the gloom. In the lacklight behind the crates we pressed ourselves against the back wall. Like the scravir, Lupei sniffed the air. Did he know we were at the farm or was he simply guessing that Emile Noir was not alone? I know only that I had never been so happy to be in an enclosed space that stank of dog shit as I was that night. The dog barked and growled, leaping up at the door, trying to claw Lupei through the gap in the planks.

As the dog stood on its hind legs howling and yelping in his face, Lupei reached a hand through the gap. He grunted loudly as he stabbed himself on a nail and withdrew his hand and stared at his palm an instant then turned his attention back to the dog. Reaching in with his other hand he touched the dog's head. The barking stopped immediately, to be replaced by a whimper and then silence. Slowly the dog sank back to all fours as Lupei continued to press his hand on its head. We watched in horror as, silhouetted against the light coming through the gap in the door, the dog's muscles shrank before our eyes, its shoulders and haunches emptying of flesh, until it could no longer support itself.

Megan opened her mouth to scream. I quickly grabbed her head with all my strength, pressing the palm of my hand across her open mouth to shut her up. It was our good fortune that the dog had decided to put up a struggle as its life was sucked away, its paws scraping frantically against the ground and the door, masking any faint sound that Megan was making. Finally, when it seemed the suffering would never end, the dog collapsed to the floor, its fur falling in clumps from its flanks to reveal ribs heaving as it gasped its last breath and was gone.

'Useless scrip.' Lupei straightened himself up and wiped his hand on his coat. He muttered something else in a language I did not recognise and walked away.

I let go of Megan. 'OK?' I hissed.

She rubbed her neck. 'That hurt.'

'Didn't know what else to do,' I whispered.

If either Megan or I had harboured lingering doubts as to who or what Thor Lupei was, or whether or not he represented a real danger, those doubts had been blown away by what we had just witnessed. We crouched in the darkness behind the pallets in the company of a dead dog, sickened and repulsed, and afraid. We would probably have stayed there until daybreak if two things hadn't happened.

The first was the vibrating of the walkie-talkie in my pocket and the second was the sound of the Hounds of Hellbane bus starting up.

'Daniel, have you found Katie?'

'Tiffany, are you OK?' I whispered.

'Yes. Where's Katie?'

'We don't know. But Lupei has Alex. He may have killed him.'

'What? Hang on a minute …'

We waited in the dark, fearing the worst. The walkie-talkie crackled and squelched then cut out.

'Let's get out,' Megan said.

We pushed the pallets aside, ran to the door, reached through the gap to pull back the bolts and stepped outside over what was left of the dog. I felt guilty; I had used an innocent creature to protect us from Lupei and it had paid with its life.

Back in the farmyard, the fire still burned fiercely but was past its peak. Terrified of what we might see, we approached the fire. No sign of another body. A couple of large skull fragments lying among the burning timbers provided the only obvious clues as to what had happened. They were all that remained of the scravir.

Of the bus all that was left were fat tyre tracks. The farmhouse front door hung open. Without expecting much, if I'm honest, I shouted Alex's name, then Noir's. Megan was already running toward the farm entrance.

'Wait!' I shouted, but Megan wasn't listening. 'Give me your torch.'

She stopped, turned, threw her torch at me and disappeared round the corner. The torch fell several metres short of me in a puddle. Rummaging in the cold water I found it and headed back to the farmhouse where I ran inside, half-expecting to find Noir dead on the stairs in a pool of blood. There was evidence of a fight, overturned chairs, broken curtain rails, slash marks in the walls, splintered bannister rails and a trail of spattered blood across the floor of the hall. But no body.

Was Noir on the bus with Lupei and Alex? If so, where was he taking them?

I felt very alone in that miserable house, with the image of Lupei sucking the life from the dog still vivid as viscera. Stumbling my way outside, I was agitated and afraid. An owl hooted. The dying fire dry-crackled, throwing huge dancing shadows against the walls of the buildings clustered around the farmyard. The wind rattled the asbestos roof of the barn. Night loitered on the edge of things, waiting for the fire to die.

I hurried past the dark gaping maw of the barn doors and was halfway to the farm entrance when I heard the brittle snap of a stick. I stopped, muscles humming with adrenalin. Someone stood in the shadow beneath the hedge.

He looked completely lost, like a five-year-old who has

lost his parents in a busy station. Didn't even lift a hand to shield his eyes from the torchlight.

'It's OK,' I approached slowly, my hands out in front of me. 'You're all right. It's me. Take it easy. There you go, mate. There you go.'

I reached out a hand and held his shoulder. I hugged him. I had found Alex.

He made no attempt to communicate as I walked him out from the shadows and down the road, away from the farm. My pockets were so crammed with all the stuff that Noir had given me that it took me a little while to find the walkie-talkie. I pressed the button and hoped that it still worked because I had no idea where Jordan had hidden the car.

'Daniel. Where are you?'

Just hearing her voice brought me close to tears.

'I've found Alex,' I gasped. 'We're on our way.'

'OK. Don't move. We're coming.'

Almost immediately the Land Rover emerged, coming down the slope ahead of us and to our right, squashing gorse and bracken as it came. As soon as the car stopped Jordan leapt out and rushed up to Alex and hugged him.

'Wow, man. We were worried sick. You OK?'

'Jordan,' Alex said, in a dull monotone, as if he were waking from a deep sleep, his eyes barely focusing.

'That's right, man,' Jordan smiled, the worry written all over his face as he exchanged glances with me.

'I'm cold, Jordan.'

We bundled Alex in with Tiffany at the back of the Land Rover. I got in after him and Jordan started the car.

'What about Katie?' Tiffany asked.

'Look at him,' Jordan lashed back. 'We have to get him back to the cottage, or to hospital. We don't even know if Katie reached the farm.'

'She's still out here. We can't abandon her!'

Megan said nothing. I could see from her face that she had retreated into herself, focused only on preserving her own life in the wake of what she had just witnessed and, knowing what she had been through, I could not blame her.

'We have to get real,' Jordan said. 'We are in some pretty shit, man, and if …'

'Shut up,' I said. 'You're both right, so here is what we do. Take Alex back. Drop him off at the hospital or whatever. Check up on Hannah. Call the police. Do all that stuff. I will wait here until you get back. If Katie shows up I'll be here.'

'They're not human,' Megan muttered to herself. 'We have to go.' She looked straight at Jordan. 'GO!' she screamed. "GET OUT NOW!'

'Shhh,' I hissed at Megan, glancing at Alex beside me, fearful of his response to Megan's hysteria.

Alex was staring at the floor, his face as blank as cardboard.

'I'll stay with you,' Tiffany volunteered.

The beautiful evening was in tatters; I wanted her to stay and I didn't want her to stay. More than anything I wanted her to be safe.

'No. Please. Go with them,' I told her. 'It's not your fault.'

'It's not your fault either, man,' Jordan said. 'We'll ring the police as soon as we are in town. Let them deal with this.'

I was as scared as the others but someone had to stay.

'Your phone was getting a signal in the farmhouse, Megan. Can I borrow it?'

She looked at me. 'Don't lose it.' She showed me the code to unlock it.

I stepped out of the car, closed the door and tapped the roof to let Jordan know he could go. As the car drove away into the night Alex turned to look at me through the car window. The half-smile playing on his lips unsettled me. Maybe Tiffany would have been safer staying with me after all.

CHAPTER 23

Whitby Lighthouse - DC Simon Cook
incident report

On 6th Nov 2016 at 02.11 a.m. I went to Whitby lighthouse following an anonymous phone call to police station at 02.08 a.m. regarding damage to one of two holiday let cottages and report of a dead body in grounds. Accompanying me was PC Jane Collet.

Upon arrival, PC Collet confirmed that the first cottage was unoccupied. I walked from parking area to second cottage and observed the front door was open and lights were on inside. Two drawers had been pulled from kitchen units and contents were spread across floor, along with broken wine glasses.

Entering other rooms, I found that east facing window to living room was broken, glass and glazing bars having been pushed outwards. Given the structure of the window and materials, I concluded that considerable force had been required to break window. One of the curtains had been ripped from rail.

Inspecting the broken window from the outside I identified numerous fragments of glass and glazing bars. Evidence of heavy impact of shoes on ground in front of window, consistent with two persons jumping from the window to the ground. The garden behind cottage is an expanse of lawn that drops down toward cliff edge. Approx. 2 metres from the cliff edge, the boundary is marked by a low dry stone wall, situated beside which was body of a deceased male. The lawn was muddy and we counted the footprints of six individuals in the vicinity of the body, including those of the deceased.

At 02.32 a.m. we were joined by forensic pathologist Dr Nigela Shaveling, who inspected the body and the scene, and collected fingerprints. Dr Shaveling observed that the emaciated condition of the body bore significant resemblance to the bodies found in Whitby town centre on morning of 5th November. The deceased appeared to have been around 80 years old. 02.37a.m. Dr Shaveling drew my attention to an item of tongue jewellery in the mouth of the deceased. I called for Scene Of Crime team to be sent. I also requested if the location of the anonymous call had been identified, to clarify whether the call had been made from the lighthouse cottages.

The occupant of the cottage is listed as Mr Darren Quincey aged 20 from London. Mr Quincey has rented the property for period 4th to 7th November. From belongings found at the property, it appears that Mr Quincey is still occupying the property and that a second male is staying at the cottage with him. Their whereabouts are unknown. I will contact Mr Quincey's next of kin and the letting agents, upon our return to the police station, to confirm whether he has left the property and to advise the letting agents of the break in.

03.42 a.m. I have been informed of the location from which the anonymous call was made. Dr Shaveling and the SOC team will remain at the lighthouse to complete their work while PC Collet and I make our way to this new location.

CHAPTER 24

Farview Farm - Daniel Murray

Sunday, 6th November

Back in the farmyard, the light of the flames comforted me, regardless of what had burned there. We are only a few hundred generations away from cavemen. As glowing embers rose and were carried away on the breeze, I warmed my hands and considered my options.

I had to work quickly; no way was I spending another night at Farview farm even though we had killed the scravir. My tent could stay but if I collected my rucksack and clothes I could return the stuff I was wearing to Tiffany's flatmate. Crossing the cattle grid into the field, I tried to imagine where I would have gone if I were Katie. On my arrival the previous night, I had gone straight to the farmhouse door and knocked but, as a female weighing fifteen or twenty kilos less than me and as a total dipstick, Katie might have viewed her choices very differently.

Having looked around to check I was alone, I unzipped the tent and crawled inside, rezipping the entrance behind me. Everything was as I had left it: mat, sleeping bag, wet socks, parka, and rucksack. Back inside a familiar space, even one no thicker than a plastic bag, I was instantly calmer; no longer in a cold godforsaken field in Yorkshire, I could as easily have been camping in Dorset in May.

I took off the soaking t-shirt and dark blue hoodie I had borrowed from Tiffany's flat and pulled dry clothes over my head. And my trusty parka. Emptying my pockets and placing the devices Emile Noir had given me onto the sleeping bag, I spent some time studying each item with the aid of Megan's torch. The drawstring pouch contained a dozen or more small glass vials like the ones in the magazine that Noir had inserted into his syringe gun. The smaller syringe revolver Noir had given me resembled the revolvers that gunslingers used in old westerns, except for the long needle it had in place of a barrel. The six-chamber cylinder was plainly designed to accommodate the glass vials nestling in the drawstring pouch. I loaded the gun and snapped the cylinder into place, feeling the weight of it in my hand and remembering the toy gun I had played with as a child.

The pages of the leather bound book appeared to contain a journal, written by hand in a foreign language and completely unintelligible except for the illustrations that occurred sporadically. There was no mistaking the drawings of scravir, on which a series of red marks had been superimposed. Did they mark the points of vulnerability? Halfway through the book were a series of drawings of Thor Lupei himself. It was unmistakeably him; the long white hair, the aquiline nose and thick white eyebrows, the pink eyes, but what the text said beneath the drawings I hadn't a clue. The last sixty or seventy pages were blank. I flicked through these anyway and was surprised when a note fell out, written in English.

Arrives: Hull 9 a.m. 3rd Nov. overnight freight ferry from Rotterdam

Could be in Whitby before midday

Sandu says TL left R 31 October (Halloween)

At least 9 scrav. He is looking for 'a good harvest'. Micăbrukóczi possibly unguarded

Contact Ylenia for ampuls before Tuesday

Which explained how Lupei had taken a double decker bus across the Channel. There was no way of knowing if the words on the note had been written by Emile Noir but they were in the same cluttered italicised hand as the writing within the book.

Zipping the book and drawstring bag into the front pouch of my rucksack, and stuffing the gun in my parka pocket, I felt tiredness overwhelming me, I had been up twenty hours and had hardly slept the previous night. I was sorely tempted to crawl into my sleeping bag and close my eyes but I had to make an effort to find Katie and get back to Whitby. I unzipped the tent, crawled outside and shouldered my rucksack; if I did find her she might be happy of some extra clothing. I would come back for the tent and the other stuff in daylight. Or maybe abandon it.

There were half a dozen outbuildings to explore but before leaving the field I thought again about the tents. Had we missed something? She would have passed them for sure. I kept the torch off, not wanting to attract attention.

Staring at the dim outlines of the tents, I noticed the campervan and remembered the movement I thought I had seen from the farmhouse window. I set off towards it, my trousers quickly damp to the knees in the long wet grass, my shoes and socks still soaking from having waded through the field with Emile Noir an hour earlier. Wasn't that how soldiers in the First World War had ended up with trench foot? What was trench foot?

The campervan was maybe sixty metres away. The slender moon had long since vanished, thick dark clouds were racing across the sky and another downpour could be only minutes away. Wind rippled the grass in trembling waves causing the campervan to resemble a boat adrift in a turbulent sea. Reaching the van I circled it carefully. The curtains were drawn behind the windscreen and in every window. A box section overhung the cab, presumably with space for a bed. There was a ladder at the back; surely lying on the roof would be too exposed.

You'd have seen her from the farm window.

Of the three doors at the back only one seemed large enough to give access to the inside, the others must be storage lockers. What if Katie had chosen to hide in a locker? Could you do that? Was there room? I stepped forward to try the handle of one of these smaller doors and was close to a rear wheel when I heard a sound coming from underneath the vehicle. I froze in my tracks. The wind and whispering grasses were cloaking the other sounds but there, on the periphery of my hearing, was the noise that had kept me awake the previous night. The sound we had heard in the lacklight of the barn; scratching, sniffing, this time accompanied by a gentle knocking as if a bone were tapping a metal box.

Call me a coward if you want but I was reluctant to stand my ground. I stepped back, slipping the rucksack silently from my shoulders and swinging it round until I could reach into the front pouch, from which I withdrew the syringe revolver. It might only be a hedgehog or a rat beneath the campervan. I was taking no chances. After a brief pause, the tapping sound resumed.

What was I hoping to achieve? Noir and I had already tried the doors of the campervan; it was locked. Better to beat a retreat and check the outbuildings. I walked backwards until I was far enough from the campervan to feel safe then turned and headed briskly away towards the farmyard. Behind me the tapping noise grew louder instead of quieter; whatever was making the noise was becoming bolder.

The various outbuildings were all smaller than the farmhouse and the cavernous barn. The first shed contained two tractors and stuff to drag along behind them; don't ask a London boy about farm equipment. The second shed was crammed with sacks and the sweet smell of rotting vegetables. There was a brick building with external padlocks on both doors.

A narrow passage led to a low barn that smelled like I imagined cows must smell. Sweet veggie farts, like boiled easy cook rice in a wet nappy.

You're weird, bruv.

The roof was made of transparent corrugated plastic sheets that allowed a little light to fall in from outside. The ground had been scraped away to leave a thousand slippery stones, broken bricks and small pools of rust-coloured water.

Walking gingerly over the slimy surface, I called out Katie's name, my feet slipping on the greasy floor as I explored the various side rooms that led off the central area. No sign of her. Could she have walked straight through the farm and carried on along the road to Hawsker Lane? But if she had then surely Jordan would have passed her in the car, unless she had been close to one of the other farms along the road and had hidden from view.

I was mulling this over as I left the low barn and re-emerged from the passage back into the farmyard.

'Stop right there, son.'

A bright torch was shining straight into my face, completely dazzling me. It was raining again. While I could not see their faces I could see their boots. There were two of them and from the markings on the vehicle in front of the farmhouse they were police officers.

'Well, bugger me, it's the Yorkshire pudding guzzler from Angie's caff. Maybe you'd like to explain what you are doing on an abandoned farm in the middle of the night? Stop. I didn't say you could move. PC Collet, cuff this gentleman and read him his rights.'

I stayed motionless as PC Collet stepped behind me and handcuffed my hands behind my back, while spouting some stuff I didn't really listen to, if I'm honest. Grabbing my arm she led me towards the police car where it quickly became obvious I would struggle to get into the vehicle with my hands cuffed and a huge rucksack on my back.

'Bloody hell,' PC Collet muttered as she undid one cuff in order to allow me to remove the rucksack which she thrust onto the back seat of the squad car.

'Bit of a late night, is it Jane?' laughed her colleague who I remembered was called Simon.

'Shurrup.' Collet answered. 'Get in,' she told me, having recuffed me with my hands in front of me.

The policeman joined me in the back. For a few moments he said nothing. He shook his head and puffed his cheeks.

'You are in deep shit, aren't you Lad?' he said finally. 'Do I take it that you are responsible for lighting this fire? Arson a life skill they teach young layabouts in London? What I don't understand is why you come two hundred and fifty miles to wreck havoc. What is wrong with Croydon?'

I said nothing.

'OK,' he continued. 'First things first, I'm DC Simon Cook and this is PC Jane Collet. What is your name?'

'Daniel Murray.'

'Brother a tennis player, is he?'

I arched an eyebrow.

'Shame, you might need access to a pot of money if the judge grants bail. So why are you here, Daniel?

'I'm camping.'

'Camping? In November? This look like a bloody campsite?'

'I booked online. My tent's over there, I can show you, if you want.'

DC Cook wiped his eyes and forehead with his hand then glanced at PC Collet who was sitting behind the wheel.

'Can you check?' Cook asked her.

PC Collet opened the car door.

'Not the sodding tent, the website.' He turned to me. 'So, how do you think we ended up here?'

'You saw the fire?'

'No.'

'My friends called you?'

'You know all about it, don't you?'

'About what?'

'A bunch of Londoners dressed as vampires come to Whitby for a laugh and a dirty weekend. Everyone gets pissed then they decide it would be fun to abduct a dosser, take him to the lighthouse, dress him up as a Goth then beat him up. Only it gets a little out of hand and the old man ends up dead. How does that sound to you?'

'Insane.'

'So you explain it.'

'Explain what?'

DC Cook waved his hand towards the fire.

It was one thing witnessing the supernatural horrors that had taken place, quite another to attempt to explain any of it to a third party.

'It's difficult,' I started.

'Try me. From the top.'

By the time I finished, the policeman had his head in his hands, rubbing his eyes. He sighed audibly and looked directly at me.

'Do you actually believe any of this shit?' he asked.

'You asked. I don't know what to believe,' I answered truthfully. 'When we met yesterday morning, you commented on my costume. The truth is I'm not into all this Goth stuff. Or steampunk. I came because my friends were coming. I booked the campsite because I couldn't afford to ...'

'So you're telling me that this music star and his band have been here dossing on a shutdown campsite with no amenities? Rather than staying in the best hotel?'

'Check the tyre marks,' I said, pointing down at the mud of the yard. 'It's a Routemaster London bus.'

DC Cook looked across at PC Collet, who stepped out of the car into the rain.

'And take a few shots in the barn while you're at it,' DC Cook called out after her.

As DC Cook made a phone call I stared outside. The policewoman was wandering about, studying the ground, intermittent flashes coming from her camera.

'Hello. Yes. Are you finished at the lighthouse? No, I would like you to come over to Farview Farm. Yes, I do know that it's connected to the lighthouse by the coastal path. This business is getting weirder by the minute and I would appreciate your professional opinion. Fifteen minutes? OK.' The policeman cut the call. 'Right lad, while we're waiting, you are going to take me to your tent. What colour did you say it was?'

'I didn't, but it's green and orange.'

DC Cook climbed out of the car and opened the door for me.

'Do I have to wear these?' I lifted my wrists to show him my handcuffs. 'It's slippery and dangerous.'

'I'll look after you, my love,' Cook cooed, in a singsong voice that suggested he was talking to a three-year-old. 'Come on, out of the bloody car.'

We skirted the dying fire. I could still see fragments of skulls in the smouldering embers but, if he saw them, Cook said nothing. I didn't mention the cattle grid and, passing through the gate into the field, the policeman almost broke a leg. Five minutes in the car hadn't helped me and I was now cold to the core. We tramped across the wet field and round the corner of the outbuildings to reveal my tent tucked in along the hedge close to the cliff top.

'It's your tent. What's inside?'

'Nothing, I put everything in the rucksack. Oh no, hang on, there's a pair of wet socks.'

DC Cook unzipped the tent and shone his torch inside.

'Cosy,' he muttered. 'OK, for the moment we'll agree that, for whatever reason, you are freezing your backside camping on a derelict farm in bloody November as part of Goth weekend. So now tell me who is in the other tents and who lit that bloody fire.'

'They're empty. Well, there's stuff in them but no-one's there.'

'And how would you know that?'

'I looked earlier. I was trying to find my friend.'

Cook shone his torch in my face.

'Right. What friend?'

'Katie. I told you when …'

At that moment DC Cook became distracted by the tapping sound coming from the centre of the field. He turned towards the campervan then back to me, indicating that I should follow him back towards the gate. When we reached it he grabbed my arm, unlocked one of the handcuffs, threaded the chain through a bar of the metal gate then snapped the cuff shut.

'Stay there,' he barked unnecessarily, before turning heel and heading towards the camper van, torch in hand.

If he hadn't shackled me to the gate I might have called out after him and warned him to be careful but, in the circumstances, freezing and once again wet and fed up with everyone and everything, I zipped it and let him walk. The only improvement to my situation was the presence of the police because, for some stupid reason, they made me feel safer. I wanted to sit down but all I could do was turn towards the fire; it was too far away to afford me any heat it did at least give me something to look at. PC Collet was nowhere to be seen. I assumed she was in the barn. Rather her than me.

I turned back towards the field. Cook had reached the campervan and was shining his torch on the side of the vehicle, creating a circle of light against which he was silhouetted, like a hilltop tree against a rising moon. He extended a hand towards the door. Locked, I thought to myself. Pointless waste of time.

Suddenly the policeman disappeared downwards, letting out a huge shout as he fell. I say fell; it looked more as if he were yanked downward with great force. He screamed for help, calling out for Jane, yelling for someone – presumably me – to do something.

A female voice to my left shouted "Simon, wha ..." but then nothing more. The policewoman did not appear. DC Cook was howling unworldly screams that chilled me to the bone. Realising that I was like a tethered goat awaiting the arrival of the tiger, I pulled frantically at my handcuffs, rattling them against the steel bars of the gate. The cuffs bit into the skin of my wrists.

The gate must be three or four metres long, far too heavy to lift off its hinges. Cook's blood curdling cries mingled with frenzied banging as if he were desperately trying to escape. I turned away from the van and focused my energies on trying to break free; having been a party to the killing of eight scravir I knew one thing for sure, if we had missed some then those that remained would show me no mercy. I ran left and right, dragging the cuffs along the bar of the gate, searching for some sign of weakness in the structure. Nothing. In the field the policeman's torchlight had vanished. Why couldn't we close our ears as easily as our eyes? I turned towards the fire. The police car stood on the far side of the fading flames. Where was the policewoman? I stared down at the cuffs; would I have the courage to rip off one of my own hands if it would save my life? Was such a thing even possible?

I was locked in this disorientating adrenalin-fuelled hell when the touch landed on my shoulder.

The primal scream that spewed from my open mouth frightened me as much as the hand weighing on my collarbone. My whole body shook in anticipation of the brutality that must surely follow. I kicked blindly behind me hoping to at least inflict injury on the creature that was about to kill me.

From far far away I heard a voice calling *no, Daniel, no* which I wrote off as the confabulation of a desperate mind.

'Daniel, stop. STOP!'

My wrists were bleeding as I wrestled frantically with the steel bars and lashed out randomly with my feet. It was as if I were a child again, defiantly pitting my eight-year-old body against the violence of my drunken father while mum shouted at him to stop. I would not die without a fight.

'STOP!'

What quality in that voice penetrated my torment and agitation and gave me a fraction of a second of conscious clarity? I don't know. The policeman was still screaming, but all at once the rage and panic of a cornered animal subsided sufficiently for me to pay attention to my surroundings. The hand on my shoulder was not yet ripping my flesh with six-inch talons. I turned hesitantly, expecting a monster, but found instead a face I recognised.

Katie.

'OK?' she said, moving her hand to my face.

I flinched and recoiled.

'OK,' she repeated.

I gasped, deep gasps clawing for air.

'How did you get here?' I blurted.

'I could ask you the same question. Where's Alex?'

'The others have gone. I stayed to find you.'

For the first time, I saw respect in Katie's eyes, and even embarrassment. I was not just an irritating prat after all.

A scream from the direction of the campervan broke the spell.

'The handcuffs,' she asked, 'Where are the keys?

'They'll kill us,'

'I know,' she nodded. 'The keys, Daniel, where are they?'

I shook my head. 'He has one set, she has the other. But they're gone. Where were you …'

'In the police car perhaps?'

I took a deep breath then threw up.

'I don't know. Maybe.'

Katie ran off without answering me.

'Wait. Where were you?

'The camper van,' she called out over her shoulder.

'Watch out! The cattle grid!'

She adjusted her stride just in time, raced into the yard and around the fire to the police car, flinging open one door after the other. Behind me DC Cook's cries were fading. Time was running out; if the creature beneath the camper van were like the ones in the barn it would be gaining strength by draining the life out of the policeman. As soon as it was done it would be onto us.

Katie was running back.

'Found these,' she said showing me a large pair of cutters.

I positioned myself so that she could get the handcuff chain between the jaws of the cutters.

She didn't have the strength.

'Hang on.' I pushed the jaws back so that they were clamping down on just one side of a single link in the chain. 'Try again.'

Katie pushed the two arms of the cutters together but still couldn't deliver the force required to snap the link.

'Wedge it. Wedge one arm under the rail,' I urged her.

She turned the cutters as I suggested then pushed with all her strength and with both hands against the other side. Finally one side of the link snapped. She adjusted the jaws against the other side of the link and started again. And suddenly I was free and we were racing away from the field, towards the fire.

There were no ignition keys in the police car. I grabbed my rucksack off the back seat and we ran on out of the farmyard and onto the open road and kept running, the wind howling in the hedge, the sky hurling water from above, and the night mustering all the dark shadows of the world.

When we saw car headlights across the fields, heading in our direction, we didn't need to speak, we found the nearest available ditch and threw ourselves in, waiting until the car had passed before picking ourselves up and continuing towards Whitby as quickly as our legs would carry us.

CHAPTER 25

Farview Farm - Dr Nigela Shaveling, Dictaphone recording.

"Sixth November at whatever unearthly hour of the morning this is. The situation is, frankly, beyond comprehension. I am in the yard at Farview Farm. I have my car's headlights on as there is no lighting on-site. If I recall correctly, the farm was abandoned several weeks ago. The squad car is parked in front of a large fire, doors open, hazard lights flashing. No sign of either DC Cook or PC Collet.

I am walking towards the fire now and it is hard to believe what I am seeing. The smell is unpleasant. Reminiscent of an abattoir. Oh my Lord, I am seeing bones. A human femur and part of a pelvis. Hang on a minute, I am now walking round to the other side … what? … what? … There are charred fragments of a human skull. This is awful. Signs of several bodies. Someone has been burning corpses. To repeat, there are human corpses in the fire.

Where are the two police officers? I am not sure it is safe to remain at this … What was that? In the field … beyond the fire … something is moving.

I have to leave. DC Cook. DC COOK! Is anybody here? Hello? HELLO. I'm sorry, I have to go.

(sound of walking then running)

It's following me. I don't know what or who it is but it is picking up speed …

(sound of running)

Get out … get out … just get in the car and … nearly there.

(sound of car door slamming)

Keys. Keys. KEYS. Oh God, where are they? For Goodness sakes!

(loud bang)

Flying fishcakes! No. No! Keep calm. Deep breath. Jacket pocket.

(loud bang followed by sound of breaking glass)

Get away! Oh, thank God.

(jangling keys)

Get in, get in. DAMN YOU.

(grunts. Sound of car engine roaring to life)

Go, go, go. Yes. OH YES!

(spinning wheels and racing engine. A gurgling sound followed by the crunch of something breaking. Car thrown into gear and powering away)

Right. Out of the yard then right and foot down. Nothing following me … I think I am OK now. Aaargh.

(sound of pounding on metal. Car screeches to a halt then engine surges and car moves. Sound of impact.)

Die. Die you bastard. Die. Yes! YES! OK, let's go. Now. Forty, fifty, sixty. Keep going. Oh my God. What was that? Next farm is up ahead. I think I'm safe now. Back to Whitby. This is unimaginable. Hang on. Up ahead … two people running on the road. They've seen me. They're running into the field. I can't leave them here. Have to stop.

(squealing brakes)

You. Over there. Listen to me. You can't stay. Too dangerous. Get up. GET UP! Yes, you. Come on. I'll give you a lift. Get in the car. Run.

(tapping sound within car)

Come on, come on, come on.

(car door opens)

Get in. Sorry about the mess. Just move stuff. Right, we're off. I'm taking you to Whitby. You look soaked. Are you hurt?

Who are you?

'Daniel, and this is Katie.'

What the hell are you doing out here? Are you in fancy dress?

'It's a long story.'

Where am I taking you?

'Henrietta Street. It's near the …'

I know where it is … Sorry, Nigela Shaveling, pathologist. We'll speak in a moment … I have to switch this damn thing off.

(click)

CHAPTER 26

Henrietta Street – Skype conversation,
Hannah Morris to Chloe Carter

'The clue is in the name, Hannah. Three kippers cottage.'

'Ha ha. Only there isn't a big cat at the Red Lion on St Marys Road, is there? But this place really stinks of fish.'

'Yeah, Katie said.'

'Someone's smoking them in a garage a few doors up. It's disgusting. Daniel actually bought some; they're wrapped in newspaper in the fridge. I'm throwing them out in the morning.'

'I love smoked mackerel.'

'They're kippers.'

'Anyway, you were going to show me what the cottage looks like.'

'Too tired. This laptop weighs a ton. Tell you what, you can see what the front room looks like. I'll do a twirl.'

'Oh, that's nice. Very cosy. So why does Alex stick Blu-Tack on the lens? Is he worried everyone will see him and Katie shagging? You look terrible by the way.'

'Thanks, Chloe. Goth makeup at four in the morning.'

(fingers roll Blu-Tack over lens)

'Hey, I was joking.'

'Tough. I'm going to bed.'

'And they still aren't back?'

(knock on door)

'Hang on, Chloe. I think that's them.'

(doorbell, creak of door opening)

'Ah, Megan, isn't it?'

'Hannah, actually.'

'Oh Hannah, I am most dreadfully sorry. Please forgive me the appalling faux-pas. I am mortified at arriving at this ungodly hour but I was most concerned to be reassured that everyone had got home safely. The bus developed a mechanical fault on the edge of town and I encouraged everyone to walk home. Ironically, the problem disappeared only minutes after they had all departed and I fear that I may ...'

'They're not back.'

'As I feared. I feel dreadful. Should I drive around to find them? The night is chill. Unfortunately in these narrow streets the bus is ...'

'You could come in and wait, if you want.'

'Really? Hannah, you are generous beyond the realms of kindness and, may I say so, radiant. Sea air agrees with you.'

(creaking door closes)

'I cannot not rest until I know they are all safe. Incidentally, I brought a few albums on CD and vinyl. A trifle, in the circumstances. Do you think that ...'

'Rad. Will you sign them? Your gig was great by the way. Just didn't fancy the bus. Sorry.'

'No need to apologise Hannah. It was presumptuous on my part to assume that my ancient fun wagon would appeal to all.'

'Do you want a coffee? There's cake if you want some.'

'Let me take that for you. Oh, your arm is so warm. Just hot water for me please, Hannah, thank you. Can I sit down?'

'Wherever you like.'

'Marvellous. Oh, your laptop is ...'

'Oh, it's OK, just close it. I was Skyping a friend in ...'

'Perfect. Come and sit with me, I would love to learn all about you while we wait.'

(Skype call ends as laptop lid is closed)

CHAPTER 27

Church Street, Whitby – Daniel Murray

Sunday, 6th November

If you had asked me just thirty-six hours earlier whether I would have enjoyed looking out over a harbour at night, with the boats rocking back and forth on the swell, streetlights reflected in the water, the wind blowing off the sea, and all that stuff, I would have said yes, it's why I came. An adventure up in t'far north where even the ferrets wear flat caps.

But there was nothing pretty, romantic or funny about the view facing us on Church Street.

'They're not still in it, are they?' Katie called out.

She was standing on the pavement, facing away from the wreckage, too distraught to venture any closer.

The Land Rover had hit the railings at speed; breaking them on one side and bending them on the other. The front half of the car was out over the rising waters and leaning at an angle of thirty degrees.

'How many people were inside?' The patholgist, Nigela Shaveling, had her face pressed against a window, trying to see inside. She wore an impatient scowl and a ill-fitting dark trouser suit. Her grey hair was a tousled neglected mess.

I walked round the car.

'Jordan, Megan, Tiffany, and Alex,' I told her. 'Four.'

'Friends of yours?' Shaveling asked, rattling a handle. 'Bloody doors are jammed.'

'Yes. Well, Tiffany is from Whitby, we've just met, and the

others are all from London.'

'Front air bags deployed. Everyone climbed out through the rear right passenger door,' Shaveling observed.

At that moment the car tipped forward, balancing ever more precariously over the harbour, the twisted railing grinding against the driver's door.

'Blood on the rear left window. Who was sitting there?'

'Alex,' I answered, remembering his curious smile as the car left the farm.

'Oh God, is he hurt?' Katie blurted. 'I don't want to see anything disgusting.'

'Don't touch anything,' Shaveling ordered us back. She produced a smart phone from her pocket and dialled. 'Yes. Shaveling. Has the car reached Farview Farm yet? Ask them to call me as soon as they arrive. Yes, of course it is bloody urgent! And send the SOC team to Church Street. Opposite the wholesalers with the red doors. A car has hit the railings and is about … so why isn't anyone here? Four people, I'm told. Not in the vehicle, no … I couldn't give a flying fig how stretched you are. … Call Chief Inspector Rawes, he is past the age where beauty sleep bestows any measureable benefits. Yes, and have him call me on this number.'

Shaveling stuffed the phone back in her pocket and looked at the two of us. 'Henrietta Street is five minutes away. On the way you can explain what or who is burning in that fire at the farm.'

'I tried explaining to the policeman. It's just a waste of time.'

'You will find me more intelligent than your average plod Daniel, and I have already seen enough this weekend to convince me that the normal parameters of reality are somewhat under siege.'

CHAPTER 28

Henrietta Street, Whitby. Phone conversation between Megan Holmwood and Chloe Carter

Sunday, 6th November

'I know it's four in the morning, and I know people are meant to be asleep Chloe, and I'm so bloody sorry I woke you up.'

'She was fine ten minutes ago. We were Skyping. She showed me the cottage on the laptop camera and we had a chat and a laugh.'

'Well now she won't wake up and we're really scared. There's like nothing we can …'

'Calm down. Shake her and …'

'I've tried bloody shaking her! Oh my God, she's not breathing. Maybe she's …'

'Megan. MEGAN. Stop and listen. She's not dead, she's sleeping, that's what you said. Ask that posh guy with the accent what's happened, he'll …'

'What posh guy?'

'The guy she opened the door to.'

'She let someone in?'

'When?' (different voice)

'Who's that?'

'It's Jordan. You're on speaker phone. We just came in together: Me, Jordan and Tiffany, Daniel's friend.'

'This was like fifteen minutes ago. There was a knock on the front door. Hannah answered it, thinking it was you, only it was this other guy. She knew him and invited him in.'

'What did he look like?'

'No idea. She covered the laptop camera with Blu-Tack – like she's totally paranoid – so I could only hear the voice. Like deep and super-polite, really posh but maybe slightly foreign. He said something about a bus breaking down, everyone walking back, bla bla, then he was checking everyone was back safely. She invited him in and ...'

'Thor Lupei!'

'What was that?'

'Jordan said it must have been Thor Lupei. He's run upstairs to check the rooms.'

'The singer?'

'No, Jordan.'

'I didn't mean ... oh, doesn't matter. Look, no disrespect, Megan, but why would a pop star come round to see a bunch of students at four in the morning? And where are Alex and Katie?'

'I'll ring you back. Tiffany has just opened the back curtains; the window is wide open. No wonder it's freezing.'

'She offered him coffee and cake. Oh, this was weird, he said her skin was warm. Thinking about it, that's really creepy, isn't it? Then the Skype connection cut out and I went back to bed.'

'I have to go, Chloe. Bye.'

CHAPTER 29

Henrietta Street, Whitby - Daniel Murray

Sunday, 6th November

Dr Shaveling dropped us off outside the cottage and continued up the hill to park at the end of the street.

Tiffany answered the door. Jordan and Megan were there but there was no sign of Alex. Katie ran forwards and hugged Tiffany, like she knew her; it was that kind of a night and we were all tired and stressed. I told the others about the police arriving at the farm, and what happened to them, and where Katie had been hiding. When Katie finally let go of her, Tiffany and I looked at each other and before embarrassment could get in the way, fell into each other's arms. Her hair smelled of fresh air and apples and the faintest hint of perfume. She held me so tightly I could feel her heartbeat. I closed my eyes. The horrors of the past few hours had multiplied my awareness of how fragile we are and the wafer thin line between life and death. In my mind's eye I saw Darren's shrunken wasted body lying in the grass by the lighthouse, his youth sucked away, his body transformed into a mummified wizened corpse. My body was trembling with fear at how close we might all have been to aging sixty years in a few minutes. I pulled Tiffany closer, wishing I could lose myself in human warmth. Her body felt full and firm and …

'Hey. HEY!' Tiffany said, pulling herself away from me. 'First date, remember?' She said in her thick Yorkshire accent.

'Sorry. I mean it, Tiffany. Oh shit. Sorry. That was really …'

'It's OK,' she smiled. 'It's OK. Just take your foot off the accelerator. All right?' She leaned forwards on her tiptoes and kissed my cheek.

Jordan had left the room. Finally I noticed Hannah, asleep on the sofa covered in a quilt. Megan knelt beside her, holding her hand and whispering to her in a low voice. Two steps behind Megan stood Katie, fiddling distractedly with her hair. Feeling eyes on her, Katie turned towards us, her face thick with worry. She tapped Megan on the shoulder.

'Where's Alex?' she asked.

Megan stared up at Katie. 'Who cares? Does Hannah look pale to you? '

I cared but I had no idea what was going on.

'Can you push the door? It's freezing,' Tiffany said to me then, turning to Katie, 'He nearly killed us. We're on Church Street and Alex, who hasn't said a word, suddenly smacks Jordan in back of head and starts shouting we're all going to die. He grabs Jordan in a headlock. Jordan's trying to drive the car while Megan and me are pulling at Alex to make him let go. The car comes off the road, up pavement and slams into the railing. There's airbags and everything and the car's hanging over the harbour and Alex just jumps out and legs it.'

'Liar,' Katie lashed out, defending Alex.

'No, that's exactly what happened.' Jordan entered the room, massaging his neck.

Katie span round towards Megan who simply nodded to confirm Katie's account.

'You're liars,' Katie muttered to herself. 'All of you. Alex isn't like that.'

'I'm not disagreeing with you,' Jordan said, 'but this was some weird shit. I've never seen him like that.'

Tiffany disappeared into the kitchen. Jordan followed her. We heard the tap running, the kettle being switched on, cups being assembled.

Megan had turned her attention back to her girlfriend. 'Hannah, wake up, it's me,' she was saying, over and over.

I pushed the front door to, leaving it on the latch, Shaveling would be arriving any second.

Katie leant forwards and put her hand on Megan's shoulder. Neither of them spoke. Megan stood up.

'It's my fault. I shouldn't have left her on her own.'

Katie shook her head. 'She'll be fine. You'll see. Are there hot water bottles somewhere? Then I'll ring Alex, he can't be far.'

'In the bathroom cupboard upstairs.'

Katie went off. Megan knelt back down. I dropped my rucksack by the table and hung my parka on the back of a chair. Behind me the front door creaked. Assuming it was Dr Shaveling, I headed towards the kitchen to help Tiffany and Jordan without looking back.

'No. No,' Megan shouted.

I stopped in my tracks and spun towards the door. Alex stood on the threshold, soaked to the skin, his wet hair matted against his face, an ugly cut bleeding down his left cheek. Apart from that he looked like Alex, no evil eyes, no satanic smile, just a worn out friend who looked confused and on the verge of collapse. I ran across, grabbed his shoulders, steered him towards the chairs gathered round the dining room table, kicking the door shut behind me to keep the heat in.

'Don't let him in,' Megan said.

I ignored her and sat Alex down.

'What happened to your arm?' I asked him.

'I think it's broken, Dan,' he said quietly, his teeth chattering and his whole body shaking. 'I was at the lighthouse with Jordan. I think I fell in the sea.'

'You're freezing.'

I turned to Jordan who was standing in the kitchen doorway, eyeing Alex with suspicion.

'Can you fetch a blanket?' I asked him. 'We need to run him a bath to warm him up.'

'We weren't at the lighthouse,' Jordan protested.

'I know. If we don't hurry he'll die of hypothermia. A blanket and a towel?'

'Yeah, all right,' Jordan said reluctantly.

Tiffany appeared behind Jordan, carrying a tray of cups, at the same time as Katie came downstairs clutching two hot water bottles. I grabbed a coffee from the tray and pushed it into Alex's hands. 'Drink this, bruv, it'll warm you up.'

Alex stared at Tiffany and Katie as if he hadn't the faintest idea who they were.

'Friends,' he muttered to himself, watching Jordan head upstairs.

'You'll be fine,' I said. 'You need to take all this wet stuff off. Stand up.'

Alex allowed me to remove his coat, which I did carefully. His left arm hung at a weird angle and I wondered if he had dislocated his shoulder. I sat him down again and removed his shoes and socks. His feet were blue with cold.

Jordan reappeared with a blanket and towel. We wrapped the blanket round Alex while Katie did her best to towel dry his hair; which was strange and brought back memories of mum drying my hair when I was seven, the last summer before she left.

'What happened to the doctor?' Katie asked me.

I shrugged. 'She's parking her car at the top of the road.'

'That was ten minutes ago.'

'You think she's got lost?'

'It's a dead end. You can't get lost.'

I suddenly had a bad feeling. 'Back in a few.'

Grabbing my parka off the back of the chair, I stepped outside and ran up the cobbled street. The temperature was still dropping. In seconds I had reached the end of the houses on my left, leaving only the handful of cottages on the right-hand side of the street, crouching in the shelter of the cliff and looking out over the harbour. Down in the jaws of the harbour itself the wind was whipping the swell into a boiling ferment, the lanthorns still disappearing intermittently beneath thick clouds of spray.

Shaveling's car was alongside others in the parking bay in front of these last exposed cottages. The car doors were closed but not locked, she obviously wasn't worried about anyone nicking the pile of books and other junk we had had to shift in order to be able to sit down. Of the pathologist herself there was no sign. The street was empty.

'Are you there?' I shouted.

On a hunch I crossed to the far end of the parking bay, where a flimsy wood and chicken wire fence marked the edge of the cliff. Far below on the beach, maybe twenty metres down an almost vertical grassy slope, were two figures. From my vantage point, the first seemed to be lying down, the second was leaning over the first. In the darkness it was hard to be sure but I thought the standing person looked up at me.

Who were they? What were they doing? There was a gap in the fence on the other side of the car. Suddenly I was alarmed. One wrong step and a person would find themselves tumbling into the void. I raced back down Henrietta Street. Tucked between two houses, a ginnel led to steep steps that dropped between walled gardens and down onto the beach. I took the steps two at a time and, at the bottom, turned right and hurried along the sand.

In the time it had taken me to reach the beach, one figure had disappeared. I approached cautiously and crouched down. The pathologist, Nigela Shaveling, lay broken on the rocks, her left leg stuck out at an impossible angle. Even in the lacklight I could see what I most dreaded to see. The gaunt face, the skull all too evident beneath skin stretched thin as parchment, the sunken cheeks, Shaveling bore all the hallmarks of having been attacked by malevolent forces. The scravir were also in the town.

Had Shaveling been pushed off the cliff? Had she fallen and then attracted unwelcome attention? I imagined tumbling down the steep grass bank. A movement in the periphery of my vision caught my eye. Further up the beach, along a protective wall, the stones themselves appeared to be rippling as if diffracted in the buckling light of a fast moving stream. I remembered the sensation I had experienced peering into the smokehouse at Fortune's kippers, the shadow that had shifted without any solid object to create it.

Where was the other person I had seen from above? How could they have moved so quickly?

Suddenly I was being dragged downwards by the throat. A hand gripped my collar, yanking me down hard until my face was just inches above Shaveling's. Her eyes opened, staring wildly into my own. Cracked lips drew back to reveal receding gums and long teeth.

'Listen to me,' Shaveling wheezed, her tongue moving with difficulty, her speech garbled. 'He is pure evil … must be stopped … or driven away … don't let him touch … you … skin to skin.'

'Who attacked you?' I asked, though I already knew the answer.

'Tall … albino … old but very strong … he sucks the …'

Shaveling's eyes closed. Her lungs heaved as she drew rasping breaths. Her grip on my collar loosened. When her eyes re-opened, the anger and urgency had gone, leaving only pain and sadness.

'Moves slowl … when he is full … the weight …'

She blinked twice. Her throat gave out a hoarse gasp and she was dead.

I had to prise her fingers apart one by one to release myself from her grip. Should I return to the cottage or chase after Shaveling's assailant? It was a measure of how conflicted I was that I still struggled to believe that Thor Lupei could be responsible for Shaveling's death. Maybe Emile Noir was right, maybe I was not to be trusted.

I strode towards the jumbled rocks at the eastern end of the beach but, when I realised that there was no easy path between them to gain access to the ramp that led up toward the far end of Henrietta Street, I turned back. Better to take the longer safer route. As I headed back I thought I briefly saw the head of someone above me, trudging up the hill, but I could not be certain.

Avoiding looking at Shaveling's broken body as I ran towards the foot of the ginnel, I reached the steps and took them two at a time. By the time I emerged on Henrietta Street I had wasted several minutes. The street was empty. Where was Lupei? I followed the street towards the sea and had once again reached the parking bays when a movement across the water caught my eye. Two hundred metres across the harbour a double decker bus was making its way along Pier Road. Passing the amusement arcades, it turned the corner at the Lifeboat Museum to head up the hill towards the Pavilion. I knew the name of the hill road only because it had struck me as funny when Tiffany had told me; they called it Khyber Pass.

Faced with two choices - to run across town alone in the hope of catching up with the Hounds of Hellbane bus or, to return to the comparative safety of the cottage – I chose the coward's option. It was one thing looking down my nose at Goths and the Dracula Experience and middle-aged Steampunks parading about in brass-coloured gasmasks, and quite another confronting single-handedly a man who could allegedly suck the flesh from another person's body just by touching them.

Entering the cottage, out of breath and with the back of my

shirt sticky with sweat, I stepped into a huge argument.

'Forget it. He shouldn't be here. He's not right in the head. Look at him.'

Megan barged past me and disappeared into the kitchen with Katie in pursuit.

'So what do you want to do, Megan?' Katie said. 'Like throw him out? In the middle of the night?'

'He needs locking up.' Megan shouted from the next room.

'OMG. Just because you don't like men?'

'That's nothing to do with it.'

'You are so sad.'

The object of their attention, Alex, was sitting quietly where I had left him. Still in bare feet, the blanket round his shoulders, staring at the carpet, muttering quietly to himself in a low monotone.

'And you are so binary and mega-sad,' Megan was saying as Katie reappeared in the kitchen doorway.

'Where's that pathologist?' Katie asked me.

My hesitation was enough.

'Oh my God,' Katie's voice rose a notch. 'What …'

'At the foot of the cliff.' I chose my words carefully. 'She fell and ….'

Megan appeared behind Katie. 'Don't walk away when I'm shouting at you.' Spotting me she came across and held out her hand. 'Phone.'

I handed it over.

'I'm talking to Dan,' Katie responded. 'Is that still allowed?'

'No, you're not, you're talking with me about Alex or I'm ringing the police.'

'Look,' Katie sighed and reached out an arm to try to calm Megan down.

'Don't touch me, you bitch,' Megan snarled and stormed off back into the kitchen, colliding with Jordan who was coming in the opposite direction to see what was happening.

'Hey. Hey. Chill, guys,' he said.

'Back off, Jordan. Is it my sexuality you're worried by or your own?'

'Hang on a minute,' Katie mouthed at me then disappeared back into the kitchen.

Jordan and I exchanged raised eyebrows.

'Where's Tiffany?' I asked him. 'We have to ring the police. She's local and …'

Jordan indicated the kitchen behind him with his thumb. I checked the front door was locked. Alex had stopped muttering to himself and was looking at Hannah sleeping beneath her blanket. I followed Jordan into the kitchen.

The kitchen would have made a reasonably-sized shower cubicle; but with five people, a Baby Belling cooker, sink and fridge all crammed together it was worse than rush hour on the Central Line

'Has anyone spoken with Darren's parents?' Jordan asked.

'Have you?' Megan responded.

'Hey! Guys, guys, we're all in this together. Yeah?'

'You're just bricking it at the thought of explaining to Darren's dad what you did to his car.' Megan sneered.

It wasn't a loud noise, just a small gasp, but, as we heard it, we looked at each other and realised our mistake. We had all come into the kitchen, leaving Hannah alone with Alex.

We raced out. Alex was leaning over Hannah, peering at her face, one hand touching her neck, the other under the quilt.

'Hands off her, you bastard,' Megan screamed, throwing herself across the room.

Alex turned slowly towards us, head tilted to one side, his gaze steady like a leopard interrupted in the act of killing. That same look that Lupei had worn while looking out at the crowd from behind the stage curtain: feral, malevolent and utterly devoid of humanity. Watch the sheep, always watch the sheep.

Megan smashed her fist in Alex's face. His body moved

with the impact of the blow but his eyes kept fixed on Megan. As she drew back her arm to strike a second blow I saw Alex's arm pulling back from under the blanket.

'No, Megan. Watch his hands! Don't let him touch you!' I yelled.

As I watched Alex, I understood the meaning of Shaveling's last words: *moves slowly when he is full.* There was something lethargic and deliberate about Alex's movements. I knew instinctively what he was doing to Hannah and I knew she was in mortal danger. If he were somehow sucking the flesh from her, the extra weight would require more energy to move. In any event, Megan had plenty of time to dodge Alex as he turned towards her. I moved round to Alex's left, as Jordan moved to his right, surrounding him and confusing him. He turned towards me and, as he did so, Jordan grabbed the table lamp and struck Alex a powerful glancing blow to the side of the head. Alex sunk to his knees, surprise in his eyes, then fell face down on the carpet. Ripping the lamp from the wall socket, Jordan used the flex to tie Alex's hands behind his back.

'There's washing line in one of the kitchen drawers,' Jordan told Tiffany. He turned back to Alex and muttered something I couldn't hear then looked up at me. 'He's one of my best friends,' Jordan said helplessly.

'I know.' I didn't know what else to say.

The situation was impossible. In little over a minute Alex was bound hands and feet and we were all breathing a little more easily. Megan rushed to her girlfriend's side to check up on her. She hesitated. I understood exactly what she was thinking; did she dare to pull back the quilt? She had to.

As she peered beneath the quilt, Megan let out a shriek of horror and fell to her knees.

'He's killed her,' she shouted as she threw herself at Alex.

Jordan and I pulled her away and restrained her while Katie and Tiffany crossed over to Hannah.

'Leave her alone,' Megan howled.

Hannah had lost a huge amount of weight. I wondered if Alex were solely responsible.

'Was she under the quilt when you arrived?' I asked.

'What's that got to do with anything?' Megan said.

'I'm thinking that Thor Lupei may have attacked her.'

'She was already under the quilt,' Tiffany said.

'It's not my fault,' Megan howled. 'How was I to know?'

'Nobody's blaming you, girl,' Jordan said gently.

'I can feel a pulse,' Tiffany said. 'Let's get her to hospital.'

'It's too late, Megan cried.

'No, Megan. Tiffany's right,' I said. 'Remember those Scravir in the barn? They weren't dead.'

'Are you saying she's a monster?'

'I'm not saying … Look … All I'm saying is … maybe the hospital can keep her alive while we find out how to help her. And Alex.'

'Like you're an expert in the supernatural now?' Megan sneered. 'Is this a cowboy thing?'

'Cowboy?' Katie said.

'You saw his costume. What does he think …'

'Shut up. Everyone just shut up,' Tiffany shouted, which shocked everyone into silence. 'I may just be the local girl who works in the chip shop but I'm not daft. If we don't stick together then we'll all end up like these two. And so will a lot of other people. Trouble is, with it being Goth Weekend and Whitby being full of outsiders, students, and posh people in frocks, no offence, bad stuff's happening and nobody's noticing, they just think it's part of the fun. Don't you get it? That's why Lupei is here. He's using Whitby and he's using us. So what you clever students up from London have to do is work out how to save your two friends and how to stop him.'

We all just stood there.

'To be fair, Dan isn't a student. He's an apprentice at …'

'Zip it, Jordan. It's not important,' I said. 'Tiffany's right. Let's get Hannah to hospital then grab a few hours sleep. I'm knackered.'

'OK, but we stick together?' Jordan said. 'They won't let us all go in the ambulance. My mum's a nurse and …'

'Call a taxi then,' I answered.

'I'll sort it,' Tiffany said. 'We'll take her to Scarborough. Whitby Hospital's too small.'

'And how long is that going to take?' Katie asked.

'Half an hour this time of night,' Tiffany explained.

'What about Alex?' Katie asked.

'He is unconscious and tied up,' I told her.

'So we're taking him with us?'

'No. We lock him up. That way he can't hurt himself … or anyone else while we're gone.'

We carried Alex to the downstairs toilet and put a blanket over him. I felt terrible but we had already seen what Alex could do in a moving vehicle and Hannah was in the greater danger. I offered to stay behind but the others, Tiffany in particular, wanted us all to stick together so I promised myself that as soon as we reached the hospital I would get them to send a doctor to the cottage.

The toilet had no window and the door opened outwards into the corridor. By wedging two bookcases and the dining room chairs into place we felt confident that there was no way that Alex could escape even if he did do a Houdini on the cords tying him up. When the taxi arrived we carried Hannah and piled in. Tiffany sat in front, chatting with the driver, who she knew.

I must have drifted off because almost immediately, it seemed, we were pulling up outside the hospital. Jordan ran inside and re-emerged with a wheel chair. Helping to lift Hannah out of the car, in the fierce wind that was rattling the lampposts, I was alarmed at how light she was. Little more than a bag of bones, but neither Jordan nor I said anything, to avoid further frightening Megan

Megan insisted on pushing the wheelchair. It had obviously been a busy night in Scarborough and there were still a dozen people in the accident and emergency waiting room, the majority of whom seemed high on drink or drugs. A bearded hipster nursing a broken arm was exchanging insults with an old woman in a parka, while his two friends threw chips at her. A wide-eyed girl about our age was staring vacantly into space, her knees bobbing up and down as she gripped the sides of her chair.

The receptionist took one look at Hannah and all hell broke loose. Within seconds a medical team arrived, transferred Hannah to a stretcher, and whisked us all off through a set of double doors. The staff were all wearing masks. As the doors closed behind us the old woman was shouting drunkenly about bloody foreigners and Aids. Using a card to open a door marked HLIU, the doctor, a youngish woman with straight blond hair, ushered us into a smaller empty waiting area where we were told to wait while they took Hannah into a side room. Megan tried to follow but found her path blocked.

'Please just sit over there with your friends, Miss,' the doctor said, in an east European accent. 'Someone will be out in a couple of minutes to ask you all questions. In meantime I must ask you all to stay here and not to wander off into hospital.'

Twenty plastic chairs, some posters on the dangers of smoking and the benefits of five-a-day veg, some weird blotchy paintings donated by the Scarborough Pet Protection Forum, and a wall-mounted disinfectant dispenser, and that was it. Interesting room. Within a minute Jordan was at the window staring out into the night. Katie had borrowed Megan's smart phone and was lost to the world, and Megan was pacing up and down like a caged tiger.

'Still glad you agreed to a blind date with a geezer from West London?' I asked Tiffany.

She grabbed my hand and squeezed it.

'OMG, they've locked us in.' Megan was rattling the doors to the unit.

'They're worried we're infectious,' Jordan explained. 'It's what they do.'

'We're not.'

'They don't know that, Megan,' Katie said, eyes glued to the phone screen. 'Guess what happened in Strictly?'

'Who gives a shit?' Megan said, grabbing her phone back. 'They have to let me be with Hannah.'

Katie opened her mouth to protest then changed her mind.

'Just calm down a bit,' Jordan advised gently.

'I am calm, bozo boy,' Megan shouted.

A door opened and the doctor stepped back into the waiting area. Looking tired and apprehensive, she studied us in turn.

'I need to talk with each of you,' she said. 'Who wants to go first?'

I raised my hand.

'Follow me.'

I followed her to a small office where the doctor sat down behind a desk while the lights came on. She removed her glasses and rubbed her eyes.

'You can sit down, Mister …?

'Murray, Daniel Murray.' I sat down.

'Good. I am Dr Ivanna Albu. So, Daniel, can you explain why you and your friends have brought young woman suffering from extreme malnutrition and a host of associated complications to my hospital at five in morning? She could not survive for more than few hours in her current condition so I assume that you bring her from other hospital. Do they know where she is? You have London accent, right? Who is young woman and what happened to her?'

'It is a very long story.'

'All I want is relevant details, please.'

'I don't know that you do.'

'Humour me. I have been on call for seventy three hours and …'

'Have you heard of Dracula and the …?'

'Do I look like idiot, Mr Murray?'

'OK, you don't want to listen,' I retorted. 'That's OK. So why don't I and my friends leave and let you experts work out for yourselves what has happened to her? Her name is Hannah Morris. She is twenty and lives on Creighton Road in South Ealing. Three hours ago she was a perfectly healthy person of normal weight. Maybe a bit fat. We brought her here to keep her safe from things you could not even begin to understand and to give her a chance to survive. I am sure you'll do a great job. I'll leave a contact number at reception. Can we go now please? We have to get back to Whitby for some shut eye.' I stood up to go.

'Until we establish what is wrong with Miss Morris I cannot let you leave building in case you are contagious.'

'OK. She's not contagious,' I said, 'and neither are we. So are you going to listen?'

Dr Albu nodded. I told her everything I knew. Almost everything. I told her about Darren and the pathologist who fell off the cliff, about Lupei's bus and the scravir, about the two police who came to the farm. I was midway through explaining about Alex and Hannah when a nurse with thick glasses and a bald head pushed the door open.

'Doctor, the patient's immediate signs have stabilised but we need you to decide what course of …'

'Five minutes, OK? As soon as I have finished here, I am with you,' Dr Albu told him.

The nurse withdrew.

'Please finish quickly,' Albu instructed me.

'That's it really. Hannah was like she is now. We tied Alex up and locked him in the downstairs toilet then came here with Hannah. We need you to come and see Alex too. I guess this is where you pick up a phone and ring the police to have us all charged with assault and taking illegal highs.'

The doctor stared at the wall and rubbed the sides of her nose with her fingertips. When she faced me her eyes betrayed three emotions: sadness, fear, and seriousness.

'It may surprise you, Mr Daniel, that woman of science has ...'

'Mr Murray. Daniel is my ...'

'Daniel, please listen. There is little time. I want you to hurry back to Whitby. Your friend is in grave danger. The story you have recounted is not unknown in my home country. When I was medical student I ...'

'Which is?'

' ... there were several accounts in regional news of similar events among destitute in one of our cities and ...'

'Which is?'

'and although I never witness personally ...'

'Which is? What country are you from?'

'Oh. Romania.'

The door flew open again.

'Doctor, we need you. Electolytes and blood pressure are all over the place.'

'OK. I'm coming. Prepare transfusion.' The Doctor scribbled on a sheet of paper, tore off a strip and handed to me. 'This is my mobile phone number. I must go to attend to your friend. Call me if you need to. Anytime. Here, scribble your number down for me.'

I wrote my number down on the paper.

'God speed, Daniel. As soon as we have news about your friend I ring you.'

'There's something else,' I said, rummaging in my pockets.

'The man with the mechanical arm gave me this.'

I handed her the small leather-bound book Emile Noir had given me.

Dr Albu flicked through the pages, pausing every now and then to stare silently, her expression betraying escalating alarm.

'Can you understand it?' I asked. 'It's all in some foreign …'

'It is Romanian and, yes, I understand. Can I keep this?'

'No. He gave it to me and …'

'No matter. Let me take some photos, OK?'

I nodded and watched as she turned the pages, taking snaps on her smart phone. Finally she looked up and gave me a tired and anxious smile.

'I believe that fate has brought us together, Mr Daniel. I call you in a few hours.'

She led me out. The nurse was waiting impatiently. Before joining him, Doctor Albu crossed the room to whisper into Megan's ear then followed the nurse. They disappeared into the side room and after a couple of seconds the nurse re-emerged and opened the door to let us out.

'I don't know what you told her,' the nurse said to me, 'but the doctor is convinced that you lot are the good guys.'

'I gave her free tickets to Whitby Goth Weekend.'

'Dr Albu is a Goth?' the nurse said incredulously.

'Think about it. Dark hair, works at night, likes gadgets and giving blood transfusions. From Romania.'

'Dark hair?'

An hour later, with the early hint of dawn painting purple on black over the sea, a taxi was finally dropping us off in Henrietta Street. From the outside, the cottage looked no different to when we left.

CHAPTER 30

Henrietta Street, Whitby - Daniel Murray

Sunday, 6th November

The girls had gone straight upstairs. Tiffany didn't need much persuading to join Megan and Katie rather than crossing town on her own. For Megan and Katie, having Tiffany there saved them from shouting at each other. Which left me and Jordan the beds in the other room. I would rather have been with Tiffany.

Dream on Danny Boy.

Jordan had already trudged upstairs when I remembered Alex. How could any of us have forgotten he was there? All I can say in our defence, my defence, is that we were dead on our feet, dazed from the long drive, emotionally spent, haunted by what had happened to Hannah. And there was no sound from the downstairs toilet to draw our attention. Maybe subconsciously we all wanted to avoid another furious argument. I don't know. There's no excuse.

Rather than call the others I wandered down the silent steps and stood alone outside the barricaded door. Everything was just as we had left it. I felt terrible. Ashamed. We had trussed one of my best friends up like a Christmas turkey and locked him in a room with no lighting and no windows. It had felt right at the time because of all the other shit that was going on but what if he had a fit? What if he died?

It was all but impossible to sustain the fear I had felt when confronted with the supernatural horrors of the previous thirty-six hours. Now all I could remember with any vividness was Alex sitting there with his slumped and injured shoulder, teeth chattering, gazing up at me with hangdog eyes and saying 'I think it's broken, Dan', in a crumpled voice.

On the other hand, maybe he was asleep, which wouldn't be a bad thing. Jordan would know, his mum was a nurse, we would decide together. I turned to go and fetch him.

The groan was tiny and pitiful. I jumped so hard I smashed my arm against the wall and gasped.

'Is that you Katie? What's happened? Why can't I move?'

His voice was weak, pleading, pathetic. Like a little boy cowering beneath a bully's hand.

'Hey. Hey. Is that Jordan?'

Barely able to stand up, I could have slept like a log in the dark barn at Farview Farm, given half a chance. Why couldn't Alex just sleep until morning? What if he started freaking everyone out again?

'Dan. Dan. It's Alex. You have to help me. Something's happened. I can't move. I'm frightened, Dan. I had this bad dream and then I woke up and now I can't …'

'Just shut up, Alex,' I snapped. 'Shut up and go to sleep. In the morning, first thing, I'll take you to the hospital.'

'It's my arm, Dan. I can't feel it anymore. You have to help me. Please. Please, Dan.'

He started crying. The big confident guy who always got the girls and made me feel inadequate on a weekly basis was blubbing like a baby and I was torn between anger, guilt and, it shames me to admit this, a tiny grain of pleasure. Maybe it would wipe that smug watch-me-shag-everything-that-moves smirk off his face. Maybe he'd stop telling people my mum had run off with the milkman.

'It hurts, Dan. I'm sorry. I know you're angry with me. You've every right. But I am sorry. Really sorry, Dan. You're the only … I promise I'll never …'

With a roar I spun round and tossed the dining room chairs aside then grabbed the biggest bookcase and started to haul it out of the way, scraping the skin off my knuckles against the wall of the corridor. Why me? Why bloody me? I just wanted to go to bed. I was totally fed up with everything and everyone. Alex for getting me into all this crap. Katie and Megan and Hannah for caring only about themselves. The bloody freezing campsite. Tiffany for brushing me off just because I touched her sodding butt cheeks. By accident. The police for being so bastard useless. The pathologist for falling off the fucking cliff. I seized the second bookcase and dragged it away from the door, bashing my elbow for good measure. Finally the corridor was clear and I could pull the toilet door open. I wasn't going to untie him, just check that he wasn't in a really bad way and let him see the light in the corridor.

I was so lost in my little bubble. Dumbo McStupid. I lifted the latch and was starting to pull the door when it flew open with such force that my arm was jarred backwards, banging against my chest, winding me. I staggered as Alex burst out of the room, smashing his head against my chin, snapping my neck back and causing me to lose my balance. As I crumpled to the floor he was already leaping over me.

'You always were a sucker, Dan,' he snarled. 'Dead meat and dumb as donuts.' He laughed and raced away up the steps.

I was still getting to my feet when I heard a scream. Ignoring my throbbing head, I charged after Alex and found him in the front room. He had pinned Tiffany to the ground (when had she come back downstairs?), and was sitting on her back, reaching out to grab her flailing arms. I threw myself at Alex, wrapping my arm around his neck and hauling him back with all my strength, but he was too strong. He prised my arm away; as he did so I felt a strange tingling sensation in my wrist. I wriggled out of his grasp. The only weapons to hand were the dining room chairs, one of which I grabbed and, swinging it in a wide arc, brought crashing down against his back. Alex turned towards me, his face contorted with rage, as I brought the chair down a second time, striking him a glancing blow across the head. He slipped off her back, clutching his temple.

'Get out,' I shouted. 'and leave Tiffany alone.'

Alex glanced down at Tiffany then up at me, a thin smile forming on his lips. Blood was trickling between his fingers.

'I said get out,' I yelled, standing over him, still holding the chair.

He rolled backwards, up onto his feet, putting distance between us. Taking three steps to the front door, he threw it back on its hinges, causing the whole house to shake. Rain poured through the open door. Lip curled, Alex bared his teeth like a feral dog. I swung the chair back, adopting the pose of a batsman awaiting strike; if he wanted it he could have it. Alex spun heel and ran out into the street, just as Jordan arrived in his pants and t-shirt.

'What the hell?'

'I thought he needed help. I opened the toilet door,' I explained lamely.

'You did what?'

'OK, so I'm stupid.'

'You said it, man. '

I closed the door.

'Don't listen to him,' Tiffany told me. 'He's all shite. Far as I'm concerned you're a hero.'

I helped her up and took her in my arms.

'There's nowt stupid about wanting to believe the best in people,' she told me. 'He's your friend. It's normal.

'We have to barricade the door,' Jordan said, looking around the room. 'In the morning we'll ring Alex's dad, I can't face doing it now.'

'Me neither,' I confessed.

I grabbed my parka and retrieved the syringe gun that Emile Noir had given me.

'Take this,' I said, handing it to Tiffany. 'If they attack you can kill them. Six shots. You stab it in and pull the trigger.'

'If what attacks?'

'The scravir. The vials contain a substance that burns them from the inside.'

'You think they're coming here?' Her voice soft as sorrow.

'Yes. No. I don't know. I just want you, Katie and Megan to have something to defend yourselves with. Megan knows how to ...'

Out of nowhere Tiffany kissed me on the mouth, leaving me tingling from the top of my head to the tips of my toes.

'You're on the side of the angels, Dan. You know that?' she said.

'Hey, cut the romance and help me with this.' Jordan had closed the door and was wrestling with the sofa.

As I helped him drag the sofa across the room, Katie appeared at the foot of the stairs, half-asleep, her hair all over the place.

'Alex wanted some fresh air,' I told her.

Katie blinked groggily.

'Come on, kid. Let's go up and chew some Zs,' Tiffany said, taking Katie's arm and steering her round. As she climbed the first step, pushing Katie in front of her, Tiffany turned and beamed me a smile that would have melted Iceland.

'Even puppies have the decency not to dribble while they do that thing with their eyes,' Jordan advised me.

I watched Tiffany's pyjama clad hips swinging; getting to really love the north wouldn't be hard at all.

We carried the armchairs and piled them up on the sofa. The door was almost hidden from view.

'What do you think?' Jordan asked, when we had finished.

'I think she's ...'

'The bloody door, durkboi.'

'Oh, yeah. I think they'll just smash the windows.'

There was no way we could protect ourselves if the scravir mounted an organised attack.

'OK, we stay downstairs and take it in turns to keep watch?' Jordan suggested. 'There's knives in the kitchen.'

'Yeah. Downstairs,' I agreed. 'You're a bastard, you know that?'

'And you're the shite in nining armour. Oh, Tiffany, let me protect you, Tiffany.'

We smiled. Jordan threw himself on the sofa and within a minute was snoring for England. I grabbed a chopping knife and a cup of coffee from the kitchen, put the television on with the sound off and watched some mad blonde, wearing too much makeup and strung out on coke, flogging a plastic box for slicing vegetables like it was the most exciting moment of her entire life ... It probably was.

The coffee mug woke me as it fell from my hands and hit the floor. Jordan was still snoring. The woman on the television had been replaced by a bald pink-tied tosser caressing a trouser press like it was his girlfriend's leg while pouring out a long stream of meaningless statistics about wattages and fibre compression ratios and colour retention parabolas.

An infomaniac.

What did humans do with their lives before shopping channels?

There was a cleaning cloth in the kitchen sink. I tugged the curtains and blinked. It was nearly eleven o'clock according to the microwave. On the patio table, through the window, two yellow-eyed seagulls were scrapping over a fish head. In the harbour below a couple of fishermen in yellow oilskins were walking about on the deck of a boat, lugging boxes.

I was making a wake-up coffee for Jordan when I had a

thought, scribbled a message for the others on the back of an envelope, stuck it to the fridge with a magnet, grabbed my parka and slipped out of the house.

Above me, gulls were tunnelling the thick morning air, diving and screaming between the chimney pots. My brisk cobbled footsteps ricocheted off cottage walls as I headed for the town centre, past the abbey steps, Justin's fudge and chocolate shop, Arguments Yard, and over the swing bridge where a stiff breeze blew in off the sea.

The Dracula Experience was closed, leaving me wondering why it ever opened before sunset. Lee Ester Alita Lee's fortune telling shed was also shut, though with her gifts she would have known the streets would be empty.

'What have you done to him?'

The voice made me jump, harsh and strident. I span round but saw no-one. Shivering, I set off again.

'What have you done to him?' the voice shouted a second time.

To my right a woman emerged from the shadows between two of the seaside shacks. She was dressed exactly as when I had first seen her, the wedding dress and white makeup that made her face look like a skull, the faded rose still clutched in her blood-caked hand. Too many weirdoes in Whitby; I was fed up with them. I spun my finger round in a little circle beside my head, in the international sign to convey the person in front of you is an idiot.

'Emile has disappeared,' the woman said, ignoring my insult. 'Without Noir we are in grave danger.' She sensed she had my attention. 'He smelled the evil on you the moment he saw you. On the bridge.'

Her voice carried the waft of a foreign accent, like a whisper of smoke.

'Who is he?' I asked her. 'Why is he chasing Lupei?'

'So you *have* met him.'

I nodded. 'Lupei caught him. Took him to his bus. I think.'

The woman's eyes grew in alarm. 'How long ago?'

'Nine, ten hours,' I answered. 'What time is it?'

'Eleven twenty. I am Ylenia.'

Where had I heard that name? I wracked my brains. Had Noir mentioned, or Lupei?

'So, Daniel, where are you going?'

How did she know my name?

'I have to go,' I muttered.

'I will accompany you, but don't touch me.' Ylenia reached into the folds of her bridal dress and pulled out a long hunting knife. 'I am armed.'

I wondered if she also carried a syringe gun. Then it hit me.

'Noir mentioned you. He came to you to collect those glass bullets for his scravir gun, didn't he?'

Ylenia nodded. 'You have seen them?' She stepped forwards. 'Let's go. You explain while we walk.'

Her arm was freezing. I offered her my parka, which she took hungrily. We hurried and by the time we reached Khyber Pass I had given her the bare bones of what had happened in the barn at Farview Farm. We took the steps up toward the whalebone arch. Ylenia didn't ask where I was taking her and I didn't volunteer an explanation; in retrospect I realise that she already knew.

At the top of the hill, a cold and stoical Captain Cook stood on his plinth staring out to sea with vacant bronze eyes. On his spattered shoulders four large herring gulls provided all the guano he needed, along with a feather muffler against the biting wind. A fifth bird decorated his head. The birds' hard eyes followed us suspiciously as we passed beneath the whalebones. Was I seagull or statue?

To the east the thin grey line where slate sea met pewter sky gave me hope; if sunlight, the power source of almost all life on the planet, could travel ninety million miles across space only to be prevented from reaching the Earth's surface by a few hundred metres of minute water droplets then maybe the little guys could sometimes beat the big guys. Maybe Thor Lupei wasn't invincible.

'You are sure he came here?' Ylenia asked as we headed down Cleveland Way.

'Just a hunch,' I answered. 'If I'm wrong ...'

Apart from a couple of delivery lorries, the road in front of the Pavilion was empty. We followed the road round on the seaward side of the building towards the main entrance and there, tucked behind another large lorry, we saw it, the black double-decker bus. There was no way it could have turned in so narrow a space; it must have reversed.

We approached cautiously. The curtains were drawn, downstairs and upstairs.

'Shall we call the police?'

'Set fire to the bus,' Ylenia said simply.

'What? Here?'

'Why did you come, Daniel?' Ylenia said, second-guessing my thoughts.

Was there a point in trying to reason with a zombie in a frock? Did all zombies consider torching buses outside public buildings part of a lazy Sunday morning? Ignoring her, I tried the doors at the back of the bus. Locked. I walked round the vehicle. Maybe he wasn't even on it. Maybe he had dumped it and fled.

'Why were you sure the bus would be here?' Ylenia asked, sticking to me like shit to shoes.

'I guessed. Last night, I saw the bus heading towards Khyber Pass from across the harbour after I found the pathologist.'

'He could have been leaving town.'

'I assumed he was returning to the Pavilion to pick up his band.'

'That was hours ago. Why is he still here?' she asked.

'I'm not a bloody psychic. Maybe the building was locked. Maybe he just parked here so he could go and suck the flesh out of people in the town. Maybe he's in the Pavilion.'

'No need to shout, Daniel.'

'I'm not shouting. OK, I am shouting but I … Oh fuck, I don't know. Wait here.'

I left Ylenia by the bus and headed round towards the stage entrance. The door was closed. I beat my fist against it. I was knocking for a third time when two things happened: footsteps on the other side and my phone pinging to announce a text.

The door swung open and a short and familiar figure stepped into view.

'Eric, hi.'

Above suitcase-sized bags, Eric's eyes were hard. His shoulders were slumped and two buttons on his shirt were undone, revealing a bulging white belly. He looked like he'd been up all night and there was no indication that he recognised me.

'Sorry,' I muttered. 'I'm looking for Thor Lupei. I'll call back later.'

Then, as if someone had flicked a switch, a smile erupted across Eric's fat face as he drew himself up to his full five foot one inches and snapped into life.

'Daniel. Come in, come in. You young people; up all night and still fresh as daisies.'

He welcomed me in with a sweep of his hand and I followed him along the now familiar corridors, weaving our way towards the dressing rooms.

'Is he here? I saw his bus so I thought …'

Eric didn't answer and I assumed that he had not heard me.

'I remember being twenty. Up to all kinds of mischief. Only young once, eh? Here we are,' Eric turned to face me, his smile full and broad.

He pushed open the door to Dressing Room Two and

ushered me in. I stepped past him into the room, which was far smaller than Room Four where Lupei had held court the previous night. As in the other dressing room, large illuminated makeup mirrors along one wall enabled visiting artistes to preen themselves prior to appearing on-stage.

'I didn't get a chance to thank …' I started.

The gentle click was followed by the sound of a key turning in a lock. I spun round. The door was shut and I was alone. I grabbed the handle and pulled. The door didn't budge. Total silence. No windows, no exit other than through the locked door. Maybe I had misheard, easily done. The door had just swung shut. Eric had gone to find Thor Lupei and would be back in a few seconds. No need to panic. Eric was as tired as I was.

I sat down and studied my face in the mirror, wondering if the night's events were written in my eyes. Did witnessing horrors transform you to other people? When you saw photos of murderers or rapists or Nazi stormtroopers you wanted their crimes to be written all over their faces, you wanted them to look different. It had to be visible in their eyes, in the shape of their mouths, in an evident evil ugliness loitering like a fetid smell. Except that it didn't, evil people looked just like everyone else. You couldn't see by looking at me that I had witnessed a man butchering stick-thin human monsters or that I had seen a human head burning on a bonfire.

It had to be a couple of minutes now. Where was Eric? Had he been asleep when I pushed the stage door bell? He must be at least sixty. Maybe he was in early onset dementia. Or drunk. Had he smelled of alcohol? It was hard to tell, the dressing rooms and the corridors stank of a thousand pints of spilled beer. I gazed at the skinny kid in the mirror and shrugged.

And then there was the other little voice whispering in my head. The one I didn't want to listen to.

When would Ylenia decide that waiting out in the cold

was stupid? The cafeteria was probably open so I would pass through the main entrance on my way out. Grab a couple of coffees. Up the stairs and out into the main hall would be the quickest route.

Wake up Daniel and face the facts.

I pulled my smart phone from my pocket and picked Jordan.

Straight to voice mail.

< I am at Pavilion. Thought Lupei might be here. Seen the bus. The doorman let me in then … >

Then he locked you in, Sucker.

< … he locked me in one of the dressing rooms. Come as soon as you read this. >

Send.

No signal.

Now what? The lights went out. I stood up. Where was the light switch? By the door? Must be on a timer. Why would it be on a timer?

Wake up, you are in deep shit.

I walked slowly towards the door, hands out in front, feeling for the door or a wall. My heart was thumping. The bastard had locked me in. Jordan was asleep, as were Tiffany, Katie, and Megan. Ylenia had probably given up and left.

Use the torch on your phone, Dinter.

I used the torch on my phone. The light switch on the wall did nothing. Having reminded myself of where everything was in the room, I switched off the torch to save the battery. It felt safer to sit on the floor with my back to the wall. I reached for my parka pocket and the syringe gun. Except that I wasn't wearing my parka, I had lent it to Ylenia and, in any event I had given the gun to Tiffany. Shit.

For the first time since I had arrived in Whitby I was on the edge. Combination of things; danger plus fear plus tiredness plus being shown to be an idiot. So many missed opportunities to escape, to walk away and catch the train back to civilisation: air pollution, commuter rage and all night doner kebabs.

Footsteps. The door flew open.

'Daniel, Daniel. I am so sorry,' Eric said standing in the doorway. 'We have had a power cut.'

'You locked me in.'

'No, no, no. A huge misunderstanding. Please, come with me.' Eric smiled reassuringly.

I climbed to my feet and crossed the room. Relieved, I decided not to complain, all that mattered was getting out into the fresh air. The sooner the better.

It was so small that I almost missed it. A tiny pinprick in the back of my thigh, like a gnat bite as I passed in front of Eric. The lights were on in the corridor, which begged the question; how there could be a power cut in a single room? I was turning back towards Eric when my whole body went limp. Collapsing to the dirty floor like a house of cards, I lay there, limbs in disarray around me, head spinning, Eric passing in front of my field of vision over and over again until I became so dizzy I had to close my eyes. The sensation didn't stop and I worried that I would throw up over myself. The floor itself was moving, like it did on a fairground carousel, and I wanted to dig my nails into the dark red lino to stop myself from fall-ing off. I tried to speak but my mouth and larynx ignored me. My body was moving; I was being dragged face down along the corridor, the sticky lino tugging at my upper lip and right nostril, the stale and acrid smell of smoke and alcohol scraping my skin. Something hit the inside of my lip, dragged along with me. The taste was making me nauseous. A cigarette butt? Old meat that had fallen out of a sandwich? I scrunched up my eyelids to protect my eyes and tried to roll over, to get my face off the floor, but my body refused to listen.

A sharp pain as my face dragged over a rough raised surface that smelled or tasted metallic. A drain cover perhaps?

Into another room. Suddenly Eric let go of my legs and they clattered to the floor, my knees knocking painfully together as they landed. He climbed over me, pausing briefly to kick me in the belly. His footsteps echoed briefly and I was alone.

From where I lay I could just about see through the open doorway. My field of view had shrunk, leaving me peering out at the world through a pulsating porthole. My ears were ringing, as if someone were using a food processor just out of my line of sight. Was I dying? What had Eric done to me?

Don't shut your eyes. Stay awake.

I wanted to blink, but what if my eyes stayed shut?

Fight it.

I counted the breezeblocks on the corridor wall and, when I reached the end, I started again. Seven lumps of concrete. Painted magnolia. Lipstick on a pig.

How had I misjudged Eric so catastrophically?

I was hyperventilating. I made an effort to calm down. My eyelids, disregarding my determination to keep them open, closed to soothe my stinging eyes. When I realised that I could re-open them it felt like victory. Is there something more pathetic than feeling happy to learn that your eyelids work?

Were there voices whispering? I strained to override the tinnitus and tunnel vision but my senses remained obstinately broken. How would I look to someone walking in and finding me? Were my limbs lying tidily? Had I wet myself? Was I dribbling? I could smell vomit; was that me or the sticky floor?

Footsteps. I tried to brace myself but, since my body was not listening, nothing happened. Shoes appeared in the doorway and walked towards me. I recognised them. Green trainers with a red diagonal stripe … Alex. It was Alex! He was there to help me. He had been weird but that was last night. Now he was feeling normal again. His trainers stopped in front of me. I heard the creak of fabric and suddenly his face was there, at an odd angle, in front of mine.

It's me. Thank God you're here, Alex. Eric injected me. Don't trust him. He's dangerous. We need to get out. There's an emergency exit, steps down between the dressing rooms. Must open out onto the footpath between the Pavilion and the cliff. You'll need to help me, I can't move and ...

I realised I wasn't speaking, my lips weren't moving. I couldn't even grunt. I blinked. I tried to muster up a facial expression, anything to let him know I was there, to let him know I was more than a pair of staring eyes, trapped inside a living corpse.

A trace of a smile formed on Alex's lips, as if he were remembering something. His eyes showed only mild boredom. His face lifted from my line of sight. The creak of his denim jeans.

Don't go. I'm here, bruv. I need you to see me. To protect me. Sorry about earlier. We were trying to protect you, and Hannah. You must understand that. We need to go home, Alex. Back to London. All of us. My train leaves this afternoon.

The sound of something being dragged. More feet in the doorway behind Alex's feet.

'Put him in this.' Eric's voice. 'Easiest way to get him out without attracting attention. You take that end.'

Eric was red in the face as he leaned over, straining to lift my legs. Alex must have had my shoulders as they picked me up and lowered me into a large box. A lid clattered into place, leaving me on my back in sudden and shocking darkness.

'Can he breathe?' Alex's voice was muffled.

'Don't be wet. Course he can breathe, there's holes. He's no use to us dead. Lift.'

The box shook.

'Bloody hell, what's he made of? Lead?'

'Just the weight of all those chips he carries on his shoulders.'

I counted the footsteps as they carried me, trying to stay

focused, hoping to retain a sense of where I was being taken. The box was dropped roughly. A key rattled in a lock. As they lifted me again, my mobile rang.

'Shit. Shouldn't we take his phone?' Alex said.

Eric laughed mirthlessly. 'What the hell for? Poor sod couldn't scratch his arse if he wanted to, never mind answer his bloody phone. By the time he can move his arms again the battery will be long dead. Turn left, it's quicker.'

The muffled sound of sea gulls told me we were outside. When they stopped walking and put me down a second time I heard a click followed by a mechanical whirring sound. Something was clipped to each end of the box and suddenly I was rising in the air, the box juddering and buckling alarmingly. I finally realised that I must be in a long drum box, like those Lupei used to transport his band. They must be lifting me by a hoist or crane mounted within the bus. The upward motion stopped abruptly to be replaced by what felt like horizontal movement, as if I were being swung round, then I was dropping again. Someone was waiting for me. As the box landed it was dragged rapidly into place, catches or cables connected to my box were released. Several mechanical sounds were occurring simultaneously and I imagined the lifting gear folding away and the roof sliding back into place.

Footsteps approached my box.

'Well done, Alex,' said a rich baritone voice. 'What would I do without you?

'He weighs a ton.'

'You and Eric were more than equal to the task. A little more housekeeping and we can leave.'

He sounded tired and out of breath; I guessed staying up all night killing and sucking the organs out of people could be a little draining, for both sides. And that was on top of performing before an adoring crowd.

'Shall I fasten the lid?' Alex's voice.

'No, no, we haven't quite finished with Dan the Man. He has an important service to perform. In fact now might be as good a time as …'

The lid came off my box and, once my eyes had adjusted, I saw I had been right; I was on the bus. The sun had appeared and floating motes of dusts were dancing in the air. A hand appeared; the fingers encrusted with silver rings, a row of skulls and grotesque leering masks just above my eyes. Adrenalin kicked in but I would not even be able to flinch if a punch were thrown. Thor Lupei leaned into view behind his fist, strands of long white hair framing his pale face, his pink eyes, his casual disinterested expression that of someone peering into an empty filing cabinet. In my head I was screaming at him to leave me alone, in the real world my face was dead as botox, my vocal chords mute as wool fibre in a carpet.

Lupei's hand dropped from view. Did I feel him reach out and touch me? I am still not sure to this day. In retrospect a human touch of any kind, even a slap or a punch, would have been welcome and comforting compared with the bizarre sensations I experienced in the moments that followed.

Vaguely at first and then with growing intensity, a wriggling heat crawled and swelled in my insides, like a jumbled mass of maggots squirming in a roadkill corpse. I could not see my belly but sensed it was alive with movement as hidden things rippled beneath its surface, the way the growing foetus scrapes its mother's belly with its foot. The seconds passed, with Lupei looming over me. My tightening skin felt taut as a blood bloated leech. My pulse thumped in my ears. Out of nowhere, the memory of a photo I had seen at school; honeypot ants with huge translucent abdomens spherical with golden liquid fed to them by other workers. Living storage containers with hard shiny faces and dead eyes, clinging to the roof of a tunnel deep inside the nest, their lives sacrificed to protect the colony against future times of drought or hunger.

My chaotic thoughts were interrupted by the gentlest of baritone sighs, the sound a happy guy makes at the end of a long day when he is finally able to take off his tight new trainers. I opened my eyes, not aware of having closed them, to find Lupei was no longer above me.

'Perfect. You may wrap him up.'

'Wrap him up?'

'The lid, Alex. Our friend needs his beauty sleep. Long journey.'

Darkness slid in to cover me. Footsteps retreating. A low sweet ripple of laughter, then silence.

Where was Ylenia? She must have seen Alex and Eric carrying me out to the bus, watched me being lifted on board. Had she called the police?

I was as detached from the world as if I had been dumped at the sunken sump of a salt mine. How long before I would start hallucinating in this terrifying isolation? I focused all my energy and my willpower on trying to move a single muscle: a toe, a finger, my jaw. Aside from my eyelids, nothing. I could not even feel where my body was in space. I knew from what I had seen when the lid was off that I was on my back but, in the dark, I had no sense of up or down. My phone ringtone kicked off again but I could only lie there waiting for it to end. Was it Tiffany, or my Dad suddenly coming on all family-minded, calling to remind me I had work in the morning? Or the doctor in Scarborough? I would never know.

When the phone did stop it made way for another sound. Sniffing and scratching close by. Was something locked inside the box with me? Was it crawling between my legs? Had it emerged from the numb soup of my abdomen? My chest heaved violently as I anticipated the horror, dripping saliva on my cheek, the fetid breath of death, the razor teeth.

'Please, you have to help me. Somebody help me,' a human voice whispered close by.

I must be hallucinating. How could there be someone in the box with me, it made no sense. An ugly scraping, like fingernails along a blackboard just centimetres from my ears. My breathing assumed the insistent rhythm of a warning light at a level crossing. Please God this was not real.

Another noise, on my left this time. A feeble tapping, sporadic at first then more urgent. Still the whispering, pleading voice asking for assistance. And then a third sound. Beneath me? More desperate scraping. A woman's muffled voice crying piteously in the darkness. They could not all be in the box with me. We must be stacked up.

The bus rattled into life. Movement and engine noise muffled the other sounds.

A wriggling in my bowels, like a tight shoal of fish sliding over each other to escape a shark. Inside my own body. Tears welled up and ran hot down my cheeks. The nightmare was swallowing me alive in its gaping maw. The ugly face of a scravir leered at me, its jaw clicking as it opened, and I prayed I was hallucinating.

For the first time in my life I understood the eager grasping claws of death. I was even willing it on, anything to end the torment. Just how many of us were there on that bus, paralysed and stacked up in blind desperate boxes?

CHAPTER 31

Ealing Hospital, London - telephone transcript

Sunday, 6th November 1.07pm

Reception:	Putting you through now, caller.
Jordan:	Mum?
Janice Barcelle:	Jordan. Thank God, where are you son?'
Jordan:	I may miss the train, there's been a ...
Janice Barcelle:	Stop right there and listen to me. I been ringing you for hours. Darren's father rung to tell me the police have reported his car been found smash up in the middle of Whitby. You kids are in a whole heap of trouble, Boy.
Jordan:	We're not kids and this whole bloodclaat weekend is ...
Janice Barcelle:	Jordan, stop and think before you open your mouth. This is a hospital line, they record everything
Jordan:	I've done nothing wrong Mum.
Janice Barcelle:	So just get on the train and come home. What time it leave?
Jordan:	Four thirty-seven but it's not that simple. Katie, Megan, Alex and Daniel are ... You remember Hannah, I introduced you at the open day? She is in hospital, and Alex has disappeared.

Janice Barcelle:	Only thing that matters to me is you.
Jordan:	Hang on, Mum, someone is knocking at the door. I have to answer it.

Sound of door opening.

Jordan:	Can I help you?'

Another voice, female, too indistinct to transcribe.

Jordan:	OK. Come in. I'm on the phone. The others are still asleep. Give me a couple of minutes. If you want to make yourself a coffee, the kitchen is through there. Mum, hi, yeah, that's the doctor from Scarborough Hospital, she's come to speak with Daniel.
Janice Bacelle:	What business have you got with a doctor from Scarborough?
Jordan:	It's along story.
Unidentified vce:	Who was at the door?
Jordan:	That doctor who saw Hannah, she's in the kitchen. Look, Mum, I have to go.
Unidentified vce:	(shouting) Where's Daniel?
Janice Barcelle:	Jordan, who is that? What happening!
Jordan:	Downstairs, I think. I heard the shower running.
Unidentified vce:	The doctor wants to talk to us all.
Janice Barcelle:	Who is that?
Jordan:	It's Tiffany, Mum. She's a friend, of Daniel's. Look, something's come up. I'll ding you again in ten minutes.'

CHAPTER 32

**Email from Miss Tiffany Harrek
to Mr Edward Harrek**

Sunday, 6th November, 10.47pm

Hi Uncle Ted,

Really happy you are reading this because it means you've woken up and mum is the happiest sister in the world and I'm the happiest niece. Mum's really brave but she was scared to death when they put you into an induced coma.

I have to tell someone about what is happening right now and I can't tell mum and dad because they've got enough to worry about. You have to promise you'll keep everything I'm about to write to yourself unless I'm dead or disappeared.

You risked your life saving Mark and the others on the boat so I know that by the time you get to the end of this email you will understand why I am doing what I am doing. With luck, we'll have had a hug before you even read this!

You're always telling me that Whitby is a dead end and that if I've any sense I'll find a way of getting out. Well I met this boy called Daniel. He's come from London for the festival. Funny thing is he doesn't even really like the Goth scene; his friend Alex invited him. You'd like Daniel, he's a bit like you: fish out of water, tall, quiet, silly in a serious kind of way, and brave. Not like lads round here. (Yes, I know I've only known him for 36 hours but it feels like forever).

Daniel came into the chippie on Friday night and we got talking and he told me he were spending the weekend camping at Farview Farm. Which didn't make sense because they closed it down, didn't they? I told him to find somewhere in town but he said he had already paid online. It were pissing down with rain and he were set on walking miles to the farm in the dark. He didn't even have a torch so I nicked the one from the storeroom at work (Andy'll kill me if he finds out) and lent it to him. God only knows how he thought he'd pitch his tent in the dark so I gave him my number in case he needed help.

Saturday morning I went with dad to change the flowers on David's grave (we all got drenched) then I stayed in while five o'clock when I went on shift. At ten o'clock Daniel rings and asks if I want to watch the bands at the Pavilion, says he can get us in at the stage door. I hadn't realised how bad the weather were. I reached the lifeboat museum when I bumped in to Daniel who were meant to be waiting for me by whalebone arch. He said there were a boat in trouble at the end of the pier. When he described the boat I realised it were you. We ran past lighthouse and saw the helicopter rescue you. (If you noticed some idiot swept off the pier, hanging in a life buoy, that were Daniel.) They said you were a hero, I were so proud of you.

When we came away from the pier, I took Daniel back to my flat to get him some dry clothes so we could go to the gig. We talked while we walked; Daniel's mum left when he were eight and his dad is agoraphobic, which is why Daniel went straight to work instead of going to university. He said his friends don't even know about his dad because he's too ashamed to tell them. I told him about losing David. It sounds silly but it were like we were meant to know each other. Anyroad Emily lent us some of Jack's clothes and we went to see the bands, which were great.

You might have heard on the radio about deaths on Friday night; three old people died of hypothermia outside. Well they were murders and I know who killed them. I don't have time to tell you the whole story, it'll all come out anyway, but if we all die in the next few hours no-one will know how dangerous Thor Lupei is or how many people he's killed or where he's gone. He's the singer with Hounds of Hellbane and like a kind of vampire but worse. You're thinking we all had a few jars too many or we've been on the wacky backy but if you're reading this it is because I have disappeared or been found dead so I need you to take it seriously, however weird it sounds. Lupei kills people by sucking the life out of them, and he's been staying on Farview Farm in the Hounds of Hellbane double decker tour bus. The old people the police found dead on Friday night weren't old people; they were young people killed by Lupei. He doesn't just kill people, he turns them into slaves somehow, which is what we think has happened to Daniel's friend Alex.

Last night we locked Alex up in the toilet of the cottage on Henrietta Street where Daniel's friends were staying, after Alex turned bad, while we took Hannah to Scarborough hospital. She's another friend. Alex had sucked away part of Hannah's body, I can't tell you how scary all this is. And two police and a pathologist woman have died. We were all so tired by the time we got back from the hospital. I stayed at the cottage with the others, I were too frightened to walk to my flat in the dark. I were asleep and it were still dark, when there were this massive bang. I charged downstairs, smack into Alex who were coming up from the basement. Somehow he'd escaped. He pinned me to the floor and after what he did to Hannah I thought I were stuffed but Daniel comes legging it upstairs, throws himself at Alex and drives him off and saves my life. Alex ran out of the front door. Jordan and Daniel barricaded the front and I went back upstairs.

We slept while lunchtime when there were banging on the front door. Downstairs Jordan were on the phone, getting a right earful, and there were this woman in the kitchen, Ivanna Albu, the doctor who were looking after Hannah at Scarborough hospital. She'd come to talk to Daniel about Thor Lupei.

Jordan thought Daniel were taking a shower but I checked and he weren't. His rucksack were by the sofa but his mobile weren't there. We guessed he had bobbed out for a walk. Ivanna the doctor said she needed us to take her to Farview straightaway; she were looking for evidence that might help Hannah recover. None of us wanted to go, but eventually we piled into Ivanna's car. I left a note for Daniel. We turned off Hawsker Lane onto the single track road and were coming up to first of the farms when Jordan started shouting at Ivanna to get off the road and hide the car. They argued a bit then Ivanna drove across a stretch of muddy grass and stopped behind a barn. Suddenly this large black car roared past, followed by a police car. We waited a minute then Ivanna put her car into reverse to get back onto the road.

Straightaway, the wheels started spinning and the car were sinking into the mud. We all climbed out and tried to push the car while Ivanna revved the engine; which were a bloody waste of time. We're still pushing when this massive yellow tractor thundered past before we had a chance to stop it and ask for help. In the end I went to the farm and lied about skidding off the road and got one of the lads to pull us out of the mud.

Megan and Katie were scared to go back to Farview because there were these weird creatures there. Megan had helped Daniel and this other guy, Emile Noir, who had killed several of them, to build a huge fire to burn them, and Katie had heard a policeman being killed by one of the monsters. So we're turning into the farm and Megan is telling the doctor to watch out for the fire and Katie is explaining that there's an abandoned police car in the yard. Only there is no big fire, there's just mud. And there's no police car either. It looked like the whole farmyard had been scraped clean by a mechanical digger. Jordan said that maybe the police car Katie saw was the one that passed us in the lane. But Katie insisted it were a crime scene; there should be that tape up all over the place and men with special suits on walking about with tweezers and stuff.

Two police had died and there were bodies in the fire. Ivanna asked if Katie had actually seen the police getting killed and Katie said no but that she had heard the screams beneath the campervan. (I saw the light and smoke from the fire with my own eyes Uncle Ted, so I know Katie and Megan weren't making it up. And Daniel had told me about it too.)

Ivanna wanted a blood sample. She explained that Daniel had let her take photos of pages in a journal that he had been given by Noir, the man with the mechanical arm. Ivanna had been able to read them and she were convinced that getting blood or DNA samples of the creatures Daniel and Megan had seen would help her understand what were happening to Hannah.

A freezing wind were whistling in off the sea. Megan took us to the barn. We grabbed sticks at the entrance; even in daylight it were dark inside. Jordan found a sickle. We moved together in a group, each of us looking in a different direction, checking for any sign of movement. Ready to leg it. Megan couldn't believe the barn were empty, no sign of the horrors of the previous night. Just the usual rubbish you find in a barn. She swore blind the creatures that this man called Emile Noir called scravir had been killed right there.

Ivanna squatted beside a darker patch of ground and touched it. She lifted her hand and smelled her fingers and said it smelled of diesel. Katie decided the police must have been covering up the evidence, but no-one could think of why they would do that.

We checked everywhere, including under a campervan in the middle of a field. There were nowt. Daniel and Katie had both heard strange noises coming from under the van, before the policeman were killed. Back in the farmyard, Jordan saw an outbuilding that had three massive new padlocks, and there were fresh tractor tyre marks outside. There were also a couple of new padlocks fitted to the front door of the farmhouse. We were thinking about whether we should break in when Megan said she knew where to find the blood sample that Ivanna were looking for. Somewhere the police wouldn't have known about and wouldn't think to look.

She took us down a path between the farmhouse and the out-buildings. The path opened out onto a garden and the back of the farmhouse. To our left were an old lean-to greenhouse and an outbuilding with a couple of whitewashed doors.

Megan said she could show us a dead dog behind one of the doors. She and Daniel had gone there, using the smell of dog shit to hide from Thor Lupei. The dog had still been alive and Thor Lupei had stabbed his hand trying to open the door. Ivanna told Megan to stop walking. In front of one of the doors were a large puddle. There were blood on the horizontal bars of the door, a thimble-sized pool had gathered in the space where a knot had fallen out of the wood. The place stank to high heaven. Ivanna took a bunch of test tubes and a pipette from her bag and collected samples first from the door and then from the puddle. As she held the first one up we could all see that the liquid in the tube weren't black, it were dark red.

As Megan were explaining how Lupei put his hand on the dog's head and sucked the life out of it, Ivanna suddenly said she understood. She said something about blood pressure; if Lupei were absorbing a person's flesh or blood into himself it must increase the blood pressure in his own body, and that would make him bleed heavily if he injured himself.

Ivanna stood up and pulled open the door to look inside. She gasped and stepped back. The stench of dog shit were over-powering. She asked someone to take a photo. While she removed her gloves, Jordan covered his nose and took a few photos before staggering away. When he had stopped throwing up he told us rats were eating the dog, like it were disgusting and exciting. I think he were embarrassed at throwing up.

As we got back in the car the rain were hammering on the roof. Ivanna said she'd drop us off then return to the hospital. We were all glad to leave Farview. All the way back I were praying that Daniel were back at the cottage, though he hadn't messaged. I even thought that maybe he'd buggered off back to London, which would have been OK if he had bothered to tell someone. I know all of this will sound mad. There's more but I am sending this now in case we lose the internet signal.

Love,
Tiff.

CHAPTER 33

Email from Miss Tiffany Harrek
to Mr Edward Harrek

Sunday, 6th November, 11.31pm

Hi again,

Here's the rest of it. When we were back at the cottage, I persuaded Ivanna to have a cup of coffee before she headed back to Scarborough with her blood samples. She were totally knackered, I don't think she'd slept since coming off shift.

The others were packing and tidying, they were meant to be out of the cottage by twelve and it were already three o'clock. That were when the phone call came from the hospital to tell Ivanna that Hannah's parents had turned up in Scarborough and were demanding that she should be transferred to a proper hospital. Ivanna hit the roof, like what were wrong with the NHS, and stuff about the risk of moving patients when they are so ill. Megan came downstairs and there were a lot of shouting. First she were shouting that Ivanna drive her to Scarborough then the next minute she were shouting Hannah were a cow and could go to hell. Megan were all over the place, to be honest, and Katie nearly walloped her at one point.

The bags were all by the door. Ivanna had had enough and were putting on her coat while Katie and I did a last tidy up in the kitchen. That were when we found Daniel's note. I think he'd stuck it to the fridge with a magnet but it slipped off and landed face down under the fridge.

Hi Guys.
Had an idea. With a bit of luck, by the time you read this Lupei will be toast. Something that pathologist said got me thinking: Lupei becomes really slow after he has attacked someone and absorbed their flesh. So that must be the best time to attack.
Going to find the bus. I think it's parked outside the Pavilion. I haven't woken you up because I need to do this alone; for some reason Lupei trusts me and will let me get close. So I'll wait for him to arrive then find a way to inject him with the small syringe gun Emile Noir gave me ... If my plan works, we've got him.
Daniel - 11.05am

Apart from the madness of chasing after Thor Lupei by himself the worst of it were that Daniel didn't even have the gun; he'd given it to me!

Katie and I were gawping at each other in horror when the front door closed. Realising that Ivanna must just have left, I rushed out and charged down the street after her. As I ran I were trying to reach Daniel on his mobile. I caught up with Ivanna and passed her the note. While she read it, she told me she had tried ringing Daniel on her way up from Scarborough. He weren't answering.

As Jordan joined us in the street, I burst into tears, angry with myself at how stupid I had been in assuming that Daniel had bobbed out for a walk. Four hours had passed since he stuck his note to the fridge door and we had done nothing to find him. Jordan was really sweet and said I shouldn't beat myself up, we had all got it wrong and what mattered were what we did now. We were wasting time, so Jordan and I raced back to grab our coats. Katie and Megan were coming out the front door, bags in hand; they had given up and just wanted to catch the train home. I gave them a piece of my mind. Can't remember what I called them but it weren't pretty. Daniel had saved Megan's life and Katie's; if the boot were on the other foot, Daniel wouldn't be running away, he'd be running to rescue them, and they knew it. But they left anyway.

Suddenly I remembered the gun, went upstairs and found it under my pillow, where I had hidden it, then Jordan grabbed his bag and we left the cottage. We were just over the swing bridge when Ivanna's car pulled up alongside, with Megan and Katie in it. They had dropped the cottage keys off at the agents. We agreed we would have one last try together to find Daniel. Two minutes later Ivanna were parking outside the Pavilion.

No sign of the Hounds of Hellbane bus. The girl at reception, Cathy Hogson, is a dozy cow. Lives on Ropery. Plastic roast chicken earrings, bleached blonde with more roots than a field of carrots, and so much war paint her face looks like two eyeballs on a leather purse. I sort of know her, she were two years above me at school. One of the 'popular' girls. Loudmouth bitch, in other words. Used to call me a Paki because of me surname. IQ in single figures.

Anyroad, she said she saw Daniel standing outside stage door on CCTV, hours ago when she'd just come on shift. She thought Eric, the back stage manager, must have let him in, so she buzzed him.

Yesterday was first time I'd met Eric. He were really friendly when he let me and Daniel in through the stage door to see the bands. Today he were anything but. He shouted at us, told us he knew nowt then threatened me. Told me he knew I were local lass and that I should forget nosy-parkering about outsiders and think about my family, if I knew what were good for me.

Ivanna tried explaining that she were a doctor at Scarborough hospital and needed to talk with Daniel as a matter of urgency, but Eric told her to get stuffed and go back to where she came from. He told me I should learn to keep my legs together and stick with my own kind. After telling Cathy to call the police if we refused to leave, he buggered off.

Cathy Hogson were grinning like an open pedal bin. I nearly clocked her but Jordan grabbed me arm and pulled me away and told me there were no point trying to reason with trash. Once we were outside, Jordan let it all out, about the bodies in the streets and Darren at the lighthouse and people going missing and the stuff on the farm and no-one giving a stuff.

Suddenly Ivanna were looking past us like she'd seen a ghost. In the road by the Pavilion were a woman with long blonde hair, haunted eyes and a face painted like a skull. It were her clothes that interested me more. Jordan thought I were talking about her wedding dress, like Miss Havisham in that Charles Dickens book. But it weren't the wedding dress; it were the fact that she were wearing Daniel's jacket. By that time she had noticed that we were looking at her she were walking briskly away. Jordan raced after her and grabbed her arm and she told him to let go or she would scream, in a thick foreign accent like Ivanna's. Ivanna said something to her in a foreign language and the woman cooled down.

They talked together for a couple of minutes then Ivanna explained that the woman were called Ylenia, a friend of

Emile Noir, the man who had killed the scravir in the barn. She had bumped into Daniel down in the harbour and he had lent her his coat, she said. They had gone to the Pavilion together and he asked her to wait while he went in to find Thor Lupei. She hung around for fifteen minutes and were about to leave when she saw two men carrying a long black box to Hounds of Hellbane bus. The box were lifted up and lowered into the top of the bus on a small crane. The men went back inside and come out with second box which also went in through the hole in the roof. Then one man climbed onto bus and the other one, who was older, short and fat, went back into the Pavilion.

We guessed the short man were Eric. Ylenia said the younger one had messy hair, a hipster beard and a bright blue and yellow jacket. Alex. Jordan wanted to go back into the Pavilion and have another little chat with Eric. (Let's go and kick the shit out of him, were how he put it). Ylenia mumbled something and Ivanna translated. The bus had left three hours ago, driven by none other than Thor Lupei. We were too late.

Jordan intruded on my misery fest by asking how Lupei could travel incognito in a black London bus. He had a point. But where would Lupei be going? Ivanna thought she knew. Daniel had let her photograph some of the pages in the journal that Emile Noir had given him. Noir and Ylenia had come to Whitby to try to catch him or kill him; they knew where he had come from and how he had travelled. And they knew where he were heading. Romania.

We should have expected it. It was too perfect, too unbelievable. What better cover could there be for Lupei than a Goth festival in Whitby? While everyone was staggering about in fancy dress, pissed as farts, pretending to be vampires, who was going to pay attention to a real killer?

Ivanna said that she knew where Lupei was going and that Ylenia were willing to come with us. Ylenia said in English that first she must collect some things from her hotel. But, as Katie pointed out, there were already five of us in Ivanna's car. Which were when Megan announced she were catching the train back to London in fifty minutes. She just took her case from the boot and left. No goodbye. Nothing. Katie and Jordan looked torn watching Megan go and, for a moment, it looked like it would just be me, the doctor, and the mad woman in a wedding dress.

I caught Jordan's eye. Katie asked what the chances were that Alex and Daniel would still be alive. I told her we had to try whatever the odds. Katie looked down the street, chewing her lip. Megan had almost reached the corner. Taking a deep breath Katie turned back towards us and gave a slight nod. We piled into the car. Jordan asked where we were going. Ylenia said Lupei must be leaving the same way he had come, on the Hull Rotterdam ferry. The ferry left at 20.30 every night from Hull; two hours drive away. We had four and a half hours to get there. If Lupei reached the Netherlands he had won; there were too many roads through Europe and he would escape. The good thing were that we had plenty of time and the quickest route passed through Scarborough so Ivanna could drop her blood samples off on the way then go on to Hull where we could raise the alarm.

Ylenia took two minutes to gather a bag from her hotel and we were off. Ivanna drove as fast as you do, Uncle Ted, she knew all the bends and dips and hidden junctions between Whitby and Scarborough. It were still blowing a gale as we ran along the edge of the moors. I hadn't understood why Ivanna had invited Ylenia to come along until she asked her to tell us what she knew about Thor Lupei. Ylenia said nothing for a minute, I thought maybe she hadn't heard or understood Ivanna, then suddenly it all poured out. (I've probably forgotten a fair bit.) In her words, Ylenia's story started when the beast arrived in the mountains above her town and destroyed everything. Before that she said her region in Romania had been happy for a hundred years and more. Local people didn't understand where Lupei came from or what he were, but they did know the legends of the vampires that have always poisoned the mountains. For her, coming to Whitby Goth Weekend and watching people having fun pretending to be vampires were as unsettling as an Indian villager going to a town in Mexico and finding people amusing themselves by dressing up as tigers.

She insisted that the vampire myths contained hidden truths that were designed to protect children from the real dangers that stalked the night. She must have known what we were thinking because she looked at me and Jordan and said we were very clever for laughing at her in our heads and thinking she was primitive for believing such things.

It were five years since Lupei had bought Micăbrukóczi castle on the hill above the town. (I know that is the right spelling because she wrote it out for us on slips of paper, in case something happened to her.) Lupei spent a fortune restoring the castle, employing local people. Even though he looked very different and dressed grandly, even though he had those striking looks of an albino, local people had been won over by Lupei's charisma, his big plans, pop star money and showmanship. Most of all people loved that he shouted loudly about the corruption of all our local politicians. He was not afraid. He talked about making the region great again and that is what people wanted to hear.

I found myself making links between Lupei and other things happening this week around the world, but then Ylenia said that the people he criticised kept quiet because Lupei were always very polite, and that he weren't a man of vulgar tastes, so not quite the same then.

Two years later the rumours started. A couple of mysterious deaths in the valley. Two young hikers were found in ditch, their bodies stick-thin like hunger strikers or famine victims. The local news published a CCTV photo taken only a week earlier showing couple in a local town, looking healthy and normal. People start talking and a reporter I knew popped up claiming that there had been similar unexplained deaths a hundred kilometres away. She also revealed that Thor Lupei were from that area. A week later she disappeared. That were three years ago. Since then further rumours emerged of strange emaciated living beings who stalked the countryside around the castle, sucking the life out of livestock. Local peasants called them scravir. There were a man who claimed to have been attacked by them while tending his flock of sheep. He claimed a creature had sucked the flesh from his leg.

Emile Noir and Ylenia are part of a network that were formed to protect their community, taking turns to keep watch on the castle from up in the forest that overlooks it. A year ago, when Emile and a friend were on watch, the scravir attacked them in the darkness. Emile and his friend, a huge middle-aged farmer called Boris, had been in the lookout with their telescopes trained on the entrances to the castle. Ylenia said the lookout is a wooden bench on the edge of cliff, at a spot called the eagle's nest; on a popular tourist path through the forest. Emile told her afterwards that he heard a mechanical scraping sound just before the attack, but assumed it was Boris rubbing his boots together to keep warm. Suddenly Boris fell face down in front of the bench, knocking over his telescope, his head just inches from the cliff edge.

Emile told Ylenia there were something weird about the way Boris' clothes sagged. It were only when Emile leaned forwards to pull Boris back and turn him over that he understood what had happened. It were too late. Boris were little more than skin and bones, his muscles sucked out of him. His left trouser leg had been pushed up and his calf were bruised and carried the marks of fingernails, as if he had been gripped by something. Emile were clocking the danger he were in at the exact moment when the scravir grabbed his wrist. In the darkness he saw a thin face with its deep eye sockets, the smiling dirty teeth, and a flaking scalp. The scravir were naked, one half of its body bloated and fat. Emile were in terrible pain but he also felt something were controlling him to keep him quiet, like a fly trapped in a spider's web.

According to Emile, he almost gave in until he saw Boris on the ground in front of him and understood that if he didn't fight he too would end up dead so Emile stood up, dragging the scravir with him to the edge of the cliff. The scravir were struggling to keep balance, weighing twice as much on one side of his body to the other, and slow to react. Emile spun round, kicking the scravir's legs from under him, causing it to lose balance and trip over Boris' body. The scravir let go of Emile's wrist, twisting round to grab an ankle instead. With his free foot Emile booted the scravir away, sending him backwards over the cliff edge. For a second Emile feared he too would fall to his death. He wrapped his good arm around the base of the bench and, clinging to the bench, kicked the hand that gripped his ankle, over and over until the scravir let go. A second later he heard the crunch; the scravir had been impaled in the trees below.

Jordan asked if that were why Emile Noir had an empty arm and Ylenia said yes, and explained that his real arm were inside the mechanical contraption. He had refused to have it amputated. I were looking at Ivanna, wondering why she had nothing to say. She were a scientist, a rational person used to practical solutions to practical problems. I were about to ask her if she believed Ylenia's story when Jordan shouted at the top of his voice.

We were still on the road to Scarborough. Smoke were pouring into the sky from a field on our left. We were approaching the crest of a hill, just after that crumbling barn you used to tell us were haunted. Ahead of us a row of chevron arrows marked a dangerous bend and a junction. There were a huge hole in the dry stone wall through which were a badly damaged red car on its roof in the field and, maybe twenty metres beyond the car engulfed in clouds of smoke and partially hidden by the slope of the land, were a tall vehicle. We had found the burning remains of the Hounds of Hellbane bus.

Ivanna Alba turned off the main road and parked on the grass. We climbed out and followed her into the field towards the upturned car to see if anyone needed help. The ground were wet and churned up with deep tyre tracks and a strange cloying smell hung in the air. A dozen gormless sheep were stood gawping. Before we could reach the car a policeman were behind us, telling us to bugger off or get arrested. He must have been sheltering behind the wall. Ivanna explained she were a doctor from Scarborough and asked what had happened. He told her one dead and one with multiple injuries, over two hours earlier. The woman had been taken to Scarborough hospital. Ivanna asked about the bus, could she take a look? He showed her a pair of handcuffs and said yes, if she wanted to spend the night at Whitby police station and then added that they were overcrowded this weekend and that many of the regulars didn't like foreigners, if she followed his drift. The nasty tosser then looked at me and said hadn't he seen me at a chippie in town? I were just about to say something when the policeman is looking straight past me and shouting "Hey. Hey you, Rastaman".

Jordan had walked off and were crossing the main road. If he heard PC Racist above the noise of the traffic he hid it well. To take his mind off Jordan, I asked the policeman if they had found two students my age on the bus, Daniel Murray and Alex (I don't know Alex's last name). The bastard asked me if they were my regulars, at which point Ivanna grabbed my arm, told him he had been very helpful – in a tone of voice that suggested the opposite – and dragged me off towards the car. Jordan were still on the other side of the road, peering over a stone wall. By the time we reached the car, he had turned away and were waiting for a gap in the traffic.

As we pulled off, heading south, we saw the bus properly for the first time. The front end were badly damaged and in the grass beside it were a pile of long black boxes. We were all thinking the same things; had Daniel been burned alive? Why did the police employ such twats? And if Daniel and Alex weren't on the bus, where were they?

Out of nowhere Jordan, who looked like he had seen a ghost, declared that there were three vehicles involved in the accident; the two we had all seen and a third that had smacked the wall on the other side of the road. In his opinion Lupei had left the scene of the accident in this missing car or van or lorry. Scraped paint on the stone wall said the vehicle were white and, according to Jordan, tyre marks showed it had turned round and headed south, back the way it came. None of which explained why he thought Lupei were driving it. His explanation, when it came, worried us all. He had looked over the wall and seen a body, a man lying in the wet bracken, his face screwed up in agony, skin as thin as clingfilm, neck no thicker than a turkey's. He looked like a broken bag of bones in a sack, Jordan said, Lupei must have sucked the life out of him and tossed him over the wall. The worst part were that he were still alive. Ivanna slammed the brakes but Jordan said it were too late, the man were practically dead and we should concentrate on saving the living. Being a doctor, Ivanna hesitated. I felt for her and said nothing. What could I possibly say? Abruptly she clenched her jaw, threw the car into gear and accelerated down the road. I took Jordan's hand and held it while he sat there. No-one could bear to speak. If Jordan were right then Thor Lupei were still out there, still killing people, still heading for Hull. What had he left on the bus? Why had he picked Whitby? All I knew for sure were that we had to do all we could to rescue Daniel and Alex. Or die trying. And I were glad I weren't alone.

Twenty minutes later we were pulling into staff parking at Scarborough hospital. Sorry, I need another break.

Xxx ;-)

Tiff

CHAPTER 34

Email from Miss Tiffany Harrek
to Mr Edward Harrek

Monday, 7th November, 00.26am

Hi Uncle Ted,

I had to go out for a breath of air, I were beginning to feel sick with the rocking about; I obviously haven't inherited the Harrek cast iron stomach!

We got to the hospital just as it were getting dark and hung around inside the main entrance area while Ivanna went off to give someone the blood samples she collected at Farview. Ylenia, the Romanian woman, had collapsed on a bench beside some old gaffer in a wheel chair, and drifted off to sleep. I still weren't clear why she had come to Whitby. What did a skinny middle-aged hippie with a skull painted on her face think she could do against someone as dangerous as Lupei and, if she really thought there were something she could do, why hadn't she done it in Romania? How many people have died in Whitby this weekend? It must be double figures.

By now we were all tired and angry. Jordan were complaining that hospital coffee were crap. I were pissed off that I must be only metres away from your ward but I couldn't visit you. Katie were annoyed with the whole world, and with Jordan and me in particular, accusing us of doing sod all to find

Hannah. Jordan told her to go and ask reception herself. So she did. They told her only family were allowed to know confidential information. She shouted that Hannah was her best friend and she had come two hundred bloody miles to see her. At which point the receptionist explained that Hannah weren't in the hospital; a private medical team had flown her off in a helicopter because her parents thought that hospitals in the north of England were as primitive as those in the rainforests of Papua New Guinea. So there you go, you might as well be in Papua New Guinea according to Hannah's toff parents.

Ivanna returned, having handed over the blood samples. She'd discovered the woman from the accident were in Intensive Care. Leaving Ylenia asleep on the bench, we followed Ivanna to the café where she said we could wait while she went off to see if the woman were conscious. Katie were being a twat. Even with a gob full of pastries she were banging on and on about how she should have gone back to London with Megan. I snapped, called her a self-indulgent southern prat and wandered off to find you. They caught me in Ophthamology and frogmarched me back to the café. Suddenly Ivanna's running towards us. She grabs Katie's arm and says we have to leg it; she knows what he's driving. It took me a second to remember who she were on about!

Back at reception we found Ylenia had gone walkabout. We shook the old man awake and asked him. Poor sod didn't even know his own name so we asked reception. No, they can't remember seeing a woman in a wedding dress with a skull painted on her face. Like what the hell *do* they notice?

I run off to check the toilets. By the time I get back there's a manager arguing with Ivanna about what she were doing in ICU interrogating a patient 'without authority'. He drags her off and we waste even more time. Finally Ivanna returns with a face like a bulldog that's just pissed on a nettle and we leave. In the car park we take Ylenia's bags out of the boot and Jordan runs back inside to leave them with reception. We are piling into the car when Ylenia is suddenly there banging on the window, she's been having a vape in the car park. Yours truly runs back inside to collect her bag.

It were six o'clock by the time we left Scarborough and headed south towards Hull while Ivanna explained what she had discovered. The woman lying in a hospital bed were called Laura. She had multiple fractures of her arm, several broken ribs, a perforated lung and God knows what else, but she were conscious. Jordan had been right. Or almost right. The accident hadn't involved two vehicles, or even three; there were four. Laura and her husband were in their car, a red Renault, in the lane waiting to come onto the main road as the Hounds of Hellbane bus approached the right-hand bend on the crest of the hill. As the bus reached the bend a small green family car were coming round the corner in the opposite direction, but the accident were caused by a large white van that had appeared suddenly, overtaking the green car on the outside of the blind bend, straight towards the bus. With no time to brake, the bus could only choose which vehicle to hit. The driver threw the bus to the left to avoid hitting the van head on. They struck each other a glancing blow like jousting knights. The bus smacked into the red car, smashing it through into the dry stone wall, then followed it into the field, hitting it a second time and flipping it over onto its roof.

When Laura woke up she were hanging upside down, held in place by her seat belt and in great pain, her husband dead beside her. She could see through the broken windscreen and in the rear view mirror. The bus had stopped down the slope.

Two people climbed out of the bus. One were tall with long white hair, she couldn't remember anything about the other person. As they walked up the slope towards her, she were thanking God that they had seen her, but they walked straight past her without even looking inside. In the rear view mirror she saw them walk on through the gap in the wall.

She thought she must have passed out because the next thing she remembered were opening her eyes and seeing a large white van parked beside the bus. She thought it could have been the van that had crashed into the bus but she weren't hundred percent sure. The two men, she now remembered they were both men, were lifting long boxes into the back of the van. There were other boxes strewn about beside the bus. The men were lifting the lids off the boxes and looking inside them and talking. Laura tried to shout out but she were too weak and in too much pain to make much noise.

Once they had finished they closed the van doors. The man with the white hair poured liquid on the boxes that were on the grass then climbed on the bus. A moment later he stepped off again, threw something at the bus and got into the van. As the van drove past Laura, who were still upside down in her car, the bus and the boxes exploded into a ball of flames. Ivanna asked Laura if she remembered the van's number plate but at that moment a nurse whipped back the curtain and caught her sitting beside the critically injured woman. As Ivanna stood up to leave, Laura grabbed her arm and appeared to be trying to say something more. Ivanna leaned in, her ear close to the woman's lips. "One green door and one white", she whispered then slumped back against the pillow.

It were quarter past six, which meant we had two and a quarter hours to cover an eighty minute journey or so we thought.

CHAPTER 35

Message to R.D.Felini

Sunday, 6th November

My dear friend,

At last my journey turns towards the scented mountains of home! Never have I been more eager than I am today to leave these dull lands that cower beneath fat bloated skies. I am weary of the dreary company of dullards; the gloomy grape-eyed gormless with their flatbread faces and breadcrumb brains. Never have a people more closely resembled the livestock in their fields; malleable, predictable, bovine and coarse.

I rejoice at least that, in spite of the many tiresome impositions and obstacles placed in our path, this year the harvest has again been bountiful, but how my heart yearns for the cool shadows that nestle within the castle walls and for the roaring fire of the grand hall.

Those lengthy preparations have repaid us handsomely, allowing us to move freely with minimal interference from the law. How well conceived the effort spent to nurture persons of interest and influence prior to the voyage! We never met of course, for it would all too easily have proved a risk to us both, but I relished the peace of mind afforded by the absolute certainty that the Chief Inspector would not lift a finger against me, understanding personally, as he does, the huge humanitarian value of our enterprise.

Predictably the weather bared its teeth and did its utmost to disrupt our work but it is a coarse unfocused brute, cloaking and hampering the activities of the good and the bad in equal measure.

Ah, the thrill of the chase! There is a brief tale I must relate. In the darkness and when the storm was in full spate, I chanced upon two foolish lovers, their underwear puddled around their ankles, indulging their primal instincts upon the harbour wall. Sheltered from the gaze of the town, they were coupling against the huge sandstone blocks that are stacked up to protect the sailors of a previous age, upon the eastern pier.

The cacophony of wind, wave and water that created a cocoon for their unbridled lust also provided the cover for my approach. I strode up and touched the pair of them without either having sensed my arrival. Each mistaking my grasping hungry fingers for the heavy caress of the other, their senses overwhelmed by the savage power of the elements, the pair continued in their lovemaking unaware of my presence until it was too late. Like a female mantid devouring her lover's head while he takes his pleasure, I supped deeply the simultaneous neural frenzies of their physical climaxes even as the heavens and seas threw themselves at the three of us.

Too late the lovers realised their mistake. By then they were weakening so quickly that neither could so much as lift a finger. Seldom in all my many years has a feast proved as sweet and complete as this. Having finished my work and still sheltered from the gaze of the town, I rolled the spent and empty bodies to the edge of the pier and kicked them into the eager raging maw of the sea then, heavy with the weight of my repast, I trudged to the end of the pier where steps lead down towards the sands that nestle within the safety of the harbour walls.

Two top hats wedged in fractured indentation of the sandstone blocks were all that remained of the lovers. For an instant, I watched them tremble in the wind and wondered idly how long it would be before they succumbed, flew up into the air and tumbled down into the frothing fatal bowels of the deep? A magical night I will fondly remember.

Anyway my friend, the job is done. I am sitting at a desk made of plastic wood in a drab magnolia-painted box, a stone's throw from a wretched monotony of a city, awaiting our imminent departure. The bus is no more, the result of an unfortunate event. We managed to salvage two thirds of the harvest and three of the band (Olas was regretably damaged beyond repair along with the bus). The rest we torched to cover our traces. We lost several scravir but that was always to be expected. I have a new acolyte, a self-serving and irritating youth who may not survive the journey I fear, and the use of an utterly unmemorable white van.

Prepare everything for my arrival. With good fortune, I will reach the castle gates at daybreak thirty-six hours from now.

Your master,

TL

CHAPTER 36

Email from Miss Tiffany Harrek
to Mr Edward Harrek

Monday, 7th November, 01.03am

The others have just woken up so I have only a few minutes left to finish writing.

Everything were fine all the way to Driffield. Seven miles from Hull we hit traffic. Nothing were moving and in minutes we had ten cars behind us and a solid wall of cars ahead of us. The road turned up ahead so we could see nothing. Jordan climbed out of the car and disappeared down the road to try to see what were going on.

Eventually he came back. Nearly two hundred cars ahead of us an articulated lorry had jack-knifed and blocked the entire road. A crane were trying to lift the lorry. We checked our phones for turn-offs and shortcuts, like everyone else, but there were nothing. We just knew that Lupei had somehow caused the accident. Always one step ahead.

Traffic though Hull to the King George Dock, when the traffic finally got moving, were easy but we had lost so much time. It were gone eight o'clock. The ferry loomed above us like a castle on a hill. Ivanna pulled up on a double yellow and ran in to the terminal. Minutes later, when she hadn't come out, I ran in after her. She were arguing with the ticket office, insisting that a dangerous man who had murdered at least five people was on her ship. Had a white van with one white door and one green door got on the ferry? Could they check their CCTV?

The manager would not delay departure without a direct request from the police. Doctors didn't count. In fact, the manager argued, if this man were on board, and if he were as dangerous as she were making out, then surely the sooner he were out of the UK the better. Then came the bombshell; she asked Ivanna where she were from. That racist speech about foreigners stealing our jobs were hurtling down the hill towards us like a rolling cheese so I pulled Ivanna away. She were gutted, to have come so far and everything.

Suddenly I had an idea. I rushed back to the ticket desk and asked if it were still OK to buy tickets as foot passengers. Boarding for foot passengers closed in eight minutes. We raced back to the car. Ivanna couldn't go, she had to work. So did I like, but saving lives and serving chips is chalk and chives. Katie threw in the towel and told Jordan if he didn't go back to London with her he were even more stupid than he looked.

Which made Jordan's mind up for him. He told Katie he'd rather spend twelve hours on a fleapit ferry to Rotterdam than four hours trapped on a train with Queen Quack. We thanked Ivanna, grabbed our bags, said goodbyes and legged it to the ticket office. The ship's horn boomed as we reached the boarding gate. In case you're wondering, I always carry my passport to get into clubs and pubs. So does Jordan. It's a young people thing. Anyroad, we've just got on board when we hear shouting; Ylenia's joining us. With Emile Noir vanished she's decided she may as well catch the ferry and help us, and then head on home to Romania.

So that's it, now you know, I'm on the Hull-Rotterdam ferry, typing on Jordan's laptop. As soon as ship left harbour Jordan threw up, turns out he'd never been on a ship before and he couldn't stand the floor moving about. I left him groaning in a foetus position in the main bar, found a steward and asked what cabin a passenger called Thor Lupei were in. Steward were as bad as ticket office in Hull. Couldn't divulge information of that sort, couldn't even confirm he were on the ship. She said I could leave a message in case the gentleman contacted them. I asked if for ten pence extra they'd tell the whole ship we were on board and loan us special flashing hats that sang "idiots seek punch in face" every thirty seconds. She didn't smile.

So I'm back in the bar with Jordan snoring next to me. Ylenia were here but she wandered off fifteen minutes ago, mumbling about getting changed, and how she felt Lupei's presence on the ship. Planet Lala that one.

Jordan and I agreed we're going down to the car decks to look around when everything quietens down. Most people with a cabin are in bed; there's maybe twenty left milling about watching football on TV. Or drinking themselves stupid.

If I don't survive, I want you to pass these emails on to some-one who can help find out what happened to us. Not sure I trust the police. Tell mum and dad that I love them heaps. Sorry I've let you all down but if you were in my shoes I know you would do just the same. I can't walk away. Daniel saved my life and I must do the same for him.

Lots of love
Tiff.

CHAPTER 37

Daniel Murray, whereabouts unknown

… I had little sense of the passing of time, drifting in and out of consciousness. My sense of smell appeared to be working; at some point over the previous hours I had clearly pissed myself. I was still immobile and still, it appeared, shut up in a box. I no longer knew if I was on my front or on my back, standing up or lying down.

I had been learning how many different colour blacks there were. Pitch black, midnight black, warm black, lacklight black, lost in a cave twenty metres from the entrance black, stuck in a box black. For now I was firmly in pitch black, still absurdly grateful that I could open and close my eyelids, even though the activity delivered no sensory data. In truth 'blink' was a big word, my eyelids moved at the breakneck speed of a tired sloth erring on the side of caution.

My sense of hearing was having a better time of it. I had been on a bus, Lupei's double decker I assumed. The bus had hit something hard then stopped. My box had floated for a while before landing on the ground. The lid had opened for a few fleeting seconds. The light had been so intense that I saw nothing until the lid was closing again. I thought I glimpsed a cloudy sky and water drops falling and the silhouette of Lupei staring into the box. Then I was plunged back into darkness. A moment later the box was slid into place somewhere. While I could not feel my body, my inner ear was still giving me a sense of spatial movement. The disconnect was disorientating and left me nauseous but my body was too numb to respond.

Doors were slammed. An engine started up, the note less throaty than the bus.

The next time I was awake I seemed to be travelling feet first up a hill, metallic sounds crunching and slapping like gunshot. The engine was straining then the hill was done and we were moving slowly, I think, before stopping altogether. The muffled sound of people shouting in a vast space. Metals clanging and reverberating.

'No, no, leave it. Everything is fine.'

Thor Lupei's voice nearby, followed by the sound of slamming doors. Again.

Fade out fade in. I had pissed myself, I could smell it. A low and monotonous hum hung in the air, hot as a headache, and I felt simultaneously full up and hungrier than I ever had in my life.

CHAPTER 38

Hull - Rotterdam ferry
- Jordan and Tiffany

Monday., 7th November.

'Where is she?'

'Who?'

'Miss Havisham,' Jordan says, lifting himself into a sitting position and massaging the long line pressed into his cheek by the edge of plastic chair he has been sleeping on. 'Bride of Dracula.'

The room is almost empty. At the bar a couple are perched unsteadily on stools, leaning in to chat. Four students are playing cards. Jordan and Tiffany are beside a small table.

'She woke up twenty minutes ago,' Tiffany says, handing Jordan his laptop. 'You OK? You want a drink?'

Jordan shakes his head, stuffs the laptop in his bag.

'She went to get changed and …'

'Into what? Let me guess,' Jordan interrupts Tiffany. 'Tinkerbell? Big Ben? One of the blue Narvi people in Avatar?'

'… and said she could feel the presence of Lupei on the ship,' Tiffany continues, ignoring the interruption. 'She believes that if she wanders around the corridors she'll sense what cabin he is in.'

'Looney tunes.'

'Are you ready?'

'Yeah,' says Jordan's mouth. The rest of his face says no.

'That's why we got on the boat, isn't it?'

'I said yeah.'

They leave the bar. The décor is exactly what a person would pick if they were feeling queasy and trying to make their mind up about whether or not to throw up; pale greens and beiges swirling and clashing beneath pulsing and jaundiced fluorescent lighting. The ship is rolling gently to enhance the vibe. Jordan looks like he needs a bucket.

Cheap plastic wood effect doors are set into the pale green walls. The cheaper cabins, in the middle of the ship, have no windows. They are boxes containing a bed, a plastic table and chair, and a sink almost large enough to rinse a toothbrush. The corridor opens onto a stairwell with a couple of lifts. They take the stairs.

Somewhere above them a woman has changed out of her wedding dress and scrubbed her face clean. She has removed her blonde wig to become brunette, slipped into jeans and a fleece, switched from prey to predator. So she hopes.

The car decks are far from full. The lighting is even harsher than on the decks above. The dark green floor is as shiny as cockroach wing cases. Every corner and edge is protected against impact with metal bars and lurid black and yellow stripes. Parked cars and vans hug the walls like limpets.

'No vans.' Jordan says, a little too loudly. 'You sure we're on the right deck?'

'Follow the arrows and see where we end up.' Tiffany whispers.

'Got you.' Jordan whispers back.

Arrows and yellow lines weave a course round blind corners. More cars. No vans. No CCTV cameras. Their footsteps ring out in the metallic void. They stop every twenty steps or so and listen. All quiet.

'Why the Gristle Gang by the way?' Tiffany asks.

'What?'

'You, Alex, and Daniel. He told me they called you the

Gristle Gang.'

Jordan laughs and shakes his head. 'It's too stupid.'

'Go on.'

For a moment Jordan is lost in thought. A smile of recollection. 'It was in year six. We were always in trouble. One lunchtime we're having school dinner and it's this rank stew. Weird meat with these huge lumps of gristle. Since we don't want to eat it we cut the gristle off. Then someone has a great idea. Can't remember who. Anyway an hour later Miss gets upset in class because the three of us have made these special rubber bands and we're using them to hold our crayons together and there's gravy clots all over the desks and ...'

'Yeah, OK, I get the picture,' Tiffany says.

The floor is vibrating as they turn a corner and the distant muffled hum of huge engines trembles the air. Up ahead another line of cars. No vans in sight. A steel exit door set into the wall. As Jordan hauls the door open, the ship rolls in the waves.

'You OK? You want to go back up?'

Jordan shakes his head. 'I'm good, but if someone stops us, what's our excuse?'

'We didn't see the signs.'

'What signs?'

'The massive *No admittance to lower decks when ship is moving* signs in the stairwell.'

'Oh, those.' He gags and spits some bile.

The temperature drops as they descend the stairs to Level 5. Tiffany zips up her fleece. The same cold light, the same ugly shiny green floor. Cars and vans dotted about like mushrooms in a cave. A couple of white vans up ahead, facing away from them. The rearmost vehicle has two white doors at the back but what about the one in front?

Tiffany stops in her tracks.

'What?'

'The clicking.'

There is a mechanical tapping sound, crisp and rhythmic as if a horse with wooden heels were following them. It stops.

'Plumbing,' Jordan suggests.

Tiffany considers this and shrugs. They step forward. The tapping sound picks up again. Suddenly they are both feeling underprepared. The gulf between idea and reality. What will they do when they find the van? What if Lupei is there? They pass the first van, slowly, torn between the opposing urges to remain hidden until the last moment, and the desire to put enough space between them and the second vehicle to turn and run if they have to. The clicking sound has also slowed. Is it an echo? Tiffany spins round, half-expecting to see something standing behind them.

'Hey,' Jordan hisses. 'Stick together.'

She nods.

Through the windscreen of the first van they see the rear of the second. No green door. The direction arrow on the floor beckons them on with a long bony finger. Twenty cars, some with trailers, many with roof boxes, before they see another van; Jordan is counting. The van is blue. In a side bay are half a dozen campervans, all white with rounded corners. Set against the green floor, Jordan imagines the vans to be ice cubes floating in a gin and tonic. An uncle in Trinidad boasts that drinking gin and tonic makes him part of the British establishment. He also believes aliens stole the bougainvillea from his back yard.

The campervans carry all the usual stupid names - Rapido, Lightning, Cheetah - names marketing people give vehicles that struggle to reach forty mph. A large brown Winnebago covered in stickers is badly parked.

The road turns back on itself so Tiffany and Jordan take a short cut between two pillars to rejoin the road further along.

Three vans parked one behind the other, all white, all facing towards them. That clicking sound again. Behind them. Like a tiger dainty on its claws.

'This is cool,' Tiffany says.

'Really? You think so?'

She shakes her head. 'You don't want to know what I think. You see an exit?'

'I get you.' Jordan heads off away from the vans, looking left and right, wishing he were wearing trainers instead of shoes. 'Yeah, down here,' he calls out to Tiffany in a stage whisper. 'Big sign.'

A loud metallic crash. They jump. With the echoes it is impossible to identify the direction of the source. A section of the overhead lighting flickers and strobes. Then cuts out.

Shadows multiply.

'Bumberclaat. This is insane, man.'

The clicking has stopped. Tiffany has a headache. Jordan is shaking with adrenalin. He remembers the regular beatings on his way to school. He was six. Always the same posse of older boys, white thugs keen to start the day with a bonding ritual. Never dared tell his mum. It only stopped when the Gristle Gang happened; three little kids standing side by side.

The windscreen of the first van is in shadow, the vehicle is spotless. Does the passenger's side carry a long scratch scraped along a stone wall?

They draw level with the driver's door. Neither Tiffany nor Jordan reaches out to open it. The dashboard is anonymous, as dull as the day it arrived in the showroom. They continue past the end of the van and turn to see the rear doors. Both white. It should make them feel better but it doesn't.

The second van is also a white Ford Transit, but with attitude. On the dashboard an ugly green skull mounted on a spring and, where black plastic meets windscreen, a collection of parking tickets. Round coffee cup stains and cigarette burns in the vinyl. The footwell and passenger seat are piled high with cardboard boxes. A crumpled burger bun bag has dripped cold chips onto the floor. The side of the van carries scratches and dents from a dozen minor accidents, including a long horizontal scratch the length of the vehicle. They approach the rear of the van, hearts in their throats. The back doors are both white and show signs of having been attacked with a crowbar.

The last van is a Citroën, its clean surfaces bright with reflected light.

'Straight out of the showroom,' Jordan observes, striding ahead. 'We keep going.'

They cannot see the extensive damage to the passenger side as they step quickly towards the light, their minds already focused on the next bay.

The return of the clicking sound stops Tiffany in her tracks. This time she knows that the noise is not the sound of plumbing. The hairs on the back of her neck are tingling.

'Jordan,' she whispers. 'Wait.'

Jordan hasn't heard her. He's striding on, keen to find fresh air; the ship's heave is bringing fresh bile to his throat.

Tiffany hesitates. She is certain, as certain as she has ever been of anything. She will not like what she sees when she turns around. Fear blooms a million tendrils that constrict her breathing. Blood thumps in her ears.

The mechanical tapping; gentle and understated, as if a giant stick insect were lurking invisible in a bush, shifting its weight. Tiffany is suddenly imagines the threat is hanging over her, clinging to the ceiling, jaws dripping saliva and sharp teeth. Slowly she lifts her gaze. Only metal pipes. In her peripheral vision spots a shadow shift on a wall.

Run! Shout! Before Jordan disappears round the corner.

Dreadheavy, dizzy, Tiffany turns slowly towards the van.

One white and one green.

Why would a new van have mismatched doors? Why is the green door ajar?

Wait for Jordan. Just wait. He will realise you aren't following him. He'll come back.

But she cannot wait. What if Daniel and Alex are in there? She takes two steps. Towards the back of the van. The clicking stops and, far from making her feel better, the silence makes her feel much much worse.

Last one to touch the door is a baby.

That's what David always used to tell her. It was easy for him, four years older than his little sister. They would be standing in a back alley at dusk, or in front of a garden shed or an outside privy and he would goad her, telling her stories of monsters even though they had never ever found one behind any of his stupid doors.

'Chicken Licken. Girls are scared as chicken shit.'

'I'm not afraid,' she would shout. 'You're a liar.'

'Best go home, scaredy pants. Back to your dollies.'

Every time she would eventually crack and run forward and pull open the door with all the strength in her six-year-old arms. And find nothing. And David would be laughing till the tears were streaming down his face. Then he would hug her and tell her she was his little lion.

That was the moment she loved and longed for. Unwittingly, David had gifted her that courage of a lion, unaware that she would draw on it to speak at his funeral when she was still only twelve years old. While all the grownups had been unable to speak for grief, Tiffany had stood in front of the whole congregation and spoken in a clear voice about her brother and the cancer hidden behind the door.

Tiffany knows she has to open the doors. Three quick steps. She grabs the handle and pulls and cannot believe what she sees. At the same instant something grabs her left ankle and she is falling to the deck. She screams. Her ankle is shooting hot. Searing pain. A second hand or claw is trying to grab her other leg. With all her strength she kicks with her free foot, raining blows on whatever it is that has grabbed her. A voiceless howl, like the wind rattling a picket fence, emanates from beneath the van as Jordan arrives, running. Without hesitation he throws himself forwards and stamps on the arms that protrude from beneath the van. Tiffany feels herself being dragged under the vehicle. Her flailing foot makes contact with something that crunches. This time the howl has a voice, guttural and primal. Jordan stamps again and again. An ugly splintering sound rips the air and Tiffany knows instinctively that it is the sound of snapping bones. For a second she fears her own leg has been broken in two. She kicks and kicks again. Jordan cries out but she keeps going, knowing her life is at stake. She winces as she feels something give. The claw gripping her is suddenly no longer attached to anything. On her back, the soles of her feet on the floor, Tiffany pushes herself backwards, away from the van, then rolls onto her side, over and over, putting distance between her and her attacker. The claw that grips her ankle relinquishes its hold and clatters away. Finally she climbs to her feet and rushes to Jordan who wraps an arm around her.

With his spare arm Jordan is holding a torch and shining it under the van. In the shadows is the scravir curled in a foetal position. It is missing one forearm, which is twitching on the floor where it fell. The second arm is also clearly broken and hanging at an unnatural angle. The scravir's face is damaged, one cheekbone has collapsed and an eyeball is hanging loose, swinging back and forth on its nerve stalk like a conker on its string.

Tiffany is bent over double, retching uncontrollably.

'What's in the van?' Jordan asks her.

Tiffany shakes her head, the little lion's courage is spent, but Jordan knows that they must follow through to the end. He shines the torch into the back of the van. He sees two large empty boxes. He prises himself away from Tiffany to climb inside the van.

'There's something in there,' she hisses but either Jordan doesn't hear her or he isn't listening.

As he crosses the threshold something grabs him and pulls him out of sight. Tiffany screams and turns to run away then, out of nowhere, she remembers her last moments with Daniel. She thrusts her hand into her jacket pocket and pulls out the syringe gun he gave her. It was because Daniel had given her the gun that he was unable to protect himself. Now she must act to save Jordan. Consumed with rage, she clambers into the back of the van, gripping the gun in front of her.

It is there, sulking in the shadows behind the door, malevolent and skeletally thin, barely human, tapping its toes impatiently on the floor of the van. Pinned beneath the scravir's scrawny leg, Jordan's arms flail about as he gasps for air. Tiffany wonders how a creature so skinny can have such strength. The scravir jerks his head towards her, his face breaking into a gap-toothed grin. His breath reeks of mould and decay. Tiffany flinches back still clutching the gun. As her eyes drop to her right hand she senses the scravir's attention shifting. She doesn't have the luxury of time. She throws herself forward, tumbling over the prostrate Jordan as she collides with the scravir, the needle of the gun penetrating its abdomen. The ghoul's howl is so loud that Tiffany fears her eardrums will burst. He pushes her back violently but she braces herself against the far wall of the van refusing to be dislodged. She grips the gun and pulls the trigger.

Nothing happens. She is losing her balance. If she falls the needle will break. The scravir sniggers, exhales fetid air over her. Jordan is choking to death. All or nothing. She grips the trigger with the index finger of both hands and pulls with all her strength, until she fears her fingers will snap. Finally, the vial cracks and the liquid spurts into the scravir's belly. The monster writhes, its limbs in spasm as its muscles waste and wither before Tiffany's eyes. It lashes out blindly, desperate to dislodge the needle. Like all living creatures it clings to life but it is too late and before her eyes it collapses, an empty sack of skin and bones.

Jordan takes a huge hacking gasp of air. He is alive! With her arms wrapped around herself, Tiffany backs away. She clambers out of the van, barely conscious of her actions. Her head is spinning, she leans against a pillar for support, the wall protecting her back. A moment later Jordan emerges. He is holding something. A card. He gives it to her.

Alex's railcard.

Without a word Jordan disappears around the side of the van. Tiffany wants to shout at him to stop but she is spent. She staggers forwards away from the wall, keeping clear of the van.

Jordan has thrown open the driver's door. There is nothing of interest in the cab, except to a forensic team who could dust for fingerprints and pick the long white hairs from the back of the driver's seat. Jordan takes a few photos on his smart phone.

'Let's go,' her voice flat as February.

Taking care not to place himself in danger, Jordan walks round the front of the van to the passenger side, the side against the wall. He returns and shows Tiffany the mess of bent metalwork and scratched paint from where the van hit the dry stone wall. Tiffany stares blankly at the phone screen, too tired to think. The syringe gun drops from her hand. Two of the five remaining vials smash on impact with the floor. Jordan scoops everything up and gently steers Tiffany away.

CHAPTER 39

On board Pride of Hull, docked at Rotterdam

Monday, 7th December

She has allowed herself to be led upstairs where she stands side by side with Jordan in the fresh air on the Skylounge Deck, at the top of the ship. Tiffany hasn't spoken since the attack.

Huge wind turbines churn a drab sky. To the east of empty terminal car parks, fifty gas towers hunch like crabs awaiting a returning tide. To the north, drizzle kisses the horizon and The Hague hangs in the balance.

From the bowels of the ship, cars emerge blinking into the dull morning, down the ramp two by two, metal avatars of a forgotten Ark. Behind the cars come the campervans. The large Winnebago waddles out.

'What kind of butt dialling dumb-arse goes on a European tour in a campervan in winter?' Jordan mutters. 'They'll freeze their bollocks off.'

Tiffany half hears him. She thinks of the hundreds of static caravans crouching on the headlands around Whitby, rattling in the winds, the rain drumming on their roofs. She remembers Daniel's fragile tent trembling in the breeze by the cliff edge on Farview Farm.

More vans appear below. Jordan wants to see who is driving the Citroën with the white door and the green door, to take photos that can be used as evidence. Tiffany is too numb to care.

The Citroën van does not appear. Articulated lorries are

snaking their way off the ship now. As the last vehicle crosses the ramp towards dry land, the ship's crew rearrange the traffic cones.

For five minutes Tiffany and Jordan stay put, staring out at nothing in particular.

'What do you want to do?' Jordan asks finally.

She turns toward him, a haunted look in her eyes. Far beneath them the foot passengers are disembarking along the covered walkway towards the terminal building. The sky sags graveyard grey, as tired as fallen arches. They came all this way for what?

'Home,' she says simply.

Jordan tries to smile reassuringly but his heart isn't in it.

'Come on,' he says, reaching to take Tiffany's arm.

She recoils, opens her mouth. It sounds as if she is starting to scream. Jordan decides it must be a ship's horn but the sound grows and he realises it is a siren. A couple of police cars and then an ambulance appear on the quay below. Lights flashing, the vehicles thunder across the ramps and into the belly of the ship.

'They must have found it,' Jordan mutters, walking towards a door that leads inside. He senses Tiffany is following.

'We need to sort out our return tickets and what not,' he tells her as the door swings shut behind them.

'We aren't even getting off the ship?' Her voice is flat.

'You want to get off the ship?'

She doesn't answer.

They return to the lounge bar. Ylenia's bag is where she left it, wedged between the wall and the back of a sofa. The bar staff are busy cleaning and stocking up for the return trip and no-one pays them attention. Tiffany lies back and closes her eyes, desperate for sleep.

Jordan finds a charging point for his phone and opens the on-board magazine on the table in front of him. How many times can you flick through pages of pointless penthouse apartments in Dubai?

At least the ship doesn't rock about while it is docked.

'I am sorry, Miss, but you have to leave the ship.'

It is a woman's voice. Tiffany opens her eyes and checks her watch. Ten o'clock. She has been asleep for an hour. Jordan is sitting beside her. A woman in uniform is standing over them.

'Your tickets please.'

Jordan leans back and lifts his backside off the sofa to reach into the pocket of his jeans. He hands over his ticket and passport.

'And yours please, Miss. This is a single, Sir.'

'We're going straight back,' he explains.

'You still need a ticket.'

'But we aren't leaving the ship,' Tiffany says.

'You *have* to leave the ship,' the woman explains, her patience is wearing thin.

Tiffany is about to protest when the bar door opens and two crewmen in fluorescent orange tabards run in, a younger guy with a hipster bread and an older guy with a beer belly the size of a space hopper. Beer belly spots the woman standing by Tiffany and Jordan. 'They need you down in reception, love,' he calls out.

The woman glances down at Tiffany and Jordan then back at Colin. 'I need you off my ship in five minutes,' she says hurrying off.

'Her ship,' Tiffany mutters scornfully as she and Jordan gather their things. Tiffany takes Ylenia's case.

'And when I say skinny I mean like anaerobic,' Beer belly is saying as they pass the bar.

'No, you don't,' says hipster beard. 'You mean anorexic.'

'Same thing.'

'Dozy sod.' Hipster beard pushes a cup of coffee across the bar towards the older man.

Jordan and Tiffany leave the bar and make their way to the main entrance on Deck Eight where a tall policeman is talking with staff at the reception desk.

'Excuse me,' someone calls out as they head down the gangway towards the terminal.

They stop and wait as the policeman catches up. He is middle-aged with a ruddy complexion and wears a black uniform with a two broad yellow stripes that run across his barrel chest and biceps. A full head taller than Jordan, and stocky, any basketball team would welcome him with open arms.

'Hello, I am Police Patrol Officer Gert Muyskens of the Rotterdam Police, I would like to ask you a few questions,' he smiles broadly. 'You are day trippers, yes?'

Tiffany says no and Jordan says yes.

Muyskens smiles. 'It is my accent, yes? I ask again. Are you day trippers?'

Tiffany lets Jordan answer. He says yes and she agrees with him.

'We're taking a walking tour so that Tiffany can see the modern architecture, the cube houses and the market,' Jordan explains.

'Good idea. And don't forget Erasmus Bridge.'

'What's happening?' Jordan asks. "We saw the police cars and an ambulance.'

Muyskens frowns. 'I cannot say anything. Sorry.'

'We just want to know if the ship will be sailing this evening or if …'

'Ah, OK. I think yes. But if there are delays the shipping company will find you accommodation. Did either of you see anything strange on the ship last night?'

Jordan shakes his head. 'We were in the upstairs lounge. Didn't book a cabin.'

'Did you see this woman?' The policeman produces a passport photo from his breast pocket and passes it to Tiffany.

Both Tiffany and Jordan do a triple take; not recognising the face, then recognising Ylenia, then trying to convey not having recognised her. She is almost unrecognisable, brunette instead of blonde and much rounder in the face.

'You look confused,' Muyskens observes.

'I thought she reminded me of someone in the bar.' Jordan says. 'But I am wrong. Has something happened?'

'Miss?'

'She's really tired,' Jordan explains. 'Couldn't sleep last night.'

'OK,' Muyskens offers Tiffany a business card. 'If you think of anything later give me a call.'

Tiffany takes the card. Jordan takes Tiffany's arm. 'Erasmus Bridge, right?'

'Correct. There are left luggage lockers in the terminal, you don't have to carry those cases with you all day.'

'Good idea. Thanks, man.'

'You take care, guys.'

Jordan and Tiffany walk to the Terminal building where Jordan buys them both tickets back to Hull on the next ferry.

'Come on, let's get some fresh air,' he says.

'What were all that about modern architecture and bridges?'

'I read it in the magazine in the bar,' Jordan explains.

'I thought he were going to arrest us.'

'Why are you carrying Ylenia's suitcase? And that was her in the photo, wasn't it?'

Tiffany nods.

Ten hours later, the shuttle bus drops Jordan and Tiffany back at the terminal. The walk turned out not to be. They spent the day drinking coffee, keeping warm, killing time, seeing Rotterdam's modern architecture through café windows.

Tiffany has stayed monosyllabic and withdrawn. Jordan has stayed at her side, his attention focused on his phone, watching the news, playing a game. In the middle of the afternoon he decided to open Ylenia's suitcase. Clothes, books, toiletries, the wedding dress and the rose, nothing that shed any light on anything. Fed up of carrying it, they dumped it in a waste bin on the edge of a park.

Dead on their feet they make their way along the walkway and back onto the ship, both hoping they can sprawl out on sofas in the lounge and sleep all the way back to Hull.

'A good time, yes?' a voice calls out behind them.

They turn to find Muyskens, the policeman, standing by the reception desk.

'Haven't you forgotten some of your luggage?' he asks.

Tiffany offers no explanation. Jordan steps in.

'You were right. Tiffany thought we needed an extra suit-case for presents, but we didn't find anything so in the end we left it in a city centre bin.'

Muysken's gaze is steady. 'I told you there are left luggage lockers in the terminal.'

'Yeah, you did,' Jordan agrees. 'We should have listened.'

For a moment it looks as if the policeman is not buying the story of the suitcase. Tiffany fiddles uncomfortably with a lock of hair. Does he know it belongs to Ylenia? What has happened to her? Have the Dutch police been talking with the Whitby police?

'I feel sick,' Tiffany says, grabbing Jordan's arm.

'We'll sit down in a minute,' Jordan reassures her.

'You have been in one of our famous coffee shops smoking cannabis?' Muyskens smiles. 'Hey, don't worry, it's OK. It is legal here. You are over eighteen, yes?'

'Bit stronger than she was expecting,' Jordan admits. 'You work long hours.'

'I have just finished. Time to go home,' Muyskens says.

'Safe journey. And remember, if you think of anything that could be useful, call me.'

The policeman walks off down the ramp. Jordan takes Tiffany upstairs where they make themselves comfortable in one of the lounges. The ship leaves in a little over an hour.

'You're such a liar,' Tiffany says.

Jordan smiles. 'It's called survival. I'm a survivor, and so are you. Get this: I just checked out Muyskens' name on the internet. He must be six foot six and his name means little mouse. How sick is that?'

Tiffany manages a half smile.

CHAPTER 40

Whitby Gazette
United in Grief

Tuesday, 8th December
Updated 2 hours ago

There have been calls for immediate action in the wake of Whitby's worst weekend in decades. In the aftermath of a weekend that has left the town united in grief, following the deaths of seven people and the disappearance of five others during the most powerful storms to batter the town in twenty years, a spokesperson for the council said that "lessons would be learned".

Opposition councillors have condemned "repeated failures" by the local authority.

"Whitby residents are upset and fed up," said Councillor George Sadwright. "We're common folk with common sense. No disrespect but if visitors haven't the basic nous to stay away from raging seas then access to the beach and harbour must be shut down altogether when storms strike during Goth Weekend to prevent further calamities."

Cllr Sadwright said the council administration must be held personally accountable because the town's reputation was at stake. "If Goth Weekend organisers refuse to take responsibility for ensuring that the event is properly managed," he added, "then the festival should be scrapped altogether."

Council leader, Cllr Peter Bickering, said that Cllr Sadwright's remarks were typical but inappropriate at a time when families are grieving the loss of loved ones.

Among the fatalities were an elderly couple said to have been swept off the harbour wall during the storm. Refusing to comment on "lurid rumours" that the victims were found in a state of partial undress, head of police, Detective Inspector David Rawes, confirmed that twelve people were either dead or missing, including two police officers whose squad car was found abandoned on the A174 north of the town.

Among the missing is 19-year-old Londoner, Darren Quincey, who had rented one of the lighthouse cottages. Police believe he fell from the cliff in the small hours of Sunday morning, following a report of a body on the shore.

D.I. Rawes said that those seeking to introduce "grisly and bogus supernatural explanations" for the tragic deaths over the weekend were grossly irresponsible. "Exploiting the misery of others for entertainment and commercial gain is disgraceful."

In a further development, police confirmed that the bus involved in an accident on the A171 south of Whitby was the vehicle used by Hounds of Hellbane, one of the festival's headline acts.

The black Routemaster bus was in flames when police arrived at the scene of the accident where one person died following a multiple collision. Another person is in the critical care centre at Scarborough Hospital. Police are trying to contact Hounds of Hellbane singer Thor Lupei. It is not known whether Lupei or the band were on the bus at the time of the accident.

CHAPTER 41

Whitby - Tiffany Harrek

Friday 18th November

I hadn't been outside all day until I left the flat to go to work, it were that cold. At the chippie we kept front door shut but even the heat from the fryers couldn't keep the biting cold from sneaking in. Every punter coming in would be shivering as they ordered, pacing up and down like caged tigers while they waited for their fish to fry. And they all wanted scraps on their chips, like the extra calories were a matter of life and death.

It were ten days since Jordan and I had arrived back in Hull. First four days I sat in my room. Light on all night. Curtains drawn all day. A chest of drawers up against the door. Jordan rang but I didn't want to talk to anyone. Eventually he texted me and I replied, to let him know I were alive.

The monsters underneath and in the van were everywhere I looked. Couldn't get them out of my mind. Stupid really; I already knew about the scravir from Daniel, Megan and Katie but seeing them myself and being attacked had changed everything. It were amazing any of us had survived, and I were slowly admitting to myself that Daniel and Alex must be dead.

Tina, my flatmate, had left the newspaper on the lino outside my door. I picked it up on a trip to the bathroom, took a photo of the article about the deaths on my phone and sent it to Jordan. It made no sense. Why were the police saying Darren had fallen off the cliff? We knew he had died in the garden.

On the plus side, no-one were blaming Jordan or the rest

of us for anything. I don't think the police had even called Jordan; he would have said. He did text me that Katie and Megan were refusing to talk with him.

On the Saturday Uncle Ted rang our landline and spoke with Tina. She banged on my door till I answered. He had read my emails before I could stop him, I'd forgotten all about them, and he wanted a chat. I told him I didn't want to talk about it. He didn't push the point, left it at telling me that my whole life were ahead of me and I shouldn't be causing waves over a lad I had only known for two days.

'It's not a crush, if that's what you're thinking,' I told him.

He just laughed that big laugh of his and told me I were just a kid and that I should ring me mam because she were worried. She knew I hadn't been at work.

It helped more than I could ever tell him, to hear that big laugh. I gave me mam a quick call and went back to work on the Monday. I were there grabbing a pile of takeaway boxes out back when the manager told me there were a woman asking for me out front. Peering round the corner of the storeroom door, I saw it were Ivanna, the doctor from Scarborough.

'Tell her I'm not here.'

'She's says it's important.'

'I'm not here.'

'Don't know what you're hiding from, Tiffany, but you're miserable as shit. What's his name?'

'Sod you.'

An hour later the chippie closed and I finished my shift. I turned the sign round from open to closed on the front door and left, turning my collar up against the cold.

I had walked just three steps before Ivanna were there in front of me.

'Hello, Tiffany. I have someone who wants to meet you,' she said.

I shook my head. All I wanted was to forget, to crawl back

under my little rock and be safe. I tried to step past her but she blocked my path.

'He's come a long way,' she said gently.

For a second I thought she meant Daniel. It were like a mountain were climbing off my back. I started daring to dream the impossible dream as tears welled up. Then her eyes lifted and met mine and I knew I were being a twat, it weren't Daniel at all. Daniel were dead.

'You can trust him. He's here to help.'

A car door opened and out climbed the little mouse. The two metre tall policeman from Rotterdam.

'Wait, Tiffany. Hear what he has to say.' Ivanna shouted after me.

He weren't in police uniform and I had no idea if he had the power to arrest me or anything but I were cornered with nowhere to run and no-one to turn to.

We took a table at the back of the café beside the Dracula experience. The place were more or less empty. Police Patrol Officer Gert Muyskens waited for the waitress to leave.

'Thank you, Miss Harrek,' he started. 'First of all, I put your mind at rest. I am not here to arrest you.'

'Tiffany.'

He smiled. 'I need your help, Tiffany. I believe that you and your friend hold vital information relating to the case I am trying to solve.'

'I doubt it.'

'When we met on the ship at Rotterdam you said …'

'We didn't see owt.'

'Forget the ship. What if I told you that in the evening of 10th November a young family were found dead in a village not far from the border with Germany. All four bodies, including those of the children aged ten and twelve, were emaciated, as if they had been starved in a prisoner of war camp. The father ran a small removals business. A removals lorry is unaccounted for. A neighbour said she had seen the mother just days earlier with one of the children, and that both appeared normal and in good health.' Muyskens paused and waited until I looked up. 'A brown Winnebago was found half a kilometre from the house. We have identified it as having been on the Hull to Rotterdam ferry on 8th November, the day you travelled.'

I shivered involuntarily.

'From the discussion I have had with Dr Albu here,' Muyskens continued, 'I am convinced that you know what I am talking about.'

'It's pointless,' I said, staring at my shoes. 'He's too strong. And the police are helping him.'

'Why do you say that?'

'They've been lying to cover up what has happened.'

'In what way?'

I shook my head, I didn't trust him. I didn't trust anyone.

Muyskens decided not to press me. He turned to Ivanna Albu. 'Have you told Tiffany what you have found?'

'One person is doing all talking,' Ivanna said, looking at me and rolling her eyes.

'OK, I shut up.'

'Those blood samples I gave to forensic lab,' Ivanna started. 'They separate DNA to identify multiple individuals involved in crimes. For example, gang rapes, or mass murder in wars. Forgive me if this is complicated and unpleasant. Specialists calculate how many contributors there are in a DNA sample collected at a crime scene. They separate Y-chromosmal haplotypes from male DNA mixtures to ...'

'Too complicated,' I shook my head.

'Yes. I explain another way. Sample I collected from door, Megan said it was blood of Thor Lupei. You remember?'

I nodded.

'Tests shows this is not blood of one person; it is blood

of many people. Maybe more than one hundred. And not just human beings. Blood of dogs and wild animals all mixed up. It is confusing and extraordinary. One hundred people cannot cut themselves on door so …'

'So all those different DNA samples all come from him?' I cut in. 'They're in his blood?'

'Exactly. Why does he carry blood from so many different people?' Her voice was loud and rising in pitch. 'And animals. Why is he not sick or dead? His body must reject foreign DNA. And another thing …'

'Wait.' I put my hand up to stop her mid-flow. 'You haven't told me why he's here,' I said, pointing at Muyskens.

'The forensic lab alerted Europol,' Ivanna explained. 'International crime cooperation. It is routine when they discover something unusual like this.'

'Don't worry, kid,' the policeman said, 'after Brexit no-one will bother you. Exchange of information will stop in the North Sea. But for now, I need you to tell me about Thor Lupei and I need you to explain why you believe the Whitby police are covering up.'

I hesitated.

'You were on the ferry to save your friend. You believe that Thor Lupei had kidnapped him. Six people died and five are missing since …'

'Seven. Seven people died. And three of the people they say are missing aren't missing, they were murdered.'

'Go on.'

'Have you read the local paper? They said the pathologist is suffering from dementia. She's not; Daniel said she were dead. He saw her on the rocks at the foot of the cliff below Henrietta Street. She were pushed off the top then attacked.'

'Do you know how or why?'

'She spoke with Daniel and Katie after she picked them up from Farview Farm. I think she had seen the dead police at the farm, and the fire. They covered all that up, so maybe they killed her. Or maybe they don't want anyone to see her body. They moved the police car from Farview Farm to north of Whitby and said the officers were missing. Talk to Katie.'

'You saw the bodies?'

'No, but Daniel and Katie saw them. I saw the fire.'

'Who are Daniel and Katie? Can I speak with them?'

'Daniel is missing. Lupei smuggled him out on the ferry. Katie is in London but she won't even talk to Jordan.'

Muyskens looked thoughtful for a moment. 'Jordan is the guy you were with on the boat? The black guy, right?'

I nodded.

'Hmm. When I showed you this photograph on the ship you both said you didn't recognise her.' He passed Tiffany the photo of Ylenia. 'That wasn't true.'

'She looks different.'

'She's thinner and has blonde hair,' Ivanna interjected, inspecting the photo.

'And she had a skull painted on her face last time I saw her,' I added.

The policeman looked confused.

'She was in costume,' Ivanna explained. 'For Whitby Goth Weekend.'

'Oh, OK. A festival?' Muyskens said. 'Vampires, loud music, black leather, real ale? That kind of thing? So you know her?'

'Only for a few hours,' I said.

He looked me in the eye. 'There's no easy way to tell you this. Her body was found on the ferry; that is why the police were called.'

I felt like someone had kicked me in the stomach. 'We thought that someone had found the dead scravir.'

Muyskens looked confused.

'The monster under the white van that Lupei stole after

he crashed the bus. One attacked me. They're like Lupei's zombies or something. The one that went for me lost a hand and an eyeball. He died under the van.

Muyskens shook his head. 'We found the Romanian lady, and two Australian tourists butchered in their cabin. We believe that it was their Winnebago that Thor Lupei stole to leave the ship. The Romanian woman was found in one of the women's toilets; her body weighed just thirty kilos. But no bodies under vans, and no zombies, sorry.'

Instinctively, I wrapped my arms around myself as I received the news that the scravir had escaped.

'I have been doing my homework,' Muyskens said softly. 'Five years ago there was a similar pattern of deaths in Denmark. During the Roskilde festival. Nothing was done because no-one could make sense of the deaths.'

'Was Lupei ...' I started.

The policeman nodded.

'So the Dutch police are helping the Whitby police?' I said.

'No, no, no. You have misunderstood. I am officially on holiday, kid. No uniform, no warrants. I'm a tourist exploring Yorkshire.'

I was confused. Ivanna looked disappointed.

'This is personal,' Muyskens' pale blue eyes fixed on the wall. 'Thirty years ago my brother Pim died. His body was found in a skip in Schaesburg during the PinkPop festival. He had left home two years earlier after a fight with my father and I hadn't seen him for all that time. According to the morgue his body weighed just forty kilos. My mother hardly recognised him.'

Muyskens looked me in the eye. 'They told her that Pim was a junkie. It was crap, and he was as tall as me. They didn't even conduct an autopsy. I promised my mum I would find the truth. That is why I am a policeman.' He stood up and, wincing at the taste of it, finished his coffee. 'The alley where Pim's body was found is less than five kilometres from where that family were murdered last week.'

Muyskens held up his open hands. 'So we all have unfinished business I think. But let me make something very clear to you. I cannot arrest someone for being a zombie or a vampire. We need proof that real offences have been committed and we need to provide evidence to link crimes to perpetrators and conspirators. Understood?'

CHAPTER 42

Micăbrukóczi

Friday 18th November

The snow had been falling all day, hanging heavy on branches of the conifer forest. It muffled the *hoop hoop* hunting calls of the boreal owls as night slid down the mountains, smothering the valley floor and choking the distant howls of the wolves.

Inside the castle, logs were spitting in the open fire, throwing dancing shadows across the vast hall. It had taken several days for the metre thick stone walls to absorb sufficient heat but finally they felt warm to the touch.

Seated in a wingback armchair facing the fire, the castle's owner was playing a Gibson 1959 Les Paul Standard. He knew the blues should really be played on his Fender 1956 Stratocaster but he was such a rebel. The notes slapped the walls, cascaded and tumbled in the flickering light.

And I feel so bad, bring me a doctor. I feel soooooooo bad.

He chuckled; half a million pounds up for a weekend's work. Deduct twenty K for the burned out bus, and another ten in expenses, add five for the gig itself. With the castle renovation complete he could spend the money on a few little luxuries. A pack of hunting dogs? A 1960s Ferrari? A bottle of 1858 Cuvée Leónie cognac? Or maybe a little human entertainment, a special party?

I feel soooo bad, won't you fetch me a doctor?

With a squeak of heavy hinges, the carved oak door at the far end of the hall swung open to reveal a wheezing and shuffling skeletal figure pushing a trolley. Beneath the bald head, the eyes were vacant of expression. The occupant of the wing-backed chair followed his servant's progress in the mirror that hung over the fireplace.

The man came to a halt beside the chair. With a perfunctory upward glance, Thor Lupei pointed at the side table.

'Cognac not cola and, since you're going back to the kitchen, bring more interesting snacks.'

The old man shifted his weight in order to get the trolley moving, there being little strength in what remained of his muscles.

'When you've finished here you can feed the honeypots,' he called after the retreating figure, resolving that he would remove the ridiculous contraption that encompassed the man's right arm without serving any real purpose.

CHAPTER 43

Whitby - Gert Muyskens

Saturday, 19th November

Used to waking up at five, Gert Muyskens slept until after nine. Sea air or the now empty minibar, he couldn't decide where the blame lay. He threw on the same clothes he had worn the day before. In the bathroom he splashed water over his face, stooped to observe his reflection in the mirror and noted that he needed a shave, then ran downstairs hoping he had not missed breakfast.

He needn't have worried; he wasn't even the last to arrive. The coffee was almost undrinkable but the waitress friendly, and a full English breakfast was quickly on its way. While he waited, he fished out his mobile and called in a favour. Like him, Antoine was a man on a mission; if there were anything to find, Antoine would sniff it out. The databases at Europol were extensive and impressive, but the jewels in the crown were the researchers and technicians from across the continent: methodical, dedicated, and relentless. And Antoine was the departmental big gouda, the real master at unearthing patterns across space and time.

The waitress returned and waited while he pushed his laptop across the table and out of the way. Muyskens stared happily at his laden plate. He knew what his doctor would say if he could see the festival of cholesterol in front of him; fried bread, three fat sausages, streaky bacon, mushrooms, black pudding, tomatoes and eggs swimming in oil. He had already had an angina scare but one cooked English breakfast in an ocean of dreary sugar-free zero-salt bran flakes wouldn't make the difference between life and death. Besides he had a busy day ahead of him, as he had decided to make the best use of his time in Whitby by visiting the various locations referred to by Tiffany and Dr Albu. He had printed up a couple of maps before leaving Rotterdam and, with Tiffany's help, had scribbled crosses and notes over them in green Biro.

Ninety minutes later Muyskens had exhausted himself climbing the steps to the Abbey, salivated outside Fortune's Kippers, peered in through the windows of the cottage the four London students had rented, and walked along the east pier and the beach, taking notes as he went.

Crossing the swing bridge he followed the road round – St. Ann's Staith, Haggersgate, Pier Road, and Khyber Pass, taking the steps up to the whalebone arch, and onto Cleveland Way to reach the Pavilion. Stepping inside, Muyskens found himself surrounded by pirates, robots, half a dozen Mad Hatters, zombies and a hundred other "half-eaten sandwiches in search of a picnic" as his cantankerous father would have called the eclectic mix of fun-seekers attending the Sci-Fi and Comic Convention.

A robot mermaid sprayed green and sporting a mechanical cardboard tail gave him the directions to reach Reception.

'Why do you want to know?' asked the bored girl at the reception desk, fiddling with earrings that Muyskens realised were miniature toilet rolls on gold-coloured hoops.

'I was hoping to have a quick word with Eric, we're coming in to fix the roof tomorrow morning and I wanted to check times with him, Cathy,' Muyskens said politely, reading the name off her badge.

'Are you Polish?'

'Wow, you have a great ear for accents,' he said, happy to indulge her ignorance and prejudice.

'All builders are Polish.'

'By the way, what is Eric's last name? I need to fill out the paperwork.'

'Well, Mr Dunn is not here. So that's that.' Cathy tilted her head to one side and stared him straight in the eye, defying him to call her a liar.

'Thank you, you have been very helpful.'

'What we're here for, love,' she sneered.

He made his way back the way he had come.

'Did you find it?'

Muyskens turned. The robot mermaid was all smiles.

'What?'

'What you were looking for.'

'Do you know where the stage entrance is?' he asked.

'Down the side at the back. I can show you. I'm Jaz.'

He followed Jaz out, immediately anxious that the girl might die of cold in her flimsy costume, green painted bare shoulders and cardboard silver tail.

'Do you want to borrow my coat?' he offered.

'Don't be silly; mermaid's are cold-blooded,' she giggled. 'You're not from round here, are you?'

'The Netherlands.'

Her expression showed she was impressed. 'There aren't any bands on today.'

'It's OK. I'm here to see Eric. The stage manager. Little guy. Maybe sixty …'

'Bright yellow jacket? Cross between Elvis and a Hobbit?' she said, stopping in front of a brown door. 'I saw him inside, half an hour ago. Have fun.'

Muyskens rang the bell and watched the girl walk away, wondering what she was when she wasn't a robot mermaid.

'Deliveries round front,' said a voice behind him.

Muyskens turned and looked down. A long way down.

'You must be Eric.'

'And you must be bloody deaf,' Eric answered.

Muyskens put his heavy boot in the path of the closing door. 'Mr Lupei sent me.'

Eric hesitated fractionally.

After thirty years policing you got a feel for these things. Muyskens pressed home his advantage. 'I have a message and a request.'

Eric leaned forward and looked left and right, checking that the tall stranger was alone, then beckoned the man inside and closed the door. As far as Muyskens was concerned, Eric had already lost.

'Well?' Eric tried to put defiance and authority into his voice but the off-duty policeman couldn't have been less interested.

'Mr Lupei is concerned that you may have felt tempted to double cross him.' Muyskens observed every flicker of emotion as it registered on Eric's face. Anger, certainly, and was there also fear? 'So why don't you explain what happened?'

Eric looked confused, torn between wanting to throw the door open and kick the man out, and the fear that there might genuinely be an issue. Had he overlooked something? 'What are you talking about?' he said, finally.

'You were careless and left a trail. Lupei is concerned that the police are all over it and it is only a matter of time before …'

Eric's demeanour changed. Caution and anxiety were replaced by contempt. 'Oh I get it; you're from the press or something. The police?' He placed a white gloved hand on the doorknob and threw the door open. 'They won't lift a finger against me. If I were you I'd watch my back. The bigger they are the harder they fall. Now fuck off.'

Muyskens retreated before Eric could reach up and bite his elbow; he had what he needed. As the door slammed behind him, Muyskens checked the digital recorder was working. Tiffany was right about Eric and other things too. He pulled his smart phone from his pocket.

'Hello. Is that the Royal College of Pathology? Yes, I do know it is the weekend. This is urgent. I am Gert Muyskens of the Rotterdam police and I want you to listen very carefully …'

He had to wait twenty minutes, which he spent standing on the west pier staring out to sea while sipping an acceptable skinny latte.

His phone rang. He answered. The receptionist at the Royal College of Pathology explained that they would not release the address of a member without a formal request from an authorised source. Muyskens called in another favour from Antoine at Europol, the friend and ex-colleague who had tipped him off about the DNA search that Ivanna had carried out.

'That's a couple of tickets to a world cup qualifier you owe me,' said the friendly voice at the other end of the line.

'Done, but I don't think it will be a Netherlands match, sadly.'

'Neither do I. I call you as soon as I have something. Still waiting for the other stuff you asked for.'

'Something else for you to investigate, Antoine. Who gets charged in a town if the coffee they serve is undrinkable? Is it the guesthouse or the mayor?'

'You're in UK. I think it's the Queen. But tread carefully, three hundred years ago women were banned from drinking coffee in England. She may still be upset about that.'

Muyskens was still smiling as he trousered his phone and walked out to the end of the pier, past the lighthouse. Through the gaps in the planks he could see a couple of fishermen on the lower deck, wrapped in thick jackets, their conversation drowned in the noise of the waves crashing against the sea wall. A small fishing boat carrying half a dozen tourists passed through the jaws of the harbour and out to sea. Watching the boat rise and fall in the swell, Muyskens wondered how long it would take a vessel of that size to reach Rotterdam? He barely heard his phone ring.

'Sorry, Antoine. I can't hear you. Ring you back,' he shouted.

He rang from inside a fish and chip shop on Pier Road.

'Nigela Shaveling lives in an apartment on the west cliff. Before I give you the address there's something else you need to know,' Antoine told him. 'Shaveling filed a report at the college on the evening of the fifth of November. It concerned her preliminary thoughts regarding a series of autopsies she performed on the bodies of three people discovered on Whitby streets following the first night of the Goth festival. I am uploading a copy of the file. OK, do you have a pen?'

Muyskens read the report sitting on a bench overlooking the harbour and quickly realised that he had an important piece of the jigsaw in his hands. Screeching gulls landed on the railings close by, staring at him with hostile yellow eyes before flying off. The sun emerged and dull winter hues shone briefly with vibrant colour, then, just as suddenly, clouds quenched the light and grey grew back. And the Dutch policeman found himself weeping.

'Penny for your thoughts.'

Muyskens turned to find himself face to face with Tiffany.

'Aren't you at work?' he said, pointlessly.

'Late shift,' she explained. 'You OK?'

A little embarrassed, he brushed the tears away on the back of his sleeve. 'Memories. The sun is shining in the last memory I have of Pim. My brother. When you get older you …'

'For me it's the smell of candyfloss,' she said. 'Even when he were dying in hospital, our kid would ask for candyfloss.'

For a moment they stared at each other, each recognising the void in the other. Muyskens reached into his jacket, found his wallet and pulled out a Polaroid snap of a tall gangly guy with a mop of blond hair standing in a park. Different hair colour (had Muyskens been blond before he turned grey?) but the family resemblance was clear. Pim wore a T-shirt that read 'Just like heaven – The Cure'.

'A great British export,' the policeman said.

Tiffany smiled, tried to think of something encouraging to say, gave up, and pointed instead at the screen of his tablet. 'What's that?'

'The smoking gun,' Muyskens answered, closing his wallet and hiding the bruise he had worn every day of his adult life. 'It's a report the pathologist wrote about the three bodies found on the Saturday morning. I'm copying it to Ivanna at the hospital. Want to walk up the hill? Shaveling's flat is on Royal Crescent.'

She shook her head and showed him the crumpled bag she was holding. 'Promised Uncle Ted I'd do him some shopping.'

'We'll speak later on then,' he said as they parted company. 'What was your brother's name?' he called out after her.

'David,' she said, both happy and sad to be voicing it aloud. 'My brother was called David.'

The renal unit was closed at weekends. Cuts and savings, the usual. Ivanna pushed open the heavy doors and entered. There was something strange about empty units in a hospital, she always thought; a pretence that all the world's problems had been solved and everyone had been cured. And yet, in twenty hours time the tide of humanity would rise again, the waiting room chairs would all be occupied, machines would hum, staff would rush, and patients would wait for answers and the chance of a better life.

As expected, the computers at the reception desk had been left to drift to sleep rather than being switched off; where there was life there was hope. She checked to see if there were CCTV cameras looking down on her but this wasn't Accident and Emergency; visitors to the renal unit didn't arrive with bruised knuckles and a skinful of grievances. Ivanna could have accessed the data she sought from any of a hundred terminals in the hospital but she had decided that using this particular computer would help her to cover her tracks. She approached her task methodically. First 2016 then 2015 … The information was not hard to find; it was simply a matter of knowing what you were looking for. She took a series of photos on her phone.

Ivanna had understood immediately what had motivated Muyskens' request; a similar notion had been swimming around in her own mind for days. She had tried to dismiss it as ridiculous. There were around 1,500 kidney transplants in England every year and around 5,400 people on the waiting list. 283 kidney transplants performed in Yorkshire the previous year, in Leeds and Sheffield, and maybe 650 people on the waiting lists. 25,000 kidney transplants across Europe in a year. What would sufferers and their families be prepared to do in their desperation?

The list covered over a hundred individuals who had been referred to the Scarborough renal unit following transplant surgery over the previous five years, including twenty-seven with addresses in Whitby. Ivanna pocketed her phone and left the unit.

'Third floor,' said the old woman, fiddling with her thinning white hair. Her green housecoat was frayed and worn and she smelled of cats' urine. 'I don't think she's in, love. Mavis said it were in the papers that she's gone gaga. Doing a Heathcliff out on the moors somewhere. What did you say your name were?'

'I didn't,' Muyskens answered, taking the stairs two at a time.

He knocked, waited a minute, knocked again, then donned latex gloves, picked the lock and let himself in. Just one of a number of skills he had acquired over the years.

No smell of death, which was a good sign. Spinster's homes, like their Bachelor equivalent, came in two types: scrupulously clean or total tip. Shaveling's flat fell into the latter category. Bookcases lined every vertical surface; in the corridors, in every room. Even the kitchen and bathroom. The overall impression was of a small public library that had been taken over by squatters. The oven was full of folders and ring binders, the hob piled high with medical magazines. The kitchen table was a jumble sale of books in cardboard boxes. Only the sink, kettle and microwave, and the large pile of takeaway containers betrayed the room's function.

Squeezing along the corridor, Muyskens found the bathroom, home to literature, and a dusty collection of comic verse. Further along was the bedroom / historical reference section. The dirty windows pockmarked with dust.

Beyond that came the lounge / biology section, a television partially concealed behind a stack of magazines: The Doctor, and The Journal of Pathology.

On the other side of the corridor was what might once have been a second bedroom, now home to an extensive medical sciences collection, with the different bookcases being organised by language: English, German, and French.

The last room was locked. Muyskens picked the lock in seconds, stepped into the room and switched on the lights.

The contrast with the rest of the apartment took his breath away. Nestling in this chaotic bibliophile hoarder's paradise was a pristine Victorian dining room cum office. Beneath the chandelier a mahogany table with elegant scrolled legs occupied the centre of the room. A crystal vase containing dried flowers rested on a diamond-shaped and tasselled mat at the centre of the table. A large dresser with bevelled glass doors displayed a gold-trimmed dinner service. Beside it was a silver statue of a swan in flight. On an escritoire lay a powerful

Apple MacBook Pro connected to a colour laser printer. An ornate trolley carried several decanters, expensive whisky bottles and crystal tumblers and glasses. In the far corner of the room was a large marble statue showing either a nude woman turning into a tree or a tree transforming the other way.

Not a book in sight.

The policeman guessed that the lock on the door was not there to keep burglars out but was Shaveling's device to protect the room from her obsessive love of paper.

He opened the laptop, expecting it to be switched off, and was surprised to see the screen awaken. More surprising still was the yellowing page displayed upon the screen. Clearly a scan of an old book, the top of the page was headed with the following words:

Being an account of the further travels
of Three Englifh Gentlemen, &c.
In the Year 1736. Never before Publifhed.

Muyskens scrolled down and read.

SECT.III
Evil in the mountainous region north of the Metropolis of *Brafsov*.

T he road was rough and we were pretty much fatigued by the time we chanced upon a poft town of no great note, betwixt *Brafsov* and our northern deftination, where we were able to refrefh ourfelves and our Servants. Our horfes and the coach wheels of our chaife had suffered greatly during the afcent and we were obliged to pass the night in a mean tavern carved into the rock in the manner of the Troglodytic farmers of the *Loire* valley in *France*. The local Women had a mafculine Air that appealed little to our Party but we were happy when the miftress of the Houfe brought us a large spread of meats, which we fell upon like ravenous wolves, and a flagon of pafsable wine that did much to raife our drooping Spirits.

The enjoyment of our Repaft was spoiled by the arrival of an old man of such diminifhed state as to cause us much difcomfiture. Drefsed in tired and torn rags, so thin was this Fellow that every bone of his skeleton was clearly vifible beneath the tranflucent parchment of his skin. He sat at the adjoining table, his sunken yellow eyes obferving us with such ugly and indecent curiofity that we were obliged to requeft the Landlord that the man be moved on.

The lady of the House then appeared and beat the man on his way with a great stick upon his back. She then returned and, upon our enquiries, provided us with a fabulous and exploded Notion as to the origins of his Condition.

A foreft Path runs betwixt the town and its neighbours in the valley below and the local Citizens are wont to travel this path to buy and sell produce: wild boar, cheefes, nuts, cherries, and mufhrooms which they exchange for wines and diverfe goods from far across *Europe*. Along the Path are subterraneous Fountains and Rivers concealed in caves and, following a season of stormy and tempeftuous Weather, reports emerged of the caves having become infefted by corrupted Creatures, predatory people who upon whom was barely any flefh. These infernal creatures fall upon People travelling alone, taking hold of an ankle or arm, and thereby sucking the living flefh from them leaving them weakened and barely able to stand.

In the local language these daemons are known as *Scravr* or *Scravir*. The old man who had been chased away was one Victim of such an attack.

We enquired of the Lady of the Houfe why the People tolerated the prefence of such debafed beings in the Town and were furprifed by her reply. She infifted the poor fellow was in fact barely two and twenty years of age, known to her in perfon as a kindly lad and on his way to meet his betrothed before peftiferous Beings happened upon him. She further contended that while some of the Infected had themfelves become as evil as the Daemons that had attacked them, and had been put to the sword and deftroyed in the grave following the Cuftoms referved for Vampyr, many Victims are but sad hufks of the People they once were, inviting the Pity of their neighbours.

We must not omit Obferving here that the Landlord did arrive and interject and claim that two perfons were known to have recovered from the wafting Contagion, following interventions from a doctor of great Erudition, and that they did double their weight and become healthy again.

One further matter of note to sate the Curiofity of our readers is that, in a low voice and once her hufband had departed, the lady of the Houfe declared that, after a particular incident, people chancing upon a body lying on the Path did find that not only had the mufcles and sinews been reduced to nothing, but also the Body itself appeared to have been emptied of its vitals.

Since the Perfon was already Dead the shrivelled body was opened and it was confirmed that heart, kidneys and other organs were absent, even though the Body bore no external signs of butchery.

Having finished reading, Muyskens stood awhile in thought. The best forensic pathologists were a special breed, scholarly and versed in the sciences but with open minds capable of sidestepping conventional thought or wisdom. The policeman tried to put himself in Shaveling's shoes on that Saturday evening two weeks' earlier. She had produced a preliminary report with its shocking findings and sent it to the Royal College of Pathology. Was that her usual practice? Were British pathologists required to file autopsy reports, including preliminary findings, immediately with their professional organisation?

The preliminary report contained opinions and conclusions that were, to put it mildly, unconventional. By sending it to the Royal College, Shaveling was risking her own reputation so why had she done it?

As he considered this, Muyskens explored the files on the desktop of Shaveling's expensive laptop, his latex covered fingertips skating across the touchpad. The desktop image was an empty seascape; grey sky meets grey sea. Aside from the historic account he had read the desktop carried just two documents: a screenshot showing a detailed chart of the weather in Whitby between midnight on Friday 4th November and midnight on 5th November, and a note detailing various times and places. Muyskens recognised many but not all the names: Henrietta Street, Arguments Yard, Flowergate, East Pier, Cleveland Way.

The rest of the laptop was password protected.

Glancing at his watch, the Dutch policeman realised he had been in Shaveling's flat for nearly twenty minutes. Should he take the laptop? What might he learn from it that he did not already know?

His phone rang. A message from Ivanna Albu containing a list of names. He scrolled the list. A name leapt out. He replied immediately, asking her to get further information about the patient named A.Dunn. He then carried on to the end of the list. Towards the bottom he had an uneasy feeling that one of the other names should also be ringing alarm bells. But which one?

Suddenly his subconscious delivered the answer to a different question. Shaveling hadn't sent the report to the Royal College of Pathology because she was required to; she had sent it in order to protect herself. So the real question was who else had she sent it to?

CHAPTER 44

Scarborough & Whitby

Saturday, 19th November

Ivanna Albu hesitated. Her shift started in twenty minutes and, at the rate she was going, it might be the last shift she worked in an English hospital. She tried to persuade herself that what she was about to do was entirely proper; one of her patients had arrived at the hospital suffering from extreme muscle wastage and a mixture of other alarming symptoms and she, as a responsible doctor, was simply exploring possible causes of the patient's condition.

The trouble with that argument was that the patient herself, Hannah Morris, had been flown out of Scarborough just twenty-four hours after being admitted, nearly two weeks ago, on the instructions of wealthy parents who thought National Health Service hospitals were incapable of providing decent healthcare for their daughter. On the other hand there was no guarantee that any European doctors would be welcome in UK hospitals in a couple of years … Ivanna gritted her teeth and did what fifteen years working to save lives told her was the right course of action.

She logged on and accessed the files for Abigail Dunn. Date of birth: 10th August 1998. First visit to the renal unit in October 2013. A total of ten visits since that date. Ivanna felt a tingle down her spine as she read where the kidney and pancreas transplant had taken place. Not in Leeds or Sheffield but in Petroşani, Romania. To cover her tracks, Ivanna trawled through the data on the patient's weight, blood tests, drug regimen, stuff that she might claim was relevant to her search for information that might relate to Hannah's condition. It was wishful thinking, the best she could hope was that no-one noticed her search.

She took photos of everything and sent them to Muyskens. As she was closing files and windows Ivanna saw the original list of twenty-seven names of patients from the Whitby area. Like Muyskens she too had a disquieting feeling about the list, a suspicion that alarm bells should be ringing.

Muyskens stood beneath the whalebone arch, staring out across the harbour towards the church of St Mary on the hill, the cottages of Henrietta Street huddled beneath it like chicks gathered for protection beneath a mother hen. To his left, Captain James Cook's bronze eyes stared towards the horizon, and the outer piers of the harbour reached out like a crab's pincers, the yellow grey of the stone against the blue grey of the sea. He breathed deep the fresh air and wondered if, finally, he might be drawing closer to solving the mystery of his brother's death as well as closing a net around the perpetrators of the current spate of murders and abductions. He was at a crossroads; turn left and walk down Cleveland Way to confront Eric Dunn or walk into town to enlist the support of the local police.

Two gulls were fighting over pride of place on Captain James Cook's head. Some days you're the statue, some days you're the seagull. Muyskens decided that today he was the seagull and that the time had come to crap on the self-important Eric.

'Less than two hours ago I told you to fuck off. You're not welcome. We voted Leave. What makes you think anything has changed?' Eric's voice was muffled through the brown metal door.

The Dutch policeman noticed the lens set into the entry panel above the doorbell button. 'I can stand out here,' he shouted at the top of his voice, 'discussing your daughter's organ transplants with you and half of Whitby, or you can open the …'

The door swung open. 'Bastard,' Eric snarled, staring up and lunging forwards. He was quick but not quick enough.

For a tall man, Muyskens was very agile. He rolled back on his heels as the blade slashed the air, catching his jacket and snaring on the zip. Eric was pulled off balance and before he could steady himself Muyskens had his wrist in a vice-like grip.

'Drop it.'

Eric dropped his head and threw himself forward to headbutt the taller man in the belly. Again Muyskens rolled aside like a matador.

'I said drop it.' This time Muyskens' voice was firm as flint. He yanked down on Eric's wrist with such force that the door-man feared his arm had been dislocated at the shoulder.

Eric dropped the knife. Muyskens glanced around him; they were alone and unobserved. He pushed Eric back into the building, picked up the knife and stepped inside, closing the door behind him. Both men were breathing hard.

'Bastard.'

'Sit down. Legs apart, hands on your head,' Muyskens ordered. 'Right. You and I are going to have a talk.'

'No. We're not.'

'When did you first meet Thor Lupei?'

'You are so dead,' sneered Eric.

'How many people have you let him kill in order to protect your daughter? What about the victims and their families?'

Eric Dunn shook his head and kept his mouth shut. Muyskens sighed and adopted a different tack.

'Do you ever wake up in the night and wonder who he

killed in order to obtain the organs that keep your daughter Abigail alive?'

'People like you know nothing about suffering so don't throw your morality at me,' Eric muttered.

'On the contrary, Eric, I was twenty when my brother was found dead, in a skip at a music festival. They told my parents that he was a heroin addict; his body was so thin. But you and I know differently, don't we? It destroyed my family. How did Lupei find you? Did he murder to order or does he have human organs just sitting about, waiting for the highest bidder?' Muyskens studied Eric's face. 'These knives are illegal in the UK,' he observed, turning the blade over in his hand. 'OK, let me set out a scenario and we'll see how close I get to the truth. You daughter falls ill. She is referred by the doctor to the specialist kidney unit in Scarborough. You find out about waiting times for donor organs and you are frightened. Out of nowhere you are contacted by someone who offers you a solution. Transplant tourism. You are desperate, you say yes and catch a plane to Romania where you make a Faustian pact with the devil. How am I doing?'

Eric looked up, smiled and shook his head pityingly.

'Even in Romania kidney transplants are not free,' Muyskens continued regardless. 'Fifteen thousand euros? Twenty five thousand?'

'In case you haven't noticed you are in England. We have our own currency.'

'Forgive me. So what shall we say: twenty thousand pounds? A lot of money. You could buy a good car for that kind of money. Or a very very nice holiday.'

Eric says nothing.

'But you don't care about a new car. You care about your daughter. Trouble is you don't have twenty thousand pounds. And the wait for a free kidney from your wonderful National Health Service is just too long. Because the extra £350 million pounds a week you were going to get from Brexit was all a lie, wasn't it?'

'Fuck off.'

'So, here's the deal,' Muyskens said. 'She can have her kidney, and a new pancreas, for free or almost free as long as you are prepared to help Thor Lupei in his charitable work. You help to ensure he is invited to Whitby to play at the Goth festival, which isn't that hard because who wouldn't want a Goth superstar playing in their town, eh? And then while he is here you help him pick his victims. A menu, you could call it. I'll have two liver stroganofs, a large kidney pie … Do people eat pancreas? In a sausage perhaps with …'

'You're a sick bastard,' Eric observed.

'Perhaps. But you helped him choose the victims and then set them up. Did you knock them out or lock them in a room for him to collect when he was ready? Either way you are an accessory, Eric.'

'And you're a foreigner breaking the law. This is England not the Netherlands so bugger off back to your miserable little country before I set police on you.'

'What did the hospital say when you showed up in Scarborough with your daughter and someone else's internal organs? Romanian transplants must be risky low quality affairs, prone to infections. It's practically the third world. Not like your glorious NHS kidneys. Did they put her in quarantine?'

'The transplants were perfect. Still are. No rejection, no relapses. Nothing. '

'I'm impressed. Did no-one pick you up on where the operation took place?'

Eric's eyes narrowed.

'The hospital in Petroşani doesn't perform transplants,' Muyskens said lightly.

'Liar.'

'You just picked the nearest town to where the operation

actually took place and hoped for the best, didn't you? The trouble is that Petroşani is too small, not much bigger than a village.'

'You think you're so fucking clever,' Eric snarled. 'The bigger they are the harder they fall, Gouda Boy. You'll be lucky to make it out of Whitby alive.'

Muyskens had what he wanted. He left Eric bound and gagged in a shower cubicle backstage. There was no way of physically locking the door so Muyskens just had to hope no-one ventured backstage for a few hours.

He left via the stairs that led up to the main hall. He waved at Jaz, the robot mermaid, who was posing for a photo with someone who looked like Sponge Bob Square Pants in a Star Trek uniform, and headed outside. There wasn't much time; Stir the hornets' nest and the stings are already on their way, as the old Dutch proverb said.

He rang Ivanna but her mobile was switched off, she was on shift. He typed a text and pressed send but his phone did not confirm whether or not the message had been sent.

It was time to contact the local police. Muyskens was on someone else's patch and sooner or later there would be trouble if he didn't show respect. He was loath to walk into the police station, given what he had heard; the alternative was a discrete word with the man at the top. He walked back across town towards the station to find a taxi.

CHAPTER 45

Daniel Murray

I don't know how many times I woke up in that box. Ten times? Twenty times? There was no way of knowing because I lost all sense of when, where and how long. Eventually, the ravenous hunger that had so gripped me faded but my body remained paralysed.

In all that time my eyes saw practically nothing because there was nothing to see. Only very occasionally would I awake to the darkest lacklight, soft like the black that nestles inside a car tyre. I had already decided that small air holes must perforate my coffin, for otherwise I would long ago have suffocated; and I concluded that these same hidden holes must permit a few random photons to sneak through.

Only my nose and ears seemed unaffected by my condition. Neither brought me anything of value. On one occasion I came round and was instantly overpowered by the acrid stench of urine. My own no doubt. If there had been food in my stomach I would have retched, but it was a long time since I had eaten and I couldn't have choked to death on my own vomit even if I wished it on myself.

The sound of my breathing frightened me. For a while the asthmatic wheeze of my lungs had been concealed beneath engine and tyre noise. When those sounds stopped I heard again the haunting groans and cries of what I took to be victims in other boxes until, one by one, they faded and I was alone. In my isolation each and every breath became invested with unbearable meaning and intensity, on the one hand providing the proof that I was alive and, on the other, reminding me that I was trapped. With nothing else to occupy my senses, my grip on reality slipped and I became convinced that every hint of an obstruction in my airwaves was the proof that I was about to die. The more I worried I grew, the more chaotic my breathing became.

For all those reasons, whenever I awoke I prayed that I might immediately fall unconscious again.

But this time it was different. Something had changed. This time a current of air was brushing my cheek and the heavy scent of flowers tickled my nostrils. The smell of urine had gone and the rise and fall of my breathing was no longer resonating in my ears. I lay there, eyes closed, certain that I must be hallucinating but desperate not to break the spell. Memories tumbled pell-mell: the storm on Whitby Pier, my school prom, staring at Tiffany across the counter of the fish and chip shop, mum teaching me to tie my shoelaces, climbing into Lupei's black Routemaster double decker bus.

The little voice in my head kept needling away; if I was not in the black plastic coffin then where was I?

The cry of a wild animal ripped the air.

I flinched.

I flinched! My body had moved! I was overwhelmed with waves of fear and ecstasy. If my muscles could move autonomically then just maybe I might be able to move them by an effort of will. Maybe I was more than a consciousness sealed in the oubliette of an unresponsive corpse.

I had forgotten how to move and struggled to believe what my nerves were telling me; my fingertips were flexing back and forth against a surface that was at once soft and taut. My hands could move from side to side but not up and down. Was I simply too weak or was something restraining me? It was time to see. My eyes had been closed for so long that they were gummed with sleep. The stabbing pain in my eyelids as I tried to open them was so intense that an involuntary groan caught in my throat. Would I tear my lids apart if I persisted? For once self-pity came to my rescue and, as I started to cry, my tears dissolved the cemented wall of sleep.

When my vision came into focus I saw a darkly patterned fabric hanging above me in the gloom. Was I in a tent? Turning my head or, more accurately, letting the weight of my head fall to the left, my face disappeared into soft fabric. A pillow?

A pillow!

I was in or on a bed. It was night. Close by curtains trailed from the ceiling to the ground, billowing languorously in an invisible current of air. Behind them lay an open window through which came such little light as there was in the room.

My breathing was slow and measured. I felt as yet no fear, only curiosity. From far away, as if I were observing myself from a great distance, I understood that fear would come soon enough. The monochromatic world of shadows before my eyes included a wall covered in a pattern of intersecting lines. Not regular enough to be wallpaper. Stone blocks perhaps? On the wall hung a large painting without a frame, a tapestry showing three deer grazing in a woodland glade. Tall vertical poles flanked the periphery of my vision; I was in a four-poster bed.

The animal cry repeated and this time I decided that it might be a bird. As my senses sharpened, my mind cleared. Fragmented memories rose to the surface: dead bodies in a barn, a lurking evil, a skull in a fire, a friend pushing me over as he rushed past me, a barking dog, a short fat man leering over me as I lay paralysed. The man's name was Eric and I was angry.

I attempted to sit up and felt a pressure holding me back. My hands and arms could only move from side to side. I wasn't on a bed, I was in the bed; tucked in and so weak that I could barely move my arms. The sheet worked free a few millimetres at a time as I kept my eyes fixed on the billowing curtain, determined to reach the window and see the view beyond. After what felt like an hour but was probably only a few minutes the sheet was sufficiently loose for me to roll onto my side, though my legs were of little help. How tired my body had become; was it days or weeks that I had spent in the box?

Panting from my exertions, I heard a new sound and held my breath to hear better. Music. The sound of an electric guitar playing the blues. My kind of music. The notes were drowning in echo as if the music were being made in a huge space far away. Where was I? Who had put me in this bed? Who had washed me and put me in pyjamas?

Abruptly the music stopped, to be replaced by a blood-curdling scream followed by a peal of uncontrolled laughter. In that moment my focus sharpened; I was not in a hotel, I was not a guest, I was not safe. I was a prisoner.

Gripping the side of the bed I wriggled myself up into a sitting position. The room, much of which lay in deep shadow, was large. Two windows, two doors. Silhouetted against a wall were various massive pieces of furniture and a large portrait.

A sudden surge of terror about my belly. I struggled franti-cally with the bedclothes, desperate to see what had happened to me. My belly looked normal. Had the feeling of bloatedness been another hallucination? The sooner I reached the window the better. I swung my legs round to stand up.

Only my legs didn't swing.

I tried a second time. Nothing. I reached my hand out to feel my thigh and gasped in horror. Beneath the pyjama fabric was only a sagging sack of skin, a bunch of tendons as thin as electric cables and a bone. Was I a scravir? Dizzy and in shock I passed out.

Fade out, fade in. Fear and anger swirled in equal measure. No-one was going to stop me from opening the curtains. Avoiding my legs, repulsed by what I had felt, I gently probed my upper body through my pyjamas. While I had lost weight, my arms and chest still carried muscle, as did my back. I still had a butt, though so much reduced that my fingers could trace the contours of my pelvis, as if I were touching an Egyptian mummy.

Get a grip. You don't have time for this.

Hauling myself to the edge of the bed, I orchestrated a fall. The sound of my empty legs hitting the floor was even uglier than the shooting pain that flooded my brain as my wasted knees clapped together, pinching the nerves. With gritted teeth I dragged myself across the floor with my hands; pulling the dead weight of my legs behind me. A rug had broken my fall. Beyond the rug, the hard stone floor was warm to the touch. It must have taken me five minutes or more to cross maybe as many metres of floor. When I reached the far wall I did not pause to catch my breath. Instead, I grabbed a curtain and pulled myself up into a sitting position then climbed hand over hand up the curtain, my entire weight carried in my fists, to drag myself to my feet. Sweat pouring down my back, I had nearly accomplished this challenge when the curtain rail buckled away from the wall and the fabric ripped and I fell back heavily beneath a tumbling pile of cloth.

I was lying there prone like a parachutist caught under his collapsed chute, swearing and wriggling, when hands grabbed me.

'Bastard.'

'Yes, you've said that.' Lupei looked at me thoughtfully. 'Daniel, Daniel. How can I explain? Circumstances. Even the very best laid plans … Hate me if you must, but for the right reasons.' He turned towards the door. 'Move him closer to the fire.'

The candlelit hall was vast and I now understood that I was in a castle. I had been dressed in my own clothes, the clothes

I had been wearing when I was kidnapped. A tall skinny man wearing only shorts and a tatty t-shirt stepped into the light. A scravir.

'The night is chill,' Lupei told me, his brow knotted with concern for my wellbeing.

I remembered the first time I had heard him use those words, the night his black double decker bus had stopped alongside me as I trudged along a rainswept Hawsker Lane.

The scravir's hands were at my back, pushing my wheelchair towards a fireplace wide enough to roast an ox.

'You see, Daniel, someone killed my merry band and, in doing so, threatened to turn a good weekend's work into an unmitigated disaster.'

The scravir positioned my chair and headed back the way he had come. I noticed that the wheelchair had only small wheels at each corner; I was not expected to be propelling myself around. As the scravir passed Lupei, the lord of the manor swung a mighty blow across his back, sending him sprawling across the floor.

'If it is a bastard you are seeking, Daniel, vent your fury on this man. He is to blame for everything. If he had not followed me to Whitby and brought destruction to Farview Farm you would not be in your reduced circumstances.'

As the scravir picked himself off the floor I saw the framework encasing his arm. It was none other than Emile Noir. If Noir recognised me he gave no sign of having done so. Was he sentient or was his mind in servitude like his body; little more than a zombie? What did Lupei's dark magic actually do to his victims? I did my best to keep my face blank; allowing Lupei to realise that I knew Noir would not be to my advantage.

'And now he is atoning for his crime,' Lupei continued, 'He had accomplices, including a mad woman who pursued me all the way to the ferry. You may have spotted her in Whitby.'

'I doubt it,'

'She wore a wedding dress. More in hope than expectation I fear.' Lupei flashed me one of his widest coat hanger smiles, evidently pleased with his wit. 'A local girl, from this region, who blabbed something deeply ill-informed about my having killed a relative of hers. They are quick to blame others for all their misfortunes in these parts. Ignorant and superstitious. In fact I do believe that …'

'Where's Alex?' I asked.

Lupei tilted his head, as predators do when calculating distances to a kill, his white hair falling like a curtain to frame his pale face. The orange light of the fire twinkled in his eyes.

'Do you like the blues?' he asked.

'Where's Alex?'

Lupei studied me a moment more, his expression a curious mix of cruelty and compassion. 'Let me show you something,' he said, clicking his fingers and standing up.

Noir stepped forward from the shadows. Lupei had already reached the doors by the time Noir had grabbed the back of my wheelchair.

The high doors of the great hall opened onto an equally grand entrance hall complete with suits of armour, the stuffed heads of stags and more exotic wildlife and a large clock that chimed six thirty as we approached. Less traditional was the row of guitars hanging like portraits in the stairwell. Lupei strode to the front door and threw it open. A bitter blast of cold air heavy with snowflakes swept in from outside. A high wall was visible some distance away, beyond the empty branches of a tall tree. An owl fell forward from the largest bough and flew away on silent wings. Snow lay thick on the ground

'Hm. We'll use the tunnel.' Lupei closed the door.

The wall ahead of us opened to reveal a lift that took us down to a passage carved out of solid rock. This passage was lined with several rows of framed photographs showing Thor Lupei standing beside a succession of people. Men in suits, women with expensive hair, young couples, beside a lake, in a hospital room, outside a castle, on a cruise ship. A child in a wheelchair held the hand of a middle-aged woman. While the child and Lupei stared into the lens, the woman only had eyes for Lupei, her face consumed with gratitude.

At the end of the passage, Noir reversed my wheelchair into the waiting lift. The doors closed and when they reopened I was wheeled out. I had expected the unexpected but I was still totally unprepared for the scene in front of me.

CHAPTER 46

Eskdale - Gert Muyskens

Saturday, 19th November

It was a large Victorian house with a large conservatory or greenhouse at one end and surrounded by an expanse of meticulously striped lawn. A large black Range Rover was parked in front of the double garage. Muyskens' shoes crunched on the gravel as he walked towards the front door, having paid the taxi driver, a large-faced man with sad brown eyes, a substantial tip to wait for him. The Dutch man climbed the stone steps, knocked three times using the large lion's head brass doorknocker, and turned to inspect the view.

The house was secluded and perched near the top of the hill with a magnificent view toward Whitby and the sea. Beneath him was the expansive pine forest through which the taxi had driven. Did the entire forest belong to the house?

'This is private property. What do you want?'

Muyskens turned to find a man almost as tall as himself, thickset, with black hair and gold-framed glasses. He exuded authority and was dressed in a tweed sports jacket, checked shirt, club tie and jodhpurs as if he had just returned from a fox hunt.

'Chief Inspector Rawes?'

'I know who I am. Who the hell are you?'

'Gert Muyskens. Rotterdam police. I was hoping …'

'I were expecting you.' The scowl softened. 'Come in.'

They were served tea and scones in the conservatory cum

greenhouse by a woman in a white apron.

'Brenda leaves in twenty minutes so you arrived just in time,' Rawes confided in Muyskens as the housemaid left. 'She works shorter hours at weekends.' Rawes spread cream and jam on a scone then left it uneaten on his plate. He put his hands together and pressed his fingertips against his lips, as if in prayer. 'So, let's start by you telling me why you are breaking every rule in the book, turning up on my patch as a foreign bobby and conducting an investigation without having the decency to talk with me first.'

'Three bodies on the Hull Rotterdam ferry,' Muyskens answered, taking a bite from his scone, 'and a trail that leads back to Whitby.'

'That doesn't answer the question.'

'Our early leads include a number of lurid stories and claims, some involving your officers. I am long in the tooth, Chief Inspector. I have learned that it is better to do a little homework before jumping in with wild accusations. And that starts with an informal look around. I believe you would do the same.'

Rawes nodded. 'Fair enough. Walk me through what you've got.'

Muyskens outlined his investigation, taking care to avoid names and references to the supernatural. He spoke of the deaths associated with music festivals, going back many years and in countries across Europe. Emaciated victims, usually written off as junkies. The condition of the body found on the ferry, a woman in her forties who had about her person a weekend pass to the Whitby Goth festival.

Throughout Muyskens' explanation, the chief inspector waved the Dutch policeman on sporadically, ate three scones and sipped his tea, but said nothing.

'I had hoped to speak with the forensic pathologist, Nigela Shaveling, but I understand she may have gone missing. Lastly, in the course of informal interviews, a number of witnesses have suggested that one or more members of your police force might be implicated in a cover up,' Muyskens concluded. 'And that is why I am here.'

David Rawes got to his feet and crossed over to the vast window overlooking the garden. He stood with his back to the Dutch policeman, staring at a group of sparrows squabbling on the bird table. In the distance the sea was just visible.

'Been here four years and I never tire of that view.' A pause. 'Well I'll say this, you have at least managed to present an interpretation of events that does not draw on Dracula, vampires and Old Mother Shipton's ghost.' Rawes turned towards Muyskens. 'You would not believe the crap I have to listen to in this town. Whitby is drowning in mumbo jumbo. Gothic horror is our main industry, since fishing went tits up, and I'm surrounded by halfwits willing to regurgitate all manner of crap. My job is to hold the line and keep a slim grip on reality.'

Rawes crossed back to his chair and sat down. 'I'm not being funny like, it's a bloody illness. Shaveling is a case in point. The woman is a forensic pathologist for fuck's sake, a scientist, a defender of reason and rationality in a complicated world.' He shook his head sadly. 'On the Saturday, when my staff were dealing with town centre packed with tourists and visitors dressed as ghouls, vampires, steam punks, zombies, human bloody skeletons and god knows what else, all drunk as farts, all clambering over tombstones in churchyards … when all that is going on I've Shaveling going native and rabbiting on about stolen organs and supernatural mumbo jumbo that belongs in a frigging comic. Now if there's a designer drug doing the rounds that we all need to know about, an ugly but rational explanation for the mayhem, then you can count me in. We are here to protect the public, you and I. I'm a common man Mr Muyskens and I deal in common sense, so if you can produce the evidence for a simple crime committed by an ordinary human being, even if it involves one or more of my own officers, I'll smother you in bloody kisses, Lad. There's always a risk of rotten apples and I pride myself on a clean ship, so here's what we do. Give me your report.'

'I haven't produced one yet.'

'OK.' Rawes produced a scrap of paper on which he scribbled. 'You go back to your hotel, produce your report, and send it to me at this email address. That way we keep it away from the station, to be on the safe side. I appreciate your coming round to see me. I take it I can reach you in Rotterdam?'

'Yes, of course, and thank you.' Muyskens stood up.

Rawes led Muyskens back through the house towards the front door. The telephone in the hall rested on a small mahogany table on which there was also two photographs of Rawes and a short woman. In the first they were arm in arm on the hill overlooking Whitby harbour. Rawes was every inch the square-jawed man, thick-framed glasses and a face used to barking orders while, beneath her flame red hair, the woman leaning on his arm had the face of someone who was perpetually sorry to be so much trouble. In the second they were standing in a formal garden.

'Your wife?' Muyskens asked.

Rawes nodded.

'Beautiful photo,' Muyskens observed.

'Hampton Court. Took Susan there in June. Imagine running a place like that. Lovely, except for those damn parakeets. Swarms of them. Should all be shot but you know how tree-huggers and bloody liberals start whinging. Like everything else in this country, going tits up because of foreigners. Still, we soon kiss goodbye to Brussels … Can't wait. No offence.'

'None taken,' Muyskens smiled genially. 'And Whitby is a beautiful town. At home everything is so flat.'

'Except the beer. Bit gaseous for my taste. Went cycling in your neck of the woods once.' Rawes opened the front door.

The taxi was still waiting.

'For cycling it is good,' Muyskens agreed, crossing the threshold. 'By the way, Chief Inspector, do you know an Eric Dunn?'

Rawes shook his head.

'The door manager at the Whitby Pavilion,' Muyskens continued. 'He pulled a knife on me this morning. It might be worth rattling his cage.'

'Put it all in the report. By the way, which way did taxi bring you?'

'Through a village on a hill. Alby?'

'Aislaby. Got you. Tell him to turn right at the gate. It's the scenic route; fabulous views overlooking the Esk. Won't take you any longer and, for a man who likes his scenery, it's well worth the trouble.'

'Sounds good.'

Rawes stood on his stone step; whether out of politeness or to ensure that the Dutch policeman left his property, Muyskens was unclear. As the taxi's tyres crunched along the gravel, Muyskens took one last look at the house. Rawes had a mobile phone pressed to his ear. Two crows landed on the lawn. Quarter to four, the sun was about to disappear.

CHAPTER 47

Scarborough - Ivanna Albu

Saturday, 19th November

Ivanna had finally got ten minutes to herself; the afternoon rush was over, a quick break before the evening shift began. She checked her phone and found Muyskens' message about going to see the head of the Whitby police, following up on Tiffany's belief that there might be corrupt local police officers.

Something was still bugging her about the list she had obtained earlier from the renal unit and Muyskens's message only exacerbated her anxiety. She sat down in a quiet corner of the cafeteria and unfolded the papers that she had tucked into her trouser pocket.

The list appeared like any other collection of random names and she wondered if she had simply been spooked by the situation, alone in the renal unit and anxious that someone might stumble in and find her there. Young, old, male, female … kidney failure could strike anyone at any time of life.

Atkinson, Bowman, Coldfoot, Cook, Cox, Dunn, Dudek, Fox, Galloway, Guerin, Heath, Layton, Lowther, Maroulis, Moore, Nixon, Ogleby, Oliver, Packington, Postgate, Prosper, Qalat, Rawlings, Smurthwaite, Snaith, Tuft, Walker.

All but four had been operated on in Yorkshire, at Leeds or Sheffield and referred to the renal unit. Of the four that remained, three had been attending the unit regularly. The fourth had attended only once, back in 2013. Was that significant? She would have to look deeper into the file to find out.

She had refolded the papers and was stuffing them back in her pockets when she realised what had been bugging her. She ran all the way back to the renal unit. If she was right the situation could be even more dangerous than she had feared.

She drummed her fingers impatiently on the desk, why did computers take so long to come out of sleep mode? Fifty seconds later she had retrieved the database and was selecting one of the twenty seven names.

10th October 2013. Arrived with a male, late fifties. She gave her name hesitantly and the couple appeared agitated. Patient complained of dizziness and loss of appetite. Doctor's address listed at Harley Street. Patient explained that her transplants (kidney and spleen) had taken place two months earlier in Europe. Declined to say in which country. Papers presented at visit were deemed inadequate and a second appointment was booked for 14th October to allow patient to find paperwork. Patient never returned. Investigation showed doctor's details to be false, as were all other contact details.

Case closed 10th November 2013.

The patient's declared name was Rawling. Ivanna had read that when people gave a false name they often did so midstream; they would start giving their real name then change their minds and modify their answer. Ivanna left the renal unit. She checked her watch; she was back on shift in five minutes. If she hurried she had just about enough time to go online and trawl through the old news stories on the Whitby Gazette; if her hunch was correct then Muyskens might be in real danger.

CHAPTER 48

Eskdale - Gert Muyskens

Saturday, 19th November

The cloud cover had broken and the last orange rays of a setting sun were piercing the gloom of the forest and strobing in the conifers as the taxi followed the single track road. Rawes was right; the view was spectacular. Thirty metres below the level of the road, the river Esk was visible through the trees, its surface bright as polished gold.

Muyskens was reasonably satisfied with the meeting. That Rawes had clearly failed to spot the darker evil elements of what had been happening in his own town the weekend of the Goth festival was no great surprise; as the man said it was his job to keep his head while others lost theirs and, in his place, Muyskens would have fought just as hard to prevent the crimes from being explained in terms of the supernatural. The Chief Inspector was pompous and over-interested in status, an occupational hazard among senior ranks in Muyskens' book, but he seemed straightforward and down to earth, and both qualities would be needed in the days ahead.

Muyskens checked that his phone had uploaded all the audio files of his conversations with Eric Dunn and David Rawes to the cloud; new technology was so much easier than taking detailed notes, and less obtrusive.

The jolt threw the phone from his hand as the driver slammed his brakes, bringing the car to a juddering halt. Directly ahead, a tractor was heading towards them, filling the entire width of the track, seemingly oblivious to the presence of the taxi.

The driver was shouting and pumping his horn as he looked around for somewhere to move the vehicle. The tractor kept on coming, its cabin too high above the taxi to see the face of the person behind the wheel. Throwing the taxi into reverse, the driver lurched backwards up the track, engine screaming as the car veered dangerously from side to side. With the trees less than a metre from the track on either side of the road and with a thirty-metre drop to the river on one side, it was imperative that they find a passing point.

Suddenly the tractor's full beam headlights were on, flooding the inside of the taxi with bright light. Moments later the weights at the front of the tractor slammed into the bonnet of the reversing car, causing the metal to buckle and bend. Inside the taxi, the driver and Muyskens were rattled about like stones in a tin. Eyes wide, the taxi driver stared over his shoulder, past the Dutch policeman, and through the rear windscreen back up the track, desperately steering the car to safety. Muyskens had retrieved his phone from the floor and was calculating his chances of survival if he threw himself out of the moving car, when the tractor hit again. This time the tractor was moving too quickly for the taxi to back away. Engine screaming, wheels spinning, the taxi was no longer under the control of its driver. A rear tyre left the track as the back of the car started to judder over the rough stones of the verge. A glancing blow against a sapling, then another. The eardrum-wincing squeal of wood against buckling metal as branches scraped the full length of the car. A slight change in the light announced a break in the trees. The tractor driver threw his steering wheel to the right, causing the taxi to spin out of control. The rear of the vehicle left the road and tipped back onto the steep slope. With a further nudge from the tractor, the car was sliding backwards, picking up speed as it clattered over rocks, hurtling down towards the river Esk in the valley below.

Glancing up, Muyskens noted that the tractor had come to a halt and that the driver's face was pressed against the window staring at him. Five seconds later the taxi reached the end of the slope and dropped three metres through the air before landing on its roof in the icy waters of the River Esk. The wheels spun for a few seconds then stopped. Gurgling gently, the water continued on its way towards the sea, the upturned car of no more significance than a large rock. A robin landed briefly on one of the tyres then flew off towards the forest.

Hidden in the trees high above the river, the tractor continued on its way as if nothing had happened.

CHAPTER 49

Micăbrukóczi, Daniel Murray

Saturday, 19th November

If we were still in the castle then I saw no sign of it. The large room, bathed in pools of subdued and coloured lighting, was unashamedly modern, with contemporary furniture and tall potted plants, a temple to Scandi-minimalism. At the far end of the room was a long and wide window that looked into a second room. Emile Noir let go of my wheelchair and Lupei himself took charge of pushing me across the room.

'I need a doctor soooo bad,' he sang a blues gently under his breath.

He positioned my wheelchair directly in front of the action.

'It is a one way window,' he explained. 'They cannot see you. Prevents distractions.'

Through the glass, a team of six dressed in gowns and face-masks were gathered around an operating table. Lights flashed on high tech machines. The vital signs of the patient – blood pressure, respiratory rate, pulse, temperature, oxygen saturation, etc. - were being traced over and over on a couple of computer monitors that hung from the ceiling. The figure on the operating table looked to be just a child.

'Eleven years old,' Lupei said softly, second-guessing my thoughts. 'She only had a few weeks to live. Thanks to you, Daniel, her life can go on.'

I turned toward him, confused.

'You have saved a dozen people over the past two days,'

Lupei continued, 'and will have helped five more by the time the surgeon has finished.'

'I don't understand.'

'You were strong as an ox, Daniel. You and your friend Alex saved the day when all hope was lost. The gifts you nurtured on our difficult journey are what is bringing new life to people like little Krysta here.'

'Where is Alex?'

'He is fine, you will see him soon enough. Like you he has some thinking to do, and he needs to recover his strength. Come, let me show you something.' Lupei tapped the glass as he spoke and the window turned opaque.

He wheeled me towards another part of the room. As we approached, a display screen lit up within the wall ahead of us. The screen showed the operating theatre behind us.

'This was taken three days ago,' Lupei explained.

There was no sound on the video clip. At first my eyes were focused on Lupei. Like the rest of the team he was wearing green scrubs, including a facemask and a hat that covered his long white hair, but his pink eyes were unmistakeable and he was a head taller than anyone else in the room. Around him the theatre team, what could be the same team who were conducting the operation behind the opaque glass at the other end of the room, were as busy as ants in a nest; attaching monitoring electrodes to the patient, positioning equipment and confirming checklists. Finally I noticed, in the middle of all this activity, the patient lying on the operating table; I could not see the face or even identify the gender. From the monitors in the background of the shot, I could see the patient was breathing and had a heartbeat; presumably asleep.

Satisfied that everything was ready, the person I took to be the surgeon, a fat man with very bushy eyebrows, turned towards Lupei and nodded. Beside him, two other members of the team manoeuvred a motorised cupboard on wheels into position. It carried what looked like a shallow Perspex or plastic tank which appeared to contain water. Lupei stepped in front of the surgeon, placed his open right hand on the unconscious patient and his left just above the Perspex tray. His eyelids fluttered as he stood quite still, as if in prayer. I sensed that everyone around him was waiting as the seconds ticked past. The timecode on the screen showed fifty seconds had elapsed when Lupei arched his head back and appeared to breath in. As he did so, the feet of the patient on the operating table flinched. Was the patient alert and aware of what was happening to him or her? Slowly Lupei's head rolled forward and, as it did so, his left hand shuddered and blood began to trickle then pour from his palm. I forgot I was sitting in a wheelchair with wasted legs and a headache the size of a walrus. I forgot I was Lupei's prisoner, held captive in a castle that could be anywhere. I forgot everything as, in horror and dark fascination, I watched matter pouring from his left hand and beginning to congeal in the Perspex tray, as if Lupei were some kind of living 3D printer.

Something resembling a shiny and slippery brown fish or an amphibian without legs was growing in the tray. Then suddenly it was done and Lupei's hand moved to the side. He arched his head back a second time and the process began all over again.

By the time he re-opened his eyes some ten minutes had passed, according to the timecode on the screen, and in the tray were seven objects. The patient, who was still hidden from view, flinched or twitched twice more over that ten minute period. Of the seven objects, five resembled each other. The last two items, though similar in colour, looked more irregular in form. I decided that they could not be living creatures because, except when directly under Lupei's hand, they did not move of their own accord. Were they parts of a body? Was Lupei ridding someone of cancerous growths? How and why were men and women of science, people with medical training, associating themselves with this bizarre and malevolent activity?

His job done, Lupei nodded to the surgeon and stepped back from the operating table. The operating theatre staff moved forward and busied themselves around the patient. A nurse moved the motorised cupboard away to the far end of the room. The surgeon also moved away and the patient was turned round towards the two exit doors to be wheeled out of theatre.

It was then that I began screaming.

The body on the operating table was me.

Instinctively my hands went to my belly, terrified of what I might find. Was I bandaged? Was my skin studded with staples? Had I ripped myself open tumbling out of bed? I raised my hands to my face expecting them to be covered in blood.

Lupei's hand grabbed my shoulder from behind. I tried to wriggle free but he was too strong for me.

'Calm down, Daniel,' Lupei said softly in his rich baritone. 'All is well. Instead of fear you should feel intense pride. Your body has saved the bodies of others. This is my body, which is given to you. Do this in remembrance of me.'

I knew those words, I had been to Sunday school when I was a child. 'No. No,' I shouted. 'This has nothing to do with the bible. This is evil. Pure evil.'

'Saving lives is evil?' Lupei countered, spinning my wheelchair round so he could look me in the eye. 'Come now. You have brought the gift of life to those on the brink of death. Do you have any idea how desperate is the need for organ transplants?'

'That's what I felt inside me on the bus, isn't it? Darren, Hannah, the dead bodies on the streets of Whitby; you don't save people, you kill them and then somehow injected their organs into me. You used me to get at my friends. You are a monster not a saint.'

Lupei stood there, taking the insults and saying nothing. Which really wound me up.

'And when you aren't killing people you're torturing them. What have you done to my legs? And the members of your band? And the man who pushed my wheelchair? How many have you tortured?'

I stopped, gasping for breath, my body tired and weak, my voice hoarse from shouting.

'May I speak?' Lupei said softly.

I glowered, like he needed my permission to do anything he wanted.

'I have carried a burden for many years, my young friend. More years than you can imagine. When I started barely literate physicians were relieving migraines by trepanning their patients, and haemorrhoids were cured by the administration of red hot irons. People barely understood what a kidney was, never mind what it did.'

'That's rubbish, you're talking about the Middle Ages not the modern world.

'Indeed I am,' he replied, looking me in the eye and letting his words sink in. 'Very perceptive of you. And now the problem is not ignorance but a shortage of donors.'

'So you kill one bunch of people to provide another bunch of people, rich people presumably, with new organs.'

'Crudely put but broadly speaking correct.'

'Who are you to play God?'

'Is God willing to play God?' Lupei asked. 'So much misery and suffering and where is he?'

'Hospitals don't kill people who donate a kidney,' I said.

Lupei stood before me, his face beaming like that of a proud parent at a school open day.

'I knew I was right selecting you, Daniel. Forgive my

failings. Too long I have been unopposed and alone, a sad creature belonging to a different darker age, governed by dark urges. Save me from that violence that haunts me.'

The conversation was doing my head in. I was confused and weak and he sensed that.

'I can return the strength to your legs and teach you the arcane mysteries my kind has protected through the ages. Join me and help me use this power for good.'

Lupei stepped past me, grabbed my wheelchair from behind and turned me round, away from the screen and towards the large window, which he tapped with his index finger. The glass turned from opaque to transparent. The operation was finishing, the surgeon was at one end of the room, preparing to leave. Other theatre staff were moving equipment around in order to wheel the patient out. The girl's face was so small. I remembered what it was like arriving at secondary school. However tough my life had been it was nothing compared with the difficulties this girl was living through.

'You are tired,' Lupei said quietly. 'When you are rested we can chat again and I will introduce you to the team.'

The door opened and the skeletal form of Emile Noir entered the room, his face blank and pale as a raw crumpet.

'Take Mr Murray back to his room,' Lupei ordered.

Noir approached head bowed. Was he conscious? Did becoming a scravir destroy the brain? Lupei left the room through another door as Noir wheeled me back the way we had come. Back in the great hall the wood panelling on one wall slid back to reveal another lift. Emerging from the lift, the wheels of my chair made no noise as we followed the corridor and stopped in front of a solid and ornate hardwood door. Noir produced a key. I was back where I had woken up.

'Emile, can you hear me? It's me, Daniel,' I whispered as he wheeled me into the room.

Nothing. I tried a different tack.

'Turn my chair,' I ordered.

My wheelchair was duly turned towards the bed.

'Come here where I can see you.'

His hands loosened their grip on the chair and he shuffled into view.

'Look at me. Can you hear me? I need your help.'

As if fighting a war with himself, Emile Noir slowly lifted his head but he would not or could not look at me.

'Do you remember? We met in Whitby.'

The muscles of Noir's face crawled beneath the thin waxy skin. His jaw clenched and unclenched. Was he trying to speak? It was as if his lips were sewn together. A frown of concentration flickered on his brow as he made a small guttural sound somewhere deep in his throat. His arms shook slightly and the sinews of his scrawny neck tightened. Finally, he managed to glance at me for maybe half a second though I saw immediately that the act of doing so was causing him great pain.

'It's OK,' I said softly. 'Forget I said anything.'

The tension dropped visibly from his shoulders as he turned away,

An animal cry outside. The owl again?

'Stop,' I called. 'I need you to move my chair.'

Noir stopped.

'I want to be by the window.'

He rolled my chair across the room then went to close the window.

'No, it's fine as it is. I want it open. You can leave now.'

He left. The key turned in the lock and I was alone. For a while I sat there lost in thought. In spite of everything I was in awe of Lupei; his power and charisma, his intelligence and artistry. All those qualities we all wish we had, or I wished I had. When Lupei spoke people listened. And he was offering me the chance to be part of it. Maybe he was right, maybe I could change him. There was evil and darkness in his method, but maybe the evil could be brought under control.

I didn't know much about science but I had heard of organ transplants and how transplant patients had to take drugs for the rest of their lives to stop their bodies rejecting the organs they had been given. And yet I survived for days with the organs of six people inside me, maybe more. What was the secret? Could I be the person who helped to revolutionise medicine?

Looking back now, I have a clarity that eluded me then and I can see the insanity that had gripped me. But then, as much as I hated Lupei for what he had done to my legs, and the misery he had caused my friends, and for what had happened to Emile Noir, I also sensed the opportunity before me. The chance to be someone.

The owl cry. So close this time. As if nature herself were beckoning me to embrace what I might become.

From my sitting position I pulled the curtains aside. I was too low to be able to see anything but, grabbing the casement stays at the bottom of the windows I was able to haul myself up until, finally I could peer out into the darkness.

As a Londoner, I was used to night skies that were never darker than orange. Even at Farview Farm, the sky to the north had been bright with the light pollution of Whitby. But here, wherever I was, fat snowflakes tumbled from a black sky. The windowsill was deep in snow and, way below, the castle grounds were also cloaked in a thick carpet of white.

I let the curtain fall into place behind my back and, as my eyes adjusted to the light, I saw that I was wrong. What I had taken for night sky was, in fact, a tree-covered mountain lying in deep shadow. High above me, above the distant serrated treeline, a blanket of dark cloud arched over the valley and the castle crouching by the skirts of the pine forest.

The casement stays squealed as I pushed the windows further open. Powdered snow fell into the room. It appeared that

I was three or four storeys up, though it was hard to be sure because the windows were set into a steeply sloping roof and I could not see the ground directly below me. The frost breeze swooped in like a wraith over a cemetery. I breathed deep the fresh mountain air and the distant howling of wolves and, in spite of the perilous nature of my situation, I felt alive.

There was another sound, a manmade noise that grew steadily. The trees across the valley became lit up in harsh white light; a vehicle was approaching. The castle gates opened and a black limousine swept inside, it's headlights swinging in a wide arc to reveal stone battlements, a row of parked cars, various outbuildings, and the huge tree from which the owl had flown. The driver parked out of view from my window and cut the engine. The silence that followed was punctuated with shouting voices. Thor Lupei appeared walking through the snow accompanied by two large men in dark jackets and a huge dog; I recognised his voice but not the language he was speaking in.

Suddenly cold and tired, I pulled the window handles towards me. Snow fell into the room as the rusty hinges screeched, the noise echoing across the castle courtyard. I threw myself back, landing heavily in the wheelchair, unsure as to whether anyone had seen me from below. When I had regained my breath and calmed down, I wrapped myself as best I could in the curtains and fell into a dreamless sleep.

CHAPTER 50

Eskdale - Tiffany Harrek

Saturday, 19 November.

Dusk chased us down the lanes, shadows leaching out from beneath the empty trees and hedgerows to submerge us in a deepening gloom. Uncle Ted had his foot down, using a lifetime's memories of every sharp turn and gradient in Eskdale to keep the car on the road. It were already twenty minutes or more since the phone call and, while neither of us said as much, we were both well aware we might already be too late.

'Not far now.'

Uncle Ted were defying doctor's orders driving a car so soon after the accident but I'd asked him because he were the one person I knew I could count on to help me without asking questions. My shift started in little over an hour, but shovelling chips into cardboard boxes weren't a career; I could take it or lose it.

We left the narrow metalled road for a dirt track that dipped away between the trees. After a minute Uncle Ted pulled up and parked, turning the car round so it faced back up the track. He grabbed a coiled rope from the back seat and we climbed out. The damp air clung to us. The track were slippery with fallen leaves as we hurried on foot towards the vague patch of lighter ground ahead. Emerging from beneath the trees onto a boggy grassy bank, we could hear the gurgling of the river.

'Old cottage is just up there.'

Tendrils of mist laced the dying grass and brambles that

snagged and tugged at our boots. The river meandered lazily, sometimes smack up against the steeply rising ground of the far bank, dense and dark with pine trees, sometimes curving away into the marshland.

'There. Look,' Uncle Ted pointed. 'That'll be what he saw.'

A tumbled down cottage lay ahead of us, its roof collapsed in on itself, its chimney leaning like an Olympic diver about to launch herself from a high board. It were too dark to say for sure whether the cottage walls had ever been pink, as I had been told; all I could say for sure were that it were light in colour.

'Over there,' I shouted, spotting something away to our right.

It was hard to be sure exactly what it were but there, in the middle of the river, lay a dark solid mass. Reaching the riverbank Uncle Ted shone a torch. The partially submerged car were on its roof, its four wheels above the waterline making eyes at us like cautious frogs peering out of a pond.

Uncle Ted who, as a North Sea fisherman, knew all about the perils of drowning didn't hesitate. He lashed one end of the rope he was carrying round a tree and the other end round his waist then stepped off the bank into the freezing water.

'It's too late,' I called out after him. 'They can't be alive, it must be nearly an hour since he rang.

He ignored me. The river were quickly up to his hips. After all the rain that had battered us for weeks, the waters ran fast and deep; if they hadn't made it out of the car they would surely both be dead. Keeping one eye on my uncle, I ventured further along the bank towards a clump of trees, more in hope than expectation.

'Are you there?' I called in a half-whisper. 'Mr Muyskens? It's me, Tiffany.'

Why were I whispering? We were in middle of bloody nowhere but I could not forget the words the Dutch policeman had used when he rang 'I cannot call the police, Tiffany. You were right.'

'Mr Muyskens,' I hissed again.

I were turning away when a faint flashing light caught my eye. I ran forwards.

'Is that you?'

The dead leaves beneath the tree shivered and fell away as the policeman sat up. He was clutching his phone. His hair was dirty and matted, his face was plastered with blood.

'Are you alone?' he asked.

'No, Uncle Ted's in the water trying to reach the car.'

'The driver is dead.'

Muyskens brushed away the leaves to reveal a man's face lying beside him. I flinched.

'Fetch your uncle, Tiffany. We must leave quickly before someone turns up.'

Muyskens' phone had photographs of everything, the car, the dead driver, the route the taxi had taken down through the trees, and the river before it got too dark. He thought he had cracked a couple of ribs and broken his arm as the taxi had fallen backwards down the hill. The way he put it, the trees had saved his life as the repeated impacts had slowed the vehicle down on its descent. The car itself had borne the brunt of the landing as they crashed out of the forest and landed upside down in the river. The driver had died instantly as the car hit the riverbed and a rock smashed against the driver's window, breaking the glass and smacking a mighty blow to the man's head. Disorientated, Muyskens had thanked the rock even as the freezing water poured into the car, knowing that the equalising pressure would enable him to open his door and escape.

But the door had not budged. As the air remaining in the car bubbled away, Muyskens found the strength to unclip his seatbelt before his head disappeared beneath the rapidly rising water. He fumbled in the gloom, found the window winder was still working and, moments later, was squeezing through the window against the current. Coming up for air, he quickly understood the situation; the car was facing up stream and he had been pushing the door against the full force of the river. He too had taken a smack to the head and, by the time he had retrieved the driver's body and collapsed on the riverbank and rung me, his hair, face and clothes were matted with blood and mud.

He were hobbling heavily as we made our way back towards the car, twice we had to catch him as he slipped on the wet leaves, but he insisted his ankle were just badly sprained and that nothing were broken. We put him on the back seat. Uncle Ted grabbed blankets from the boot of the car and a small bottle of rum from the glove box. Muyskens let me wrap the blankets round him and took no persuading to take a long swig of rum. I climbed in front. The car soon warmed up and we were only just out of Sleights when I heard snoring from the back seat.

Muyskens instructions were that we should take him to Scarborough hospital. Whether that was to receive medical attention, to see Ivanna, or simply to escape from Whitby, or a combination of all three wasn't clear. We were about half-way there when the snoring stopped. Seconds later we heard Muyskens talking on his phone, first in French, then in what I assumed must be Dutch, and then in English.

'OK,' he said, sitting up, his voice stronger than before. 'We make progress. How far are we from the hospital?'

CHAPTER 51

Micăbrukóczi - Daniel Murray

Saturday, 19th November.

'Maestru Lupei is a wise man and does much good for our region. Do not listen to those who tell you different.'

The fat surgeon gripped my hand. Above his handlebar moustache and beneath eyebrows thick as hedgerows, his dark eyes probed my soul as he leaned down towards me. With his spare hand he shovelled another cake into his mouth.

'Come, I have someone who wants to meet you,' he said, crumbs dropping from his lips.

He didn't wait for me to say yes. I thought I recognised the person pushing my wheelchair as one of the nurses from the operating theatre but, with them wearing scrubs and masks, it was just a hunch. We left the buffet party, or whatever it was, with the surgeon accepting the praise of various people who I took to be relatives of the patients. Out in the corridor, we passed the doors to the operating theatre. Further down, the surgeon stopped outside a door and knocked.

The couple stood up as we entered the room. Both were immaculately dressed, him in a smart blue suit and tie, and her in a pretty dress, red lipstick, perfect hair and heavy gold earrings. She wore leopard skin stilettoes and was clutching a matching bag. The surgeon crossed the room and spoke with them in a foreign language. As he spoke all three faces turned towards me. The couple smiled, their eyes dancing with gratitude and joy. Beside them, tucked up in bed and propped up on pillows, was the girl I had seen in the operating theatre. On the far side of the bed a nurse busied herself taking readings of the monitoring machines in the corner of the room.

'Domnu Murray,' the woman said. 'Please accept all our thanks. We are forever in your debt.'

I turned back towards the parents. Were they the people who had arrived in the black limousine? What did Dommu mean?

'Doctor Ardelean has explained everything,' the man said. 'As we say here in Romania "Voia este în tine". In English you would say if there is a will, there is a way. We cannot express how overjoyed we are to meet you.'

So I was in Romania. I didn't know what to say so I simply smiled back.

'Mama,' the girl said sleepily.

The mother leaned over her daughter and whispered in her ear. The girl tried to lift her head from the pillow but the nurse stepped in and gently pushed her back.

'She must rest,' the surgeon explained in English. 'The girl would like to see you,' he said to me, grabbing the handles of the wheelchair and pushing me forwards.

The parents moved aside to let us pass. When I was level with the top of the bed, the mother leaned in and touched the girl's hand. Her eyes opened and she looked into mine.

'Mother says I owe you my life,' she said simply in faltering English.

How do you answer something like that? Can you say 'your new kidney was stolen from someone who was murdered at a music festival? I'm only here because I was stuffed full of other people's organs against my will and locked in a box?' I couldn't. I simply smiled and said thank you.

The surgeon wheeled me back to the great hall. We arrived as Thor Lupei appeared from another direction, dressed in black. Snowflakes clung to the shoulders of his long leather coat. The two men spoke briefly in what I now guessed might be Romanian; glancing over at me from time to time as they spoke.

'And now I must leave you,' Doctor Ardelean said. 'Welcome among us, Daniel Murray. I look forward to working with you again.' He gave a formal nod, a gesture that he repeated for Thor Lupei, and via the twin doors, which he pulled closed behind him.

'You made an excellent impression on our good doctor. A celebratory drink?' Lupei asked. 'You enjoyed the slivovitz, if I recall.'

Where had I heard that name before? It made me think of warming up after being drenched and cold. And then it hit me; the Hounds of Hellbane bus the night Lupei picked me up.

'Is that where we are, Moravia? It's that damson brandy, isn't it?'

'Marvellous memory but, no, you are quite wrong; Moravia is in the Czech Republic.' Lupei poured two glasses from a cut crystal decanter and offered me one. 'I propose a toast. To the future.'

Things were moving too fast. Lupei was making assumptions and I was still unsure that I was ready.

'You promised me several things,' I said, not taking the glass from him.

His eyes narrowed a fraction. 'Go on,' he said, a touch of weariness in his voice.

'My legs. And we were going to talk about how to do all this without killing people.'

'Is that all?' he said, his face brightening.

'Alex. I want to see Alex and talk with him.'

'I understand your eagerness. Let's do things in sequence, Daniel.' Lupei swallowed his drink in one and placed mine on the small table beside the fireplace. He removed the long leather coat and rolled up the sleeves of his shirt. 'If you are to be my apprentice then we must awaken creierul anticilor, the brain of the ancients. Give me your hand.'

I grasped his large pale hand without thinking to refuse and immediately felt a tingling that hovered in my own hand for a few seconds then suddenly leapt up my arm, along my collarbone and up the vertebrae of my neck, to end up, in the middle of my head.

'The medulla oblongata, midbrain and pons. Can you feel them?' the soft rich baritone voice enquired.

My eyes were closed, though I could not remember deciding to close them. There was something totally weird about experiencing a sense of pressure inside my head, as if a fingertip were lightly stroking the inside of my brain.

'Yes?'

'Good. To acquire my craft you must learn to travel at will through the human body, as familiar with its contours and edifices, its lumps and conduits, its treasures and repositories, as one might be at home with the rooms and possessions in a house. Imagine the veins and nerves to be like the electrical system or plumbing, the stomach is the dining room, the bladder is the bathroom, and so on. We are currently in the library, if you will. Now come with me.'

We were on the move, leaving the middle of my brain and following the twists and turns of a conduit that led downwards. I became aware of a pulsing double rhythm and, once I recognised this as my own heartbeat, I began to panic.

'Stay calm, Daniel. All is well.'

As I focused on relaxing, my heart rate slowed. Forgive me but it is impossible to clearly describe what I was feeling because it was so outside ordinary experience. Imagine a tube train progressing through a tunnel or the roots of a plant spreading through the soil, speeded up thousands of times. I was feeling points of warmth tunnelling through my body, probing, caressing, turning back as if having taken a wrong turn in a maze then surging forward. Lupei reached my heart, pushing through a valve as if passing through a revolving door. The man who could empty a human body of its organs was somehow inside my heart. A surge of adrenalin had me gasping for air, overcome with absolute fear, convinced I was about to die. I felt a hand on my shoulder gripping me firmly.

'You are quite safe, Daniel. Ride the wave.'

I could not ride the wave, my entire body was in mortal fear for its life. My heart was thumping so quickly it might explode. Just as I released an involuntary moan, the sensation of being invaded disappeared; Lupei's presence in my body was gone. I sat there endeavouring to bring my breathing back under control, aware of sweat trickling down the small of my back and tears streaming down my cheeks. When finally I opened my eyes, I looked up at Thor Lupei whose face broke into one of his coat hanger smiles. All apex predator teeth.

'Excellent. Now drink,' he said. 'Then we eat and after that you will practice awakening the creierul anticilor that lies within you.'

I shook my head. 'I'm just an ordinary person, I can't do that.'

Lupei arched a pale eyebrow. 'Really? Do you know how few people have experienced what you have just lived through and survived to tell the tale? I chose you, Daniel. Trust me.'

He handed me the glass of brandy.

'We will eat in ten minutes. I'll send someone to bring you to the dining room.'

He turned heel and left the hall. I turned my attention to the fireplace and stared deeply into the dancing flames. I thought of home. How long would it be before my absence was noted? They would have noticed at work, of course. Mr Rogers would have sacked me in my absence. The bastard had been looking for an excuse all along; my face didn't fit according to him. Which was code for you don't grovel enough. Well, sod him.

Maybe I didn't need his poxy job. It would be a year before my dad noticed, as soon as he had met Sheila I had disappeared off his radar; he hadn't even asked where my bedsit was.

Which left Tiffany. But who was I kidding? I had known her for two and a half days; dream on, Daniel, you useless plonker. Sure, she seemed different to all the others and I had felt things for her I hadn't ever felt before, not for anyone, not in my whole life. And I didn't mean sex. Well I did but I meant more than that. Although it seemed stupid to even think it, the moment I saw Tiffany in that fish and chip shop I imagined spending the rest of my life with her. To her I had maybe just been an interesting weekend. If that. She'd have others.

I took my hand away from the back of my head, conscious that I had been rubbing it for quite a while. A hot itching sensation throbbed beneath my scalp, like a weird migraine inside my skull, which made no sense because there are no pain receptors in the brain. Abruptly, the sensation ebbed away.

What did I have to lose? I couldn't pretend there weren't dangers because I had seen for myself just how callous, brutal and lethal Lupei could be. In the old days they used to take canaries down into the mines to warn them if there were dangerous gases leaking in the tunnels. First hint of carbon monoxide and the canary would drop dead. I was knee deep in canaries, but the prospect of being someone special was overriding my caution and my sense of right and wrong. I sort of understood that once I knew Lupei's secrets I would not be allowed to walk away, but maybe Alex and I would be able to think of something together. Alex was in the same situation and, no doubt, thinking things over just like me. Did he know I was OK? Had he asked to see me? Had Lupei sucked the muscles from Alex's legs? One way or another I had to find my friend.

Unless I could persuade Lupei to fix my legs I wasn't going anywhere and any dreams of escape would remain dreams.

I felt the hand close on one of the handles of my wheel-chair. I turned expectantly; maybe Emile Noir would help me.

The bony hand on my wheelchair was not Noir's but that of a huge scravir. The grey face leering at me had never been handsome, with a smile that resembled a tear in a sheet of paper and sunken bloodshot eyes that conveyed only a dull bestial brutality. The thinning hair on this ghoul's head reminded me of the matted sickly coat of the abandoned dog I had found in the shed on Farview Farm. One of his nostrils appeared to have fallen off, further accentuating the impression that I was looking at a living skull rather than at a human face. His body was as thin as a stick insect's but where Noir looked weak this man looked lean and wiry.

'You're taking me to the dining room,' I said loudly.

The torn paper grin grew broader.

CHAPTER 52

Eskdale - David Rawes

Saturday, 19 November.

They parked the 4x4 on the bend where another vehicle had parked recently enough to have left tyre marks in the fallen leaves. The passenger got out and stood waiting, torch in hand, while the driver went around the back of the car to don wellington boots and grab a bag of tools. The two men set off down the muddy track, the car's indicators flashing behind them as the doors locked.

The magic hour was long gone, it was pitch black, cold and it was raining. Neither man spoke. When the shorter man slipped and fell the other didn't break his stride; he wasn't there to mollycoddle a halfwit who couldn't be bothered to look where he put his boots. Pulling up the collar of his long Driza-bone oilskin coat, David Rawes forged ahead, knowing the river was close by. The other man got to his feet, pulling his sodden flat cap into position as he ran to catch up.

They found the car easily enough, on its back in the middle of the river, facing upstream, and, a few minutes later, they found the body of the taxi driver. Had the driver crawled out of the wreckage only to die on the riverbank? Was his passenger dead, trapped inside the car?

'At the back or in the passenger seat?' Rawes asked.

'Back, I think. I told you, it were dark. I couldn't see much.'

'Hope you can swim, Alistair'

'It's bloody freezing.'

'Get in.'

The two men waded into the river, moving methodically, testing each foothold on the slimy stones before shifting their body weight, to avoid being swept away. Reaching the upturned car, Rawes wedged his tool bag between a rear wheel and its axle.

'Driver's window is smashed,' Alistair shouted over the noise of the water.

Rawes shone his torch into the water, there was no body behind the driver's seat. 'Go round the other side and pray the bugger's still strapped in and floating upside down.'

'It's too dangerous,' Alistair protested. 'I drove tractor and pushed them off the track, like you asked. That's it.'

Rawes shook his head and leaned towards the farmer. 'You should have thought of all that before you started molesting young girls. You're my bitch now so get round that car and see if the Dutchman is inside,' he growled.

The farmer had no choice. Muttering under his breath that it would have been easier to do the time for his crime than be forever a victim of blackmail, he advanced against the full force of the water that now pinned his legs against the bumper. Reaching the far corner of the bonnet, he grabbed the wheel arch as his feet were swept from under him.

Rawes was smirking as Alistair's flat cap fell off his head and was carried away in the swirling water.

Hand over hand, his fingernails bending back as he clung to whatever he could grab hold of, Alistair edged toward the passenger side door. Water were fucking freezing, his balls must have shrunk to the size of peppercorns. He pulled his torch out of his jacket and directed the beam under the water. The passenger's door was intact.

'Nowt down here,' he shouted, looking up. Where had Rawes gone?

'Over here.' Rawes shouted.

Alistair turned. Rawes had moved and was now standing at the back of the vehicle, protected from the current.

Alistair clenched his jaw and carried on, clinging to the exhaust pipes of the upturned vehicle; soonest done soonest mended. A few more steps. He shone the torch into the water. Nothing. He looked towards Rawes who had moved again and was now at the corner of the car, just a couple of metres between the two men.

'It's empty.'

'Take a proper look,' Rawes shouted. 'Get your bloody head down there and check the back seat.'

The farmer's hatred was written all over his face as he took a deep breath and ducked beneath the surface. The water thundered and gurgled in his ears. The rear window was missing, broken or open, it wasn't clear which. And the back seat was empty. The passenger must have got out. Shit.

It wasn't his fault. He had done what was asked of him. How was he to know the car would roll backwards down a steep bank, crash down into the river, land on its sodding roof, and still not kill the bloody occupants?

Alistair threw himself back into the land of the living, the white noise rush of the river flooding his ears as he straightened up and his head came out of the water. He spluttered and grabbed a huge lungful of air at exactly the moment the tyre wrench crashed down onto the back of his head, fracturing his skull and knocking him unconscious. His hand released the exhaust pipe and his body fell away from the car and was quickly caught in the current, floating downstream at increasing speed towards Whitby harbour and the sea.

The rain was falling heavier than ever. Rawes toyed briefly with the idea of leaving the wrench there in the river, but that was stupid. It wouldn't take a halfway decent pathologist more than a few minutes to match the farmer's skull fracture to the tyre wrench. Rawes rinsed the tyre wrench in the current, put it back in his tool bag, then waded back to the riverbank. He hesitated by the body of the taxi driver. On balance it would be better if the driver had never made it out of the river, so Rawes dragged the body out from under the trees and rolled it into the water.

Only when he had trudged all the way back to his car did Rawes remove his gloves. Sheltering beneath the open boot door, he climbed out of his wet clothes. For a moment he stood on the track stark naked while he dried himself off then climbed into the spare set of clothes he had stashed away. The wet clothes went into a couple of black bin liners.

It wasn't late, just after ten to six, but he let himself in rather than ring the doorbell. No sense in disturbing her, she had been through enough already.

'Is that you, darling? It starts in twenty minutes. The Chuckle Brothers are on this week. Then it's Strictly from Blackpool. I do hope there's a good tango.'

Her voice, drifting into the hall through the open lounge door, was as beautiful as a blackbird's. The light was flickering in colour and brightness; she had forgotten to switch on the lights and was watching the television in the dark.

'I'll be through in a minute, my love,' he answered, heading for the back kitchen. 'A few things to do. Have you taken your tablets?'

He stuffed everything in the washing machine, found the manual and programmed it. As the water started to trickle into the drum, Rawes got busy on his mobile; he hadn't finished with the Dutch policeman. Not by a long chalk.

CHAPTER 53

Scarborough

Saturday, 19 November.

She was waiting for them at the deliveries entrance of Scarborough Hospital. As soon as she identified Tiffany stepping out of the car, Ivanna pushed open the door and walked out into the drizzle, pushing the wheelchair ahead of her.

'You cannot come in like that,' she told the middle-aged man who was dripping wet from head to toe.

'He's my uncle,' Tiffany protested.

'It's OK, love. I'll stay in the car,' Uncle Ted said, heading back across the car park. 'I'll turn heater up.'

'If anyone asks, your name is Andrew Western. 12 Porret Lane, Port Mulgrave,' Ivanna told Muyskens as she wheeled him briskly inside and down the corridor towards Accident and Emergency. 'I have already signed you in.' She turned towards Tiffany. 'You can sit in A&E waiting area. It's a busy night. Three very drunk women. Keep head down and eyes open please.' She smiled reassuringly. 'I collect you as soon as I can.'

Ivanna took the policeman to one of the treatment rooms. While she attended to his injuries, the pair filled each other in on the day's discoveries.

'I am prescribing painkillers for your rib fractures. No jogging, weightlifting, or press-ups. Use an icepack for twenty minutes every hour for next two days then …'

'Where am I going to find an ice-pack?'

'I give you,' Ivanna answered. 'When you reach hotel drink everything in minibar to make room for ice-pack. Ankle please.'

'Getting drunk sounds good to me,' Muyskens smiled and winced as Ivanna manipulated his left foot back and forth. 'You were right about Petroşani, by the way. Eric Dunn has never been there. His daughter's transplants took place somewhere else.'

'And now we know region of Romania where Lupei is hiding. Ylenia was right. Ankle is bruised, not broken. Walking OK with stick, no running.'

'My friend at Europol is checking the audio I sent him,' Muyskens said, wincing as Ivanna started to clean his head wound. 'Rawes is smarter than the doorman but I am sure his wife has received an organ transplant through Thor Lupei.'

'I agree.'

'Both men owe the lives of their loved ones to Lupei. That is his power over them. I think this pattern is repeated across Europe. A network of sleeper cells created over decades. That is how he is protected from the law.'

'So where is pathologist,' Ivanna asked. 'Has she run away?'

Muyskens shook his head. 'Shaveling is dead.'

The door was thrown open and Tiffany fell into the room.

'He's here,' she gasped as she picked herself up. 'The fat one from the Pavilion.'

Ivanna was already tossing things into a bag as Muyskens shifted himself off the bed and back into the wheelchair.

'He's talking with the reception staff.'

'Did he see you?' Muyskens asked.

'Don't think so. How would he know to come here?'

It was a good question. There was only one reasonable explanation. David Rawes had discovered that Muyskens' body was not floating in the upturned taxi. Putting two and two together, he had decided that someone had helped the Dutchman, then deduced that Muyskens was likely to require hospital treatment. More interesting to Muyskens was the revelation that Rawes and Eric Dunn knew each other and would act together to protect Lupei.

'Reception staff do not have my name?' he sought reassurance from Ivanna. 'And no-one saw us enter the hospital?'

'There are CCTV cameras. I cannot promise that no-one has seen us.'

'Are we feeling lucky?' Muyskens asked.

The two women stared back at him, tension written across their faces.

'Finish your work, Doctor,' Muyskens instructed Ivanna. 'Then we go.'

Too late. Seconds later the door flew open and three men built like walruses on steroids squeezed into the room. Framed behind them in the doorway was the diminutive Humpty Dumpty figure of Eric Dunn.

'Right lads, bundle them up and carry them to the van,' Eric said. He shook his head pityingly at the sight of the Dutch policeman lying on the bed. 'You're going to be so sorry you're still alive, you useless wanker,' he snarled.

CHAPTER 54

Micăbrukóczi - Daniel Murray

Saturday, 19 November.

The scravir left me in my wheelchair in front of a pair of tall hardwood doors. I wondered if the doctor I had met earlier knew of the existence of the scravirs. It was unlikely that the young couple or their daughter had ever witnessed the ugly creatures that inhabited the underbelly of Thor Lupei's world.

The banqueting hall was the embodiment of medieval elegance. Ancient tapestries glowed in the flickering candlelight. The walls were covered in geometric designs in blue, yellow and green, painted directly onto the warm yellow stone. A huge dark wooden coffer carved with fruit and woodland animals and birds ran along a wall beneath a row of gothic windows. The carving was so good you could imagine the creatures coming to life. The floor was a lattice of interlocking diamonds, brown and white. A mountain of logs blazed in the fireplace.

We sat at opposite ends of the long table, some five metres apart.

The food was all a bit posh for me, if I'm honest. But delicious. There was a light brown soup that smelled of hazelnuts and mushrooms, with bouquet of flowers made from herbs and cream floating on the top. Two tiny roast birds served in latticed vegetable nests and chips no thicker than matchstick. A pear tart with chocolate ice cream encircled by a picket fence of white chocolate.

All served on plates and bowls that appeared to have been designed for that particular dish and no other.

As we ate, Thor Lupei took pleasure explaining the background of each wine (there was a different one with each of the seven courses), telling me the country, the village, and even from which end of the vineyard the grapes originated. He lavished praise on the chefs and serving staff and introduced me to his sommelier, not skipping a beat when it became clear he would have to explain to me what a sommelier was.

The serving staff of four, including the wine waiter, were not scravir, though the two men were lame. I wondered whether Lupei had had a hand in their condition, removing a muscle here or there to slow them down. The two women looked to be about my age, the men older, maybe in their forties. Were they here of their own free will? Did they gain special advantage for themselves or their families by working at the castle? One thing was certain, none of them was ready to make eye contact with me or Lupei. They smiled gratefully when he complimented them or the food, and otherwise worked heads bowed.

Lupei revelled in having an audience. He detailed the renovation of the castle, the modernist architect he had flown in from California, the furniture craftsmen he had employed in India and Brazil, and introduced me to the history of the region. He recounted anecdotes of the people whose lives he had saved and how they in turn were saving the cultures of Europe. He asked me my opinion on subjects he knew that I knew nothing about: the conservation of wild flowers in alpine meadows, the architectural styles of European castles through the centuries and then, when it was clear I had little to say, he would fill the time with his own opinions.

I was happy to sit there and stuff my face. It didn't take a genius to understand what was going on; I was being sold the life of a medieval lord and it was very obviously a better life than I would ever expect to live.

One of the serving girls arrived with a tray on which were a long and savage-looking knife, two spoons and three glass bowls, the largest of which contained a large fuzzy wooden melon.

'Perfect. Perfect. Thank you Maria,' Lupei chuckled in his deep baritone. 'I know I do not have to tell you what this is, Daniel.'

'Cupuaçu,' I answered, remembering my first experience of tasting it before the Hounds of Hellbane went on stage at Whitby Pavilion. 'From the Brazilian rainforest.'

'To the very top of the class. My most able student.'

Lupei took the fruit from the bowl and placed it on the wooden table then grabbed the knife and swung it violently like a machete, splitting the cupuaçu in half to reveal the brain-like pulp within. He served himself, scooping the flesh out into one of the bowls then beckoned the serving girl to carry the tray down to me.

'Eat every last morsel. It will protect you when we finally get down to work,' he advised.

Maybe the wine had numbed my taste buds. Maybe the wine had been spiked. The cupuaçu I scooped from its hard shell tasted sour, quite unlike the first time I had tried it. There was, however, the same dizzying kaleidoscope of flavours: pineapple, chocolate, mangos, aniseed, and the heat of chillies. I felt it permeate my body almost immediately, like a drug, like coffee or a spliff.

When I had finished and last dishes taken away we were left alone with a bottle of cognac that looked as if it had been carved out of a rock crystal, and a large wood box.

'You're a man who appreciates the very best the world has to offer, Daniel, so I give you a Clos du Griffier vieux cognac, a King of Denmark cigar, and Lookin' Good from blues legend Magic Sam.'

Lupei pressed a button somewhere and suddenly the

mesmeric rhythms of a blues guitar were bouncing off the walls in a cascade of raw energy, as airy and sticky as a spider's web. The cognac flowed through me like lava in a volcano. I said no to the cigar; I had never smoked one before and my head was already spinning. I felt curiously detached from my body. When the music ended Lupei leapt to his feet.

'And now the fun begins,' he announced.

He crossed the room and took hold of my wheelchair. The huge scravir was waiting for us out in the corridor. Lupei handed over control of the wheelchair and strode off purposefully, singing a blues song, his long white hair dancing at his back.

'I need a doctor, I need him soooo bad ...'

The scravir took me to the lift and the underground tunnel that led back to the medical centre, but this time we followed a different route and ended up in the operating theatre itself with its pristine gleaming surfaces and its forest of electronic cables, machines and screens.

Lupei was waiting for us at the back of the room, holding open a second door, to the right of the huge window through which I had watched the operation hours earlier. We passed through the doorway into a passage lined with rough-hewn stone, leading gently downwards. Ten metres or so along the passage the stone blocks ended and we were in a tunnel leading through solid rock. Whether gouged out by human hand or by an ancient underground watercourse, I could not tell.

'There have been humans here since Neolithic times,' Lupei said over his shoulder as he led the way. 'Each successive civilisation has simply built up over the ruins of the past, as it always does.'

It was a perfect metaphor, to be following a man who seemed to belong in a previous century along a path that led backwards in time. The passage turned to the left as it spiralled in a wide arc down into the bowels of the earth. Such light as there was came indirectly from fittings hidden behind over-hangs, reflecting a warm yellow glow off the surfaces of the rock. Numerous side passages led off into velvet darkness and it no longer felt like we were in a castle at all but rather in a warren of prehistoric caves. My head swimming and completely disorientated, I felt detached from the rest of my life.

The path levelled out finally and ended at the mouth of a large cave. Where the passage was lit in yellow or orange light, within the cave a single narrow shaft of cold blue light provided the only source of illumination. It was focused entirely on an operating table that occupied the very centre of the space. The rest of the cave lay in shadow. In the air hung the dank odour of decay. As the scravir wheeled me towards this operating table the wheels of the wheelchair caught against something. Set into the floor was a wooden trap door with a large iron ring that, presumably, served as the handle. The scravir pulled the wheelchair back and found a way round the obstacle. We passed in front of the table and continued to the other side of the cave where I was left in my chair with my back to the centre of the room.

'Don't worry, Daniel,' Lupei smiled, sensing my apprehension. 'You are not in any danger.'

Lupei said something in a foreign language. I turned and, straining my neck, saw in my peripheral vision the scravir exit through the second of the three entrances to the cave.

We were alone and now I understood with sudden clarity that this was to be my moment of truth, my opportunity to shape my destiny. I was to be a gladiator in an arena, given the tools to defend myself then tossed in with my opponent and left to live or die.

A rhythmic squeaking noise accompanied the approach of what I took to be a wheelchair. Out of nowhere I was over-whelmed by a sickening realisation. How dumb and naive I had been. It wasn't me who was about to be placed on the operating table, but Alex. Lupei was going to pit us against each other.

Refuse! Tell him to go to hell!

My wheelchair lacking the large rear wheels to enable me to turn myself about, I could do nothing. Straining my neck round I caught sight of the other wheelchair enter the cave, pushed laboriously by the tall scravir, but could not see its occupant.

'Ah, perfect.' Lupei's baritone filled the cave. 'We lift into position. Carefully. Mind the head. Good. Now fetch Daniel.'

Lupei's back prevented my seeing Alex's face as I was pushed towards the table.

You don't have to do this.

So how are you going to stop him? Maybe Alex will operate on you.

No, Alex will refuse.

Really?

Was Alex awake? Was he in pain? Lupei stepped aside as we reached him. The figure on the table was covered in a sheet.

'Good, the work is done. Go back to your hole,' Lupei ordered the scravir.

For a fleeting second it seemed that an expression of resentment were forming on the face of the scravir then the glare vanished to be replaced by a look of subservience and, finally, by the blank expression of an automaton or zombie. With Lupei's hard stare still upon him, the scravir bowed and withdrew. I turned my attention back to the table.

'Is he dead?' I asked.

'Is who dead?'

'Alex.'

Lupei gave me a curious look then followed my gaze and burst out laughing. He whipped the sheet away like a conjurer concluding a magic trick, to reveal a bald middle-aged man lying on the table. His face was long, with a weak chin, a cruel mouth, and several days' stubble. His hands were thick and calloused. He was built like a rugby player or a weightlifter.

'Is he alive?' I asked.

'Is who alive?'

'This man.'

'He is unconscious.'

'Who is he?'

'It is not important, Daniel.'

'It is to me.'

A flicker of irritation crossed Lupei's face. 'This scoundrel is a murderer and a rapist called Marku. The regional prison has been only too glad to send him over to us because he killed a prison guard two weeks ago.' Lupei paused to look me in the eye. 'Can we continue?'

I nodded.

'Thank you. You are grace and equanimity personified. So let me explain the principles of what we are going to do.'

'I'd rather just get on with it,' I said.

'Excellent.'

I'm not sure why I said what I said, I think I was trying to avoid thinking, if that makes any sense. My emotions were all over the place. I was about to step into the dark side and I was completely stuffed. Stuffed if I did and stuffed if I didn't. If I didn't do what Lupei wanted I'd be stuck in a wheelchair forever. No, that wasn't true, I'd probably be dead in a week. Why would he want me to return to a normal life, knowing what I knew? It wouldn't happen.

And then there was the other side of me, wanting to know his secrets. Who wouldn't? This man could save lives or end them as he saw fit. He was like a god. He turned science on its head and had access to power people dreamed of. He was rich. He was a rock star. He owned a castle. People listened to him.

'I want you to take hold of the man's hand,' Lupei said.

I did as he instructed. The hand was rough and strong.

'I am taking hold of his other hand.'

He needn't have told me. The second he grabbed the man hand it was like electricity shooting up my arm. I jerked back in my chair.

'Relax, Daniel, and follow the flow.'

The initial surge of energy had been replaced by a localised tingling. My vision was distracting me so I closed my eyes. At school we learned about proprioceptors and how they give a sense of where the body is in space, enabling you to bring your fingertips together when blindfolded, for example. Or to know where your limbs are even when in total darkness.

At that moment I was simultaneously feeling both a tingling in my left hand … and in someone else's right hand.

'Good. That's it. Now follow me,' Lupei instructed.

My eyes closed, I felt Lupei's focus rise up the man's arm, moving slowly like a fly walking across the skin. Beneath his shirtsleeve, on his upper arm, the man had an old tattoo of a wolf's head and his arteries were as thick as drinking straws; he was either a weightlifter or a street brawler. Against the flow of blood we surfed the systemic arteries back towards the aorta and the heart. The man arched his back as we passed through the aortic valve and into the left ventricle of his heart then, as quickly as we arrived, we left through the same valve, heading down through the body along other arteries until we were somehow in one of the man's legs.

I know this will all sound totally mad. How could I see tattoos that were hidden from view? How did I know that I was travelling along a man's arteries when I did not even know where my own arteries were? All I can say is that, under Lupei's direction, that is what I felt.

'Brace yourself, Daniel.'

I groaned out loud as my legs were engulfed in flames, a pain so excruciating that I was on the cusp of passing out when, abruptly, the sensation vanished as quickly as it had appeared and Lupei was speaking softly in that low rich baritone.

'Relax. Take deep breaths. You are in good company. Dante reacted just as you did. We met after the battle of Campaldino when he was not much older than you are now. He was a Guelfi, fighting with the Whites, and stumbled across me as darkness fell. I was busy removing organs of the slain on the field and he would have killed me if it had not been my good fortune to be plundering a group of Ghibelini corpses.'

Lupei's voice soothed me. I still hadn't opened my eyes.

'I was heavy with the fruit of my labours as we sat on the edge of the forest and ate bread and drank wine. The shadows grew long while we talked and it was clear that he had an inquisitive mind, unusual for the period. Before long the wine had loosened our tongues and I found myself telling him far more than I should have for they were dangerous times and a man could be hanged from a tree for as little as stealing a basket of olives.' Lupei paused. 'Are you ready to continue, Daniel?'

'What happened to my legs?' I asked.

'Use your free hand to touch your thighs.'

The last time I had touched my legs I had been both frightened and disgusted. Reluctantly, tentatively, I did as he instructed. While they were still painfully thin, my legs had swollen with muscle. Instinctively I lifted my heels off the footrests, proof that I had functioning calf muscles. Could I walk again?

'Now you will finish the job,' Lupei told me.

I opened my eyes and stared at him. His suggestion was ridiculous, I had absolutely no idea how to do what he did so effortlessly.

'I will guide you,' he said, reading my thoughts.

He was back inside my head.

'Medulla oblongata, midbrain and pons. Can you feel this? And this?'

I nodded and re-closed my eyes to aid my concentration. I could feel the inside of my brain as you might feel your tongue without moving it.

'I awaken creierul anticilor, the brain of the ancients. That which we understand we can control'

As Lupei spoke, the centre of my brain lit up from within like a lighthouse shining out over the dark sea of consciousness.

'Now fly! Through your body. I am following you. Yes. No, not that way, out through your hand. There. Find his blood vessels, they are the roads between cities. His heart, spleen, stomach, kidneys, testicular artery, common iliac artery, femoral artery. OK. Stop.'

The weight of the unconscious murderer's thigh was all around me. How did I know that? I felt my own heartbeat adjust its tempo until it was in synchrony with the double beat of the murderer's heart. At the same moment a surge of energy drew itself together in my brain and reached outward like a ghostly hand, grabbing a handful of the other man's flesh. It was as if I were wearing a virtual reality helmet and watching a hand emerge from the man's thigh and sweep down away from the table to enter my own thigh where I sat in the wheel-chair. The same burning sensation I had experienced minutes earlier flooded my nervous system as the virtual hand loosened its grasp and the muscle was released into my own legs.

'Now you do it, Daniel. Alone.' Lupei commanded me.

With sweat pouring down the small of my back, a left hand weary of clinging on to the hand of the man on the table, and a headache the size of Romania, I struggled to take control of the ghostly hand, attempting to move it back up towards the table as it kept slipping from my mental grasp, like setting jelly seeping between the fingers, or like those claw crane grabber machines in amusement arcades that never quite gather up the cuddly toy. The seconds passed as I fumbled then, slowly I lifted my ghostly limb and swung it over the table and into the man's thigh. Exhausted, I took a deep breath and opened my eyes.

'Wonderful. You learn quickly.' Lupei was looking down at me, a huge smile across his face. 'At last I have found the perfect student. You have no idea how long I have waited for this moment nor how rare your talent is.'

'I need a few minutes,' I said.

He gave a small sweep of his hand, brushing my worries aside. 'As long as you like.'

'Can you finish what you were telling me about a battle-field?' I asked. 'Wasn't Dante way back in history?'

'Very good. Yes, the battle of Campaldino took place on a hot day in early June in 1289. I was travelling through the region. In every town and village people had been shouting for weeks as tensions mounted, exchanging stories of atrocities that had been carried out in other towns by those they disliked or distrusted. Some true, some lies. In the taverns and market squares men were spoiling for a fight, good men and women consumed with suspicion, convinced that peace was to be found at the end of a sword. Outsiders kept to the shadows, fearful that they would be singled out and have their throats slit as spies.'

I was already feeling more relaxed, the tension slipping from my shoulders, the headache subsiding slowly. Lupei's voice and imposing presence were soothing, even though his story was dark.

'As you can imagine, Daniel, it was difficult for me to blend in. Albinos have been stigmatised and bullied and mur-dered in all places over the centuries. The ignorant dismember us and use our bones and hair for magic potions to this day in Africa. And my height was even more unusual in the distant past. Fortunately, I have always been good at languages. I have had plenty of time to learn. Mi ritrovai per una silva oscura, chè la diritta era smaritta.'

I had no idea what he had said but in his rich baritone the words sounded beautiful.

'Fortunately, my special gifts enabled me to locate safe houses and protection, then as now. Back then the world of science barely existed and medicine was crude. People lived with pain to a degree that this age cannot begin to understand. Can you imagine being so consumed with the torment of kidney stones that you are prepared to allow a man who does not even understand the function of blood to shove a fist up your backside in order to massage your kidneys from within in a desperate bid to force the pain from your body? Well in the thirteenth century that passed as medicine. Sad souls carried abscesses the size of their own heads on the sides of their faces from the moment they awoke till the moment they fell finally to fitful sleep. Those with seizures would seek solace from quacks who drilled holes in the skull to let out evil spirits.'

The look on my face persuaded Lupei that he had provided enough examples.

'It was a world without either tranquilisers or painkillers and it was into that world that I brought relief and new life; replacing diseased kidneys and lungs, even teeth. You are right; I have over time become consumed with the orgasmic rush of penetrating a body and divesting it of its organs and tissues but you and I, together, will find a way forward.'

As Lupei spoke I saw, in my peripheral vision, a skeletally thin silhouette at the entrance to the cave. Black against the faint orange glow. The scravir shuffled forwards in that slow and deliberate clanking gait, disappearing from view behind Lupei's back.

'Here is an interesting detail, Daniel,' Lupei said. 'Did you know that before writing his Divine Comedy, which I flatter myself was influenced in part by our discussion that night, Dante joined the Physicians and Apothecaries Guild? I sensed in him what I sense in you, a latent ability to access creierul anticilor. We had so little time, he and I, in that war torn moment of barbarity. It is the tragedy of my condition that everyone I have ever known has shared only an instant with me. Human life is as fleeting as flowers in a vase but you, I can give you …'

As Lupei spoke I saw a shifting in the shadows over his head. I was still only beginning to make sense of what my eyes were seeing, while listening to his voice, when the shadow moved precipitously downwards. There was a sickening crunch as Lupei's voice stopped in mid-sentence. Mouth still open, uttering a small gasp and with a look of total surprise on his face, Lupei started to sink downward like those slow motion films of tower blocks collapsing after they have been dynamited.

He was still holding one of the murderer's hands on the operating table. And so was I. Through that conduit I felt an overwhelming surge of force that threw me back in my wheelchair. I couldn't breathe and it felt that my heart had stopped beating as adrenalin invaded my entire nervous system. The murderer's eyes had opened and his body began to twitch as if in a fit. If I did not let go of the murderer's hand I would die from this overwhelming assault on my body. But I could not let go. Lupei was still sinking, still staring at me. Behind him a face was emerging. A scravir. Not the huge evil brute who had wheeled me into the cave but someone else. I was beginning to lose consciousness for lack of air. The face behind Lupei was familiar. I tried to speak. My larynx would only let out a choked guttural grunt. The scravir's eyes moved away from me towards the body on the table and the hands that linked us all together. The scravir's arm, encased in some kind of cage or framework, rose into view. In his hand a long blade penetrated the narrow blue pool of light, gleamed and sent a blinding shaft of light directly at my eyes as it fell downwards in an arc towards the operating table. Milliseconds later the blade connected with its intended goal. There was a second sickening crunch as metal sliced into muscle, tendon, and bone. I heard a second gasp from Thor Lupei and all at once the block on my heart and lungs ended. My autonomic systems kicked in. I took a huge lungful of air and my heart recommenced its thumping rage within my chest. My hand let go of the murderer and my chair fell backwards as my legs spasmed and my back arched.

I lay there, head throbbing, still in my wheelchair, knees above my head, dizzy and confused. On the operating table above me the murderer's body thrashed about like a crab on its back trying desperately to flip itself over. The scravir squatted beside me and I recoiled, convinced I was about to die.

'Daniel. Daniel,' the words were hoarse and almost unintelligible, delivered laboriously one syllable at a time. 'You must go.'

I looked up into the scravir's face, my vision spinning sickeningly from right to left.

'Listen to me,' the scravir said. 'I am Emile Noir.'

'You killed him,' I hissed in anger. 'He is teaching me and Alex to …'

'Alex is dead.'

'You're lying. Thor is helping him and …'

'Alex is dead.'

At that instant I wanted to kill Noir; the bitter husk of a man who understood nothing. Yes, there was a bad side to Lupei, there is a bad side to everyone. But there was also a good side, a side that had helped thousands of people over centuries. A side that would bring hope to those who suffered.

I rolled myself backwards and out of my wheelchair. Painfully and tentatively I gathered my strength and, clinging to a leg of the operating table, I pulled myself up until I was on my feet. Noir had also hauled himself up. We faced each other, the wheelchair between us, the prostrated figure of Thor Lupei on the floor behind Noir. Fists clenched I took a step towards Noir. My legs were weak but serviceable. He had the machete but I had the upper body strength.

'Wait. I can prove Alex is dead.' The words issued from Noir's mouth as slowly as slugs crossing a step.

He turned away from me and crossed the cave. Squatting down with his back to me and placing the machete beside him, he grabbed something on the floor. There was the hollow sound of something rattling against wood. If I moved quickly I could reach him and break his stringy neck before he had a chance to react. Lupei's body was twitching; he was still alive. I must hurry. I walked with the stiffness of a heron. Five steps and I was behind Noir and already raising my fist when he turned towards me.

'I am too weak,' he said. 'You must help me. Your life depends on it.'

He shuffled to his left to give me space to join him on the floor. In front of me was the trapdoor that had caught the wheels of my chair as the scravir had brought me into the cave. Noir was holding the large iron ring, leaving enough space for me to help him. I hesitated. Should I kill him or see what he wanted me to see? Why could he talk now when before he was tongue-tied? Why should I waste time listening to him? What could he know? It was a trap. Maybe he hoped to push me through the trapdoor.

'Trust me,' he said. 'Did I betray you at Farview Farm?' His eyes revealed only concern and compassion.

Grinding my teeth, I glanced over at Thor Lupei then back at Emile Noir.

'I am already a dead man,' Noir said, reading my thoughts. 'I am trying to save you and you can save others.'

I grabbed the ring and helped him lift the trapdoor. The hinges squealed as the heavy door lifted to reveal a black void and an ugly, sweet and fetid stench.

'Alex is down there,' Noir told me. 'In the oubliette.'

'Liar.'

There was nothing to see. Why should I believe him? Behind us Lupei was stirring. Suddenly Noir jerked back like a puppet on a string. His mouth opened to speak but no words came out. His eyes shifted towards Lupei then back at me, pleading, beseeching me to act. Was he only able to speak while Lupei had been unconscious? Slowly, deliberately he unbuttoned the shabby shirt that covered his ribs and started trying to remove it. He wasn't strong or agile enough and gave up. His hand went instead to his pocket from which he retrieved a box of matches. He fixed me with a stare of desperation.

I understood. With the machete I carefully tore the shirt from his back, tied it in a knot and grabbed a handful of matches from the box. I lit one and held it to the fabric. It burned brightly for a few seconds then flickered and went out. Noir pointed at his other pocket. In it I found a hip flask, unscrewed the top and smelled the contents. Brandy warmed by the feeble beating of his heart. Pouring the alcohol over the shirt, I grabbed a handful of matches this time and struck them all at once. Holding the shirt at arm's length I brought the flame to the wet material. Fire engulfed the fabric and when the heat became unbearable I dropped the shirt through the open trapdoor.

Some three or four metres beneath the trapdoor the ground was covered in bodies, lit by the hellish light of the flames. Emaciated corpses lying tangled and interlaced. The smell was disgusting. Rotting flesh clung to some of the bodies, others were skeletons. Among the dead were both men and women. There were even children. Some corpses were in modern clothes but others wore fragments of costumes that belonged in a dim and remote past.

Noir was pointing down to my left. I followed the direction of his finger. The trainers and the jeans. My ears were ringing as if a huge orchestra were playing a chaotic downward glissando that had no end. I hesitated then forced myself to follow the jeans upwards, passing over a familiar t-shirt until, finally, I saw his hipster bearded face. Blank dull eyes stared up at me, seeing nothing. Tinnitus fogged my thoughts, a mad rush of a dozen vacuum cleaners and washing machines screaming inside my head.

Then his arm flinched. My heart surged. Alex was alive.

'You see that?' I shouted. 'We've got to help him.'

There had to be a way down, a ladder, a rope, a hidden staircase. Noir was ignoring me. Thor Lupei would know what to do.

I could see Alex was trying to roll over and push himself up, he must be in terrible pain. My friend needed me. Somehow, injured or not, I had to get down there. I pushed Noir aside and shuffled across to get a different view of the oubliette, maybe I would see the foot of the steps that would give me a sense of how to reach him.

My new vantage point did bring an insight but not the one I was looking for. I now saw into the gap beside Alex's left arm. Sharp yellow teeth were clamped down on his little finger, tugging and tearing the skin. A rat the size of a cat was shaking its head back and forth as it ripped the flesh from Alex's hand. Alex wasn't alive, or trying to prop himself up, or moving his arm, he was simply suffering the indignity of having his body pulled about and eaten by rodents.

Alex was dead.

The more I stared into this vision of hell the more I saw. There weren't only dead bodies down there. Beside the scurrying rats there were other movements too; intermingled with the fetid lattice of corpses were maybe half a dozen scravir crawling mechanically like spider crabs across an ocean floor.

I was numb, like someone floating high above a landscape, seeing fields and trees and people walking, but all too far away to hear, to smell, to sense, to touch. I was an observer, a silent drone, cold and clinical and without a heart.

And yet I could hear Alex's voice from far away in time, urging me to join him in the river where he was already swimming, encouraging me to let go of my fears. Two twelve-year-olds on the cusp of adolescence.

Tears were rolling, tickling my cheeks as they found each other and merged into larger tears that fell through the open trapdoor, to be consumed by the flames. Alex couldn't be dead. It was ridiculous, him lying implausibly among cadavers and skeletons, as meaningless as discovering him trapped in a still life in an art gallery, tucked in among the fruit in a bowl painted two centuries ago.

Movement drew my eye. Noir had somehow got to his feet and was trudging towards Lupei. As I sat there, unable to find the motivation to do anything, destroyed by the succession of betrayals and lies, emptied of the will to live, consumed with grief, I watched Noir grab Lupei's shoulder and begin to drag him backwards across the floor towards the trapdoor. Lupei's long white hair was matted with blood. What had he been promising me when Noir had struck? Noir was no longer paying me any attention, all the strength in his body and all his mental energy were consumed in the single purpose of dragging Lupei through the trapdoor to his death.

Watching Noir's willingness to lay down his own life to rid the world of Lupei, my mind tormented by what lay beneath the trapdoor, I was still torn. In my mind's eye I saw Hannah's emaciated body on the sofa in the cottage in Whitby, Megan weeping gently beside her. I saw Darren's body in the garden by the lighthouse. I heard Lupei telling me to watch the sheep. Could there be compassion in a world where an individual could exercise power over life and death without restraint?

Noir had reached the lip of the trapdoor. He glanced at me. His jaw clenched but he could not speak. His eyes told me to go while I could. I shuffled back from the trapdoor as Noir lowered his legs into the void then swung himself backwards, his body falling through the gap. The weight of his body dragged Lupei in a rush towards the trapdoor until his head was out over the void. Beneath him Noir's body swung to and fro over the dancing flames. The fire had spread through the fraying rags below and several scravir were now animated and staring up towards the trapdoor.

Lupei's eyes opened and he stared into mine with frightening intensity.

'Kill him, Daniel, and save us both.'

As he spoke, Lupei's hand reached gently towards me. At first I imagined he was wanting something to hold onto, someone to help pull him away from his predicament, the comfort of human touch. Then all at once I understood. He was not reaching out for me to save him, he was reaching out to grab me and to empty my body to bring him strength. In that instant I understood the amoral impulse that had propelled him through the centuries. I recoiled.

Lupei roared his fury, his hand lunging towards me. His rage ignited my own; *he* had killed Alex. It was *his* fault.

From beneath Lupei came the sound of a sharp crack. I hauled myself to my feet and saw through the trapdoor that one of Noir's arms had snapped, he was now holding Lupei with a single hand. Lupei arched his back, trying to roll onto his side, threatening to dislodge Noir's remaining grip.

I could not dare to touch Lupei because of his immense power. Instead I grabbed the wheelchair and swung it round. Positioning it between myself and Lupei's feet, I pushed with all my strength. Lupei screamed as his back was pushed out over the void. His legs kicked out at the wheelchair seeking to dislodge it from my grasp. I held firm. My skinny weak legs aching from the strain, I inched forwards, step by halting step, with gritted teeth, my face contorted in grief and anger.

'Don't throw it all away Daniel,' Lupei shouted. 'I am promising you the Earth. You and I together. Alex was weak. You are the one. He would have betrayed us.'

'Liar,' I screamed back, pushing with all my strength.

'You have no right. Stop,' Lupei ordered me. 'I will give you whatever you ...'

Suddenly the wheelchair was moving quickly and I had to drop to the floor. There was a loud clattering through the trap door as Lupei disappeared through into the oubliette. A thump as Noir's body hit the pile of bodies, followed by Lupei landing on top of Noir. The wheelchair was hanging in the balance over the trapdoor, wheels spinning slowly. I was on my knees catching my breath, too tired to move.

It is one of the universal laws that everything must move from a position of high entropy to one of lower entropy. The wheelchair followed its destiny. One minute it was in the cave, the next it was falling through the air to crash down onto the bodies below.

The new arrivals in the oubliette had dislodged and shifted the contents and a fresh wave of foul air flooded the cave. On the operating table the murderer's body had stopped twitching. For a few seconds I leaned against the table, begging my head to stop spinning.

At the far side of the cave was what looked to be a filing cabinet. Keen as I was to leave the gruesome crypt, I staggered across to explore what the cabinet contained. The answer was not very much, dust and an assortment of glass vials, but I was rewarded with the discovery of a small torch which, in the circumstances, seemed as great a prize as it was possible to imagine. Keeping clear of the open trapdoor, and ignoring the bestial cacophony of snarling, splintering bones, and noisy eating emanating from the pit, I squatted to grab the machete Noir had used to attack Lupei and left the cave.

To my left the passage continued downwards into the

bowels of the earth. There was no lighting beyond this point. I decided not to shine the torch for fear of attracting the horrors that surely lurked in the darkness below. I turned right and followed the winding passage up and away from the ancient past and towards the present, mindful of the danger of damaging my Lowry-stickman-thin legs.

I had progressed only a few steps along the passage when a loud crash followed by a primal howl behind me reminded me that I was not alone.

CHAPTER 55

North Yorkshire

Saturday, 19 November.

Covered in bruises, Tiffany had rolled herself away from the other two and was peering through a hole to get a sense of their whereabouts. They appeared to be in a field.

All three had been tied up with industrial tape before being tossed into the back of a van that had then driven away at speed, though not before the stage door manager had given the policeman a vicious kicking. The van was pretty corroded and peppered with small holes, the sidewalls allowing in a certain amount of light, and it was this that had enabled the three kidnap victims to see each other and enabled Tiffany, as a local lass, to recognise the Red Lion Inn at Cloughton as they sped past. She told the other two that they were heading north, back towards Whitby.

Muyskens was in a foetal position close to a wheel arch with Ivanna beside him, whispering in his ear. They had been parked on a steep slope for a little while; Tiffany's hands and watch were behind her back buried beneath a thick winding of tape so there was no way of telling the time. The last few hundred metres had been over very bumpy ground that had tossed them in all directions until the driver, presumably Eric, had parked the vehicle, cut the engine, and climbed out.

The voices, those of the men who had abducted them, rose above the noise of the wind from time to time. They must be a little distance away because she could not make out what was being said. An occasional shout or laugh stood out. Where they waiting for someone to arrive or something to happen?

Tiffany wondered where Jordan was. She had texted him hours ago, immediately after receiving Muyskens' desperate phone call from the river bank. She trusted Jordan completely, they had saved each others' lives, and believed must be well on his way from London, but he would never find her.

She wondered what had happened to her uncle Ted. At least he hadn't played the hero and thrown himself at the three bouncers; the state he was in he would have ended up dead. Maybe he had fallen asleep in the car park and been totally unaware of what had happened. Maybe he had walked into A&E looking for her.

'Is that car?' Ivanna said in the darkness.

Tiffany strained her ears. 'Yes. It could be my uncle.'

The noise grew then faded as a vehicle.drew up alongside the van and cut its engine. Tiffany was shivering with cold.

Minutes passed. The driver's door of the van opened.

'Well, fucking ring him then,' said a voice outside.

'No point. I told you, he weren't shifting before the end of Strictly.' Eric's voice. 'They always watch it together. No matter what.'

'I don't believe this crap,' the first voice was suddenly an octave higher in anger.

The palm of a hand slapped the side of the van. Tiffany flinched.

'Calm down. I told you, you don't have to hang about.'

'Oh right. And where's our money, Pal?'

'I'll be round by midnight.'

'I wouldn't want to be you if you fuck up.'

'Here, you can all have a couple of pints on me while you're waiting,' Eric said.

'It's not a deposit?'

'It's not a deposit.'

The sound of footsteps, someone walking away.

'And you're one hundred percent that this van isn't traceable?' Eric's voice.

'Everything's traceable. Your boss should know that, he's a bloody copper.'

'You know what I mean. You're good lads. See you in the Dragon.'

More raised voices. A car engine started up. Eric climbed back into the van and turned the engine on but the van didn't move. Tiffany guessed he just wanted the heater on.

CHAPTER 56

Micăbrukóczi - Daniel Murray

Saturday, 19 November.

The curve of the tunnel and the smoke from the fire in the oubliette left me unable to see more than a few metres ahead or behind. The lighting in the tunnel had failed. Torch in hand, I staggered upwards on feeble legs, at the mercy of pursuing enemies who, if they caught me, would tear me limb from limb as casually as crows dismember roadkill. The hell horror scene beneath the trapdoor was seared into my brain. My head was thumping.

How much further must I walk before the tunnel's slow snake coil released me back into the castle? Where did the dark side passages lead? What if I missed the exit? Would I miss the castle altogether and continue walking upwards until I ended up at the peak of a blizzard shrouded mountain, dying of hypothermia surrounded by howling wolves?

At last a rock feature I recognised; an overhang that resembled an old woman's downcast face. I had seen this feature earlier, on the way down while being pushed in my wheelchair. Spirits raised, I passed the feature, stopped and turned to see it from the opposite direction, only to discover it was not visible from the other side so I could not possibly have seen it before.

Face it, you're lost.

I set off again with smarting eyes and aching lungs.

Where's your key?

I focused on the rhythm of my steps, my tired feet shuffling stone scattered ground.

Get real. Even if you reach the surface, you'll need a key.

I cursed my inner voice and focused on my immediate challenge; to increase the distance between me and the horrors below.

The scream, when it came, seemed to belch from the very rock itself.

I froze, my senses straining like hounds on a leash, whitened knuckles gripping the machete. The rough lumpen surfaces of the passage provided nothing in the way of echo. How far away had the noise originated? Did the danger lie ahead or behind?

The machete cut a wild arc as I swung it to loosen my shoulder. I transferred the small torch to my mouth, clamping it in my jaws, and swung the machete again, this time with both arms to gauge my strength. This time the tip of the blade caught the rock wall, jarring my wrists, the metallic ring of steel on stone signalling my presence to whoever was tracking me. Cursing my stupidity, I took the torch back in hand to stop myself from gagging, and staggered forwards, gasping for breath.

To my left the tunnel wall contained an open door. The torch beam revealed a short side passage at the end of which was a space stacked with medical equipment, a wheelchair, display screens, a trolley. Waves of tiredness washed over me. Days spent lying in a box had weakened me and the urge to hide while the danger passed by was overwhelming. I was saved from myself by a movement beneath the wheelchair. A huge rat was staring up at me, its head tilted to one side in the manner of a vulture considering which end of a cadaver looks most tempting. A second even larger rat emerged. I turned and continued on my way.

Forty seven steps later (yes, I was counting them), I saw

light ahead. I paused, resting a shoulder against the tunnel wall. My lungs burned from the unaccustomed exercise, the smoke and the falling oxygen levels. A headache the size of Everest. I could barely lift the machete let alone swing it.

The seconds slick slow slipped one over the other like eels in a barrel as I braced myself for my showdown with death. How many scravir were there? Would they come from one direction or both? The flickering light must originate fron the burning torches they carried. Would I die engulfed in flames like a heretic burnt at the stake?

Slowly I realised that the pattern of flickering light was constant, mechanical, repeating. Could burning torches do that? And why wasn't the light becoming brighter? And where were the advancing footsteps?

Not torches but electric light. The recessed lights on the ceiling must have come back on in at least the top end of the tunnel. The flickering was disorienting but better than no light at all. I relaxed a fraction, stepped forwards purposefully and dared to dream of escape.

When a current of cold air brushed the hairs on the back of my neck, I spun on my heel, machete raised, expecting a scravir at my back.

The passage was empty. Or was it? Had the smoking shed in Whitby been empty when shifting shadows had slunk between the hanging racks of kippers? Had I not already witnessed enough to know that the ghouls hunting me down need not be bound by the laws of physics?

Bullshit! Focus on what is real.

I searched for a rational explanation and eventually my fingers felt it. Nestling in a crease in the rock to my right was a narrow vent. Through it chill air was seeping into the passage. The air smelled fresh.

I must be finally close to the surface!

'DANIEL!'

The voice was much louder than before. Had Lupei had somehow risen from the pit? No, the voice was high in pitch and as dry as parchment. Who then? The leering ripped-paper smiling, flaking scalped scravir who had pushed my wheelchair perhaps?

If I couldn't outpace him I had to outwit him.

Just ahead a wooden door stood ajar. Another side passage. I pushed the door open and stepped into the shadows, swinging the door back into place behind me. Moments later someone or something passed on the other side of the door, heading up.

Simply following in its footsteps would be madness; I must either wait or find an alternative.

At my back was a second door, of reinforced steel, like you'd see securing a bank vault in a film. I turned the handle and heard multiple bolts moving in the rock. The hinges squeaked as I hauled the door open. I shone my torch into the darkness and saw a cave stacked high with musical equipment: drum kits, amplifiers, guitars, keyboards. On a large table in the centre of the cave were various stage props: a top hat, sunglasses, silver rings, and a huge leather belt with a buckle in the form of a satanic ram. Lupei's stage clothes hung from pegs on the wall. "There's a few bob in that lot", my dad would have said, and no-one was going to miss any of it, least of all Thor Lupei. I took the sunglasses and rings, tied the belt around my waist, placed my machete on the table and rummaged in the drawers underneath. The torch beam picked out a dozen Hellbane branded plectrums and two custom machine heads. If I made it out of the castle alive, a pocketful of rock and roll memorabilia might generate a bit of cash on eBay. Might even pay for my flight home.

I was heading for the exit, weapon and torch in hand, swag in my pocket, when I heard the voice.

'Help me.'

A woman's voice, muffled and afraid.

There were two doors, the one through which I had entered and another, just as heavily reinforced, on the opposite side of the cave. I crossed the cave slowly, uncertain as to whether I was simply imagining things, and stood by this second door, keeping one eye on my only avenue of escape. Silence. It must just be tiredness. Or fear.

I don't know why but I tried the handle of the door; to satisfy myself that nothing could come out and attack me I suppose.

'Help me!'

I leapt back. The voice was loud and hoarse through the door.

'He left me here to die. Let me out. Please.'

'There's no key,' I answered truthfully.

'He keeps it in one of the drawers, beneath the table.'

How would she know that?

'The drawer is noisy,' she said, as if second-guessing my thoughts. 'Wood on wood. We hear the drawer being opened and the key being taken out. Before we get fed.'

'We?' I said, alarmed.

A moment's hesitation.

'There were two of us,' the voice said. 'He took her and tortured her. He'll kill me next.'

No, I thought to myself, Lupei wasn't going to kill anyone anymore. I looked at the table and then at the doors. How would I live with myself if I escaped knowing I had left a woman to die of starvation in a prison cell beneath the castle? But if I rescued her it might be at the cost of my own life as I was barely in a state to save myself. What state was she in?

She was sobbing and, for some reason, I thought of Tiffany, though I had not seen her cry.

The drawer did contain a bunch of keys. I found the right one at the fourth attempt. As I turned it in the lock I was thinking how I would explain to her that I was leaving straightaway and that I could not wait for her, she would have to make her own way out.

Unless she knew the castle better than I did and was able to help us both escape. In which case …

The key tumbled the lock. I swung the handle. The bolts drew back and suddenly the door flew open, smacking me in the face and throwing me onto my back. I howled as my head hit the floor, and I was barely beginning to roll onto my side when not one but three figures poured out, maws open and dripping with saliva.

Scravir.

In normal circumstances I could have jumped to my feet and hoped to outrun these emaciated walking cadavers but , with my skinny shanks barely thicker than theirs, I was no more agile than they were. The best I could do was to push myself backwards until I was under the table in the middle of the cave. I switched off my torch. At one end of the table were three sets of legs in fraying clothes, barely visible in the lack-light. The fetid stink of shit and decomposition filled the air.

'Pull him out,' a voice snarled.

'He's armed,' rasped another voice in a whisper as dead as dust.

'So am I,' said a third voice, clicking something I could not see.

The other voices joined in a cacophony of wheezing that must be laughter. A fist smacked down on the tabletop.

'You can come out of your own accord or …' started the first voice.

'… or we'll pull you out and tear the flesh off your bones in strips,' said the third voice.

'If the little fuckwit's touched my guitars I'll chew his face off,' rasped the second voice.

'The boss might not be so pleased.'

'Screw the boss.'

Were these the Hounds of Hellbane; the musicians in Lupei's band? But there should be four of them. I had a flash-back to the first time I had seen scravir, in the barn on Farview Farm. Had Noir killed one of them? Was that why Lupei seemed to take such pleasure torturing him?

I couldn't understand how one of these three monsters had impersonated a woman's voice. My legs were tucked up under me to prevent them from grabbing me and hauling me out. I was breathing so quickly that I was hyperventilating. Maybe I could distract them. I pulled the guitar machine heads from my pocket and threw them into the darkness. The scravir all turned towards the noise, giving me my opportunity to scramble out from under the table and run to the door.

Unfortunately, I simply didn't have the strength or the speed and was forced to give up without even having made it out from under the table. I shuffled back to the safe spot in the middle. The scravir were whispering amongst themselves. Suddenly they split up, two of them walking round the table, one on each side. They were surrounding me. I would have to lash out with the machete and pray my aim was true. I scraped the blade across the floor, metal against stone, in the hope that it would make the scravir think twice. All movement around the edges of the table ceased immediately. Total silence. I turned my head this way and that, trying to gauge from which direction the attack would start. Sweat was dripping into my eyes, and my hands were shaking.

Triggered by a signal I could not see, three sunken angular faces appeared simultaneously as the Hounds of Hellbane bent over to get a look at me under the table.

'Get him,' hissed a voice.

They lunged together, like wolves. I slashed at the closest hand, slicing it down the middle and leaving two fingers and half a palm dangling. A spray of blood spattered my face as I spun round to face the other threats. Someone was howling in agony and it wasn't me. Long hard nails tore into my shoulder. I flinched back, swinging the machete wildly, missing my target and jarring my arm as the blade buried itself in the wood of the table leg and jammed. With both hands I tugged desperately at the machete, rocking it to and fro to try and dislodge it then, all at once, I did a King Arthur with Excalibur and the blade flew out. I spun round, terrified that I was about to be grabbed and dragged out. Movement in my peripheral vision. I brought the heel of the machete handle down as hard as I could onto a bare foot that had come within range. There was an audible crunch of bones and ligaments and a cry of anguish as the foot was withdrawn.

The attack ceased and the scravir regrouped at one end of the table. The respite was only temporary. More whispering. I reached my hand up to my shoulder and felt blood, hot and viscous on my back. I tried to imagine what I would do next if I were in their position.

I guessed right.

Fat lot of good it did me.

They couldn't reach me under the table so the answer was obvious, even to a scravir. Move the table. But it was even worse than I had imagined because rather than simply pulling the table aside they were lifting it from the side furthest away from the exit door, tipping it up and thereby simultaneously removing my protection and blocking off my path of escape.

Machete in front of me, I was calm, resolute and ready. If this was how it would end, torn apart by a pack of skeletal ghouls in a cave beneath a castle on a mountain in a remote corner of Romania that I would never see, then I was going to take one or more of the bastards with me.

Stuff was sliding and crashing against the back of the drawers as one side of the table rose higher. There was another sound, one I couldn't make sense of. The shortest scravir leaned forward, nostrils flaring as he breathed in, the predator smelling the quarry to fuel his violence. He smacked his lips and bared his teeth.

At that same instant there was a dramatic increase in light. I could not see the source, but I saw the reaction. Behind me the doors to the passage slammed against the wall. The scravir's face no longer registered appetite but fear, then a visceral loathing. A guttural snarl erupted from his mouth. He turned his head towards the other members of the band. All three were making feral grunts.

The strength of the roar behind me chilled my bones. The end of the table was no longer rising. The scravir let it go and it crashed back to the floor and the whole room erupted into noise and action as the scravir threw themselves at whoever or whatever had entered.

I did not wait. As a body crashed onto the table above me and obscenities rained like confetti, I slid backwards from under the table, out towards the exit door. Oblivious to me, the Hounds of Hellbane were hurling themselves at the huge ugly scravir who had pushed my wheelchair. He must have found me missing in the castle and returned to the passage to kill me. Now all four monsters, I could not bring myself to call them men, were locked in a primal bloody bare-fisted fight to the death. It was as if millions of years of evolution had been wiped away and wild dogs were taking on a leopard.

With the wall for support, I hauled myself to my feet and shuffled unnoticed out of the cave as fast as my weak limbs would allow. I ran up the passage, ignoring both the pain and the danger, knowing that if I fell I might never get up again; it was all or nothing. Behind me the screams, howls and shouts continued. In seconds I was back in the section of passage that was lined with dressed stone and moments later, I reached the door at end of the passage, pushed it open and staggered into the operating theatre.

There was a large cabinet against a wall. I dragged it across to the door, wedging it beneath the door handle. My whole body shaking with my exertions, I spent several minutes more hauling everything that moved across the floor and up against the cabinet, to prevent anyone shifting the door.

Finally, exhausted, I sank to my knees as my lungs scraped and shovelled for oxygen. I would have stayed there all night, in a dreamlike state detached from reality, but for two things: the sound of a telephone and the sudden and violent shaking of the door handle from the other side. The first reminded me that there was an outside world and the second that I had not yet escaped to it. Aching all over, I climbed to my feet and tried to think.

I was not alone in the castle. For a start, the little girl who had received the transplant was only a few metres away down the corridor and there must therefore be medical staff close by. Then there were the villagers who had served Lupei and I our meal. Did they live in the castle or travel up from the village? If these people knew what had happened to Lupei would they cheer or be fuelled with rage and attack me?

The activity and muffled shouts suggested it could be a while before the door was broken down but I was seriously paranoid about the long one-way mirror that dominated the far wall. Was someone looking at me?

There were probably faster routes or better routes; I took the only one I knew. I emerged from the lift into the photo-lined underground passage that linked the medical block to the main part of the castle. Maybe I should take some of the photos; chances were they were all of recipients of human organs that Lupei had taken from his victims.

One of the photos leapt out at me. I wondered why I hadn't noticed it before. It showed a middle-aged couple standing with Lupei. The man was tall and well-built and had the kind of face that is used to barking out orders. Beside him, between the two men, was a red-haired short woman. Where he was all stiff upper lip, cold and unapproachable, she was looking simultaneously grateful and apologetic, as if she was sorry to be so much trouble. Lupei was as tall as the other man. His lips wore a thin smile that said here is another couple who owe me big time. Which was, no doubt, why the other man looked unhappy. But the thing that had caught my eye lay behind the faces staring into the lens; a backdrop of red rooftops arranged in rows above each other, with steps climbing a hill, winding back and forth like smoke from a chimney. The shadow of a cliff. A graveyard and a church.

Whitby.

I took the frame and several others from the wall and ripped the photos from them, rolled them up and shoved them in my pocket. I didn't know who any of these people were but others would.

Moments later I hobbled into the Great Hall where I sat down in one of the wing back armchairs in front of the huge fireplace. With hindsight, I now wonder what was wrong with my head. I had just escaped from the underground labyrinth and was anything but safe. The only explanation that makes any sense is that the drugs Lupei must have given me had muddled my thinking, preventing me from sustaining a sense of danger or any other emotion for more than a few seconds at a time. Though the fire was no longer roaring, flames were dancing on half a dozen logs and I was grateful of both the warmth and the opportunity to rest. Machete resting on my lap, I imagined what kind of life I might have had as Lupei's protégé, and was on the verge of drifting to sleep when a shriek jerked me back to me senses. The machete tumbled to the floor along with the armful of logs that a maid was carrying to the fireplace.

'Please forgive,' she pleaded, gathering up the fallen wood and avoiding my gaze. 'I did not know anyone one was … you surprise me.'

'Maria?' I said, recognising her from the dining room.

She nodded.

'I need your help,' I said as an idea came to me.

She glanced briefly in my direction.

'Do you know the sub-levels beneath the operating theatre?' I asked.

She shook her head. Her body language spoke not of ignorance but of fear.

'I am working there with Mr Lupei and he has sent me to retrieve some items for him from his office. Could you show me the way? I followed his instructions but the castle is confusing. I am worried he will be angry if I do not return quickly.'

The sympathy in her eyes betrayed that she well understood the importance of not messing up instructions from the boss.

'Come. I show,' she said.

I followed her out of the Great Hall and along a succession of corridors, through a courtyard where snow the size of cornflakes tumbled as if in a giant snow globe. Then back inside and into another unmodernised section of the castle where the temperature was barely warmer than outside. Up a flight of stone stairs. She waited for me at the top as I climbed slowly, hanging on to the balustrade.

'You are feeling better?' Maria said as we walked along a wide corridor lined with suits of armour, and medieval weapons hanging on the walls.

'Yes,' I answered, guessing that she was commenting on the fact that I was no longer in the wheelchair. 'I am tired but improving.'

'The master is a clever man.'

'A great man,' I agreed. 'Has he always lived in this castle?'

'A few years.'

She didn't volunteer any further information. Presently we stopped in front of a huge oak door carved with wolves and wild birds. Maria stood waiting and I realised that I was expected to produce a key. I made a show of patting my pockets and looking crestfallen.

'It must have fallen into the armchair by the fire. I am so stupid. I'll run back.'

She could see I was in no state to run. She leaned towards me. I imagined she was going to kiss me, which I wouldn't have minded as she was beautiful, in an undernourished and haunted kind of a way, but instead of planting a kiss on my cheek she reached out a hand and touched a stone at my back. With a faint click, the stone swung open like the door of a safe in a bank vault to reveal a hidden space in which nestled an ancient key.

'Promise you say nothing to the master,' she said, retrieving the key and placing it in my hand before pushing back the stone. 'Secret. You and me.'

I nodded vigorously. 'Of course, thank you.' How she knew of the existence of the hidden key was none of my business.

'When you leave you must put key back.'

'Please come with me into the room to find the …'

'No.' Maria shook her head, looking suddenly very fearful. 'All those who entered this room without his permission have died. Very dark magic. You will be safe because he has asked you to go in,' she smiled reassuringly, 'but I cannot enter.'

She left me in front of the door. As she turned the corner at the end of the corridor she turned back. I waved and made a show of putting the long and ornate key into the lock. Then she was gone.

Why had I lied? Why hadn't I asked Maria to help me escape? I might already have been in a car heading away from the castle and towards freedom. I could have told her that Lupei was dead in the oubliette and then she too might have fled. What was I hoping to find behind the door?

Fame, I suppose. Fame and justice. If I was not to be Lupei's apprentice then I wanted to be the person who revealed the true story of what had happened. Doesn't everyone want recognition? A modicum of immortality? To be a hero and not just a survivor.

I was being harsh on myself. It wasn't just about me. If I had had my smart phone I would have taken photos of every-thing, evidence to hand over to people who would step in and sort things out. I owed that to Alex and his parents, to Hannah and Darren, and to all the other victims. Behind the door there would be the proof of what had happened. Lupei had to have kept records. A computer database. Lists of harvested organs. Lists of transplant recipients.

'All those who entered this room without his permission have died. Very dark magic. You will be safe because he has asked you to go in.'

Was Maria mocking me? Had she known I was lying?

Too bad. Too late. I had to open the door and finish the job. Or die trying.

CHAPTER 57

Micăbrukóczi - Daniel Murray

Saturday, 19 November.

The carving on the oak door was exquisite, even more beautiful than the wooden coffer in the banqueting hall. At eye level was a crow's head, its eyeball staring directly at me. It was half-buried in the wood but looked as though it might pull itself from the tree as easily as lifting its head from mud. From the bottom of the door a wild boar gazed up at me through an evil squinting eye, ready to bury its tusks in my calves. Even the robin perched on a branch above the boar's head seemed to be plotting to stab me in the ear with its beak.

It's just a bloody door. Get a grip you useless tosser.

I turned the key in the lock. The door opened with a soft hiss, like when you unscrew the top of a half-empty bottle of cola. Withdrawing the key I crossed the threshold.

A soft yellow darkness. Three fat candles a metre tall were clustered at the far side of the room, their flames guttering and shivering in the draft I had created opening the door. A sweet aroma of honey hung in the air. Gently, I pushed the door closed, noticing that the back was blank save for the other half of the crow's face that was staring into the room just as it was staring into the corridor.

Lupei's study was almost silent and almost empty save for four pieces of furniture. A table occupied the centre of the room, a single slab of solid oak resting on two plain, rough hewn and sturdy sets of trestles, as in seen in medieval paintings. Laid across the top, and embroidered with heraldic symbols, a heavy blood-red cloth trailed over the two ends but left a clear view beneath the table. One symbol in particular drew my eye. It showed what looked like the head of a bird of prey, the beak tugging on a loose bag on which were written a jumble of letters in a jagged script that resembled a collection of tiny bones. I had seen it before but where?

Behind the table, facing the door, an ornately carved high-backed wooden chair. Black with age. Chair and door appeared to have been carved by the same hand. A wolf's head stared out of the centre of the chair back surrounded by leaves as if peering out from behind a bush. Two crows perched on the top rail. The armrests were wrapped around with snakes, and the legs ended in large feet as furry as a lion's.

Flanking the chair were two large chests. Behind the chair, recessed at the back of a ledge the depth of the castle walls, was the room's single window; tall as a coffin. There was no curtain, no carpet, no soft furnishings of any kind, save the tablecloth. No computers, no technology, no plugs, no electricity. It could have been a monk's cell. Last year, a hundred years ago, a millennium ago.

I said the room was almost silent because I thought at first that it was breathing, before concluding I must be hearing my own breath. For an empty space the room was strangely dead, as if no echo had ever happened there. I stood a while, looking and thinking. Should I stay or should I go?

Should I stay or should I go?

The Clash song was suddenly all over me, pounding my mind with that in your face guitar hook. Mum's favourite song. Why had I not thought to wonder why until it was too late?

I took a step towards the table. What did Lupei do in this locked empty room? Was it really his study or had Maria simply made a mistake? One thing was clear, there was nothing that could hurt or kill anyone apart from the superstition or fear you brought into the room with you.

Yeah, cling to that, Sucker.

Fleur de lys, lion, swan, diamonds, stripes, and crosses. An eagle, a wolf. Blue, ochre, gold, red. A fish, a ram, a black tower. How long had Lupei had the cloth and what did the symbols mean? I tried to imagine him sitting at this table for a thousand years. Was what he had told me true or was he simply one of the world's biggest tricksters? The lack of a computer was a major disappointment because it meant there was no easy path to glory, no spreadsheet listing each and every murder, transplant, and debt.

I should have counted my losses there and then and left. But it is only human to be nosy.

Homo Narratus. Chase the glory, finish the story.

The chests seemed to be screaming if you don't open us you'll never know. To which the reply should have been, I never needed to know until now so it won't matter that I never opened you.

The chests could both have been locked.

But they weren't.

Compared with the door and the chair, the chests were remarkably plain; thick and crudely fashioned metal. They were secured by rows of hasps and loops, five on each lid, though no padlocks were in evidence. Huge iron hoops were fitted at the ends of each chest. I grabbed a handle with both hands and could barely lift the iron box more than a few millimetres; it was hard to imagine even four individuals being able to carrying them any great distance. Holding a couple of the hasps I heaved the lid up. It must have weighed twenty five kilos or more and, once open, I could see why. The underside or inside of the lid was an exercise in medieval engineering as solid and complex as a steam train. By the dancing light of the candles I stared at the maze of plates, spring-loaded lock bolts, bars, and other moving parts, a scene so intricate that it resembled an aerial view of a medieval city, with its straight roads, curling paths, city walls and buildings all laid out. A total of eight lock bolts ran in three directions to secure the lid and keep out thieves and, from the inside, it was clear that a single key operated all the bolts at once. Lowering the lid to explore the outside once again, I could see no keyhole. How could a key be used without a keyhole? I ran my hands over the surface and finally worked it out; one of the large rivet heads at the back of the lid could be rotated out of alignment to reveal a secret keyhole. My nosiness satisfied, I grabbed one of the candles, reopened the chest and peered at the contents within.

Even in the course of my nineteen years on the planet I had managed to acquire enough crap to fill a couple of rooms: old toys, school photos, clothes, books, an empty aquarium, a bunch of footballs, old Airfix models Dad had insisted I would enjoy, four pairs of trainers, things Mum or Granddad had given me, etc. etc. At home I had a top notch "floordrobe" you had to wade across, shin deep, to reach the bed. Until Dad had thrown it all out.

Lupei had next to nothing. I opened the other chest. It was of similar construction and contained four objects. I lifted everything out of the chests, placing each item on the table and positioning two of the candles beside them to provide some light. It was like peering over the lip of a precipice at the flow of European history. I could not help myself. I could not leave the door open in case I was discovered and I could not take everything with me without a shopping trolley.

A baby's hat, made of wool. Tiny, fragile and pink. Had Lupei been a father? Had his own mother put it on his infant head? Hidden within the hat was a folded sheet of ancient paper. I eased it out and gently opened it. Rough to the touch. Inside a lock of fine golden hair and a flower, yellow with age that crumbled to dust as I shifted the stem to reveal the writing beneath. I recognised some of the letters. Latin or Italian or French? I could not be sure. Who had written them? A lover? A wife? If thirty years together became as fleeting as a one-night stand, in a life of a thousand years, why had Lupei preserved this moment? Why did it matter to him? Pink had not always been for girls. 'Wally' Wallace, our history teacher, had once told us that for centuries it was the other way round, pink for boys and blue for girls, which was why the Virgin Mary was always depicted wearing blue in old paintings.

Wrapped in red velvet was a dagger with a gleaming battle-scarred blade the length of my forearm. The pommel at the base was engraved with a double-headed eagle. I had learned about such things in a video game. On the table beside the dagger I had placed a musical instrument with a body the shape of an onion or shallot. It had fifteen strings, arranged in pairs except for the top string. I guessed it was a lute and it made sense of Lupei's passion for guitars and the blues. I imagined him strumming a lute in Renaissance Italy.

The fourth item was a small pottery flask in the stylised shape of a cow. It seemed so ancient that it frightened me. It was hard enough thinking of Lupei as a thousand years old; the flask looked like it belonged in ancient Egypt or Babylon. I had seen similar things at the British Museum when I was six and Mum had taken me 'to get a bit of culture before it's too late'. (Dad had refused to go; said we had enough old junk at home.)

Beside the flask was a small round brass case. Engraved on the lid stood a crow, its head tilted to one side as if in thought, while on the underside was a large black dot around which were words in a language I could not read. I fumbled the catch and lifted the lid expecting to find the hour and minute hands of a old watch but found instead a tiny crow, its wings outstretched over a compass rose. Shifting the transit lock on the compass case released the crow which, hovering like a sparrowhawk, turned smoothly to face northwards. Not knowing what lay ahead if I ever managed to escape, I closed the lid and dropped the compass in my pocket.

Next was a walking stick made of gnarled and very dark wood. Beneath a round handle that made the stick a handy weapon was a silver collar on which were engraved eleven names, including Thor Lupei's. A date was also engraved, Juli 1720, a location, Frederiksborg, and what I assumed must be a motto, Für immer Zusammen. I tried to picture Lupei as a member of a team. What had happened that month? Was he on a walking holiday? Was this the scene of another battle where Lupei had wandered among the corpses stealing organs or providing lifesaving services to the injured?

Finally there were two large leatherbound books, big as cushions. Covers distressed with age, pockmarked like the backs of an old peasant's hands. The first, bound in rich brown leather, had metal cornerpieces to protect the book from damage and was kept closed by two ornate clasps. Inside the pages felt springy and a little rough beneath my fingertips. The paper seemed to have veins meandering across the surface and I guessed it was probably not paper at all but hundreds of pages of dried animal skin.

A noise stopped me in my tracks. The sound of breathing. I stayed completely still but the only sound was the faintest sputtering of the candlewicks. That and the blood pulsing in my ears.

The text on the first few pages was arranged in columns, all in Latin, the dates written in Roman numerals, C M L X and I. As I turned the pages, the language of the text changed, the numerals went from Roman to what I imagined to be Arabic but the columns remained: first the date then a place name and country, I guessed, followed by a description that varied hugely in length. I never learned a foreign language, I slept through French at school, but I thought I recognised a few words in

Latin, German, French, Spanish or Italian, and English. There was a section where the place names were written in with capital Ns and Rs written backwards alongside other weird letters that might be Russian, and another section where the writing looked like drunk ants had been squashed onto the pages.

The first entry in English was about three quarters of the way through the book. 10th May 1857. Joseph Stairs, bank manager of London Road, Southwark, received a kidney. Fee £24. I wondered what £24 amounted to in the mid-nineteenth century; for the poor it was probably a year's wages. London Road was not far from where my mum had worked for peanuts when I was a kid.

Lupei must have been living in London because there followed a series of entries all in the same very small and tidy handwriting, thirty-seven in all, a little over a page. Many entries were only one line long. Widower in Shoreditch, four small children, missing spleen and lame in left leg. The last London entry was dated the 18th of December of that same year; a Lady Mabel Merchant whose liver was failing subsequent to an illness she succumbed to in India. No fee was listed and the address was listed as the East India Club, St James Square. Husband Sir Edward Merchant, retired Lieutenant-Colonel. The entry ended with the note that 'E.M advised earthquake had taken place in Naples on 16th inst.' I wondered what Lupei received instead of money.

The next entry appeared to be Italian on 23 di gennaio 1858, which I assumed must be January. Il Signorino Giovanni Lanaro, undici anni. Napoli. Rene.

So Lupei, ever the opportunist, appeared to have left London and headed straight towards the catastrophe.

I still couldn't decide whether he was a saint, walking towards danger to help the sick, or a ghoul preying on the misfortune of others. I suspect he had never been able to decide either.

An average of around thirty names to a page. Roughly three pages or ninety transplant recipients per year. One hundred and twenty seven pages, from that first entry in English to the end of the book, so almost over three and a half thousand transplant recipients. The last entry in the book was dated August 1899. The whole book contained maybe five or six hundred pages. It was mind-boggling.

The second book started where the first one finished, which begged the question as to how or why this book was so old. Maybe the answer lay in the fact that the second book was written in two directions simultaneously, with the transplant information starting at the back of the book turned upside down. Page after page. Country after country. All the way from 1900 to 2016. The other way up, the book was unintelligible because the writing was all in what I assumed must be code; a dense succession of numbers and letters that went on page after page without paragraphs or other breaks of any kind.

A gentle sigh brought me to a stop a second time.

The kind of sound you make when clearing your throat with a view to talking after being silent for several hours. Was it me? Was I wheezing? In my peripheral vision something moved. I spun round. The flame of the candle still on the floor in the corner of the room was dancing as if someone had gently breathed on it, causing shadows to ripple across the wall.

I returned to the book, determined to see whether there was anything worth taking with me before I freaked myself out.

Flicking forwards through the upside down book I passed 1950, 1960, the 80s and 90s, 2000. 2005. 2010. Oslo, Rotterdam, London, Rome, Geneva, Marseille, Barcelona, Prague, Bielsko-Biala. And finally, eleven pages from the final entry, there it was. The word Whitby.

7th July 2013. Susan Rawes, Greystones House, Aislaby. Kdny & Spln. Husband Chief Inspector David Rawes Whitby police.

I didn't know the man but it explained a lot. The Goth festival wasn't Lupei's first association with Whitby.

Since I could not carry the entire book and had no way of taking photos, I had only one option: rip as many pages out of the book as I could carry, roll them up and take them with me. I flicked back to the beginning of 2000: 50 pages in all.

This time I knew I wasn't making stuff up. Alongside the sound of someone snorting, the table moved, like a shiver. I leaned and peered under table. The elaborately carved trestle legs were still there at opposite ends, one set carved in the form of a dog's legs and the other like a deer or another hoofed animal. But that was it; there was nothing in the room that had not been there when I entered.

Get a grip.

The pages would not tear, something to do with them being animal skin and not paper I guessed. I sat down in the chair, resting the book between my legs as I grabbed a whole bunch of pages and heaved. Maybe I could rip out a whole section and be done with it. Failing that I could slash a few pages free with the sword. All I knew was that I wasn't bloody leaving without some proof of what Lupei had been doing over the years.

Books are made up of mini books all stitched together and glued to the spine. I knew that because I had wasted a happy hour dismantling a leather bound book when I was nine; it had been the only way I could think of that day to get my loving clip around the ear from my old bugger of a granddad.

Inspecting the book closely I saw that each minibook was made of eight sheets of paper. Folded in half and stitched down the middle that made thirty-two sides. I grabbed one of these sections. With my energies focused on one specific group of stitches, the ancient glue began to give and the pages came slowly away from the spine. With one section removed I moved on to the next. Discounting the blank pages and the pages of code, if I could remove three sections I would have at least thirty-five pages of transplant recipients. Nine hundred names.

I was still doing the maths in my head when the frightening truth hit me, metaphorically and literally.

The trestle table legs had not been elaborately carved when I had stepped into the room; they had been plain lumps of wood. So why had I just seen dog's legs and hooves under the table?

As I was processing this fact something bit the back of my head. I howled and threw my head forward to escape, eliciting a feral growl from whatever had my hair and a strip of my scalp in its jaws. At the same instant I was kicked in the shins, so violently that I thought a bone had snapped. I pulled frantically at the pages of the book, desperate to rip the pages out and make my escape.

When something started to curl around my forearms I realised the depth of my reckless folly.

Across the room the door had come alive. The crow was shrieking an alarm call, the wild boar's head had appeared on the inside of the door and was squealing malevolently. It was simultaneously ridiculous and terrifying. I had been deluding myself, rationalising everything, giving it a scientific twist, keeping everything in the modern world, seeing Lupei as a weird kind of doctor, talking to myself about transplants. But there was nothing rational about Lupei's world, it was a grotesque parody of reality, a hellhole packed with oubliettes, flesh sucking monsters, the ghoulish scravir, and now a nightmare of writhing snakes rising up from wooden chairs that threatened to kill me or eat me alive. I yanked my arms away from the arms of the chair, in the same movement finally ripping the second clump of pages from the book and, in so doing, lost my balance and fell forward onto the table which buckled in the middle as if made of melting chocolate. The blood-red cloth fell over me as the candle tipped over and clocked me on the side of the head.

Think, Daniel, think.

Had Maria seen the bodies of those who had snuck into Lupei's study? How had they died and many people had died in his trap over the centuries? Many more than Maria was aware of, I guessed. The more I struggled the more entangled I became. Something was snapping at my ankles. The room had become a cacophony of grunts, barks, and shrieks. I kicked out blindly, smashing my legs against the chair.

Something was burning. The smoke was biting my eyes and clawing at my lungs. The fallen candle must have set fire to the cloth that enveloped me. Lupei had made all this happen. A voice in my head whispered that if I had the talent he had told me I possessed, could I make it unhappen? Awaken creierul anticilor, the brain of the ancients.

I stopped struggling and focused all my energies within myself. I imagined Lupei's hand holding mine as he guided me though my body towards the medulla oblongata and pons.

'The medulla oblongata, midbrain and pons. Can you feel them?'

I felt only the pain in my legs, at the back of my head, and the burning of my gasping lungs.

Focus.

Eyes closed, I located my fingers in space, following on from there to my wrists, forearms, elbows, biceps, shoulder joint, collar bone … then lost the feeling and had to start again from the beginning. One the third attempt I was about to give up when I felt that slight glow I had experienced when Lupei had been guiding me. Refusing to panic, resisting all the other sensations flowing through my body, I journeyed up towards my spinal chord and finally up into my head. The veins and nerves were like the electrical system in a house, he had told me, the ancient brain nestled at the heart of everything.

I arrived at the primal centre of my own consciousness like a fireman attending a fire. My mid brain and pons were a screaming inferno of primal suffering. Suddenly there it was, a bright lighthouse shining out over the dark sea of consciousness. This surge of energy drew itself together, rapidly gathering strength and substance until I could project it outward like a ghostly hand, pushing back at the wolf behind my head, the snakes coiling towards my wrists, the hooved legs kicking at my shins, the fire spreading toward my face. My various assailants, caught completely by surprise, hesitated and I seized the initiative. Still clutching the fistful of pages I had torn from the book I allowed my body to fall back from the collapsing table and onto the floor, pulling my head back and away from the burning cloth.

In the lacklight it was hard to make proper sense of the growling evil that surrounded me but I knew what I must do. The door was a writhing mass and I surely had only seconds to save myself. I grabbed the dagger and clambered up onto the chair, stepping onto one of the armrests and, as the chair began to tip over I crossed over to the window ledge, taking a ferocious peck in the calf from one of the crows. I was now a metre above the floor and beyond the reach of the kicking legs of the trestle table. The wolf in the chair back was howling in fury. From my vantage point I saw that the chests had shapeshifted into thickset creatures resembling wild boars. The trestle legs had shaken off the burning cloth and were racing round the room, kicking out in all directions. Whatever powers I had drawn on to bring me a moment's respite would not be sufficient to get me across the room and past the door so I took the only other course of action open to me. Thrusting the vellum pages down into my trousers, I slashed at the window with the dagger and threw myself out into the night.

Out of the fire onto the skidpan.

I found myself on a steep and icy roof in a swirling blizzard, immediately losing my footing, crashing down onto my back-side. I rolled onto my front and stabbed frantically at the tiles as I started to slide down towards the edge of the roof. If I failed to smash through I was a dead man. No longer caring who heard me I screamed at the top of my voice as my feet passed over the edge. And caught on a gutter! I tried to push myself back up but legs were still too weak to be of service. My body was a slave to gravity. I persevered, what else could I do? Finally I broke a tile, the blade of the dagger buried itself in the battening beneath, and I came to a halt.

Clinging to the dagger with both hands, I lay there gasp-ing. Bloated snowflakes jumbled the sky and landed inches from my face like timid creatures gathering cautiously around a dangerous but dying predator. Slowly my breathing returned to normal and I regained what little strength I possessed.

The cold brought clarity; move or freeze. Leaning back-wards as far as I dared to see over the lip of the roof, I discov-ered that I was only five metres or so above the ground. Even more amazing was the realisation that the roof I was clinging to was on an outer wall of the castle. A narrow road led from the castle towards the cover of the forest. If I could reach the ground without breaking my legs I'd be in the forest in a few seconds. I'd be free!

Immediately beneath me a thick snowdrift had built up against the castle wall, partially covering what looked like a swathe of large bushes. Bending my knees and keeping one hand on the dagger, I lowered myself slowly towards the edge, sliding down the tiles on my belly until I could grab the lip of the roof with my free hand to steady myself. The lead gutter-ing was so cold I was afraid that my hand would stick to it.

Looking again, the snowdrift seemed deeper further along the roof but it could simply be that the ground rose up next to the castle wall. I was going to have to take my chances. I counted backwards from ten and let myself fall over the edge.

You couldn't see the thorns from up above. Just as well. By the time I picked myself up I was bleeding in at least a dozen places but nothing was broken. I checked the vellum pages and the photographs that I had shoved down my trousers were all OK. Flicking through, I found I had escaped with at least thirty-eight pages. More than I had dared to hope. I retrieved the dagger that I had tossed away from me before falling and hobbled to the road. Tyre tracks. All I had to do was to follow them and sooner or later I must reach a farm or a village.

In less than a minute I had reached the edge of the forest where, before stepping into the shadows, I retrieved the stolen compass from my pocket in order to get my bearings. The tiny crow spun obligingly to face north, from which I deduced that the road ahead led north west.

I was lowering the compass lid when I felt a curious tingling in my fingertips. Flipping the case in my hand I discovered that the black spot on the base was warm to the touch. I turned the instrument back again, one finger still pressed against the spot. To my amazement the crow immediately spun round until its beak no longer faced north but, instead, pointed towards Lupei's castle. The bird held its position for a second then juddered back and forth pointing first this way then that. What was the device detecting? Scravir? Another, even greater, danger? Frightened and exposed out in the open, I snapped the lid shut and stepped beneath the gloom of the tree canopy.

I turned to look back at the castle one last time. Its massive bulk lurked low on its haunches in the lacklight landscape like a predator about to spring an attack. I was suddenly overwhelmed by the feeling that I was abandoning Alex. How could I leave without him? I was the only person in the world who knew where he was. Maybe I was wrong, maybe he was still alive, alone, calling my name in the darkness. Maybe I should go back.

At that moment a wolf howled. Primal and raw. Within seconds she was joined by the rest of the pack somewhere out on the mountain, their cries crashing around me like raining meteors, and I understood that if I did not snap out of my torpor and act decisively to save myself then I too would be bare bones by daybreak and both of us would have vanished without a trace.

'Sorry, Bruv,' I muttered pointlessly, shuffling away.

It was dark beneath the trees and, even in the cold, there was a strong smell of pine. I was protected against the worst of the weather and, if a car was sent out to catch me, there were plenty of places to hide. If wolves or bears came they would find me easy prey, but I would at least have tried to escape. Dying at the claws and jaws of nature could not be worse than the deaths faced by Alex and Emile Noir and how many thousands of others.

The road led upwards for a hundred metres, which alarmed me somewhat, then finally began to descend. Lupei's dagger in hand, with lifting spirits and the sense that at last my luck was turning, I shuffled along as fast as my weak legs would carry me.

CHAPTER 58

The Hague

Saturday, 19 November.

It was a quiet night at Europol's headquarters on Eisenhower-laan in The Hague. Antoine was in the kitchen selecting coffee beans to see him through to the end of his shift. An exquisite Jamaican blue mountain dark roast combined with a Vietnamese Dalat highlands robusta peaberry low temperature dark roast would give a strong caffeine high. Finely ground for the maximum hit and into the machine. A few moments later a steam hiss announced the imminent arrival of the perfect espresso.

His boss had finally been persuaded that investing in a decent coffee machine would deliver tangible results, particularly for staff working the night shifts. Unfortunately, word had quickly spread through the building.

'Hey. Hey! Don't touch my beans,' Antoine said.

'OK. Relax.'

'No, not OK. You can use the machine but you bring your own beans.'

John from the contact team waved a bag of ground coffee in Antoine's face. 'Now OK?'

Antoine grunted his grudging assent. 'There's chocolate cake on the table. Hervé's birthday.'

'Thanks. I used to like this shift, you know?' John said, grabbing a piece of cake. 'Peace and quiet and a chance to get things done. Not anymore. Guess what? This kid just rang and wasted my life with some cock and bull story about monsters who steal organs from living people. Says he's escaped from a castle somewhere. Thinks he may be Romania. Claims he was abducted from Whitby in England, days possibly weeks ago, in a London bus. You know the red double deckers? Trafalgar Square? Only this one is painted black because it's evil. Kid's so out of his tree I explain Europol doesn't take calls from the public, suggest he rings a drugs helpline and …'

'How long ago did this happen?' Antoine had forgotten his cup of coffee and was staring intently at the other guy.

'Dunno. I just put the phone down. Two maybe three … Hey. Hey!'

Antoine was dragging John by the sleeve. 'Forget the coffee. I need the number that he called from. Right now.'

The men ran out of the kitchen and through the vast open plan area beyond.

'You know, Antoine, you could just put a sign up saying *coffee machine broken* or maybe you could lock the kitchen door,' the other guy said, struggling to keep up.

'Yeah sure, like *the machine is broken. And that beautiful smell spreading through the building, that's a hallucination.* Something like that, right?'

'Something like that. I'd have understood. And we could have avoided this running through the building punishment bullshit.'

CHAPTER 59

North Yorkshire

Saturday, 19 November.

'How is he?' Tiffany asked Ivanna.

'I'm still here,' Muyskens said weakly, determined to answer for himself.

For the eleventh time Tiffany banged her head repeatedly on the wall of the van directly behind the driver's seat. 'Let us out, you bastard,' she shouted. 'Or at least give us blankets.'

Eric ignored her but she knew he was there. The engine was running and the radio was playing hits from the 1970s. Earlier she had smelled cigarette smoke seeping through one of the many holes in the rust bucket van. If her legs hadn't been bound together, Tiffany was convinced she could have kicked her way out.

They were all - Tiffany, Ivanna, and Gert Muyskens – side by side against the wall to the back of the cab because it was marginally warmer than the exterior walls now Eric had the heater on.

Muyskens was wheezing. Ivanna had given him various medications at the hospital but, one by one, they were wearing off. Ivanna herself had said nothing for over an hour. Tiffany, on the other hand, had been singing all her favourite songs, partly to keep her spirits up but mostly to annoy Eric by preventing him from hearing the van radio.

Suddenly the van's engine was cut and the music stopped. The driver's door opened, Eric stepped outside and slammed the door behind him.

'Now we're talking!' Tiffany shouted. 'Come and open frigging doors.'

'Save your energy,' Muyskens said quietly. 'You will need it to survive.'

She was about to respond when they heard the sound of another vehicle approaching. The car's engine revved a couple of times, still some distance away, then stopped. A door slammed.

'Not driving my Range Rover over this shit,' a gruff Yorkshire voice called out. 'Where are they?'

'On bloody Mars' Eric answered. 'Where d'you think they are?'

'Don't get lippy, you're not tall enough.'

They could hear every word from inside the van.

'That's Rawes,' Muyskens whispered.

'You haven't been sat here listening to that cow singing and screaming for the past hour and a half.'

'I've had troubles of my own. Watching that lardy Labour MP dance is like watching a drunk old tart pushing a trolley with a dodgy wheel round Morrisons.'

'There speaks a Tory.'

'Nowt to do with politics, we just want to watch dancers who know a salsa is not a messy dip with random floating bits of tomato. Anyway, business. They're in the van?'

'Release the handbrake and let the slope and the cliff do the rest,' Eric said. 'What's with the plastic trousers and jacket? Don't they pay you properly?

'Halfwit. You don't think it would look a little suspicious, a van tumbling onto the rock with three people locked in the back?'

'So what is the plan, Chief Inspector?'

'Let me think.'

'We can't just let them …'

'I said let me think!' Rawes lashed out.

'Don't be a fool, Chief Inspector,' Muyskens shouted inside the van. 'There's been enough killing.'

David Rawes glanced at the van and walked away into the field. The situation had spiralled out of control. You did what you had to do to save a loved one and you kissed your arse goodbye. Knee-deep in shit and downhill all the way. Lupei had never formally threatened him, he didn't have to. Rawes knew he should have taken early retirement when it was offered. They could have sold up and buggered off to Brazil.

He turned back towards the van. A small orange glow betrayed where Eric Dunn was standing, having a fag. Dog eat dog. It wasn't fair, the doorman had problems of his own, but as Rawes' physics teacher had been fond of saying "Life isn't sodding fair, Rawes. Get over it."

He pulled on his plastic gloves and wandered back to the van. Further up the coast the Whitby lighthouse was keeping boats from the rocks.

'I need you to check the van is clean,' he told Eric.

'I've done it.'

'Well do it again. Glove box, under the seats, behind the seats, ashtray.'

Eric shook his head pityingly but didn't argue. He opened the driver's door and leaned inside. There was nothing under the driver's seat. He straightened up and was reaching towards the ashtray at the exact moment the spanner smacked him enough to crack his skull and rip a slice of his scalp. He fell forwards without a word. Rawes trousered the spanner then lifted Eric's ankles and pushed him into the van.

'What's happening?' a woman's voice asked anxiously from inside the back of the van.

Rawes didn't reply. He could not reach the handbrake to release it from the driver's side because Dunn's body was slouched over it. He went round the back, checking that there weren't any obstacles between the van and the edge of the cliff. There weren't.

As he pulled open the passenger door his phone rang. Probably Susan to find out if he wanted a hot water bottle. He stepped back from the van to hoik up his plastic jacket and retrieve his mobile, he was not leaving any fibres for forensics.

It wasn't Susan. The police station were calling.

'This had better be important,' he barked.

It was. Rawes stood there listening for the best part of two minutes. He asked a couple of questions and listened some more. He thanked the new duty officer, whose name he still couldn't remember, and shoved the phone back in his pocket.

The cows must be all of a mile away but you could smell them in the darkness. He remembered seeing a cow silhouetted on a hill as a boy, its breath forming a tiny cloud in front of its face in the sunrise. Funny how life turned out. Rawes pinched his nose and scrunched up his face. Chest trembling with emotion, he took three deep sighing breaths in the darkness then, mind made up, he walked away up the hill away from the van to his Range Rover. The wheels span as he threw the car into gear. He took the field gate at such a speed that he scraped the side of the car, and didn't give a toss. The headlights lit up the dry stone walls of the lane for a brief moment before the night rushed back across the field to envelop the van in a velvet lacklight cocoon.

CHAPTER 60

Humberside Airport, Grimsby - Tiffany Harrek

Sunday, 20 November.

I were so excited. So were Jordan. Like a couple of kids at a fairground, which is quite amazing when you consider we were sitting in arrivals at Humberside Airport near Grimsby. No disrespect but Lincolnshire makes Hull seem like Paris.

Gert, it seemed stupid carrying on calling the Dutch policeman by his surname after all we'd been through, had been tipped off by his friend at Europol who told him that Daniel were flying out of Bucharest. Gert had also been told that Whitby police wanted to interview him, but it weren't Whitby police who told him; I don't know what were going on there. No, that's not true, I suppose I do really.

It were Gert who found Rawes.

After Rawes left the field we had waited for Eric to release the handbrake and send us to our deaths, but nothing happened. The police finally arrived and released us, saying they'd had an anonymous tip-off. As they led us to the squad car I saw Eric's body lying in the front of the van.

We waited for the SOC team to arrive. Listen to her, like I'm a detective all of a sudden. The *Scene Of Crime* team. Anyway, once the team arrived the police officers drove us - Ivanna, Gert and me - to the police station and took statements. It were obvious to a blind bat that we hadn't killed Eric Dunn, since police had found us locked in the back of the van, but they still wanted to know everything we could tell them.

I told them next to nothing other than suggesting that they should talk with Chief Inspector Rawes since he were in on it. By that time my parents had turned up at the police station with a lawyer.

I didn't know what Ivanna and Gert had told them because they kept us apart. It were midnight by the time I got home. Mum wouldn't let me stay in my bedsit so I were tucked up with a hot water bottle and a mug of hot chocolate when Gert rang my mobile asking if I would get Uncle Ted to take him back to the Chief Inspector's house. Mum told him to naff off.

Following morning Gert rang again. He had found a taxi to take him to the Rawes mansion. There were no-one in the house; they were both in the garage, sitting in the Range Rover. Dead as doorknobs. The engine was running and a hosepipe were sticking out of the exhaust and into the car. Suicide. Gert touched nothing, rang the police and waited. There were a note upside down on the dashboard. When they turned up, the Whitby police were furious with him, bloody foreigners meddling in other people's affairs. The usual crap. He were bundled into a squad car and driven back to Whitby with strict instructions not to leave the town until he were told he could do so.

They refused to tell him what were on the note but by then we had a pretty good idea of what must have happened. Antoine, Gert's friend at Europol, had said that Whitby police had been advised that Daniel had turned up in Romania with a story of being abducted from Whitby during the Goth festival. He were alone. No Alex. They also said that he had a list of names of local people involved with Thor Lupei.

Gert said Rawes must have known the net was closing in and what he feared most of all were leaving his wife alone while he were tried and thrown in prison. With her medical condition, and the legal bills, and the disgrace, Rawes must have decided she could not survive without him. It were the end of the road so he killed them both. Last act of a desperate man.

Gert also said he were convinced it must have been Rawes who gave the anonymous tip-off about us all being locked in the van; decided he didn't want any more deaths on his conscience. How he disguised his voice to his own bloody police station were anyone's guess.

Anyroad, the flight landed on time and we were stood behind the barrier between people holding scraps of paper or fancy iPads with names scribbled on them. Jordan shared his earphones with me and we were listening to some retro reggae beats to keep our spirits up. Police and Thieves by Junior Murvin. "Keeping things topical, you know I mean," as Jordan put it, in his best Jamaican patois.

And suddenly he were there. It sounds daft but I were crying and laughing at the same time. Jordan were shouting and jumping up and down and the earphone were ripped out of my ear.

Although Daniel looked tired he was also looking pretty cool. He was wearing a cool fur-lined parka and a thick grey cardigan and a blue beanie hat.

'Wow man, Romania must be seriously funky. Those are sick shreds.' Jordan said.

'The police in Bucharest said my clothes stank and I wouldn't be allowed on the plane so they marched me down to a big shop in town. Some woman picked this stuff out. They even bought me a razor so I could have a shave.'

'Watch out, Tiffany,' Jordan teased me. 'This guy is dropping jaws internationally.'

'Yeah, all right,' Daniel said turning red. 'Hi Tiffany. You're looking really …'

'Hot?' Jordan suggested.

At that moment he looked to me just like the lad who had waltzed into the chippie two weeks' earlier, eyes soft, face open and gentle.

'No, not that. Well, you are that. Obviously. But I meant … you look beautiful and …'

'Shurrup,' I said grabbing him and hugging him tight. 'We tried to save you. We even spent the night running about on the Zeebrugge ferry.'

'OK, that'll do for now,' said a voice.

Behind us were two police officers, I recognised the fat one with straw-coloured hair from the police station but hadn't seen the policewoman before. I don't think I had ever seen anyone look as disinterested as this woman looked, like she had been asked to watch a Yorkshire pudding mix resting for half an hour.

It were only then that I noticed the other man standing behind Daniel, grey eyes, moustache, dark suit, crew cut, anonymous to the point of being invisible.

'I have to ask you to say goodbye to your friends, Mr Murray. They will be able to see you when we have concluded the interviews,' said the fat policeman, collecting an envelope from the grey-eyed man who must be his Romanian counterpart.

'Can't we have just ten minutes natter and a cup of coffee?' I asked.

The policewoman shook her head. Her expression suggested she got a kick out of being able to ruin someone else's evening.

'Catch you later, bruv,' Jordan called out after Daniel as they escorted him away.

'Don't worry, you'll be all right,' I shouted.

Daniel raised a hand to show that he had heard us. The automatic doors opened and closed and they were gone.

'He look all right to you?' I asked Jordan.

'Better than expected, to be honest.'

CHAPTER 61

Whitby - Tiffany Harrek

Wednesday, 23rd November

Three days later I were back at work. Jordan had gone home. We'd both been interviewed again by the police, as had Ivanna and Gert Muyskens. I had spoken briefly with Gert who were in his hotel with a heavy cold, nursing his injuries and waiting for a doctor to tell him he could go home. No-one really seemed to know what were going on or when they would release Daniel.

Then, suddenly, he were there on the other side of the counter.

'Just chips, please.' He smiled the same way he had smiled that Friday night when it had been pouring with rain and he had come in on his way to Farview Farm. 'Fancy a walk?'

'Do you need me to stay?' I shouted over the fish fryer as I shovelled chips onto a tray. 'It's half nine. Street's empty.'

'Where's Tom?'

'Out back.'

'OK, fetch him out front, Tiff, and you can bugger off.'

'Charming,' I said. 'Give me a minute,' I told Dan, handing him the cardboard tray.

He were waiting outside beneath the glow of a lamp post.

'I stink of chips,' I said, giving him a peck on the cheek.

'I'm eating chips,' he answered, handing me a small shopping bag. 'It's a present. From Oddsons' Seven Wonders.'

He watched as I opened the bag.

'It was that or the macramé nipple clamps and I thought this was less likely to offend,' he explained, blushing.

'I'll have to grow some armpit hair before I can braid it.'

'Something to look forward to then?'

We laughed and walked past the amusement arcade and out along the pier. The sea were calmer than it had been for weeks, its surface heaving gently between the harbour jaws like the chest of a sleeping dog.

'So is that it?' I asked. 'Have police finished with you? Are you free to go?'

'Not sure, Tiffany. Not sure they know. They're all over the place. Headless chickens. They took a statement, asked a whole load of questions about Alex and Darren and what had happened at Farview Farm.'

'What about Eric and Rawes and Lupei?'

Daniel stared out across the harbour at the backs of the cottages on Henrietta Street. I joined him at the handrail. Lights shone in various windows. A group of drunks were singing raucously, their voices drifting across the water.

'Not sure they were listening to a word I said.' Daniel turned towards me. 'What's new? I've been thinking, if you had a chance to leave Whitby and make a new life somewhere, would you take it?'

'Depends.'

He nodded slightly as if to say he understood and turned back towards the waters of the harbour.

'I'm a nobody,' he continued. 'I know that. Shitty job, shitty bedsit. I bet no-one even noticed I'd ...'

I grabbed him, pulled him toward me and kissed him on the lips. To shut him up. 'Jordan and I took the ferry to find you. Self-pity doesn't suit you.'

'I didn't mean ...' He found my hand and squeezed it. 'You know coming here to Whitby changed everything.'

A car engine revved wildly outside the amusement arcade.

'I want to make something of myself, Tiffany. I thought just saving up and buying a house before Alex did would be enough, but now he's dead and all that seems like so much crap. We only live once.'

'Wow, that's deep.'

He released my hand, his eyes thick with anger.

'Hey, relax. Only teasing,' I smiled. 'What did he do to you?'

The anger evaporated. Daniel's shoulders slumped.

'Where is Lupei?' I asked. 'And what happened to Alex? How do you know that he's …'

Daniel's face became a confusing mixture of emotions: sadness, anger, vulnerability, defiance.

'I can't …' Another pause. 'He's dead. I saw his body in the pit.'

'Alex?'

He nodded.

'And Lupei?'

In that instant I understood how far he were from the shore, how his experiences had distanced him, how long it would take to bring him back. It were all too raw.

'It's OK,' I said, turning to avoid his glare. 'No rush.'

'Sorry. You're shivering. I'll walk you back.'

'OK.'

Climbing the steps to the whalebone arch Daniel were silent, listening as I told him about Ivanna and the Dutch policeman and how Muyskens had found the bodies of David Rawes and his wife and how we knew that the doorman at the Pavilion and the chief inspector had both been compromised by their relationship with Lupei.

We stopped to catch our breath under the whalebone. Someone was walking their dog on the beach beneath Henrietta Street across the harbour.

'I found an old book in the castle,' Daniel said, breaking his silence. 'Went back centuries. Thousands of names. I ripped a few pages out and handed them over to the Europol guys who picked me up in Bucharest. Over a hundred names of transplant recipients. The Whitby police chief was on the list.'

I had a thousand questions. How long had he spent in that box? How had he escaped? How big were the castle? But I didn't press him, he would tell me more when he were ready.

'I have to ring Alex's parents. Let them know.'

'Jordan had an email from Hannah,' I told him. 'She's in Australia. Her parents took her out of the country. She's slowly recovering but they say it will take months, maybe a year.'

'Doctors think they know everything but they haven't a clue,' Daniel said then turned and passed under the whalebone.

On Cliff Street, I stopped outside the flat to find my keys. 'Thanks, Dan,' I said.

'Can I stay here?' he asked. 'On the sofa, I mean,' he added, seeing my face.

'I don't know. Maybe in a few days. It's not that ...'

'I understand. Time to get a wheelbarrow full of garlic to put around the bed. In case I went over to the dark side while I was in Transylvania.'

'You were in Transylvania?'

He shrugged and gave a hollow humourless laugh. 'I was taken to the castle in a plastic coffin. It's OK, I wouldn't trust me if I were you.'

'It's not that.' I reached out and took his hands in my own.

'It *is* that. I shouldn't have asked. You know, Tiffany, I meant everything I said earlier. I'm going to prove to you that I am ... Look, I'm sorry, about everything that happened, but it wasn't my fault ... and you are as beautiful as the moment I first saw you.'

He leaned forward and kissed my cheek. We stood there, hesitant, torn a thousand ways, flotsam in the aftermath of something bigger than ourselves.

Daniel remembered something and reached into his pocket.

'You know that torch?' he said. 'The one you gave me to light the path to Farview?'

'That stupid fish?'

He nodded. 'This shines a different kind of light. On danger and evil.' He looked about to add something then changed his mind. 'You'll work it out.'

The round brass case he pressed into my hand was warm from his pocket. A brief smile, then he turned heel and strode away down the street.

'Where are you staying, love?' I called out after him.

'Some bed and breakfast,' he shouted back without turning round. 'Bram Cottage.'

I listened to the slap of his shoes as he passed under the lamppost, his hair lit up briefly then lost to the darkness, torn between the urge to call him back and the knowledge that I were right to take my time. The good ones are prepared to wait as my nan would say. Call him in the morning.

I prised open the case lid. A compass. The needle was a beautiful black crow. Tiny with wings outstretched over a dark landscape. I released the catch and it spun erratically for a moment as if uncertain of its function, then turned to face north.

The following morning, it were gone eleven o'clock before I hauled myself out of bed. I wolfed my breakfast while looking up Bram Cottage online.

The owner, an old woman with a purple rinse, headscarf, plastic gloves and a nylon housecoat, stood in the doorway but didn't invite me in. The smell of toast hung in the air. A radio were playing *Someday I'll fly away* by Randy Crawford. One of mum's favourite songs.

'He left at eight thirty. Police paid the bill in advance.'

'He left?'

I turned away, gutted and confused.

'Came back mind.'

I spun back.

'About an hour ago. To collect a parcel.' A smug smile played on her cherry red lips.

The bitch is enjoying this. Keep calm, Tiff.

'What were it?'

'A cardboard box. Come in one of them white vans.'

'I meant what were *in* the parcel?'

It were all over her face; whether to fake she were insulted that I were calling her nosy, or carry on toying with me.

'A large fuzzy potato.'

'A potato?' I wanted to clock her.

'He looked happy as haggis. Said it were a fruit from Brazil. I told him that if they call that a fruit I can understand why they still run around in grass skirts and blowpipes. He called me a daft old cow and buggered off.'

'Did he say where he were going?' I asked.

'Why would he do that, love? Do I look like his mum?'

'God, I hope not.'

Ten minutes later I was on the first floor in a small hotel up on the cliff, not far from Cliff Street. The door opened.

'Can I come in?'

'Is it raining? I can smell it in your hair,' Gert Muyskens said. He was standing in his coat. His bags were by the door.

'Your cold must be gone.'

'Shame ribs take a little longer. Would you like a coffee? Sorry a tea, you English prefer your tea.'

'Coffee,' I said. 'I've come for advice.'

'Yes, I was worried that you might,' he smiled softly. 'Let me push the taxi back half an hour.'

'Sorry.'

'Sit down. I'll put the kettle on. You should read this.

It were a newspaper clipping, in some foreign language. At

the top were a photo of a young black girl.

'The translation is on the second sheet,' Gert said before I got my words out.

Voodoo violence at migrant camp

Rotterdam police are investigating claims of sorcery and murder in a makeshift migrant camp that recently appeared near the docks.

A fifteen-year-old African girl, identified only as Grace, is receiving police protection following an incident in the early hours of Wednesday evening. Several tents and shelters were set on fire in a dispute. Witnesses alleged that the young woman had used witchcraft to steal the flesh from other migrants'.

"Last week this girl was as thin as a sheet of paper," claimed Amir, one of the migrants collecting his belongings from the wreckage of a shelter. "Now look at her. She is as plump as a pomegranate. Two of my friends have died. Strong men reduced to skin and bones. The girl is a witch."

Police have declined to comment.

'Last October. What do you think?' Gert asked, pointing at the clipping and passing me a mug of coffee. 'Thor Lupei?'

I shrugged. 'It isn't voodoo, is it?

He shook his head. We both knew what it was.

We sat at the small round table by the window overlooking

the street and I told him about Daniel. Gert sipped his coffee, wrinkled his nose and pushed the cup away. He listened patiently, asking occasional questions, until I had told him not only about the previous night but practically every conversation I had ever had with Daniel. I understood why he were a good police officer.

'So this advice?' Gert said finally.

'What should I do?'

'What *can* you do? You told me that he has left Whitby without giving you an address or a phone number. Unless the Whitby police choose to give you his contact details, if they have them, you will have to wait for Daniel to contact you.'

'I'm worried. For him.'

Gert stared at me for what seemed like eternity. I sensed he was deciding about something, but what? Finally he let out a long sigh.

'I am going to tell you something in confidence,' he started, but his mobile phone interrupted him. 'Antoine, bonjour,' he said. He listened then stood up and walked to the other side of the room, speaking softly in Dutch or German or French, I weren't sure which. He sat on the bed, scratching his head with his free hand. His tone of voice suggested he were having trouble believing what he were hearing. He glanced over at me and smiled, as if to say everything were OK and not to worry, but his eyes weren't smiling, only his mouth.

'Ya, OK, bedankt.' Gert trousered his phone and sat there staring at the floor.

'What is it? Bad news?' I asked.

'Stront. Stront, Shit.' Gert said, his face screwed up in frustration. He stood up, paced up and down then came back to the table and sat down. His legs were bobbing up and down as he stared at me or through me, I weren't sure which.

'Vloek. Why didn't I see that coming?' He spat the words through clenched teeth.

'What?'

'That was my friend at Europol. They have just been contacted by the Romanian police. What did Daniel tell you about his escape?'

'Nothing much. The police had picked him up, bought him some clothes, put him on the plane.'

Gert shook his head. 'No, no, before that.'

'Nothing. I didn't want to pry. Thought I'd wait till he …'

'They interviewed him on the plane from Bucharest to Amsterdam. Antoine and a Romanian police officer. Daniel told them he had escaped from the castle after a fight with Lupei. He said he ran through the forest until he found a farm where they let him in, gave him something to eat and helped him make phone calls.'

Gert paused, lost in thought. Suddenly he noticed me waiting.

'Romanian police have visited all the local farms and no-one admits ever having seen Daniel.'

'Didn't the police go to the farm to pick him up?' I asked.

'No, they picked him up on the road three kilometres outside a village in the valley.'

'So what's the problem?'

'This afternoon after they had checked the last farm they came back down towards the village and noticed a vehicle buried in a snowdrift in a forest clearing some twenty metres from the road. In the car was a middle-aged man, frozen and dead.'

'What has that got to do with Daniel? Are you saying it has something to do with him?'

'The man was thin as a rake, his arms and legs little more than sticks.'

'He had been attacked by Lupei?'

'Daniel told Antoine that Lupei is dead.'

'A scravir then. Lupei brought the scravir to Whitby.

Maybe there are more in the castle.'

Gert shook his head again. 'No. No. They found the phone.'

'What phone?'

'It was the phone Daniel used to make the phone call. In the car. The dead man's phone.'

'Sorry, I don't understand. Start again. From the top.'

———————————

Acknowledgements

Special thanks to Mary for her endless patience as I ran and reran through the plot with her. Those who live with those who write have to put up with a great deal.

And thanks also to Whitby for not complaining once as I ran and reran the cobbled streets, soaking and skulking the lacklit corners, dodging and diving the loudly Goths, and breathing deep the salt smoke whispering by Fortune's Kippers on Henrietta Street.

This special town loiters long after moonfall in the imaginations of all who venture in.

Injini Press thanks Chris, Fiona, Angela and Tom at Whitby's wonderful independent bookshops and online guides for helping to launch SCRAVIR and make this book such a success. And a huge thank you to Peter for proofreading.

If you have loved this book you can, on the following pages, read samples of SCRAVIR II, the forthcoming SCRAVIR III, and C.M.Vassie's The Whitby TRAP. You can also learn more about the books and about Whitby itself on our website.

www.injinipress.co.uk

... and we would relish your review !

www.injinipress.co.uk/product/scravir-while-whitby-sleeps

Daniel shakes his head. 'Something they give us at college. On our language course.'

'Read that for me then.' Jonah pushes one of the pages under Daniel's nose.

The letters are as unintelligible as they have been on every other occasion Daniel has looked at them.

ҀѦҺѲѦꙶѱЅѲЄҺѦⲚЅІѦЄѦⲚ
ⲚℲІѦⲚѦЅⲚⲚЅѦꙶѦІѦѦѦІҀѦ
ҺѲҺТЄѦⲚⲚѦѦѦꙆЅѱІⲚѦꙆЅ
ѱꙆЅꙦІЅⲚⲚҀѦⲚЄⲚⲚІЅҀѦЅ
ѦТѦꙶѦⲚЅѦꙅІЅІⲚѦⲚꙦЄⲚѦІ
ⲌЄѦꙦꙦѦꙦѦҀѦҺⲚℲꙶⲚѱЄѦ
ⲚⲚѱѦТЄІℲꙶѦⲘЅꙶѦѦѱІꙶⲚ
ⲚЅѦꙶѦⲘⲘѦѲѦꙶѱⲚЅℲІѦѦІ

On the floor with his arms tied behind his back, Daniel is forced to confabulate. 'They only just give it us. They said some of it is in Latin, and some in German or Italian. Don't know what that bit is written in. That's all I know. I think they give us a dictionary to …'

Jonah stares hard into Daniel's eyes. 'What your name, Blood?'

'Daniel.'

'And Daniel in the lion's den, they thought they would never see him again,' Jonah sings an old reggae song softly in his deep bass voice. 'Oh no, what a la la bam bam bam.' Jonah's teeth are smiling but there isn't the slightest flicker of mirth in his tired eyes. 'You a thief, Blood?'

'I told you; it's the homework they gave us. It just looks old. They photocopied it or something.'

'I'm stupid because I'm black, right? That look like Latin or German to you?'

'What?'

C M VASSIE

Jonah puts the torch back on the table, reaches into one of the pockets of his coats and produces a lighter. He squats on his haunches in front of Daniel, clicks the lighter and a small flame begins to dance.

'Guess I'm going to burn your homework, Blood. They'll print another one off for you, won't they?'

The flame licks the chill air like a hunting dog straining on its leash. Russian roulette. Daniel hopes his face isn't betraying panic. If he tells his captor what the pages represent he loses all control of the situation … and the journal. If he says nothing then …

The decision is taken from him as Jonah lights a corner of a page. A cool whisper of blue narrow flame creeps along the edge of the parchment like poison gas drifting along a trench.

'Stop,' Daniel shouts.

Jonah arches an eyebrow.

'Just stop. Put it out!'

Jonah smothers the page in the folds of his coats. The two men stare at each other.

'Well?' Jonah says eventually.

'I stole it,' Daniel confesses.

'And?'

Daniel looks confused momentarily.

Jonah clicks the lighter and the flame reappears. He holds all the cards.

'OK. It's old. I stole it from this guy's house along with some other stuff. I wanted to find out what it was before trying to sell it. In case it's worth a few bob, you know? I swear. That's all I got.'

Jonah shakes his head sadly. 'Going to be a long night, Blood.'

more reader reviews
of the Scravir books

C.M.VASSIE

SCRAVIR III

Coming soon - Autumn 2025 ...

Here are three short extracts from Scravir III, the epic conclusion of Scravir books.

... He is sure of it now. The castle senses his presence. It is thrilled that he has shaken off the other two. Daniel feels it in his bones. The blunt blind walls are alive and sucking him towards the last room like iron filings are drawn to a magnet. It is his destiny.

But what of the Gothic archway to his immediate left?

No secrets.

Be my guest. Breathe my dank corridors and climb my spinning steps. You want a kingdom? Fall up into my arms.

The opening is a dark maw, a bright black void that in its very blackness beckons Daniel to itself in an inverse of the impulse that draws a moth to a flame. Without reasoning, without questioning his motivation, Daniel steps beneath the arch and enters a narrow passage that ends almost immediately at the foot of a spiralling stone staircase. Finger-thin arrowslits in the curving wall seep the faintest winter light into the gloom.

As he climbs Daniel is enveloped in a whispering cacophony of emotions. Loss, longing, pain, fear. These feelings escalate with every passing step until, barely two rotations up, he is dizzy with them. He pauses and, to steady himself, reaches out to rest a hand against the cold curving wall but the anguish only intensifies, as if it is emanating directly from the stones themselves.

He is catapulted back in time.

He is in Whitby lying in a box on the top deck of Lupei's black double decker bus. Someone is calling out, *Please, you have to help me.* Feeble tapping, voices pleading in the darkness. All of them paralysed and stacked up in blind boxes. He relives the memory of the wriggling in his abdomen, stolen human organs sliding over each other like agitated fish in a keep net. Organs implanted by Thor Lupei.

He withdraws his hand and the pain subsides. What evil is secreted here? What will he find at the top of the stairs?

This too is your destiny.

Not one without the other, Daniel.

Daniel continues up the steps, hands by his sides, each footstep heavier than the last. Sick with dread, his heart heaving hurting straining, he climbs. He no longer has a choice.

A clicking sound, soft, mechanical, brittle.

With only shadows ahead of him now, he ascends the slow spinning lacklit void unable to see either the steps or his feet. He only knows he has reached the top of the staircase when his foot reaching out for the next step up finds only air and slams down too far, tipping him off-balance, throwing him forwards He faceplants onto a cold hard floor.

C M VASSIE

The clicking fades momentarily. Daniel lies still, cheek against stone, the pleading voices now oozing directly into his face. A wasteland of suffering, mumbling, pleading, whispering.

Then the clicking sounds return and swell and, out of nowhere, Daniel recalls a nature documentary where ten thousand crabs crawled over each other in the acid darkness around a deep sea vent.

He pushes himself up on an elbow and, desperate for light, retrieves his smart phone from his pocket and presses the button.

A medley of colourful app icons light up his face.

The clicking intensifies. He is still blind to what surrounds him but now he is revealing himself to whatever shares this space with him. He is making himself a target! He swipes wildly for the button to activate the torch and, finally, the light switches from his face to the space around him and he screams.

... I was born during the reign of Aoric in the mountains of what the Romans called Dacia Inferior. Far into the future it would be called Romania. We lived deep in the forest three days' walk from their fort in Buridava. Twice the whole village moved to keep us away from the soldiers.

My father Vidigoia, named after our Thervingian hero who was killed in battle, was a woodsman when not being a warrior. My mother was called Branwen. She was beautiful with long black hair and big blue eyes. She looked after us, me and my three siblings. I was the youngest.

The mountain forests were a place of both refuge and fear and my mother would beat us if we ventured too far. The golden rule was that we must always be close enough to shout for help because there were many bears and wolves. The adults would scare us with stories about ghost men, men who were like people but thin as skeletons. They lived in caves and would eat children if they caught them.

My siblings would take me with them to find mushrooms in the autumn sunshine. The air was still thick with bees and I was excited because I hoped we would also find a hive full of honey. We ran beneath the trees, stamping our feet hard to shake the ground and scare off any snakes, and climbed the mountain to the waterfall where we were sometimes allowed to splash about.

The sun was shining and there were lots of berries and my sister Wilda laughed when I insisted I hadn't eaten any. Why is your face purple with berry juice then, she asked? I was very cross to have been betrayed by the berries. I must have been four years old.

My mother was shouting. My brother Eriulf, who had the loudest voice, shouted back that we were fine. Because he was eight he was allowed to carry a real knife. It was heavy and as long as my arm and I was very jealous. We crossed the stream and when we reached the overhanging rocks I shivered. The air was damp and we were happy to find many mushrooms growing in the moss and leaf litter. We were so busy filling our basket that we forget to keep a lookout for wild animals.

It was my sister Beyla who found him sleeping by the tree. We should all have run away but he looked so peaceful with his fluffy round ears and his big black nose. We didn't poke it or make a noise or anything. The mother bear must have been up in the tree because suddenly she was next to us. She was huge and she smacked Beyla and Eriulf so hard they flew in the air and by the time they landed they were dead and Wilda was running away screaming for the adults to help us. The baby bear sat up beside me and together we watched his mother race after Wilda. I just knew it was going to be bad.

C M VASSIE

Everything seemed to happen at once. A hand with a rock hit the baby bear so hard that its head made a cracking noise and it fell down and there was blood everywhere. I closed my eyes waiting for the rock to hit me but instead I felt myself being picked up and pressed hard against something warm that smelled really bad. Then I was moving fast and someone was running. When I tried to open my eyes I could only see dirty skin and rags right up against my face. It sounded like there were several people calling out as they ran but if they were speaking real words then I couldn't understand what they were saying. My body was being shaken about like a dead rabbit on a hunter's spear and I decided it was best not to move or make a sound. They were climbing up among the rocks. I wondered how long it would be before the mother bear turned back from killing Wilda and caught up with us all. She must have seen her dead cub by now and would be very angry.

But she didn't catch us and after a while we were moving less quickly and I dared to open one eye again to see what was happening.

There were four ghost people. I was sure that is what they were because they were so thin, their limbs thin as sticks. I had escaped the bear only to be eaten by ghost men! One of them must have been a ghost woman because she had breasts that swung left and right, as empty as socks. She was carrying the dead bear cub and, beside her, hanging over the shoulder of one of the men, was Eriulf, his head shaking back and forth, his mouth hanging open.

We were hurrying now close to a rock face, and then the rock was above our heads and suddenly it was dark. I was dropped on the floor beside Eriulf and the dead bear cub and I lay there for a few minutes not daring to turn my head or move my body. If I looked up from the top of my eyes I could see the entrance to the cave. There were two ghost men standing there, carrying spears. If I got up quickly and ran then maybe

I could get past them and run home.

But where was home? What if I got lost in the forest? Wouldn't the bear mother be out there looking for me? I reached out a hand very very slowly until I could reach Eriulf's hand and I held it tightly, tears rolling down my face. Please let him not be dead. If only he would wake up. He was eight and would be bound to have a good plan, even if he had lost his knife. Together we would escape and get home and ...

I was grabbed by the neck and yanked up into the air. The face looking down at me was fuzzy and rough as a moss-covered rock. The mouth was smiling but contained only two yellow teeth. The skin was flaking and the yellow eyes had red lines like blood.

I wriggled to get away from his foul-smelling breath. The ghost man grunted and dropped me to the ground. He kicked me. Before I could think to roll away he touched me with a bony fingertip and immediately my arms and legs felt too tired to move. I watch him walk away. I waited and waited until I was so tired I fell asleep ...

... Biter leapt away from me, clutching her head, her eyes black with hate and locked on mine. I was still angry but cowering now, convinced that she was about to strike me. I had never really thought about the stories that eyes can tell until that moment. As we gazed at each other I felt I could read her mind. I saw her anger, her desire to smash me against the floor, and then there were other thoughts passing over each other like snakes in a nest: surprise, discovery, pride, fear and calculation. Finally she gave a little nod of acknowledgement and walked away to tidy the cave.

From that day onwards, taking care that none of the others would observe us, she began to use those rare opportunities when we were alone to teach me the hidden skills of the ghost men. We began with small animals - rats, squirrels and rabbits - that we would catch in the forest. I remembered that my parents kept a cat that I had watched in fascination as the mother cat would catch a mouse, injure it and then place it among her litter of kittens to teach them how to hunt and kill. Biter did the same with me, encouraging me to practice focusing the energy in my head and sending it through my hand into a penned creature. Once we trusted each other she would put a hand on my arm and focus her energy through me and into the prey so that I might feel what she was doing. By the following summer I was able to project power from my head down through my fingers and into an animal. While I was unable to do anymore than this it was clear that a threshold had been crossed when the animal, a squirrel, turned to looked at me, wide-eyed, with such a look of fear that I immediately withdrew my hand in shock at my own accomplishment.

Biter looked me with a mixture of pride and concern, as if she too were wondering where this might all lead.

It was several weeks before we were once again alone, the ghost men having gone hunting up in the high mountains where there was little call for the services of a nine-year-old boy, even as bait. I had by now become aware that I was no longer the plaything they had seized five years earlier. I was taller and stronger and understood instinctively that a time would come, maybe quite soon, when my value to the group would have gone.

I would become a threat. What would happen then? Did Biter sense that too? Was she preparing me for that moment? ...

Also by C.M.Vassie

The
WHITBY
TRAP

The time travelling adventure from C.M.Vassie, bestselling author of the Scravir books.

"Exciting, thought-provoking, weird and intense in all the best ways."

It is 2022. Derek is drowning in the dreary routine of his job, his love life, his friends, everything ... a weekend break in a Whitby cottage is just another excuse to get drunk but waking up on a whaling ship in a snowstorm, with a hangover the size of Yorkshire, is a bit of a jolt.

While Derek is lost on the Jurassic Coast, his friends – Amy and Sarah - are desperately seeking him in the early 19th century. Even the simplest things are a struggle in a town where people work twenty hours a day to survive.

With betrayals, double-dealing, wild experiments, piracy, love and loss ... the strange duckfoot pistol in the hands of the eccentric snuff-snorting sleuth who breaks into their lodgings is the least of the women's problems.

What exactly is happening beneath the old town hall. Is there any way back? Why would you go back?

PLESIOSAURUS MACROCEPHALUS.
Scale 1" = 1 foot.

Reviews of The Whitby Trap

"Great read really enjoyed this book, history and imagination combined. Well worth a look."
C Mcnamara

"The Whitby Trap' is one of the best books on Whitby I have ever read. Can't wait for the next!!"
J Lund

"Yet another gripping read from C.M.Vassie. a great page Turner from being to end."
E Lancaster

"Readers who enjoyed Vassie's previous novel Scravir will be in for a treat with The Whitby Trap. This all-action adventure thriller set in the present-day slips through cracks in the timeline, taking us back to two hundred years ago, and then millions of years to the Jurassic Coast. An epic time-travelling page-turner from Vassie which captures the sounds and sights of Whitby now and in the past."
Esk Valley News

"Fabulous book. Well written – you are hooked after just reading the first few pages."
P Cooper

"One of the best books I've read so far."
J Martin

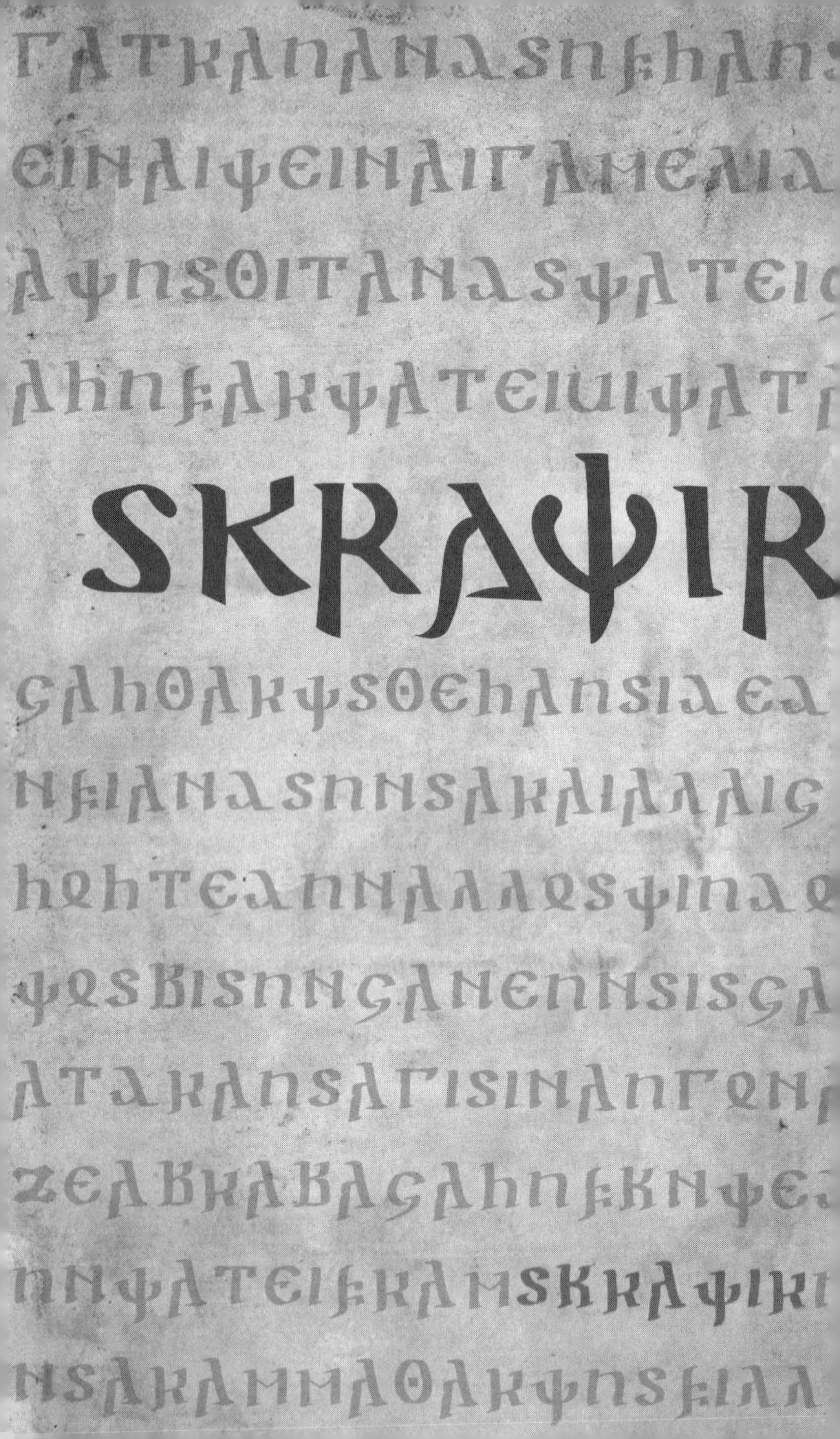